THE OLD and THE NEW
BIBLE STORIES RETOLD

THE OLD and THE NEW
BIBLE STORIES RETOLD BY

DAVID
KOSSOFF

GRAND RAPIDS, MICHIGAN 49530

ZONDERVAN™

The Old and The New

ISBN 0-007-12808-8

Bible Stories first published in Great Britain in 1968 by
William Collins & Co. Ltd
Copyright © 1968 by David Kossoff
A catalogue record for this book is available from the British Library
ISBN 0-00-626560-X

The Book of Witnesses first published in Great Britain in 1971 by
William Collins Sons & Co. Ltd
Copyright © 1971 by David Kossoff
A catalogue record for this book is available from the British Library
ISBN 0-00-626560-X

David Kossoff asserts the moral right to be identified as the author of this work.

Bible Stories by David Kossoff is published in Great Britain by arrangement with
the British Broadcasting Corporation.

CONDITIONS OF SALE

Interior design by Susan Ambs

Printed and bound in the United Kingdom

02 03 04 05 06 07 08 /❖ OMN/ 10 9 8 7 6 5 4 3 2 1

CONTENTS

FOREWORD
William Barclay

There is no more difficult task than to make the old new and the familiar interesting. This is specially true of the Bible stories which many of us have been hearing from childhood. The Bible presents another problem. We often have the feeling, perhaps unconsciously, that the world of the Bible is an unreal world removed from the kind of ordinary world and ordinary people we know. The biblical characters tend to move in a world where the people are like characters in a fairy tale, remote from the 20th century. They never become real people and the narrative of events never seems to move in the live actual world.

This is the reason why I have read with such pleasure and delight David Kossoff's *Bible Stories*. To my mind there is no doubt at all that he makes these stories come alive. He has the gift of making old stories new for he is a born story teller.

But there is something in his book even more interesting than that. Gilbert Murray has said that if we are to interpret anyone's writing we must at least to some extent repeat and share the experience of that person. This is to say that we must enter into their minds, see with their eyes, speak in their words, and above all think with their thoughts. This is precisely what Mr Kossoff succeeds in doing. He has an astonishing insight into the mind of the characters involved and the way in which he makes them speak and think is both vivid and authentic. He not only tells what one might call an external story but he enters into the internal being of the characters he is describing.

I can think of no better way to make the Bible stories real to children, and to adults, than to present them with this book.

THE OLD

BIBLE STORIES

David Kossoff's *Bible Stories* was published in 1968. The book became, and still is, a runaway bestseller.

This unusual and remarkable success story began quietly. Late in 1963, Kossoff, an award-winning actor and an occasional writer and teller of his own stories, was invited by the BBC to contribute and perform 'A Story from the Bible' on television. He took great care with this, his first story from the scriptures, and chose Jonah. It made a great impact and the letters poured in. BBC Radio, sensing a new voice, offered the old-established 'Five to Ten' morning programme for an experimental month.

It was an immediate success. He became a sort of institution. Soon he was given his own television series. His audience was huge; addictive. Soon, too, by demand, records. One of his favourite stories, Adam and Eve, was given a musical setting by Wilfred Josephs, 'for Narrator and Orchestra', with a Festival Hall premiere! He began to do 'public tellings' of his stories. These performances called 'As According to Kossoff' quickly became the most asked for of his one-man shows. His 'story-tellings' in schools to young children are as famous.

CONTENTS

Chapter 1

IN THE BEGINNING

Try to imagine, if you can, what it is like to have no possessions at all, nothing, not even the language of the country you've just arrived in as a refugee. Mind you, very few people are able to imagine such a thing, though there are thousands of men and women and children alive now who could tell you from experience what it is like to have nothing at all.

To understand the first story in the Bible, we have to imagine something a hundred times harder. Not just to *have* nothing at all, but when there *was* nothing at all. The very beginning of time. The dawn of history. Page one. Nothing at all. The earth, as the Bible itself beautifully puts it, 'without form, and void. Only (even more beautifully) the Spirit of God moving over the face of the waters'. An emptiness; formless; a dark, endless waste of water. No living thing. No plant or tree. Nothing. Only God.

The Bible tells a million stories of what God did later. Miracles. Mighty happenings and small matters, judgments and punishments, second chances, endless forgivings, great grace, mercies beyond counting. All to do with people. But this is before all that. Before people. Before anything at all. A void – and God. God had done no miracles, made no judgments, and punished nobody. Nobody to punish, or judge, or forgive, or show mercy to. No seas to part, no bushes to burn, no tablets of law to hand down, no slaves to free, nobody for God to bless or arrange a miracle for or make a prophet of. Nothing. A void.

It must have been dull for God. I've thought so since a child. I was the sort of child who liked to know why and I once asked a learned uncle why God made the world.

My uncle thought hard. My aunt too. I waited. They were both clever.

Then my uncle said, 'Well, he had to do something. To occupy himself.' And my aunt said, 'You ask *why?* Tell me, why *not?*' . . .

And the thought was planted. And grew into a picture in the mind. A picture I have to this day. A picture of God looking out over an endless dark sea. A God who'd been by himself for a long time. A quiet, thoughtful God, feeling sort of empty. A bit bored perhaps. Maybe even lonely. Sitting silent, still. And then suddenly thinking, 'I know, I'll make a world. I need to do something. To occupy myself. Why not?'

Mind you, before God started to make the world, he gave it a lot of thought. Big job. Not much to go on. No previous experience in such work. No really good materials either. Just a vast midnight, always dark, covering a great waste of nothing but water.

'Right,' said God. 'First things first! Some light to work by. Let there be light!' And there was.

'Pleasant effect,' thought God and turned it off and on a few times. He could see that permanent light might not be so good after all, so he said, 'Some of each. Turn and turn about. Sometimes more dark, sometimes more light. Light will be called Day and the dark time will be called Night. One of each together will be called *a* day. Good.'

Then God looked at the endless water. 'Too much,' he said and decided to halve it. But where to put the other half? Nowhere to *empty* it. So he pointed upwards and the water heaved and lifted and boiled upwards into a gorgeous roof over the water below. Every colour, every kind of cloud. God looked up. 'I will call that Heaven,' he said. 'Beautiful. It looks a nice place to live.' And he moved in.

From above God could see everything. No different from today really. Except that then there was less to look at. Unbroken water, you remember.

So God drew on the water with his finger and the land came up. It was interesting to draw the different shapes. 'All the pieces of land,' said God, 'will be called Earth and all the water will be called the Seas.'

All the shapes of Earth looked rather bare so God thought about it for a while and then covered all the bareness with trees and plants and vegetation of every kind. 'And every kind,' he said, 'will contain its own seed, and thus continue.'

Then God thought of a way to improve on his Day and Night invention, which was a bit hard on the eyes in its sudden change. He hung outside his home two globes of light. One large, to look after the Day and the other smaller, for the Night. No sudden changes; as one dimmed, the other came on. Nice effect. Also he named them. The larger he called Sun, and the smaller, Moon. Then he made a million smaller moons and called them stars.

God was enjoying himself. The greatest artist of them all was having fun and not feeling so lonely.

'Next,' said God, 'things that move. That fly, and crawl, and swim, and walk.' And he used every colour and shape and texture that came into his mind. Huge sea-monsters, tiny birds, exquisite insects, delicate dancing creatures, and slow, heavy ones. Nothing was forgotten. Not a feather, not a fin. Remembering his arrangement for the plants he gave to the living things their seeds too. 'Multiply,' he said. 'Fill the seas and the sky and the land. There's plenty of room.'

God was pleased with his work but had an odd feeling still of loneliness. Of something still to do. He sat looking down into a calm lake, down at his own reflection. Then he smiled. 'That's it,' he said. 'I'll make someone to talk to. A man. He can look like me.'

Adam and Eve

Now, when God decided to make a man to live in the brand-new world he'd just created, he hadn't thought much about it other than that he would use himself as model and do the work with his own hands. All the animals, plants, birds and fishes he'd sort of *imagined* and said, 'Let there be', and there they were; but the man, the most exciting, he wanted to *make*. Special job.

So he looked around for a suitable material and chose mud. Not because he knew what we were all going to turn out like but because mud is good for modelling. We don't know what colour the mud was. May have been black, of course. Or yellow.

Anyway, God worked quietly and happily until he'd made a fairly good likeness and then he let it dry. It. Not he; it. A statue, lying down, made of mud. Wet dust. Then God bent over and blew gently into the nostrils of the statue, and it changed and became skin and bone and hair; and then its chest moved and its eyes blinked and it got unsteadily to its feet and they looked at each other.

God was pleased with his work. 'Your name is Adam,' he said, 'and you will live in a garden where the trees and plants are not only beautiful but will give you everything you need for food. We'll go there now.'

God had chosen the site for his first man's home with great care. A place he called Eden, well watered and mild. And it *was* beautiful. He showed Adam round rather proudly.

'You will be in charge,' he told him, 'to look after everything and to grow things for yourself. Keep things tidy. I am very fond of this garden,' said God. 'I often walk here in the evenings. I hope you'll be very happy.' He turned and then turned back. 'Oh, one more thing. There are two trees in the garden that you must not touch in any way. Fruit trees. There, right in the middle.' Then God left and Adam settled in. A sort of gardener. He had no one to learn from.

But God forgot nothing. Such skills as Adam needed were given to him. His hands were shown how.

God visited often and one day told Adam he had a new job for him. 'Before I made you,' said God, 'I made all the animals and birds and so on. Well, none of them has any names, so I'm going to arrange that every animal and bird will visit the garden in turn and you can decide what to call them. Also – and this is important – look among them for a helper, a companion for yourself. Sometimes you seem a bit lonely and we don't want that, do we?'

Adam did all that God said, but although he admired many of the creatures there was not one he felt he could make a real friend of. He was drawn to animals that he'd called Dog and Cat and Horse, but only to a limited extent were they company for him. He told God.

So God put Adam into a deep sleep and, whilst he was under this anaesthetic, did a little surgery on him. He removed a rib and healed the wound and from the rib made a new sort of creature. Not an animal, not a bird; in fact rather like Adam, but with little differences. Softer, rounder. 'That should do it,' said God. Then he woke Adam and showed it to him.

Adam was astonished.

'It's called a Woman,' said God. 'I named it myself. A companion for you. You are a male, she is female. All I told you about your garden you can tell her.'

Adam was very pleased to have someone to talk to at last. 'I shall call you Eve,' he said, 'and the first thing about this garden that you must know is that you must not touch the fruit of the two trees in the middle. Anything else; not those.'

Well, the time passed quickly. Adam and Eve enjoyed each other's company and they had a simple primitive innocence that indeed was God-given. They lived in the sun. Quite naked, but they knew nothing of clothes anyway. Like babies on a beach. Neither touched the two trees.

Now, when God had made all the animals, he also gave them very different levels of intelligence, or cunning, or craftiness. Some more, some less. One of the creatures who seemed to get a double share of cunning and craftiness was the serpent. 'More subtle,' says the Bible, 'than any other creature.'

A serpent lived in the garden (many animals did) and it used to watch Eve as she, curious, would look up into the two forbidden trees. 'The fruit is delicious,' it said to her one day. 'Delicious. A rare experience. Try it.'

Eve looked at the serpent. 'If we eat, or even touch it,' she said, 'we shall die.'

'Nonsense,' said the serpent. 'The tree is magic and, if you eat some of the fruit, not only will you *not* die but you will be much wiser in every way.' He had a smooth tongue, the serpent, and eventually Eve picked some of the fruit and talked Adam into eating some too. Then they waited to be wiser.

Poor Adam and Eve! The wisdom in the tree was the knowledge of right and wrong. So right away they knew with their new wisdom that they'd done wrong – and were ashamed. With their new wisdom they looked at each other and were no longer innocent primitives. No longer babies on a beach. They saw themselves guilty – and naked. They hid their bodies from each other with garments made of leaves and they hid themselves from God, who walked often in the garden.

But God knew. 'Where are you, Adam?' he said. 'Why did you hide?'

Adam came out. 'Well,' he said, 'I heard you about and I wasn't dressed.'

'Why,' said God, 'are you wearing those leaves?'

'Well,' said Adam, 'you can't go around naked, it's not right.'

'How,' said God, 'do you know you were naked, or what naked means, or what is right, or wrong?'

Well, Adam blamed Eve and she blamed the serpent.

God listened. So soon disobedience, so soon the need to punish. 'You will leave the garden' he told them, 'and never come back. Because of your disobedience life will be harder for all who come after you. For women childbirth will have pain, and men will have to work, to toil and sweat. Paradise like this garden will have to be earned, it will not again be given free. And all will return to the material which I used to make you – dust. Dust to dust.'

God was not angry; he was sad. It had begun to go wrong. There was worse to come. A whole Bible full!

Cain and Abel

Now, when God threw Adam and Eve out of the garden of Eden, it was not only because they had disobeyed him and eaten the fruit of the tree of knowledge of Good and Evil. No, God was afraid they would also eat from the tree of Life, and live for ever. He didn't want that; in fact, after that business with the serpent, he wished he'd never made them at all. However, God is merciful and doesn't hold things against people. So he didn't as it were write them off. He found them somewhere else to live and showed them how to use skins instead of leaves for clothes.

Then God had the idea that maybe a new pair of people would be an improvement. So he remembered how he'd given to the plants and animals and birds and fishes their own seeds so that they could multiply. Even insects. 'Seems to work well with birds and bees,' thought God. 'I'll arrange something similar for Adam and Eve.'

It worked well for them too and soon they had two sons. Cain and Abel. Different types they were, as brothers often are. When they were old enough Cain worked the land with his father and Abel was the shepherd. Rather gentle, quiet person. Thoughtful. Cain was none of these things. Quick-tempered, violent, jealous, quarrelsome. He had an evil streak. Adam had often to act as peacemaker between his sons.

Adam remembered well his fall from grace and the beautiful garden. He had good reason to be grateful for God's mercy and he brought his sons up to fear God and to show respect. At certain times of the year sacrifices were offered. Abel loved these simple ceremonies; Cain less so.

God observed Cain's attitude on a number of these occasions and did nothing. But then one day he both rejected Cain's offering and told him off.

Cain burned. He watched his brother's sacrifice accepted and saw Abel's simple happiness. When Abel went back to his flock, Cain followed him. And in a lonely, hidden place he killed him. Then he went away from that place back to his own field. His anger died away and fear crept in. The wind died away too and the trees grew quiet. Everything grew quiet. No birds sang.

Then God spoke. 'Cain, where is Abel your brother?'

Cain was sweating. He blustered, 'I don't know,' he said. 'Am I my brother's keeper?'

God didn't waste too many words. Cain's punishment was terrible. He was made a wanderer, a fugitive. He had no place to go to and no God to turn to. He felt the face of God and the hand of every man to be against him.

But God made him live long and marked him so that men would know that though he had killed his brother they must not kill him in return. All life was to be sacred. Even Cain's.

More Trouble

So. We began with a picture of God, rather lonely, sitting in the dark dawn of time, and deciding to make a world. And working hard at it and being pleased with his work. And then making a man, and from a man a woman, and from them two sons. One family. A mother led into wickedness who took her husband with her; and a firstborn who murdered his brother. One family. It's difficult to resist another picture. Of God watching Cain walk away from him and thinking, sadly, 'Maybe making a world wasn't such a good idea after all.'

And for the next hundred years or so he had no reason to change his mind. In fact, things got so bad that even God was discouraged. He picked Noah and his family and decided to go back to page one. The story of Noah and the ark and how he saved a pair of every living species from drowning has been told so often that I don't propose to tell it again now, only to remind you that, when the waters subsided and the ark finally rested on Ararat and Noah and all the animals came out, God promised

Noah that he would never do it again, and then hoped for the best.

The years passed and then God had the Babylon business to look after. Up till then the whole world had one language, nice and simple. But purely to protect himself and to stop the people at Babylon from building that idiotic tower of theirs God fixed it so that everyone spoke differently. Confusion and suspicion ever since!

So. God had thought Noah worthwhile and had chosen him and his family for special work. But even after Noah God was still a bit wary of these 'people' he'd made and the Tower of Babel made him even more so. He watched and waited for someone really special to turn up. He waited about four hundred years, a fair time, even for God. But this had to be the right one, for this person was going to start a *new* kind of people, God hoped, so he chose carefully. As we shall see.

Chapter 2

THE FAVOURED FAMILY

Abraham, Isaac and Israel

Now, you would think that God would pick someone young to start a new kind of people. Someone who hadn't seen much; who was perhaps mystic, deeply religious; who lived remote from worldly things. Well, God chose a middle-aged man who'd lived in large cities all his life. A mature man with a good-looking wife, no children, and well used to the good things. He had a good business, a fine home and many servants. His name was Abraham. Into whose mind God spoke of fantastic things, and who listened with perfect faith. Abraham, who did not question; and when God said up and go he upped and went.

But understand first the sort of life he went from. By 'large cities' I didn't mean a bigger than usual collection of tents and mud-huts. Not at all. Abraham was born in the City of Ur near the Persian Gulf where the River Euphrates empties. After he was married he moved with his wife, his father and his nephew, whom he was bringing up, to another city far north called Haran. Both Ur and Haran were civilized and sophisticated places. Fine houses, rich plantations, elegant cultured people who knew of music and poetry and mathematics. People who dressed in beautiful clothes and had jewellery made of gold and silver and every kind of precious stone. These cities had many temples. Well, the people had many gods. Gods of all shapes and sizes. Gods they could see and touch. Familiar gods. No home complete without three or four. Regularly dusted.

So you can imagine what Abraham's family said when he told them that the GOD that spoke to him was a voice only: No idol;

no *thing;* just a voice. They thought he was mad.

'Tell me again, my son,' said old Terah, his father, 'you say a god spoke to you. Which god? Which one?'

'The only one,' said Abraham. 'Don't ask me how I know he is the only real one, I can't tell you, I just know. All the other gods *we* made. This one made *us* – and everything else too. He made the world. I'm sure of it.'

'Tell me again what he *said,*' said Terah.

Abraham spoke gently and patiently for he loved his old father and knew he was upset. 'He said I was to leave your house and go where he would lead me. He said he would make my name famous and my family into a great nation.'

The old man shook his head sadly. 'Your family?' he said. 'You have no children. And no sense either to remind poor Sarah of the fact. She has longed for a child as long as I have longed for a grandson.'

Abraham crossed to his wife. She was near to tears. 'Forgive me,' he said, 'but I must go because I believe. I cannot explain but I believe the words. Will you come with me?'

Sarah took his hand. 'Without a child, you are my whole life. What will be will be. I'll come.' Then she smiled. She had a little humour, had Sarah. 'Your god says he'll show you where to go, and that he'll make you famous. He doesn't say anything about doing your cooking and washing.' She kissed Abraham. 'It may be that you *will* be famous,' she said, 'but it won't be for looking after yourself, you're hopeless!'

The young man, Lot, had listened to everything without speaking. He knew his uncle Abraham rather well. He looked on him almost as a father since his own had died. He was part of Abraham's family and he had a good job in Abraham's firm. Import-Export business. One of the biggest in the City. Beautiful house in town; another down by the river; lovely possessions; many servants. All this to be left? Walked away from? Maybe his old grandfather was right. Maybe his uncle Abraham *had* gone mad. Then Lot raised his head from all this thinking and his eyes met those of his uncle. Abraham's eyes were not mad. They were calm, affectionate, a little amused. Abraham was known and respected throughout the City as an honest, shrewd and far-sighted man. Not young, remember, well into middle age. But active and strong – and he knew about people. He knew about his nephew Lot too. Liked him.

'Well, son,' said Abraham, 'what about you? Grandfather won't be coming, I'm giving him the river house and four servants. Everything else we are taking with us. I need a second-in-command who knows my ways. What do you say?'

Lot grinned. 'I say, Yes please,' he said.

Whither Bound?

Well, it took weeks. There was a great deal to do. Abraham seemed never to sleep and often ran Lot to a standstill. The business and the big house were sold. Camels and mules were bought. Flocks of cattle, sheep and goats were made ready. Drovers and shepherds were hired. Also more servants and craftsmen of all kinds. All were encouraged to bring their families, for Abraham told no lies. In answer to the question 'Where?' he answered, 'I don't know yet.'

Two days before the great caravan left he said, 'South.' And south they went.

Now, there came a morning not all that different from any other morning when Sarah, Abraham's wife, decided to have a little nag. Mind you, she had fairly good reason. Listen.

'Abraham,' she said, 'I am not a complaining woman, I've not any cause to be. But frankly I'm a bit scared. When you came home one night and told me we were going to sell up and move because a voice had told you to, and I said whose voice, and you said the voice of God, and I said which one, and you said the only one, I didn't argue. You are not mad and not young and we are not poor and, if you want to pull up your roots, it's my place to help and I did. I won't say you haven't done it well, we are like a small village travelling from place to place, you've thought of everything. But when are we going to *arrive?* We've been weeks and weeks on the road. Hundreds of miles. Passed through some lovely places too. Damascus was a dream. But every time I thought we were there, you said no. In two places you built great monuments because the voice spoke to you there. But we didn't settle. We went on. And,' said Sarah, 'here were are in Canaan in the middle of a famine!'

Abraham looked at his handsome wife, still a beautiful woman, no longer young but full of vigour and character. He felt a bit tired.

'Yes,' he said, 'a famine and a great many mouths to feed. We will go down through the Negev desert to Egypt. It will be hard but we've no choice. There will be great heat and little water. We have, with rationing, sufficient food. There will be bandits but I have armed all the men. In Egypt there is no famine.' He stopped and Sarah waited. She knew he was not finished and was puzzled by what she sensed was a slight embarrassment in Abraham.

'One more thing,' he said. 'It is said that Pharaoh King of Egypt, not past his youth, looks only to the north for the women of his house. He is not attracted to young girls but to mature women. He has been known to kill a husband to get the wife, to destroy a family to steal the mother. We are from the north, and you are beautiful, my Sarah.'

'What can we do?' said Sarah.

'It may be,' said Abraham, 'that a spinster sister will attract the king less than another man's wife. We will say you are my sister and you will dress plainly and keep out of sight.'

It didn't work. Abraham and Sarah hadn't been in Egypt more than a week before Pharaoh had them over for dinner and told Abraham that his sister was to be given the honour of joining the harem right away. As second favourite. 'Your sister will live like a queen,' said Pharaoh, 'and you will be rich beyond your dreams. Cattle, servants, gold and silver, jewels. I pay well.'

He did too. And got nothing for it. God looked after the whole thing. Sarah moved into the palace and Abraham was paid off. Pharaoh gave a huge party to celebrate his latest wife and in the middle of a rather cocky speech was stricken by a sort of paralysis. So were all the other men of the court. And it went on. The women of the court nearly went mad with boredom. Pharaoh's soothsayers finally told him they thought the trouble had some magical connection with the latest wife. 'Maybe,' they said, 'the lady Sarah is protected by a god – or is betrothed to a god. Maybe her brother Abraham is a magician in league with some god.' They weren't far off. 'Get rid of her,' they said, 'and her brother. Ask for nothing back. Tell them to go back up north where they came from!'

Poor Pharaoh. He gave the orders and began to feel a bit better. When Abraham and Sarah went to his sickroom to say goodbye, he looked from one to the other.

'You don't look like brother and sister,' he said. 'I think you're man and wife. Oh well,' he said, 'never mind, whatever you are your family god knows his business.' He was right. As we have seen.

Fair Shares

Well, Abraham and Sarah and Lot his nephew made their way back to Bethel – somewhere in the middle of what we now call Israel. The journey down to Egypt and back because of the famine seemed now like a bad dream. Although the great flocks and presents given them by Pharaoh were real enough. It wasn't long before these great flocks of cattle and sheep and asses and camels began to give Abraham a deal of worry. The country round Bethel did not really provide good enough pasture for all those animals, many of which Abraham had given to Lot as a wedding present. Finding good grazing was difficult, and there was much bad blood between the herdsmen and shepherds of the two men. Not between them personally; Abraham had brought Lot up and treated him almost like a son, having no children of his own. And Lot respected his uncle.

So one day Abraham said to Lot, 'Tomorrow we will ride out into the country and stand on the highest hill and look to every side. As long as your herds and flocks are with mine there will be trouble, therefore let us separate. If you choose the east I will move west, if you want the country to the north I will go south.'

Lot listened and knew his uncle was talking good sense. When they came back from their ride he took some men and journeyed east. He was gone some days and when he returned he'd made up his mind. 'The Jordan Valley,' he said to Abraham. 'Plenty of room and plenty of water. Also,' he said, 'I've decided I've done enough travelling, so I'm going to live in a town. There are two, and they seem quite lively places. Plenty going on.'

'Oh,' said Abraham, 'what are they called?'

'Sodom and Gomorrah,' said Lot.

Well, the dividing up and the sharing out and the farewells all duly took place and Lot went east. Abraham after a while went south to Hebron and settled there. He missed his nephew but knew that he'd done the right thing.

Time passed and Abraham learned little of Lot other than that he'd chosen the town of Sodom to live in. Which for quite a long while seemed a good choice. It was a wicked place with a bad reputation but Lot kept out of things and lived as Abraham had taught him. He was rich, had a nice wife and a couple of small daughters.

Then suddenly one day, a day of confusion and terror, Lot found himself a prisoner of war! His home and the whole town looted and he and all the other captives being marched north. It was a rebellion, a civil war. One of his servants escaped and made his way south to Abraham who, although a man of peace, didn't like the family interfered with. So he gathered together all the men who worked for him, over three hundred of them, and went off to war. He made up in cunning what he lacked in numbers and had fought off enough bandits in his time to know how best to use a small force. Nice thought; middle-aged Abraham a first-class commando-leader. But he was. He chased, and caught up, and harried, and attacked by night, and after about two hundred miles of this he turned the tables completely and Lot and his neighbours and their families took all their looted belongings back home to Sodom.

Abraham and his men helped also to take back the great treasures stolen from the King of Sodom. Who of course was very grateful, especially as his own troops had not done so well in the defence of his city. The King wanted to heap gifts on Abraham, gave a huge party for him, but Abraham wouldn't take a penny. 'Reward the men,' he said. 'They fought for you. I fought for myself and to save a kinsman. It would be dishonest for me to accept anything. You see,' said Abraham, 'I was never in any danger. God made me a sort of promise. Not very detailed, but it certainly didn't include getting killed fighting for you.'

God listened to all this and was pleased, and decided to be a little more detailed with Abraham about that promise.

The Promise

One day when Abraham was sitting quietly outside his tent in the cool of the evening he began to get the tense yet drowsy feeling that he knew from experience meant that God was going to speak to him. He wasn't frightened, and when he felt a sort of velvety black darkness close his eyes and surround him he reckoned that what was about to be said must be more important than usual. It was, although a lot of it he didn't fully understand. God again told him that his descendants would be a special people and live in a beautiful land. 'But first,' said God, 'they will be slaves in a foreign land for four hundred years or so and I will free them from their bondage with plagues and miracles. They will walk through a sea and eat food dropped from heaven.' God continued for some time in this rather serious prophetic way and then after a while Abraham woke up.

He woke as always with a tiny nagging thought in his mind about the word 'descendants'. He and Sarah his wife were childless – and Sarah was well past the age for having babies. It was a subject that Abraham had learnt to avoid with Sarah. She also believed in God, and was very pleased that her husband had been singled out by God, but she too couldn't make sense of that word 'descendant'.

One day she said to Abraham, 'Look, it's ten years since God told us to leave Haran and go wherever he said. We've been to a fair number of places but we seem pretty settled here in Hebron. Well,' she said, 'I've been thinking about this descendant thing. It can't mean *my* son, it must mean a son of your house. Now I know you've never wanted a concubine – it's a great compliment – but I want you to consider Hagar my maid. You know her well and she's a nice young woman who, I'm sure, will give you a fine son.' Then poor Sarah, a bit choked up, went to her room.

Well, it took a long time to convince Abraham, but no alternative arrangement was suggested by God and Hagar was duly delivered of a bouncing boy. She was told it would be a boy by an angel, who also told her that the boy would be a 'wild ass of a man' with many enemies and an enemy to many. The angel also told her that the wild ass would have twelve sons who would become a great multitude. And they did. They are called Arabs.

But Abraham thought that this fine baby, whom he called Ishmael, was the one, the son, the first descendant, the beginning of the coming true of God's promise. And God let him think so until Ishmael was twelve years old. Abraham and Sarah were quite elderly now and lived quietly and contentedly. Well perhaps not so much in Sarah's case. She'd never really got over having no children and sometimes when she looked at Ishmael and his mother she felt very sad indeed. God, who was preparing quite an important statement to give to Abraham, noticed this one day, and decided that something ought to be done for steadfast old Sarah. So when the statement was finished he went to see Abraham, in a dream.

'Now,' said God, 'nearly twenty-five years have gone by and I'm very pleased indeed with the way you've obeyed me and looked after things. I made you then a promise that you shall father a multitude of nations and you will. I said that a land shall be yours; it is *this* land of Canaan, for ever. The land I promised. The promised land. Your son and his sons and their sons shall have no other God but me.'

'Indeed,' said Abraham, 'I have brought Ishmael up to believe in only one God!'

'Ah yes,' said God, 'Ishmael. But he is not the one. Ishmael also shall be a great nation but the son I speak of will be *Sarah's* son. Who will be born this time next year.'

The dream faded and Abraham awoke and thought and, as morning came, he looked at Sarah sleeping. A beautiful woman; but a white-haired beautiful *old* woman. A marvellous wife Sarah had been to him. A son for Sarah! It would hurt her feelings even to suggest such a thing at her time of life. So he decided not to. Stupid of him really. God has his ways of telling people the things he wants them to know. As we shall see.

Don't Laugh!

Now, Abraham and Sarah lived rather quietly in their old age, so Abraham was rather surprised one day when three rather tired hungry-looking people suddenly came round the house. He just looked up and there they were. Surprised or not, Abraham knew the laws of hospitality. He made the men come in and rest in the garden. He had a servant bring water so they could wash and refresh themselves. He asked them whether they would like to eat in the garden and arranged that a good meal was prepared. While they waited for the food to arrive he and the three men talked together. They gave no details of where they were from but said that they were on their way to the two towns of Sodom and Gomorrah. Abraham was interested and told them about his nephew Lot, who lived in Sodom with his wife and two daughters.

One of the men, the tallest, then said, oddly, 'We know. You brought him up well. He remembers and lives decently. A rare thing in Sodom. Or Gommorah.'

Abraham was astonished for he'd said nothing about how he'd brought Lot up. And the men had said they were going *for the first time* to Sodom and Gomorrah. Indeed they'd said they didn't even know the way. Abraham began to have a strange feeling, but before he could say anything the tall man said, 'Where is Sarah your wife?'

Abraham blinked. He hadn't mentioned Sarah's name. At that moment Sarah was just bringing the food out. She heard her name and stopped. Just inside the house. Unseen. The tall man then said, 'We shall pass this way next spring and Sarah shall have a son.' Abraham was now sure that his visitors were from God and he sat silent. And so did they. And into that silence they heard old Sarah laugh. A sad sort of laugh, with tears in it.

The tall man got up and helped Sarah and the servant bring in the food. When the servant had gone, he said gently, 'Sarah, is anything too hard for God? Why did you laugh?' Sarah was about to laugh again, then she looked up into the tall man's face and didn't.

Friend of God

After the men had eaten, Abraham showed them the road to Sodom and gave them Lot's address and they left him. He stood awhile and pondered. He was an old man and next spring his old wife was going to give him a son. He had no more doubts about it. He felt God to be very near. He was right. But when God spoke it made him jump.

'I feel it only right to tell you, my old friend,' said God, 'that I am going to destroy the towns of Sodom and Gomorrah. The people are wicked and cruel and worthless. Your nephew Lot and his family will be all right; the three men will see to that. But everyone else – finish.'

Abraham was shocked. This seemed suddenly a new sort of God bent on a sort of wholesale revenge. There was a silence and then God asked Abraham what was up.

Abraham decided to risk it. 'Thank you for saving Lot,' he said, 'but what of the other good men? There must be *some* worth saving. Or is it too complicated to sort out?'

There was a silence and Abraham thought he had gone too far.

Then God said, 'If I find fifty good men I'll spare the lot. All right?'

Abraham said, 'I've heard it's a pretty wicked place there; what if you only find forty?'

Another silence. 'All right,' said God, 'forty.'

'Er, thirty?' said Abraham.

'I'll forget the whole thing if I find thirty,' said God, without anger.

Abraham took a deep breath. There *may* only be ten,' he said.

God chuckled. 'Abraham,' he said, 'I wasn't wrong about you. All right, ten.'

Well, by this time the three angels were well on their way. The two towns lay just below them. Further away, looking oily and still, the dark water of the Dead Sea. Around them the dead-looking hills with the strange shapes, rather bare jagged hills, made of lava, and limestone. Hills erupted, and sinister. It was evening and the air was oppressive and close.

'Well,' said the tallest of the three angels, 'there they are, Sodom and Gomorrah. God has just told Abraham that if we find even ten good men down there the wiping-out is off. The towns and the people will be spared.'

'Will we find ten?' said one of the others.

'No,' said the tall angel. 'Only one. Abraham's nephew Lot. He and his wife and daughters will be saved. No one else. The arrangement stands. Well,' he said, 'I'm off. You handle this one between you.' And he was gone.

Fire and Brimstone

The tall angel was gone and the other two angels, both disguised as rather dusty travellers, went on down into the valley and into Sodom and to the house of Lot. He was outside getting some air. Around him to every side the noise of the nightly wickedness and debauchery was beginning to increase. Lot got to his feet. Brought up well by Uncle Abraham he offered the two men food and rest. 'Come in,' he said, 'for safety's sake. Lately in Sodom no stranger is safe. The robbing and killing of travellers has become a sort of sport. In the night it's much worse, the gangs are out, they are mad with drink and drugs. Come in, please,' he said, 'I know your arrival has been noticed.'

The two men entered the house and Lot bolted the door. They washed and Lot's wife made them a meal.

Night fell and the noise in the streets grew louder. Lot was nervous for he could hear a great mob gathering outside his house. He shuttered the windows. The two men sat quietly. Lot's wife and daughters stood white and trembling. A stone hit the shutters and then another. A great banging on the door began and the mob roared for the two men to be brought out. Lot tried to speak to them but it just made things worse. The mob ringleader, a huge bearded man, crushed Lot against the door. 'We were only going to burn your visitors,' he shouted, 'now we'll burn you all!' Suddenly the door behind Lot opened and his two guests were on either side of him. There was a great animal shout from the mob and they surged forward. And stopped. And stumbled; and there was no shouting. One of the men took Lot's arm. 'Come inside,' he said. 'They are all blind. It was necessary.'

The man closed the door on the nightmare scene outside and said, 'Pack your things; not too much. God is about to destroy this town and Gomorrah completely. No one will survive. The sea will engulf what is left after the fire has come down. You will leave at dawn.'

And as day broke the two men and Lot and his family left the house. There was a terrible hush in the streets. Here and there groups of people, groping, sightless. They left the town and as they climbed the road out of the valley a great earth-shaking rumbling began. The hills on either side of the two towns erupted and the air was filled with falling rocks and clouds of ash. Then the hills overflowed and split and a sea of red-hot molten lava poured down into the valley. It was difficult to see or hear or breathe. Lot looked round and saw his wife standing still a little way below him. As he shouted to her a shower of stones and fire enveloped her. His own clothes began to smoulder. One of the men appeared out of the smoke. 'Come,' he said, 'she should not have stopped, or looked back.'

Long after, when Lot went to the spot where he'd last seen his wife, there was a rough stone standing on end where it had rolled, or dropped from the sky. Like most of the rock in the valley it was white and crystalline, and in the sun it glittered ... like salt.

Son and Heir

Well, Abraham and Sarah, who had moved so often in the past twenty-five years, moved again. And this time not because God had said so, but because Abraham was being extra-considerate to Sarah who was soon to present him with a son and heir.

Sarah had brooded rather after that awful business at Sodom and Gomorrah when his nephew Lot had lost his wife. Sarah had brought Lot up, and this trouble had worried her. So Abraham and Sarah moved south, down to Beersheba, with all they possessed. Flocks, servants, everything, a whole village of people. Abraham was a cattleman, and rich. Also he was old and wise and rather special and people liked him at sight. Not surprising really, for God had chosen him very carefully indeed.

They all settled into Beersheba quite quickly and Abraham improved the wells and planted trees and made friends and waited for his son to arrive. Sarah, who didn't like to be laughed at, had told no one of God's promise, but servants have sharp ears, and proud old Abraham had dropped a word or two, and by the time the baby was due the whole place was buzzing with excitement. This was no freakish thing, no devil's work, this was a miracle promised by God.

And the day came, a calm cool beautiful day, and Sarah was delivered of a boy. The promised son. The 'descendant' who was to continue the line of Abraham and make a new and special people. All promised by God. Sarah, old Sarah, looked at her son and wept with joy. She'd waited so long.

Abraham named his baby son Isaac, which sounds rather like the Hebrew word for laughter. Certainly there was much laughter. A fat, healthy baby, no halo, quite ordinary. Slept a lot and was made much of. The celebrations went on for days. People came from far and wide and Abraham would point out gently to his rather heathen visitors that to *this* God, the *only* God, *nothing* was impossible. God would listen to his old lieutenant and smile.

Now, you might ask, where did all this leave young Ishmael, Abraham's son by Hagar, the concubine chosen for him by Sarah? Well, Ishmael was now about fourteen years old and a fine lad. He loved his new brother and spent a lot of time amusing baby Isaac. Abraham was pleased to see it, but less pleased at the atmosphere of tension that began between Sarah and the much younger Hagar.

Abraham waited for Sarah to speak her thoughts and one day she came out with it. 'I know it was my idea,' she said, 'that you should have a son by Hagar my servant, but the way things have worked out I don't want my servant's son to be equal to mine. *My* son is your true heir; God said so.'

Abraham was troubled by all this but knew better than to argue with a woman's logic so he told it all to God, who listened and said, 'Sarah is right, and you are to do as she says. Send Hagar and Ishmael away, but don't you worry for either of them, I will look after everything. Ishmael will be the father of twelve princes and they also will become a great nation.' They did too. We call them Arabs.

Abraham was comforted by this and he arranged everything in his usual kind and considerate way. Then he and Sarah settled down to enjoy to the full every minute of the growing up of the son they'd waited so long for. The seasons came and went and baby Isaac grew into a fine boy. His old parents were careful not to spoil him and he was a credit to them. Abraham prayed his thanks to God every day but heard little *from* God for years. But one night God spoke to him again. And what God said was something that brought all his happiness to an abrupt and sudden end.

'God Will Provide'

God had spoken to Abraham quite clearly. 'Take your son Isaac,' he said, 'your only son, whom you love, take him to a mountain I will show you and offer him as a sacrifice. A burnt offering.'

It had been no dream. It was many years since God had spoken in the night to Abraham but the old man knew it was no dream. And now he sat, a large-framed, still active man and his chin was sunk in his beard.

Old Sarah looked at him and then looked again. She knew that he was under some strain. The old couple were very close and since the miraculous birth of young Isaac to them in their old age they had lived in a glow of happiness. Sarah didn't say anything for she knew that if she was to know what was troubling Abraham he would tell her without asking.

Poor Abraham. He was very troubled indeed but this trouble he could *not* share with Sarah. He raised his eyes and met hers. 'I have to go on a journey,' he said carefully. 'I have to go and make a special offering to God who gave us our son Isaac. I will take the boy with me and two of the young men of the house.'

'How long will you be away?' said Sarah.

Abraham got to his feet. 'I'm not sure,' he said. 'It is an order from God. A week perhaps. God spoke of a mountain. None near here.'

The next morning early the young men saddled the asses, packed the food and cut the wood for the sacrificial fire, and they set off. Isaac, on his first long journey, was excited and chattered away. He was about eleven, a good-looking intelligent boy who was determined to enjoy the whole thing. With the two young men for company he didn't notice how silent his father was. Old Abraham rode a little ahead and they stopped only to eat and sleep.

On the third day they came to the base of a high mountain and Abraham dismounted. 'Stay here with the asses,' he said to the two young men. 'I will take the pot of fire and Isaac can carry the fire-wood.'

It was midday. The old man and the boy climbed steadily till the young men could no longer see them. They came at last to a little level clearing and Abraham stopped. 'Here,' he said.

In the middle of the clearing was a great stone with a flattish top. 'Pile the wood on there,' he said.

The boy worked hard and then jumped down and came across to Abraham. 'Father,' he said, 'we forgot to bring a lamb for the sacrifice.'

Abraham looked into the face of his beloved son. 'God will provide the lamb,' he said. 'And now I want you to do as I say without question; as I obey God without question.'

Isaac stood still and Abraham tied up his hands and feet. Then Isaac looked into his father's eyes and saw they were wet with tears and the boy knew it wasn't a game. He kept silent as Abraham bound his eyes. Then he felt himself lifted gently and placed upon the pile of wood. He heard his father strop the knive on the great stone and he heard his father in a choked voice try to pray and give it up. He felt his father's left hand steady him and a movement as though the right hand, the knife hand, was raised high. Then the boy heard his father say, 'I am here, Lord.'

There was a little silence then, as though his father was listening. Then he felt a tear fall on his face and a kiss and he was lifted down. The cloth was taken from his eyes and he looked into his father's face.

Old Abraham pointed. 'Look, my son,' he said. And there, caught in a thicket by his horns, was a ram. 'You see,' said Abraham, rather unsteadily, 'just like I said. God himself provided the lamb. Come, you can help. It must be painless and perfect.'

And when it was done, the old man and the young boy, hand in hand, walked down the mountain.

Isaac and Rebekah

Well, Isaac was all the closer to his father after that. You can imagine. And to his mother. He grew to be a handsome young man, who adored and respected his old parents and gently took over the reins of Abraham's huge cattle business. When Sarah tentatively hinted at marriage, Isaac would chuckle and call her a marriage-broker. 'And where,' he would say, 'would I find a wife like you?'

When Isaac was twenty-seven years old, his beloved mother died and he and Abraham bought some land just north of Beersheba for a burying-place and there old Sarah's body was laid to rest. Abraham mourned a long time and came to lean more and more on Isaac.

The years passed and one day the old man called his oldest servant to him. 'Eliezer,' he said, 'I think I've been a bit selfish; this mourning for the past has gone on too long, and so has my keeping Isaac by my side. He doesn't complain, he's a marvellous man, but it's time he was married. Last night I dreamt his wife came from Haran where I come from. It is an omen, for I don't want him to marry a woman of Canaan. So, old friend,' said Abraham, 'will you take a caravan of ten camels and gifts of every kind and go north to Haran. Trust God. He will guide you to the wife for my son, for my son belongs to God.'

It was a long journey for old Eliezer and took many weeks, but all went well and God overlooked the whole thing. They arrived at Haran in the evening and rested by the well. Eliezer got off his camel, very stiff, and closed his tired old eyes. He began to doze when a voice woke him. A young woman's voice, who offered him a drink of water. 'And while you rest,' she said, 'I'll see that the camels are watered.' She was beautiful and pleasant and Eliezer's quest was over. Her name was Rebekah and her grandfather was Abraham's brother. She took the old man home with her, he distributed the rich gifts of his master and proposed on behalf of his master's son. He also told the long story of Abraham's work for God over the last fifty years. The family talked together and then left it up to Rebekah. 'Will you go?' they asked her. 'Yes,' she said, 'I will.' She took only an old nurse as companion and they left the next day.

It was Isaac's habit, in the cool of the evening, to walk and think in a pleasant small meadow near his house. There were trees and flowers and long shadows. And it was here that Rebekah first saw her gentle-voiced handsome husband. Isaac was in his late thirties and a mature and sensible man but he fell in love with the abandon of a boy and Rebekah returned his love.

Eliezer went to Abraham and related the whole journey. 'A fantastic coincidence,' he told him, 'that I should find this lovely amiable girl right off – and she turns out to be your own grandniece! Amazing!'

Old Abraham lifted his head and smile. 'Old friend,' he said, 'you were an unbeliever when I took you into my service and you are an unbeliever still. What coincidence? Why amazing? I told you before you went that God would guide you. You were never alone – as I am never alone. And my son Isaac and his sons and their sons will never be alone. Because you see,' said Abraham, 'God is interested in this family.'

Isaac's Sons

The Bible tells us that Abraham died in a good old age, full of years. When he died Isaac's twin sons were fifteen years old. Their names were Jacob and Esau.

Rebekah had waited a long time to be a mother. Nearly twenty years. After his marriage Isaac had moved nearer the coast. A place called Gerar, where his old father too had lived for a time. Like his old father, Isaac was in the cattle business. And like his father he became rich. So rich that people started to get jealous. Some of the Gerar people, who were called Philistines – a nasty lot, we shall hear more of them – took to blocking up his wells and so on. So Isaac and Rebekah moved. No small job with thousands of head of cattle and sheep and a big staff. They tried a number of places but the Philistines kept turning up with their well-blocking tricks. Eventually they came back to Beersheba. The Philistines had filled in the wells there since Isaac's childhood, so it was all to dig again. But Isaac was fond of the place and that night he prayed extra hard. He told God that if he could see his way clear to give them all a bit of peace it would be very acceptable. 'Rebekah,' he told God, 'is miserable enough about being childless, let alone this Philistine business with the wells.' God listened and then said to Isaac, 'All right! Beersheba. This place. Make your home here. There'll be no more trouble with the Philistines. Leave it to me.'

So there they settled. Isaac and his vast herds and flocks and huge household. And Rebekah. Still no children. And they'd been married nearly twenty years. But God had not forgotten and one happy day Rebekah was sure she was going to have a child. Well, she didn't have an easy time. Towards the end of her pregnancy she was feeling so rough that she said to God, 'If this is what I've waited for so long I must tell you I don't think I can live through it.' Then God explained, although it didn't mean a lot at the time. But one point he cleared up right away. 'It's twins,' he told poor Rebekah, 'and not just two babies. They will be two nations; two peoples. One will be stronger, and,' he said, 'the elder shall serve the younger.' Well, the prophecy part of what God said didn't disturb Rebekah much, although I'm sure she remembered it later on when the boys had their big quarrel. So Rebekah at last had her family and everyone was very happy for her.

An odd thing happened when they were born. It was said that the second twin was born gripping the heel of the first. In those days such things were taken notice of and people tried to work out what they meant. This omen had them all a bit puzzled. Could have meant that Jacob was tenacious – the kind that hangs on. Certainly that would have been proved right. He was the younger by about one minute and that minute caused a lot of trouble. Out of that minute came strange and wonderful happenings – great promises from God himself, double dealings, two clear cases of fraud, great anger, and great forgiveness. But it all started because Jacob was younger than his twin by one minute.

Very different they grew up to be, the two boys. Even in appearance. Esau was a powerful, muscular sort of boy; red-haired; not very clever, but an active, outdoor, rough and tough kind of lad. Not given to any deep thinking. Not like Jacob. Jacob was a very thoughtful quiet person. He stayed home – and Rebekah, who hardly saw Esau except at meal-times, found Jacob good company. They became very close indeed.

Esau's Birthright

Rebekah was the sort of woman who will treat all her children with fairness and equality but who will have a great possessive protective love for only one. We all know people like that. Not really happy people. And Rebekah wasn't happy either. It was that birthright business. In those days the eldest son was like the firstborn of a King, the inheritor by right of birth. By birthright. Think what that meant to Rebekah. Here was her favourite, Jacob, who was clever, good at figures, farsighted, and who was obviously the better one to take over the business when Isaac retired, but who couldn't because his brother Esau was one minute or so older and thus by right of birth the firstborn. She wouldn't have minded so much but Esau didn't really care one way or the other. As long as he could hunt and be in the open and mix with the cowmen and shepherds he was happy. Always a strong, reliable, obliging fellow. People liked him. People didn't like Jacob as much. He was a bit secretive was Jacob. Kept himself to himself. Very close to Rebekah; held everyone else away.

And so they grew up. And as Rebekah favoured Jacob, so Isaac rather favoured Esau. It goes like that in families. He liked this hairy, bearded ruffian, who had no clever talk but gave off a sort of loving warmth. Jacob used to watch his father and his brother together and became absolutely obsessed with the thought of how much better suited he was to succeed his father than his brother Esau.

One day Jacob was in the kitchen with his mother cooking up a long-time speciality of his. A sort of meat and lentil stew. As skilful as Esau was at hunting meat so equally skilful was Jacob at cooking it. Esau hadn't been home for days. Suddenly there were shouts outside and a very dirty, very tired, absolutely starving Esau lurched in. 'What's that marvellous smell?' he said. 'I haven't eaten for two days – I know what it is,' he said, 'it's that stew! It's like a dream come true – at this minute worth more than gold!'

Jacob, who hadn't spoken since his brother had burst in, straightened up. 'Never mind about gold,' he said, 'is it worth your birthright?'

Jacob's eyes were oddly bright; he looked a bit mad. Rebekah watched everything silently. Jacob said clearly, 'You can have as much stew as you can eat if you give me what you don't want anyway – your right to succeed Dad – your birthright.'

Esau looked from his brother to his Mother. 'If I don't eat soon,' he said, 'I'll die – and a fat lot of good my birthright'll be then.'

Jacob picked up a ladle and a large bowl. 'D'you swear?' he said.

Esau, who now was way out of his depth, said, 'Yes, I swear. Now for goodness' sake dish up!'

Jacob filled the bowl and Rebekah handed it to Esau. 'Eat,'

she said, 'and remember, to swear a promise is serious and I was here and witnessed everything. Say nothing to your Father. I'll tell him.'

But she didn't tell Isaac. Which was wrong. As we shall see.

The Blessing

Now, we didn't give a lot of time to the selling of his birthright by Esau to Jacob for a bowl of meat-and-vegetable stew. Or mess of pottage, if that sounds more familiar. More familiar; less appetizing. Well, the reason was that the detail of the happening is not important. Jacob and Rebekah his mother played a sort of wishful-thinking trick on Esau. It meant little and did them no good at all. But it shows us how much Jacob wanted what Esau possessed just by being a minute or so older. The right to succeed his father in the business. He just *knew* he was best suited for the job. And Rebekah his mother thought so too. Hence the nonsense with the bowl of stew. Don't dwell on it too much; the later, far more serious business of the blessing is more worth your attention.

Now, this blessing affair took place long after; when Jacob and Esau were grown men. And their father Isaac was really rather old. He had been forty when he was married and was all of sixty when the twins were born. Now he was in his late eighties and rather frail, and blind too.

Now, like a good many old people, Isaac didn't do much with his day. He slept a lot and looked forward to his meals. With no sight, his sense of taste was important to his contentment. He had favourite dishes. One of them was a savoury sort of casserole made with baby goat and herbs. Although there were goats among his own flocks, he preferred, he said, 'the wild hill goats that Esau hunts'. One day old Isaac asked Esau to try to catch a goat or two so that this favourite dish of his could be prepared. Esau, who was off on a day's hunt, said he would do his best. He kissed his old Dad and Isaac breathed in the coarse warm smell of his favourite son. It was long since he'd seen Esau, but the feel and smell of him was loved and familiar. Esau turned to his mother and said, 'I'll be back tonight or early tomorrow. I'll have the baby goats with me. I know where to go for them.'

Rebekah stood still for a moment and then like a flash the idea came. The scheme that was to change all their lives. And it did; but not the way she meant it to. She ran from the tent and found Jacob. 'Listen,' she said, 'and do everything I say. Your father just sent Esau to hunt wild goat for his favourite meal. And I know that your father is giving a lot of thought lately to the giving of the blessing.' Jacob stared at his mother. The giving of the blessing was the handing on to the firstborn the authority of the head of the family and with it the land and the flocks and the herds and the whole tribal leadership.

'The giving of the blessing,' murmured Jacob, 'is it time?'

Rebekah came closer. 'Your father is old and weak and he knows he has not got much longer to live and he's blind. Blind,' she said. 'Go at once to the flock and bring two baby goats. Your father shall have his beloved dish from *your* hands, not your brother's. Your voices are similar and you shall dress in your brother's clothes so that when you are near to your father he will smell the wool and fur. Serve your father and ask for the blessing after the wine and prayers. Try not to say too much. The blessing cannot be twice given or taken back. It must be this way. Abraham the founder, Isaac your father, Jacob the son. I know I'm right, Jacob. Not Esau.'

She stopped. 'What are you afraid of?' she said. 'Would I tell you wrong? You are my life!'

Jacob said slowly, 'I've watched my father with Esau. They sit close together. Often my father puts his hand on my brother's head or on his arm. Esau's hair is long, to his shoulders, and his arms are hairy. Mine are smooth and my hair is short and my neck bare. My father is certain to feel the difference when he places his hands during the blessing.'

Rebekah thought for a moment. 'Animal skins,' she said, 'long-haired fur for the back of your head and short-haired fur for your arms. Go for the goats. Leave everything else to me.'

And the whole shameful business worked perfectly. Old blind Isaac was a bit surprised that his splendid meal turned up so soon. But Jacob, copying Esau's voice, said that God had blessed the hunt. While Jacob served his father, the old man's doubts were stilled. He could smell Esau's coarse robes and he could feel the hairy arms and when he placed his hand lovingly on his son's neck he could feel the long hair. One thing though, rather unusual, he could feel his son trembling. Esau was not the trembling kind, a noisy happy rough sort of man, Esau, afraid of nothing.

'Why do you tremble my son?' said old Isaac moving his hand up onto his son's head. Jacob, muffling his voice in his sleeve said, 'Leave your hand on my head father and give me the blessing.' And the old man did. And when it was done, this important unchangeable thing, he heard his son and Rebekah his wife say Amen and quietly leave him.

The old man, sleepy with food and wine and very content, dozed a little. Then he was awakened by Esau, this time the real one, and soon a confused nightmare that he couldn't see was going on round his old head. When Esau realized what had happened at first he cried like a wounded animal, for he loved his old father and set as much store by the love in the great blessing as the honour and authority it contained. The old man, whose blind eyes were now wet with tears would have given anything to take back his blessing, but they both knew he could not. So they sat together awhile and then Esau asked his father to bless him too. 'Have you only one blessing?' he said. Old Isaac steadied himself and explained that Esau must serve Jacob now, but one day, 'one day,' he said, 'you shall be free of this yoke.' Esau kissed his father and went to find Rebekah. She looked at him silently. 'While my father is alive,' he said, 'Jacob is safe. When father dies I will kill Jacob. And you,' he said to his mother, 'and you I will never forgive.'

Jacob in Exile

Now, you might say, if this Jacob was one of the great elders of the Bible, the father of the twelve tribes and all that, son and grandson of men close to God, where was God while Jacob was behaving so disgracefully? Didn't he care about Jacob? Well, believe me, God was there and he cared. Jacob, you see, had to learn humility and some of God's lessons were going to be a bit rough. Look at Jacob's scheming to rob his twin brother Esau of their father's blessing. It had succeeded. Isaac had blessed Jacob with the blessing of the firstborn instead of Esau. Very crafty of Jacob. A lot of good it did him. His poor blind old father heart-broken and hurt. His brother had sworn to kill him. And his mother, who had really planned and plotted the whole thing, was now urging him to flee for his life away from all he'd hoped by his trick to inherit. 'You must go at once,' she said. 'Go far away – to Padan-Aram to your uncle, he will give you a home until your brother Esau may forgive you.'

And so Jacob left Beersheba and the huge flocks and herds which were his father's, and he left alone in the clothes he stood up in. He left in a hurry and in fear. He was full of shame and deserved to be. As he walked through his father's lands he wept. He walked all day and as night fell he found himself in a sort of rocky hollow. It was chilly and he was very tired. He found a smooth stone to use as a pillow and lay down. He felt absolutely forsaken. His mind kept on going over the day and sleep just would not come.

It was pitch dark; dead quiet. Perfect conditions for a vision – or a special sort of dream. Till he died Jacob was not sure which it was. It began with a feeling through his closed eyes that there was a great glowing light above him. He half opened his eyes and at first he couldn't make anything out at all. Then he got used to the light, and the light seemed to be a pure gold sunbeam that reached from the black midnight sky down to the hollow where he lay. Not straight down but like a sloping, steep road from earth to heaven. On it there seemed to be people. Tall beautiful people in robes the colour of the light. They seemed to glide and float, some going up, some down. 'They are angels,' said Jacob to himself and felt his eyes drawn up to the top of the beam where it seemed as bright as the sun. He tried to close his eyes. Not because the light was hurting them, but because he knew suddenly that he was looking into the face of God and to stare didn't seem right. And God spoke. 'Jacob,' he said, 'you are not alone. I am with you and always will be. You shall own great lands and your descendants will be a multitude that will spread through the world. Wherever you go I will never forsake you.'

Slowly the great glow faded and was gone. Jacob was stiff and cold but he felt comforted and safe. When morning came, he took the stone he'd used for a pillow and set it in the ground as an altar, praying his thanks to God, and then continued his journey.

It took a long time, many days, but at last he came to what was in those days called the Land of the People of the East. Top corner of Syria; near Turkey. A long way. He came at last to a well and was pleased to see it for he was parched. There were some shepherds there and they told him his long journey was over. This was the well nearest Haran. The shepherds actually knew Jacob's uncle. One of them, a big friendly chap, said to Jacob, 'If you wait around here one of Laban's own shepherds will be along. Owns a lot of sheep Laban does. They're all watered here.' And sure enough soon there was the sound of sheep bells and a cloud of dust and a large flock arrived. Jacob made his way across to the shepherd and just as he was about to speak the shepherd turned and Jacob looked into the face of the most beautiful girl he'd ever seen. Wonderful moment. Love at first sight on both sides.

She was Rachel, Laban's younger daughter. Jacob's cousin in fact. She took him home with her and he met the family. Laban was the brother of Jacob's mother and was like her both in appearance *and* nature. Pleasant enough, but a rather hard calculating man. Very shrewd. Rachel's older sister was named Leah. Rather plain girl who didn't look as if she was going to find a husband very easily. Jacob settled into the household very quickly. He was soon very useful to Laban because he knew a great deal about sheep and cattle farming, he'd grown up in it.

After about a month Laban, who was delighted with this clever nephew who'd happened along right out of the blue, offered Jacob a more secure job. 'All very well,' he said, 'me being your uncle and all that, but you ought to have some wages.' No fool, Laban; this wasn't generosity, he knew he had a good man and wanted to keep him. Jacob thought about it. This was now his home and he wasn't complaining. He was in love and occupied and happy. So he told Laban that he would work for seven years just for his keep, if he could marry Rachel at the end of that time. Laban agreed right away. And why not indeed!

But when the seven years were up he played a nasty trick on Jacob. When the ceremony was over and the bride lifted her heavy veil, it wasn't beautiful Rachel – it was plain Leah. Jacob hit the roof and began to have a sneaking idea that, although God was on his side, his side weren't doing too well. 'Now look,' said Laban, 'don't get excited. Poor Leah is the elder and if her younger sister gets married first she'll *never* get a husband. It's like that round these parts. Next week you can marry Rachel and do another seven years.' Well, what else could Jacob do?

So Jacob served his two lots of seven years and some on top. Laban was now very rich indeed and owed a great deal to Jacob. And he knew it. So did Jacob; who really still only worked there. Hadn't been made a partner or anything. So Jacob with a little help from God started to work a little for himself and crafty old Laban watched himself being outsmarted time and time again.

The years passed and now *Jacob* was the biggest sheep and cattle man for miles around.

And one day Jacob decided to go back home. He was enormously rich, he had two wives, two concubines, eleven sons and a daughter, huge flocks and crowds of servants but also he was homesick. He gathered his family together and said, 'We go tomorrow.' And they did. Remarkable journey. In many ways. As we shall see.

Wrestling with God

Now, things may not always have been easy between Jacob and his uncle Laban. Both crafty characters. But now that Jacob had started the journey home, he began to worry about his brother Esau. The thought of Esau began to cost him a lot of sleep. He woke one morning very low, depressed, full of pessimistic thoughts. He'd hardly slept and was feeling very much alone. And when you're feeling very alone is a good time to talk to God. Which Jacob decided to do.

'God,' he said, 'I'm frightened. Twenty years ago I ran for my life from my brother's anger. My brother Esau swore to kill me and I deserved it. You know what I did to him and I've been ashamed ever since. I shall never forget that first night on the run all by myself and you sent that dream or vision or whatever it was and you gave me your personal promise to look after me. Wonderful the confidence it's given me all these years away from home. Frankly,' said Jacob, 'I was a bit surprised you bothered with me after that business with Esau – especially as I was in the wrong. When you spoke to me that night I had nothing – and nobody. Now I have a big family and many servants and more cattle and sheep and horses than most people have ever seen. I know it's all your doing and, believe me, I'm very grateful. And when you sent an angel to tell me to pack everything and go back home I did everything you said. I didn't argue; I never have. You've got your own ways of doing things and your own reasons. And I'm sure that telling me to go back home has good sense behind it. And believe me I want to. But my brother Esau is on my mind. A few days ago I sent some of my men on my fastest horses to take a message to Esau. My men got back today and I now have my brother Esau's reply. Look, God, I'm sorry to go on so long but the point is that he is coming to meet me with four hundred men. Four hundred. We are not half that number and we have many women and children and I'm afraid for them. God, you said you'd look after us on this journey home but I must tell you I'm scared stiff. I'd be grateful for any suggestions.'

First thing God did was to give Jacob a good night's sleep. When Jacob awoke God's suggestion was clear in his mind. He got up and got started on it right away. He called his herders together and told them to count out from their flocks two hundred and twenty goats, two hundred and twenty sheep, thirty camels and their young, forty cows and ten bulls and thirty asses. 'All animals in separate herds,' he said, 'and at least one hour between herds. The goats are to leave first. Next sheep. And so on. When the first one meets Esau my brother he is to be told the herd is a present from me and that I am following. Each herder will say the same and hand over the animals. Start now.'

All this took most of the day and with the rest of his servants and workers Jacob set to moving his huge caravan across the shallow stream where they'd been camped for two days. The last to leave was his wife Rachel. She loved her Jacob and knew him very well. They stood together quietly. He explained to her, although he didn't need to really (she was no fool), that he hoped to appease Esau with the great train of presents so that when they met there would be a chance of forgiveness. He kissed Rachel. 'Go to the children,' he said. 'I shall stay this side of the stream tonight. I've a feeling God wants me to.' When Rachel had gone Jacob lay down. It was soon pitch dark. Across the stream, far off, the lights of the camp went out one by one. Jacob waited. Wide awake. His mind churned and raced. Time passed. No vision occurred; no dream came. Jacob got to his feet and decided to cross the stream and join everything he possessed and loved.

But he couldn't. Something, or somebody, blocked every move he made. He could see nothing. The man, if it was a man, made no sound. Hands gripped his arms, and shoulders as strong as his own pushed against him. Jacob was a strong man and his terror made him twice as strong. To get across that stream to everything he loved – his family, his children – was now the most important thing in his life. He fought till the breath in him sang like the wind. It went on and on, this nightmare, and as the sky at last began to lighten the Being suddenly stooped and Jacob screamed as his thigh was dislocated. The pain was terrible and Jacob, exhausted, collapsed against the hands that had wrestled with him for so long. The hands now were firm and gentle and lowered him to the ground. Then a voice spoke. 'Jacob,' it said, 'you have striven with God and with man – and with yourself – and you have done well. From now on your name shall be Israel and your descendants shall be called Israelites.'

Jacob fainted with the pain of his thigh. When he came to, the pain had gone but his leg was twisted and stiff, so that he knew it had been no dream. And Jacob – or Israel – limped across the stream. There were things to do. Twisted thigh or not, new name or not, he still didn't know how Esau was going to be when they met. He ordered the camp to be tidied and that his children be dressed in their best. Food was to be prepared and plenty of wine. After all Esau had four hundred men with him. Jacob tried his best not to worry too much about those four hundred men.

Suddenly there was a shout. Esau and his men had been sighted. Jacob lined up his children and behind them the women of the camp. He waited tensely till Esau dismounted then he went forward, bowing low at every ten paces. This was not only extremely formal but very difficult with his new limp. But Jacob was taking no chances. He needn't have worried. Esau ran forward and took his twin brother Jacob in his great arms and laughed and cried with the joy of finding him again after all these years. There was so much to tell. Esau was marvellous with the children and they responded right away to the rich kind warmth that came from this new uncle.

When everyone had eaten the two brothers looked at each other. Jacob, who had had great trouble making Esau accept the presents, felt that God was very near. Maybe, he thought sleepily, Esau with his goodness and kind eyes and his warm tolerant forgiving nature was a sort of *lesson* from God. As was his twisted leg and his new name. And you know, somehow I don't think Jacob was very far wrong. Do you?

The Sons of Israel

Now, you'd think that, when Jacob had sons of his own, the one thing he'd certainly try to avoid was making the same mistake as his mother had done. You'd think he'd have said to himself, 'All right, I was Mother's boy. And a lot of good it did me. Exiled; worked for years without wages for an uncle I didn't like; lived in fear of my brother's revenge for a quarter of a century. No, there'll be no favourites among *my* lot!'

Well, he may have said it. But he didn't take much notice. He was worse than his mother. With her it was simple; she had twins, she preferred Jacob to Esau. Jacob had thirteen children; twelve sons and a daughter. And the apple of his eye was Joseph. Son number eleven. Mind you, we must be fair, Joseph was the child of Rachel, Jacob's first and true love. You remember he worked seven years for Rachel, and then her father switched sisters and Jacob was landed with her elder sister Leah – and eventually two concubines as well. And Leah and the two concubines between them had had ten sons and a daughter before poor Rachel had even started. Very sweet and gentle woman, Rachel. She longed to have a child and at last she did. And that baby, the eleventh son, was called Joseph. She later had another son, making twelve in all, from all the ladies.

However, to get back to his father's rather ill-judged favouritism of Joseph. Jacob's business was livestock. A huge concern. Cattle, sheep, goats, asses, camels, everything. Very rich man indeed. Not city people. They lived well, but far out in the country. The boys grew up rough and tough. Jacob was a cattle farmer, and his sons were herdsmen and shepherds, and everybody worked. The younger sons did a shorter day, and Joseph was the second youngest. Not that Jacob needed any excuse to keep his favourite near him. Jacob's word was law and his love blinded him to the jealous feelings of his other sons. Mind you, Joseph *was* different from his brothers. He was gentle and quiet, where they were coarse and loud-voiced. He was clever, and learned things quickly, and was a logical and pleasant person. He enjoyed his life, and respected his father, and grew into a handsome, well-built seventeen-year-old whom most people liked a lot. Most people. Not his elder brothers; they couldn't bear him. But Joseph could shut out their dislike by enclosing himself in dreams.

Yes, Joseph was a dreamer. A visionary. And his brothers would jeer and roar with laughter at what they called his dream-talk. Sometimes, though, when at the evening meal he told of his dreams, there was no laughter and no jeering. Just a ring of dark hard eyes. For his brothers construed some of his dreams as meaning that they would all one day be his servants. That he, Joseph, would reign and that they, older than he, would be subject. It may be that God was sending Joseph these prophetic dreams. It would have helped a bit if God had sent also a little tact. Even old Jacob was rather put out once or twice by what seemed to be the obvious meaning of Joseph's dreams. But in Jacob's eyes Joseph could do no wrong. Silly, really, for favouritism always causes trouble in families. At a time when nearly everyone wore a sort of overall of rough-weave or skins, Jacob had made for Joseph a beautiful *coat* of specially woven fine cloth using many different colours – and with *sleeves*. The brothers were livid. Sleeves were for princes – an idiotic present for the young dream-talker!

Jacob was oblivious of the bad atmosphere and one day – one bad day – he sent for Joseph. 'I want you to go and see if all is well with your brothers,' he said. 'They are with the flock at

Shechem.' Joseph went and found that the flock and his brothers had moved on to a place called Dothan, so he followed. Dothan was about fifty miles from home and in those days it took a fair time. His brothers spotted him before he saw them. They were hot and tired from the sun and the shearing, and the sight of Joseph was just about the last straw. One of those mad, hate-filled, wild-eyed conspiracies began. 'We'll kill him' they said, 'we'll say a wild animal did it. We'll toss his body down a pit. Him and his blasted dreams!'

Now the eldest of the brothers was called Reuben and he calmed down first. Also he was fond of his Dad and knew that Joseph's death would just about kill the old man. 'No,' he said, 'no killing. Toss him in a pit for a day or two to teach him respect, but no blood!' He was quite a decent fellow, Reuben, and his plan was to pull Joseph out of the pit when the others had moved on with the flocks. And the others listened. When Joseph arrived his brothers roughed him up a bit and got rid of a lot of stored-up irritation but did him no great harm. Then they took his beautiful coat away from him and put him into a dry well with steep smooth walls and took the rope away.

Brotherly Love

Joseph lay there, rather bruised. The well was pretty deep and he could not hear a sound from above. He'd no idea how long he'd lain there or what was going on.

Good thing too. For what was going on among his brothers was all bad. Reuben wasn't there, he'd gone to check how things were going with the shearing at the far-off points of the great flocks. He was the eldest and in charge. His brothers were together and were settling down to a meal. One of them was a powerful quick-thinking man called Judah. Just as he was dipping his hand into the big pot of food he looked up. Far off he could see a caravan of traders approaching. He knew by the time of year that they would be from Gilead on their way down to Egypt.

'Now listen,' said Judah to his brothers, 'I've an idea that will get Joseph out of our hair for good. Reuben was right, killing him would have been wrong – so we'll not kill him. We'll obey Reuben – and we'll show a profit! We'll *sell* him.'

His brothers looked at him. They knew Judah to be a bit wild – of violent temper, but not mad. And a good, crafty trader.

'Yes! Sell him,' said Judah. He pointed to the approaching line of camels and men. 'Look,' he said, 'I know that lot, their main business is in oils and herbs. They do a lot in medicine-roots and skins and wool too. But they'll deal in anything if the price is right – even slaves! Well,' he said – and he grinned like a wolfe, 'why don't we sell them a *slave*, cheap?'

And it was done. Joseph was up out of the pit and stumbling away on stiff legs behind a camel before he knew what was happening. Judah shared out the money and they finished their meal. They laughed a lot and drank a lot and stayed up very late and all felt very clever.

Then, next day, Reuben got back. Judah, swaggering a bit, told him all about the deal and held out Reuben's tenth share to him. Reuben stood still and looked at his brothers. 'Very clever,' he said, 'thank you for telling me. Have you yet decided which one of you will tell our father?' Suddenly nobody wanted to look at anybody else. 'This will just about kill the old man,' said Reuben. 'All right, Joseph was the youngest and the favourite and we didn't like him but this is a terrible thing we've done.'

Judah was now very ashamed. 'Well, not you,' he said, 'you weren't here.' Reuben looked at his brother. 'What difference?' he said. 'Now listen, we won't tell Dad the truth; we'll kill a goat and smear the blood on Joseph's coat. We'll tear the coat too, and we'll tell Dad that we found it on our way back. Joseph left home after we did and travelled alone. Dad will think he was killed and eaten by wild animals.' Reuben looked down at his feet. 'Not far wrong,' he said. And began to say the prayer for the dead.

Well, the news did nearly kill old Jacob. Nobody could comfort him. He sat with the torn and bloodstained coat across his knees and wept and mourned. A light had gone from his life. He didn't know it but the light had not gone out. It had gone to Egypt. Where we shall go too.

Potiphar's Wife

Well, there stood Joseph – in a slave market in Egypt. His feet were blistered and raw. He was filthy and thirsty and exhausted. He seemed to have been walking for days and days. And now he was up for sale. Fairly high price; for he was young, and well-built and intelligent. The traders were offering him as a house-servant, not a field-slave or labourer.

Joseph stood still and as straight as he could. He closed his eyes against the glare for a while. When he opened them again he met the gaze of a handsome tall man dressed in the uniform of a soldier. He was the Captain of the personal guard of the Pharaoh. His name was Potiphar and he was used to judging the quality of men at first glance. He asked the price, paid it, and walked away. Joseph was handed over into the officer's house-hold within the hour. He was fed and he was given a small room and new clothes. He bathed and shaved and slept like a log for nearly a whole day. He was adaptable was Joseph, made of the best of things, always optimistic, always had a strong feeling God was on his side. Wasn't far wrong. God had biggish plans for Joseph and got started right away. Potiphar began to find out he'd seemingly bought a great bargain in his new house-servant. This Joseph could read and write and had a fine logical mind. Left to handle something tricky he used rare good judgment. He could handle men without raising his voice. Soon Potiphar was leaving more and more to Joseph. His household had never been so well run. Eventually Potiphar made Joseph head man. Overseer in charge of everything. He had great affection for Joseph and treated him almost like a son.

Potiphar's wife, however, had rather different ideas. Very

attractive woman she was, rather younger than her husband. She also appreciated her beautifully-run household and her perfectly-cooked meals, and her well-trained staff. She also appreciated her overseer. And who wouldn't? Joseph was now in his early twenties. Tall, dark and very handsome.

He treated his master's wife with perfect manners and deep respect. Which was the last thing she wanted. She didn't want Joseph's perfect manners and respect, she wanted Joseph! She tried every trick she knew, but Joseph was grateful to Potiphar and was a loyal and principled man. Well, the lady turned nasty. She stole one of Joseph's robes, had it found in her room, told a lot of lies about how he'd tried to force his attentions upon her, and how she'd fought bravely for her honour and how he'd fled leaving his robe behind – a very corny story. But often the most unlikely stories are believed and this story, remember, was told by a lady who had not only been spurned but who was also a first-class liar.

Well, Potiphar believed it; every word. And he threw Joseph into prison and his wife into history. So. This chapter leaves Joseph even worse off than we found him. But we shall see.

Dreams Come True

Well, the years have gone by. Joseph is still in prison but it's not too bad at all. Just lately he had been thinking a lot about dreams and their meanings, and about God who seemed to be a lot in his dreams and who seemed to put into Joseph's mind the clear meanings of them. A sort of correspondence between God and Joseph it seemed to be. Mind you, to have God for a close friend didn't necessarily mean it was going to be roses all the way. Look at Joseph. Favourite son of Jacob; good. Ten elder brothers hated him because of it; bad. They'd sold him into slavery; very bad. Bought by a good master he'd risen to be his master's right-hand man; good. Plotted against by his master's wife who wanted him for *her* right-hand man; bad. But not so bad. Joseph didn't waste time looking back. He was young, about twenty-eight. He was strong, fit, and could think clearly and never complained. Also, as I said, he had God on his side and knew it.

It was the King's prison. Not any less a prison but a rather better class of people. Joseph had been in prison quite a long time. Four to five years. There'd been no trial or anything. Unlikely in that prison. It all rather depended on the King's pleasure whether you came out or not – and the King didn't even *know* about Joseph. It was the King's Captain of the Guard who'd put Joseph away. And as right-hand man to an officer of the King, Joseph was *entitled* to the special prison. All right. He wasn't complaining. The pattern had repeated itself sort of. He was now right-hand man to the chief jailer. He pretty well ran the place. He knew every prisoner and they all liked and trusted him. He had, as my father used to say, time for people. If you were troubled and you spoke to Joseph, the trouble right away got smaller, the frightening dream might turn out to have a quite unfrightening meaning.

Well, one morning there was rather a flurry. Two members of the King's private household were admitted to prison. Pharaoh's chief baker and Pharaoh's chief butler. How they'd offended the King with their buttling and baking we don't know, but there they were – prisoners. Both a bit scared and both turning, as everyone did, to Joseph for reassurance.

Some months passed and Joseph got to know his butler and baker rather well, and from them a very clear picture of the King and his court. The two men came back often to the subject of the King's birthday and of the King's custom of forgiving wrong-doers on his birthday. They were both a bit tight-lipped about what they'd done but were setting a lot of store on getting a birthday pardon. Three days before the birthday both came to Joseph in a bit of a state. They'd both had very vivid dreams and had heard that Joseph could interpret dreams. Joseph listened as always, quietly and sympathetically; he never now questioned the thought that God was handling the dreams department. He waited for the now familiar 'sure' feeling and turned first to the butler.

'The vine and its three branches and the grapes and wine mean that in three days' time Pharaoh will forgive you and you'll get your job back. You will again be in charge of the King's table and the King's wine.'

The butler was overjoyed and promised to put in a word for Joseph to get him pardoned too. 'Leave it to me,' he said, 'I won't forget!'

Joseph now turned to the baker, who was a small man, rather rat-like, shifty type, about whom the word was that he *had* run a sort of racket with stolen flour and wheat.

'Well,' said the little man, 'good for me too?'

Joseph felt sad. 'Er – no,' he said. 'One thing is the same, your life will change in three days' time too. It will end. There will be no pardon. I don't know what you did to make Pharaoh cross but you are to be hanged for it.' And he was.

More Dreams

Well, the butler forgot his promise. People do. But about two years later God jogged his memory a little. So let us sit a while in the company of Pharaoh King of Egypt. Quite a nice man. Bit of a worrier. Superstitious. Believed in all sorts of nonsense. The palace was absolutely littered with idols and gods. But this particular morning the King was getting no comfort from any of them. He was seated (as is only right) on his throne, and around him were about two dozen of the top magicians and wise men of all Egypt. They all sat in a rather uncomfortable silence. Then the King spoke.

'I brought you all here,' he said, 'at considerable expense; you've been here about a week and a half, and you've come up with nothing. The two dreams I brought you here to interpret I've had twice again since you've been here. There's not one of you that's a penn'orth of help at all. I've given each one of you private audiences and a more contradictory load of rubbish I've never heard in all my life!'

Then the King turned to his butler. 'Stop fidgeting,' he said, 'stand still. What's the matter?'

The butler, who knew the King rather well, came nearer. 'My Lord,' he said, 'I've just remembered something which may help. About two years ago I made you cross about something and you threw me into the palace jail.'

'Well?' said the King. 'On my birthday I forgave you and you got your job back.'

'Ah yes,' said the butler, 'but the baker, whom you'd thrown into jail with me, you hanged. Same day. On your birthday.'

'Well?' said the King. 'He was crooked, you were a fool. So?'

'Well,' said the butler, 'the baker and I were told what you were going to do three days *before* your birthday.'

'No one knew,' said the King. 'I didn't make up my mind until I'd opened my presents.'

'We were told,' said the butler, 'by another prisoner who interpreted our dreams. A young man he was. In charge of other prisoners. A Hebrew. Name of Joseph. I promised to say a word for him but forgot. I feel a bit bad about it.'

'So you should,' said the King. 'Get him.' And very soon Joseph stood before Pharaoh. He stood quietly, waiting for God to help him with the meaning of Pharaoh's dreams.

Then he got that familiar 'sure' feeling and began to speak. 'The two dreams are one dream,' he said. 'Two messages from my God. The real God. There's only one. He has done you a great favour really. He has told you what is coming. It is this. There will be seven years of great plenty and rich crops in all Egypt followed by another seven years of famine.'

Pharaoh sat very still. 'I knew it was bad,' he said. 'Does your God send any other message?'

Joseph went on. 'Appoint overseers in every part of the land to gather and store one fifth of every crop of grain. Build great granaries and storehouses. The good years must create the reserves for the famine years. New planting to be done. Better farming. Every effort made to increase yield. All overseers to be in charge of local area managers. They in charge of state marshals, the marshals responsible to one man. That man Pharaoh shall appoint. End of message.'

Pharaoh, who had not moved, stood up. He took a gold chain from his neck and put it on Joseph's. 'You are the man,' he said. 'Your God is no fool. Stay to dinner. You start work tomorrow.'

Corn in Egypt

Well, another ten years have passed. We are still in Egypt. Everything that Joseph has told Pharaoh was going to happen has happened. There have been seven years of rich crops and now it is the middle of the seven years of famine. The advice given by God to Joseph, and passed on to Pharaoh, has been followed. Great storehouses and reserves have been built up and a first-class rationing system is in operation. Nobody gets fat but neither does anyone starve. Joseph has been in charge of everything. He is now forty years old. He is married and has two small sons. A tall handsome man who lives and looks like what he has become, an Egyptian Prince of the Court. More than half his life now he'd been in Egypt.

Joseph did not often recall the first half of his life. When he did, it was with mixed feelings. He recalled the love of Jacob his father; too much love, perhaps, for it had made his ten elder brothers jealous. He recalled how they had sold him to slavers who had brought him to Egypt. Only one brother dwelt in his mind with real warmth. That was his younger brother Benjamin, the baby of the family and his real brother, the others were half-brothers. Just lately Joseph had been wondering whether the famine was as bad in Canaan where his father and brothers lived. At least he thought they lived, for he'd had no contact with them for twenty years or more. A long way away; three to four hundred miles to Canaan.

Well, that very day Joseph was to find out. Three times a week the storehouses sold grain to people not covered by the rationing system. Border-dwellers, wandering desert tribes and such.

Joseph made a point of looking in on these deals. First applications were made to his office at the palace. When he got there
on the morning I'm speaking of, a group of obvious non-
Egyptians were waiting. There were ten. Joseph knew them at
once. They were his brothers. He counted again quickly. No
Benjamin. The brother he most wanted to see again was not
with them.

The ten brothers bowed low before Joseph. Nothing about
this richly dressed Egyptian with his gold ornaments and badges
of office and black wig suggested to them the badly bruised
seventeen-year-old they'd sold as a slave over twenty years ago.
They had come, they told Joseph, to buy grain, a long journey,
their families were starving, they had money, they were from
Canaan, the sons of Jacob, the ten sons of Jacob. Now Joseph
had no reason to love his brothers but neither was he vengeful.
However, seeing his brothers made his desire to see Benjamin
very strong suddenly. And in Egypt he had great power. After
Reuben the eldest brother had finished speaking, Joseph let the
silence go on for a while, then spoke.

'Because I fear God,' he said, 'he gives me special knowledge
and I know that there were *twelve* sons of Jacob, not ten.'

The brothers were thunderstruck. Reuben was the first able
to speak. 'Lord,' he said, 'our father indeed had twelve sons, the
youngest is at home with him, the other . . .'

'The other?' said Joseph.

Poor Reuben, who'd not even been there when Joseph had
been sold and who was really the best of the bunch, was full
of shame, and fear too, of this magical person. At last he said,
'The other . . . is no more.'

Joseph left another silence. His mind was now made up. 'All
right,' he said, 'fill your bags with grain and pay in silver.
Provisions will be given you for your return journey. Provisions
for nine. One of you will stay here in prison until you return
again bringing your youngest brother with you.' The ten brothers were now pale and afraid.

Joseph rose from his throne and just couldn't resist it. 'I know also from God,' he said, 'that the brother you shall bring back with you is called Benjamin.' Well, you can imagine.

Separate Tables

The brothers went back to Canaan and once again it was Reuben's job to tell their old father of a missing son, and of the strange Egyptian who had kept him as a hostage. 'The top man he was,' said Reuben, 'handsome, tall, dark, typical Egyptian. Gave us all the grain we wanted, food for the journey home, asked a fair price and had good manners. Said that God gave him special knowledge; said he knew you had twelve sons, not ten; said we were to take Benjamin to him when we went back – and put poor Simeon in prison to make sure we did. Said that that would prove we weren't spies. Doesn't make sense. If he thought we were spies why let nine of us go? Fantastic the way he knew all about us!'

When Reuben finished speaking, old Jacob sat quiet. Then he said, 'And you say that when you opened the bags of grain your money was there? It is beyond understanding. I do not want Benjamin to go. Joseph went once on a journey and he was eaten by wild beasts. I cannot risk my Benjamin's life. Who knows what this Egyptian wants of us?'

Well, the weeks went by and at last the grain was all used and the old man called his sons together. 'Famine is in the land,' he said, 'and only from Egypt can we buy grain. If it must be, it must. Benjamin shall go. Take to the man gifts of fruits of the land and take back the money returned to you and more money for the new purchases. And I will pray that God will look after us all.'

When the brothers arrived at the great palace where Joseph lived, they were taken not to the grain-office but to Joseph's own living quarters. They were given fresh clothing and told to get cleaned up because they were to lunch with the master. At noon the master, Joseph, entered the great dining room where his brothers waited – they a group of bearded Hebrews, he the right hand of Pharaoh and every inch an Egyptian. The brothers, convinced of his magic powers, bent low. Joseph told them to rise. Benjamin, who was Joseph's true brother – the others were half-brothers – felt an odd affinity somehow with this splendidly dressed prince of the Court. He was sensitive, was Benjamin, and felt somehow that the Prince was highly nervous, near to tears almost. He wasn't far wrong.

Joseph beckoned him forward. 'You are Benjamin,' he said. 'Tell me, how is your father?'

But before Benjamin could answer, the Prince had gone. The Prince had gone into a small room and was in most unprincely tears. Poor Joseph! He longed to reveal who he was, but somehow knew it was not yet the right time. Yet, seeing his younger brother, he was filled with love. He wiped his eyes and calmed down after a minute or two and went back to his guests. They, uncertain, hadn't moved. Joseph, aware of the many servants, watched himself, and the lunch was served.

Famine or not, it was a splendid meal. Odd in one respect. Separate tables. At that time no Egyptian could eat with a Hebrew. Rather like today. Still it was an agreeable, cheerful occasion. Simeon, released from prison, enjoyed it as much as his brothers.

A Different Judah

When the banquet was over they all set off back to Canaan. But Joseph was not quite finished with his brothers yet. They'd not gone far when they heard the sound of horses' hooves behind them.

'Hullo,' said Judah, 'who's this in a hurry?'

It was a party of armed men with orders to search the brothers' goods for a valuable silver goblet missing from the great dining hall where they'd had lunch. It was the master's own, the men said. The brothers were frightened and when the goblet was found in Benjamin's grain sack they were even more so. They knew it was a frame-up but there was nothing they could do.

The brothers were surrounded by the men and taken back to the city. Soon they stood before Joseph again. Now he seemed remote and strange. Richly dressed, every inch an Egyptian, second only to the King. Summary justice. No trial. Just the sentence.

'The goblet,' said Joseph, 'was mighty Pharaoh's and a gift to me. To steal from Pharaoh is to die. But in this case the thief shall be made a slave to serve me. For ever.'

He pointed at Benjamin. 'This one alone is guilty; the others may go free.'

And Joseph waited. He wondered which brother would speak first.

They all seemed shocked, dazed.

Then Judah stepped forward. It was Judah, a wild, violent Judah who had been the leader in the selling of Joseph to the slavers all those years ago. Now it was a different Judah.

'My Lord,' he said, 'we know that Benjamin is innocent. If anyone is to be punished, it should be us, not him, for long ago we sinned against God and against our father. This Benjamin is the son of our father's old age and the only son left of Rachel, our father's true love. We are the sons of other mothers. Our father would die if we return without Benjamin. We once, long ago, returned without Joseph, who was Rachel's firstborn, and our father mourned for many years. My Lord,' said Judah, 'take me for slave and let Benjamin go.'

At this point Joseph broke down. He told them who he was – and the joy and happiness is impossible to describe. He would not let them look back with shame. He was full of grace. 'It was God's will,' he said, 'God sent me to Egypt. To preserve life, to save you and many others from the famine in the land. God showed me how to make the fat years provide for the lean. God made me equal to the King. Go,' said Joseph, 'and bring your families and all you own here to Egypt. And give my love to my father and bring him too. Tell him that Pharaoh has offered the most fertile land in Egypt for Israel and his children to live in.'

The brothers took the message. Jacob wiped away his tears. 'It is enough,' he said, 'Joseph is alive. I will see him again before I die.' And the great gathering-together began, and at last the huge cavalcade was on its way. Pharaoh had even sent wagons from Egypt. They must have been the most gorgeous furniture vans in history!

Israel in Egypt

Now, Jacob, like many old people, was the most sorry to pull up his roots. And God knew it, and a few nights later God appeared to Jacob and told him, as many times before, not to worry. 'Because,' said God, 'I am going to look after the whole thing. Your twelve sons will become a great nation. You remember how just before Benjamin was born I changed your name to Israel? Now go back to sleep, you've got a great time coming.'

And it was a great time. Pharaoh was happy to welcome the family of his great friend Joseph. 'Give them the best,' he said. 'Let them eat the fat of the land.' First one to use that phrase, Pharaoh was. Very friendly chap. No fool either, this Egyptian. He was fully aware of how many assorted skills this crowd of Hebrews were bringing into his country. They liked him and he liked them. Particularly old Jacob. He observed the loving respect shown by Joseph and copied it. And when, seventeen years later, Jacob died, you would have thought it was Pharaoh's own father. The whole of Egypt went into mourning. And when the body was embalmed and taken north to the family tomb in Canaan, there were thousands of Egyptians in the sad, weeping procession.

The funeral ceremonies went on for weeks. Sorry to go on so long about it; it's the thought of all those Hebrews and Egyptians living so happily together. And they did – and for many years too. God did look after Jacob's sons, and their sons, and their sons too. Joseph lived to a ripe old age. Like old Jacob before him he was close to God and was used by God to show the future. Although the second youngest, he was very much the head of the family, and just before he died, he said a rather puzzling thing to them all. He said, 'The land which God promised to Abraham, Isaac, and Jacob is not this land. One day God will come and take you out of this land to the land he promised. The Promised Land.' And one day God did. As we shall see.

Chapter 3

BIRTHPANGS OF A NATION

The years went by and the picture changed. Over four hundred years went by and the original twelve sons of Jacob had become many thousands of people. Not very happy people. For the original Pharaoh's descendant, the present one, was not quite so friendly. In fact he was an absolute horror. He thought of forced labour camps about three thousand years before Hitler did, and used the Hebrews of Goshen (the fertile district which had been allotted to them by his ancestor) pretty well as slaves. They were set to clearing land and making bricks and building a great new city. 'Work 'em to death,' said Pharaoh. 'There are too many of 'em.'

But the outdoor life was a healthy one. And the Hebrew birthrate increased. So one day Pharaoh thought up a new one. A terrible thing. 'From now on,' he said, 'every boy-baby born to the Hebrews is to be killed, drowned in the River Nile.' The order of a madman. But there were plenty of Egyptian spies and secret police to see it done. Great game. Quite enlivened their day for them. Of course not every birth was discovered. No birth certificates or hospitals. Very few doctors available to these thousands of slaves. Women helped each other and the midwives were Hebrew and told lies in their reports to the police. But it was at best a postponement and when, after a month or two, the baby was found (there were frequent raids), it would be worse, much worse.

That was what Amram was thinking as he made his way home from work one night. Back-breaking work, treated like an animal and kept near to starvation like the rest of his people.

But Amram was lucky in one way. He could come home at night. A hovel; half a house; two tiny rooms; but home. Thousands of his kinsmen had no home. They lived in great camps up north near the delta, where Pharaoh was building his great new capital, to be called Rameses after him.

Amram stopped at the low door where he lived. 'It will be terrible for us too,' he thought to himself, 'terrible. Lovely baby. Nearly three months old and never seen the sun. Hidden, wrapped up, kept quiet. But now no longer easy to keep quiet.' He looked to both sides and went in. He went through to the rear room. By a small oil lamp sat his family. His wife Jochebed and his daughter Miriam who was eleven and his small son Aaron who was three and fast asleep. Amram glanced upwards at the ceiling. Between it and the roof rafters above it the baby was hidden. He sat down and looked at his wife and daughter. He thought again how alike they were. The same firm jaw, the same steady dark eyes, the same capable hands. Both had the same patience and love of children. Both gave off a sort of warmth. Amram relaxed a little and then paused. He was sensitive to his wife and daughter and tonight they were giving off a different sort of feeling. A sort of suppressed excitement.

Jochebed and Miriam moved closer to Amram. His wife's eyes were bright. 'I prayed,' she said, 'and a plan came. It must have been in my mind for months. Before the baby was born I noticed that many mothers made tiny coffins for their babies. Of reeds. Sometimes they would get caught in the bulrushes. The guards ignore them. I'm going to make one for *our* baby.'

'A coffin?' said Amram.

'No!' said Jochebed. 'Not a coffin, a floating cradle. I'll make it waterproof with pitch and oiled linen and I'll make *certain* it will be caught in the bulrushes – and I know *where* too.'

Amram stared at his wife and waited.

'Miriam, your clever daughter, has made friends with one of the serving-maids of Pharaoh's daughter. She is not like her father. She longs to be married and have children but no suitors are encouraged at the Palace. Every day she bathes in the river not half a mile from here. It is a secluded place about thirty yards long with a screen of tall bulrushes at each end. After she bathes the Princess walks up and down.'

Now Amram was sitting very still.

'In two days' time,' said Jochebed, 'the Princess will find a live baby in the rushes. The most beautiful baby she's ever seen. He will be clean and sweet and she will love him at sight. Who could fail to? Tomorrow I make the cradle.'

'And then?' said Amram.

'Then,' said his wife rather placidly, 'our Miriam, who will be nearby washing clothes in the river, will ask the Princess whether she would like to have a woman look after the baby for her in secret. The Princess will say yes, and Miriam will run and fetch me.'

Jochebed leaned forward and kissed her dazed husband.

'And I,' she said, 'will be the first woman in history to be both mother and foster-mother to the same child at the same time! You'll see,' she said, 'it will come to pass.'

A Prince of Egypt

Well, the plan worked perfectly, and soon Jochebed was being paid *wages* to look after her own baby until he could be taken by the Princess to live at Court. He would be an Egyptian. But that was to come. In the meantime, thought Jochebed, he's mine, and he's *alive*. She brought him up carefully and the Princess visited regularly and secretly.

But a day came when the Princess told Jochebed that the boy would from then on live at the Palace. He would be brought up and educated as an Egyptian. She was no fool the Princess and in some ways a bit like Jochebed. 'It may be,' she said, 'that you have cared for and loved the boy because you yourself lost a son like him; that when I found a baby, you had that day lost a baby.'

The two women looked at each other.

Then the Princess said, 'The boy has been safe with you. I promise he shall be safe with me.'

Jochebed, who was near to tears, said, 'One thing, Princess. We are Hebrews and this house is a Hebrew house and the boy has a Hebrew name.'

'Yes,' said the Princess. 'At court that won't do. I shall call him Moses, which is more Egyptian than Hebrew.'

And that's not a bad description of the boy who grew to manhood at Court. Moses, more Egyptian than Hebrew. He was a quiet sort of youth and inclined to be shy. He was thoughtful and modest. He used to visit Jochebed when he could; and one day, when she was sure of his discretion, she told him what he'd suspected for a long time. That she was his mother; and that her son, the friendly cheerful Aaron, was his brother; and that Miriam, older than both Aaron and himself was his sister.

His father, the quiet Amram, looked at Moses and was proud of this tall, strong young man with the rather serious face. 'Well, my son,' he said, 'so you are one of us. A Hebrew. Yet you live in an Egyptian Palace and an Egyptian Princess is like a mother to you. What you have learned today about us and yourself will not change anything, except perhaps the way you think about us slaves.' A wise man, Amram.

And he was right. Moses began to spend more and more time away from the idleness of the Palace. Dressed in the clothes of an Egyptian, carrying the staff that showed he was of the Court, he could go anywhere and see everything. And almost wherever he went, he saw great cruelty. He trained himself to show no emotion when he saw the appalling treatment of his brother Hebrews. And in his mind he now called them brothers. No emotion. Until one day he found in himself a rage and fury that left him shocked and trembling and left a sadistic Egyptian guard dead at his feet.

Moses was scared; to kill a guard was punishable by death, member of the Court or not. He steadied himself and looked around. No one else was about. Moses lifted the guard's body and carried it to a nearby gully and buried it and went and stayed the night in the poor quarter of the city with Amram his father.

The next day when he returned to Court he knew something was wrong. The Princess was waiting for him. 'You must go at once,' she said. 'My father Pharaoh knows about the guard. In this matter I can't protect you. He cannot make exceptions and he has no love for you as I have. Go at once.' And Moses did.

Midian and Marriage

Moses left Egypt right away. We'll go with him; in fact we'll go a bit ahead of him. To a place far from Egypt. In the country of Midian. A small village. The home of the village priest. A man called Jethro. He was sitting outside his house and waiting for his seven daughters to come home. They looked after his flock for him. Flock of sheep, not people, *he* looked after *that* lot. He was a bit worried, for the girls had used a pasture that day where the water was scarce and the other shepherds all men and rather rough. The last time they had gone there the girls had been treated very rudely and made to wait till last. Jethro dozed a little and suddenly woke in the middle of a great clatter of excitement. His daughters were all round him and all talking at once.

Yes, they said, they *were* back earlier than expected, they *had* gone to the new place, the shepherds *had* been rude – in fact had told them all to go somewhere else! Used bad language. 'One of them,' said Zippora, the prettiest of the girls, 'even tried to lay his hands on me, and then was picked up and talked to by this man.'

'Picked up? Talked to?' said Jethro. 'What man? And all keep quiet except Zippora.'

'This man,' she said, 'he seemed to appear from nowhere. He was dressed like an Egyptian. He stepped between us, held the shepherd's arms tight to his sides and just lifted him about six inches off the ground. This brought their eyes level and then the

Egyptian, without temper, talked to him. The other shepherds did nothing, they were afraid. Then the Egyptian gave them back their friend and he and they watered the flock for us. And here we are.'

Jethro looked at his rather flushed daughter, 'Anything else?' he said. 'Yes,' said Zippora, 'he is the handsomest man I ever saw, and his eyes are brown, and his name is Moses, and he's coming to supper.' And Moses did.

Jethro, although proud of his fine bevy of daughters, was very pleased to have another man at his table; and so indeed were the girls. They chattered and told the adventure ten times over till Moses, who was rather a modest man, got rather pink. Jethro shooed his daughters off to bed and he and Moses went out and sat in the garden. Jethro had met very few Egyptians but felt that this one was far from typical. And he was right. The Egyptian was no Egyptian but an Israelite, a member (as Moses explained to him) of a slave race.

'Were *you* a slave?' asked Jethro.

Moses smiled. 'No,' he said, 'I lived in the Palace of Pharaoh and his daughter was like a mother to me.' And he told Jethro the rest of his remarkable story.

Both men sat still and quiet for a while. Then Jethro made up his mind. 'Live with us,' he said. 'Be my son' – then he remembered how Zippora had looked at Moses during supper – 'or son-in-law,' he said. No fool Jethro. And that's how it worked out.

The Burning Bush

Moses and Zippora were married and soon had a son and then another. Moses was happy. He liked his wise old father-in-law and his six sisters-in-law. He lived simply. He looked after Jethro's sheep and enjoyed being a shepherd. Often he would go far afield and be away for days. Solitude didn't bother him. On one of these trips he came to a place called Horeb, a pretty sizeable mountain. As the sheep climbed, Moses followed them. Soon he was high above the plain. Suddenly he saw an amazing sight. Not a vision; a real thing. But unbelievable. It was a bush, burning fiercely, with a roaring sound. Nothing near to it was alight but the fantastic thing was that the bush itself stood in the flames unharmed. Not a branch or a leaf changed in any way. Moses remembered suddenly that this mountain was called by people the Mountain of God. As this thought came into his mind, so, equally clearly, he heard a voice. It spoke from the middle of the flames. It said rather an odd thing. It said, 'Take off your shoes.' And then, when Moses just stared, it said, 'Take *off* your shoes. This place is holy.'

Moses did so, and began to have a pretty good idea who was speaking.

He was right. 'This is God,' said the voice, 'don't be afraid, and if you must cover your head with your coat, leave it loose. We have to have a talk and I don't want you to miss anything. You needn't stand so stiff; sit on that rock.' Moses sat down trembling. The bush burned. 'Comfortable?' said God. 'Good. Now listen. I've decided to do something about bringing the children of Israel out of Egypt. They are having a bad time.'

'I come from Egypt,' said Moses.

'I know that,' said God, 'and you're going back to Egypt. I want you to go and talk to Pharaoh for me.'

'I don't want to make excuses,' said Moses, 'but some years ago, as you probably know, I killed a man in Egypt. I'll go back if you say, but Pharaoh may remember.'

'I don't think so,' said God, 'he's been dead for some years. There's a new one. Even worse. The worst yet. I tell you (said God) even with my help you're going to have a hard time.'

Moses said, 'I don't want to question your judgment, Lord, but are you sure I'm the best choice? I'm not a very good speaker, in fact when I'm nervous I stammer.'

'I've noticed that,' said God. 'So I've fixed that your brother Aaron will go with you.'

Moses felt a bit comforted by this – and pleased too – for he'd not seen or heard of his brother since he'd fled from Egypt. He sat quiet and realized that his life was going to be very different from now on. God kept quiet too and then asked Moses what he was worried about *now*.

'Well,' said Moses, 'it's this. If I go to Pharaoh and ask him to free the slaves and tell him the request comes from the middle of a burning bush halfway up a mountain, he's liable either to laugh or to get very cross. Shouldn't I have a note or something?'

'Good point,' said God. 'But not a note. That wouldn't impress him either. Very fond of a bit of magic the Egyptians are. All right then (said God) that shepherd's crook you hold, throw it down on the ground, you've finished being a shepherd, you work for me now.'

Moses threw down the staff, and, as it hit the ground, it turned into a snake. Moses jumped. He hated snakes.

'Keep calm,' said God. 'Take it by the tail.' And, as Moses did, it turned back into his staff.

'Right,' said God, 'that's sign number one. Now put your hand inside your coat and keep it there while you count ten. When you take it out, it will be the white scaly hand of a leper.'

Moses did, and it was. 'Put the hand back,' said God, 'and count ten again and the hand will come out perfectly healed.' Moses did so, and when he saw his own hand back again, he said, 'Thank God' – and then felt a bit silly.

God chuckled and said, 'Perfectly all right. That's number two. Now go home and pack. Get some rest (said God) for you and I have some interesting times coming.'

'Let my People Go'

Well, we are back in Egypt. In Goshen or, as Pharaoh called it, the slave province. Outside a sort of small meeting-hall sat two men, rather depressed. One was Moses and the other was his brother Aaron.

'I didn't even get a chance to show Pharaoh the magic which God gave me,' said Moses. 'Never *seen* a man in such a temper.

Pharaoh went crazy. Said he'd never heard of my God and how dare I interfere with all his building work and brick production.'

'What happened then?' said Aaron.

'Well, then he got really nasty,' said Moses. 'He's cut down the food and increased the hours per week.'

'When was this?' said Aaron.

'About five days ago,' said Moses. 'I've just made things worse. I feel I've done it all wrong. God knows what I should do now.'

'If God knows,' said Aaron, 'perhaps we ought to ask him.'

So they sat and waited till God spoke and, when he did, Moses told him all about it.

'Cheer up,' said God, 'I told you this job wasn't going to be easy. Go and see Pharaoh again. This time no matter how rude he gets, you do the magic. Just the first trick this time. See how it goes.'

Well, Moses and Aaron did as God said. They asked for an appointment and rather to their surprise got one.

The day came and Aaron and Moses stood together before the great throne. Hundreds of people seemed to be present. No Pharaoh. Courtiers, servants, soldiers, priests, officials, and many strangely dressed men with tall staffs of office, each one different. 'They are the court sorcerers and magicians,' said Moses nervously. 'I think we are to be made fun of. Bow your head Aaron,' he said, 'here comes Pharaoh.'

Well, there were great crashings of gongs and blasts on trumpets and music and rose petals thrown about and it all took about twenty minutes, but at last Pharaoh was safely sitting on his throne. There was a silence.

'Speak,' said Pharaoh.

'I don't want to make you cross again,' said Moses to the King, 'but my God said I was to show you a sort of miracle-sign as a kind of credential.'

'Carry on,' said Pharaoh.

Moses took his shepherd's crook and threw it down on the

floor. For one horrible moment he thought it wasn't going to work and then the staff turned into a wicked-looking snake. One or two of the women drew back a little. Nobody seemed very impressed. Pharaoh looked a bit bored and then he motioned his magicians and sorcerers forward. They stood in a half circle round Moses and his snake and they all threw *their* staffs down – and all *their* staffs turned into snakes.

Moses could hardly believe his eyes. 'What on earth happens *now?*' he whispered to Aaron.

Aaron said, 'Look, your snake is eating theirs, but it doesn't seem to be impressing the King. I think we're going to be thrown out again.' And they were.

Moses wasn't too worried, he had a strong idea that it was not the end of the matter. He was right. God had hardly started. Three weeks later Pharaoh held a special meeting. All the sorcerers and magicians and soothsayers were there, waiting. Blast of trumpets (rather shorter than usual), and Pharaoh walked in. He got straight down to business.

'As you know,' he said, 'when this Moses first came to me about freeing the slaves I threw him out and made his beloved slaves work harder. Then he did that walking-stick-into-snake thing and you all did the same and I threw him out again. Then he turned all the water into blood and we had to dig new wells for a week. Well,' said Pharaoh, 'all these so-called miracles *you* lot have been able to do. Now, Moses tells me, we are to have gnats and flies. Can you match that too?'

The magicians looked at each other and were silent.

'And there's something else,' said Pharaoh. 'Moses said that the province of Goshen where the Jews live won't be affected. He said this God of his will make what he called a "division". Anybody want to say anything?'

The head magician stepped forward and said, 'None of this is possible or *we* could do it.'

Then there was a great buzzing and humming and everyone was madly scratching and swatting. Pharaoh checked up on the division. It was true. No insects in Goshen. He sent for Moses and agreed to everything. The gnats and flies vanished. Then Pharaoh went back on his word and kept *on* breaking his promises. God made the plagues worse and worse and each time Pharaoh said the slaves could go and then when God stopped the plague he said they couldn't. Must have been mad. Well, he was, of course. He brought down terrible things on his people. Their cattle died, they were infected with awful sores, their crops were destroyed by great electrical storms and hailstones as big as fists. And nothing could be salvaged because then millions of locusts came and ate everything up. Then when the locusts passed, a terrible black fog came and nobody could see anyone else and the people just sat in misery for three days.

Every day reports came in to Pharaoh about the division. All said the same. In Goshen where the slaves lived there had been no black fog, no locusts, no lightning and hail, no sores, no cattle death, nothing. When the darkness went away Moses again went to Pharaoh and again Pharaoh went back on his word. The two men looked at each other. Pharaoh's eyes were full of hate. Moses felt sad. He had just received orders from God regarding the next and final plague. He held up his hand. 'I have to tell you,' he said, 'that in ten days' time at midnight all the firstborn in Egypt will die. The firstborn of every single family. Yours too. Whether or not you will let the slaves go is now out of your hands. They leave the next morning.'

Then Moses left the great palace and called together the elders and leaders of the slaves and told *them*. 'And,' said Moses, 'we all have our orders too. Every family is to prepare the same meal that night. Roast lamb. When the lamb is killed some of its blood is to be daubed on the lintel and doorposts of every Hebrew house so that when the Angels of Death pass through Egypt that night they will see the blood and pass over those houses. And this deliverance,' said Moses, 'is to be celebrated every year from now on for ever and will be called the "Passover".'

And at midnight on the tenth night to every Egyptian family came a death and to every Hebrew slave came freedom.

Bread from Heaven

After that terrible night when God sent death to all the first-born of Egypt, the children of Israel just left. No one stopped or hindered them in any way. They danced, they sang, they laughed. They were full of trust and hope and joy.

It didn't last long. In no time at all they started to complain. First it was the route, into rather bare, unfriendly country. Then it was the food and then the lack of water. The miracle of the deliverance was soon forgotten.

Mind you, pretty soon they had something really *worth* worrying about. An old enemy. Pharaoh, when he rose from weeping over his own dead firstborn son, decided to get nasty. So he called out his thousands of chariots and soldiers and went after the children of Israel. They'd reached the shores of the Red Sea and now there was water in front of them, and behind them, coming up fast, the chariots full of armed men. They were full of panic. God told Moses what to do and he did it. He waved his staff over the sea and the sea parted and the people walked on dry land on the bottom of the sea. On either side of them were great walls of water held up by God. Ahead of them, to comfort them, was a huge glowing cloud set there by God. When they were halfway across the Egyptians reached the shore and went straight on down after them. God waited until every chariot and soldier was below land-level and then let down the walls of water and drowned the lot of them. Ahead, unharmed, walked the children of Israel. Saved by a great miracle.

But in less than a week they were complaining again. The water where they'd camped was undrinkable, the walking was hard on the feet. 'Maybe,' they said, 'we would have been better off back in Egypt.' Moses stood for quite a lot of this nonsense and then had a word with God. God fixed the water right away. He showed Moses a certain tree near the oasis and told him to throw it in. Moses did so and the water became sweet and the people cheered up. Moses didn't hurry them; they were city dwellers after all, slaves or not, and this desert journey was going to be tough.

After a week or two they went on and the complaints soon began again. They now remembered, it seemed, only the *good* things of Egypt, the oven-baked bread, the plentiful meat and fish. *Very* rose-coloured glasses. By the time they'd been six weeks out of slavery they were holding anti-Moses meetings. Mind you, they were all very hungry. The food they'd brought was finished and the country was bare. Then God sent for Moses. 'Tell the people,' he said, 'that there will be poultry for supper and fresh cereal for breakfast. The cereal will have to be gathered from the ground before sun-up, so get everyone up early.'

Moses, who had perfect faith, told the people. Everybody waited to see what 'poultry for supper' meant. The hot sun burned down; lunchtime came and went. Thousands of hungry people. Then, as the sun began to go down, supper flew in. A great flock of quail delivered themselves straight into the camp. There was plenty for everyone and the people ate well and thanked Moses. He told them all to go to bed early. Next morning, just as it got light, he got them all up to gather their breakfast. As the light increased and the dew lifted, the people at first could see nothing. But then they saw that the ground was covered with what looked like fine frosted cornflakes. A child bent down and tasted it, and said it was like honey but crisp. The people began to gather it, saying to each other, 'What is it?' And that became its name, what-is-it, or, as they said it in Hebrew, *Manna*. And every morning the *manna* was there. It didn't keep, but it was there fresh every morning. Every man gathered his own and everyone had to get up early before the sun got at it.

The Law

Moses looked at the people bent to their task the next morning and thought, 'Early rising, exercise for the back *and* a balanced diet. God must be toning them up for something.' Well, God was. But not right away. The days turned into weeks and the people and their problems kept Moses very busy. He began to look pretty tired. And felt it too. One evening he had a guest to cheer him up a bit. His father-in-law Jethro had come to visit him and had spent the whole day in the great camp and had asked questions and listened to everyone. Moses was fond of him and respected the wisdom of the wise old priest. Jethro looked at Moses with no less affection and began to speak. 'You're doing too much,' he said, 'the people must start to govern themselves. You've done all you promised. You freed them from their slavery in Egypt, you brought them safely across the Red Sea and drowned all their enemies (I wish I'd been there to see it), you arranged the daily arrival of manna from Heaven for them and you've found a way of making fresh water by banging on a rock with your stick. You've even won a battle with the Amalekites for them.'

'Not me,' said Moses, 'not me, God.'

'They can't see God,' said Jethro, 'they can see you. You're easier to complain to than God. You're nearer. Yes,' said Jethro, 'you are doing too much. It's ridiculous that you should have to listen to every grievance and dispute and spend hours and hours on trivialities. Now here's what you have to do. You are to appoint leaders. Honest men who will do all this work for you. You will deal only with great matters. No one but you can talk to God and God is entitled to an uncluttered mind in his head man.'

Moses listened to all this and acted upon it and the people became better organized. It left Moses free to arrange the next part of the journey. This was to the great plain at the foot of Mount Sinai and when the people arrived there they had been three months out of Egypt. 'At this place,' God told Moses, 'on this mountain, I will start to make these children of my beloved Israel into a special people. I will give them through your mouth laws and statutes which will govern every day of their lives. From birth to death. All this will take a long time. Get the people ready.'

Moses told the people to pray and prepare themselves for two days and to be ready on the plain below the mountain on the morning of the third day. Everyone was, and it was something to see. First a sort of hush and then great thunderings and lightnings came from the mountain. It quaked and heaved and great flames and smoke went right up to heaven. Then the sound of a million trumpets began and went on, louder and louder, till the people thought their heads would burst, and then, suddenly it was quiet and still, and Moses began the lessons from God.

First came the ten great rules of behaviour and after these commandments began the lesser rules, in great detail. The people were dazed and frightened. So God asked Moses to go up to the top of the mountain into the great black cloud where they could talk quietly together. It took a long time; Moses was up there nearly seven weeks. God permitted him to take all the notes he needed but God insisted upon writing the first ten commandments himself. With his finger, on two tablets of stone.

When it was time to go Moses turned to God and said, 'You are angry, Lord. Why?'

And God said, 'The people have already disobeyed me. They've broken their promises and are down there worshipping an idol!'

'An *idol!*' said Moses.

'Yes,' said God, 'they put together all their bits of gold and have made an animal idol. A calf. And they are offering sacrifices to it! Well,' said God, 'that's enough. I'm going to wipe them out!'

Moses was afraid but spoke. 'They broke their promise to you Lord,' he said, 'because they are human and fools. How can you break your promise to them? You are God.' And God calmed down and Moses left him.

But Moses was no God and by the time he reached the foot of the mountain and saw the golden calf he was in a violent temper. The drunken, dancing, singing people looked up and there stood Moses on a rock just above them. He looked ten feet tall. Absolute shocked silence. Then Moses raised his arms and hurled the tablets of the Law down at the calf. They fell short and smashed to pieces. Moses felt that his own life was broken too. He walked down and through the people, who parted for him just as the Red Sea had once parted for them.

Forty Years On

Days passed and still Moses sat discouraged and alone. The camp was very subdued and quiet. The people knew they'd gone too far and kept away from Moses – and from the foot of the mountain where Moses had smashed the stone tablets. The tablets regarding the right way to live. The people were afraid and ashamed. God's own finger had written those laws, it was said, and his revenge was likely to be dreadful. Not so long before they'd seen what he did to the Egyptians.

But God was not thinking of revenge. He was rethinking the whole project of teaching this people to *deserve* to be his chosen. The next day he called on Moses. 'No revenge,' he said, 'the promise about giving them a beautiful land to live in still stands. But they must learn to live humbly and quietly and to obey my laws. I will give you another set of tablets and an exact design for the tabernacle to keep them in. Everyone shall contribute to its making and it will be holy and perfect and called the Ark. It will require many different materials, from acacia wood and goats' hair to gold and onyx. It will be carried from place to place for the rest of the journey and your brother Aaron shall be the priest in charge. At every place it will be the centre of the camp and of the people's lives. Above it reaching to Heaven I will set a cloud. When the cloud moves on the people will move on. Not until.'

All this was done and the people followed the cloud and journeyed on and at last came to the borders of Canaan. God told Moses to send out twelve men, one from each tribe, to spy out the land and bring back reports about it. Off they went all in different directions to spy out the nature of the land which

God had promised to the twelve tribes of Israel. Well, the twelve men came back at last and all agreed that the land was rich and had everything, a land they said, 'flowing with milk and honey'. 'But,' they told the people, 'the cities of the land are like forts – like mountains. Many different tribes live in the land, each tribe tens of thousands! And the people of the tribes are huge! Giants!' And every time they told their story they alarmed the Israelites more, who again showed no faith and grew full of fear and anger against Moses who had 'brought them all this way – to be killed by giants!' They held meetings full of madness. 'Let us choose a leader,' they screamed, 'and go back to Egypt!'

Moses wept. But the Lord tapped him on the shoulder. 'Moses,' said God, 'I brought them out of slavery, I drowned their enemies in the sea. I gave them food and drink in the desert. I showed them miracles. And *still* they have no faith in me.'

Moses waited. God sounded more sad than angry.

'Moses,' said God, 'take them all back into the wilderness for another forty years. During that time the lessons will go on, and every person over twenty who spoke against me today will die. Their children shall enter the land, not they.'

And so it was. Not even Moses lived to enter that promised land. But, a little before he died, God gave him a sight of it from a nearby mountain. Even after forty years the Bible says that his eye was bright and his vigour unimpaired. Imagine! Still energetic and clearheaded after all those years in the wilderness training the children of Israel to become fit for the land which God had promised them. It needed a marvellous man to stay with them at all after the way they'd let him down. And Moses was. A marvellous man. In fact never since then, the Bible says, has there been a prophet in Israel like Moses, whom God knew face to face.

The New Man

Now, it's never an easy job to take over the reins from a great man; to have to step into a great man's shoes. Imagine what it must have been like to take over from Moses, the man who had delivered the children of Israel from the power of Pharaoh, who had brought them through the Red Sea and across the desert, who had performed miracles at every turn, who had talked face to face with God, and who had finally led the people for forty years in the wilderness until they arrived for the second time on the borders of the Promised Land.

But Moses was, after all, only a man; he had to die some time, someone had to step into his shoes. And God had marked two possible successors forty years before the appointment would become vacant! Typical. Practical. Like the whole idea of the forty-year delay, during which the people could be made fit for the land which had been promised them. You remember how, when they had first reached the borders of the Promised Land, Moses sent twelve men to spy out the country? And how what they reported frightened the people who, as so often before, showed no faith in God or Moses? And neither did ten of the twelve – remember? Well, one of the two spies who believed absolutely in the promise of God was called Joshua and the other was a man called Caleb. They remained friends all their lives. And, of course, they had plenty of time to get to know one another; forty years in the wilderness.

The great camp of Israel was sleeping. It was the end of a long night and soon the new day would dawn, the day which would mean the end of their wanderings. Only the sentries stayed awake. The sentries and the two men waiting eagerly in the leader's tent. Powerful, middle-aged, prime-of-life men. They were Joshua and Caleb.

They sat in silence. Joshua thinking over yet again all that had happened to him lately. Not just being leader of the people in place of Moses. He'd known he was going to get that job for some time. No, special things had happened, not just the new job. He felt he'd been made over into a new sort of man to fit the job.

It had begun with Moses blessing him just before he died and then, not long after, God himself had spoken; not through

Moses, as for so long, but to him, personally, clearly. Orders, plans, encouragement, confidence in him. He'd felt ten feet tall. And now, with Caleb, he sat quiet. Waiting for spies to return and report.

Soon, silently, well trained by Joshua, the spies came in. As over forty years before he and Caleb had returned after spying out the Promised Land to report to Moses. Joshua's spies, two men, had not gone far. Across the River Jordan to Jericho. The objective, the first place to be dealt with in the taking over of the Promised Land. Not easy, for it was a walled city, like a great fortress. Huge, thick, high walls, so thick and high that many houses were built into the walls. Joshua's spies had known their job; those houses built into the walls had been their way in and their way out.

'A woman helped us,' said one of the men, 'a woman called Rahab. A prostitute; very good-hearted practical person. She hid us, made up lies to cover our escape and told us a great many things.'

'What things?' said Joshua.

'Well,' said the man, 'they're scared stiff of us. The children of Israel are famous! They know of what God did for us recently when we won the two big battles and how he divided the Red Sea and so on. Anyway,' said the man, 'we did a deal with the woman. We promised that, when we take Jericho, neither she nor any of her family will be harmed. Was that all right?'

'Quite all right,' said Joshua and sent the men off to bed.

Making an Impression

Joshua and Caleb talked. Taking Jericho was the second thing; the crossing of the River Jordan was the first. No bridges and no boats; and many thousands of people. He and Caleb, who had absolute faith, didn't waste time worrying. They completed their plans for moving the people down to the plains near the river.

It took about three days and Joshua's officers were everywhere. The people, very different now from the frightened slaves of two generations ago, were fit and excited. The tablets of the Law and the beautiful Ark which contained them were moved to the river bank in charge of priests and of one man from each of the twelve tribes which made up the people.

Then God spoke. 'Joshua,' he said, 'like their fathers before them, the children of Israel will need to be impressed all the time. So as you now carry the staff of my beloved Moses who did miracles for them, I will help *you* do a miracle or two. One of the best remembered is the parting of the Red Sea. Well,' said God, 'as time is short and I want you to make a big impression quickly, you can part the waters of the Jordan for me. We'll start now.'

And it began to be the greatest day in Joshua's life. He had never lacked faith and, as the right hand of Moses, he had seen many miraculous happenings. But never before had he realized how shrewd God is in his dealings with *people.* Joshua, since taking over Moses' job had felt a bit inferior (who wouldn't?) and the children of Israel, although they respected him, had let him know pretty clearly that he wasn't the old man. But now God had decided to show the people that Joshua, whom he'd chosen, was equal to great Moses.

God stage-managed it so beautifully. He'd put the priests and one man from each of the twelve tribes and the holy Ark of the Law down by the side of the great River Jordan in full flood. Well away from them, on rising ground, where they could see everything, the people. Between, Joshua. Instructed by God, he'd raised his staff, Moses' staff, and the priests and men carrying the holy Ark had moved down to the water's edge. As their feet touched the water, the water retreated and, as the Red Sea forty years before had divided for Moses, so had the Jordan halted and piled up in a great glistening wall for Joshua. The priests and their precious burden stopped halfway across and the people passed over in front of them, singing, praying. Then the priests followed and, when the last man was on dry land, the water came down with a roar like thunder.

From that wonderful day Joshua felt like a king and the people treated him like one.

The Walls of Jericho

Soon Joshua's spies told him that news of the children of Israel crossing the Jordan dry-shod had gone through the land like a wind and the many hostile tribes and kings now feared them. Joshua held great prayer-meetings and told the people that God had now forgiven them for their parents' ingratitude after Egypt. The years in the wilderness were over. Clean slate. Fresh start. One more big change, Joshua told them. 'In a day or two,' he said, 'we celebrate the Passover; from then on no more *manna* from heaven every day. We are now in the Promised Land, a land of milk and honey, and we are to eat the produce of this land.'

All this came to pass and, as so often lately, Joshua saw the wisdom of God.

'He's making them work a little now,' he thought. 'Not too easy. Lot of battles yet. Big things ahead.'

The biggest thing ahead was the city of Jericho. A walled city. Like a fortress. And, since the news of the Jordan, shut and barred and impregnable. By all accounts prepared for a long siege too – as the people of Israel were not.

Joshua spent a lot of time looking at the city of Jericho from some high ground. Alone. Thoughtful. It was a problem. One day he sat thinking of how Moses had told him the story of the burning bush and how a voice had said, 'Take off your shoes, this place is holy.' As Joshua wondered why, in the midst of all his worries, he should think of this particular story, a voice beside him said, 'Take off your shoes, this place is holy.' And he had an inkling that his worries about Jericho were about to be sorted out. He looked round and it was a man with a sword. Good-looking; no wings or anything but pretty definitely an angel. Joshua took off his shoes and listened to the battle-plan for Jericho brought from God by this rather splendid officer. Joshua listened carefully.

After outlining the procedure in detail the angel asked him if he had any questions.

'Well, no,' said Joshua. 'I was going to ask if you were joking. But somehow I don't think that you are.'

'I'm not,' said the angel. 'Goodbye. You're going to have an interesting week.'

He was right. On the first day Joshua had called the people together and begun the first part of the angel's battle-plan. He tried not to feel silly. 'Everyone – priests, army, everyone – we are going to walk round Jericho. Once a day for six days. No talking.'

And it was done. Every day the silent walk right round the great walled city of Jericho had taken place. Silent except for the continuous blowing of seven ramshorn trumpets and the sound of thousands of feet. An odd silence too from *inside* the walls. The people of Jericho had heard of this newly-out-of-the-wilderness people of Israel with their all-powerful God who parted rivers and seas for them, and they were fearful. But the seventh day was the one. If Joshua hadn't seen it with his own eyes, he wouldn't have believed it. Again the walk, but on the seventh day *seven* times round and then, as signal, a great sustained note on all trumpets and the people began to shout at the tops of their voices. At first Joshua thought nothing would happen but then the earth rumbled almost as if shouting itself, and the great walls of the city split and crumbled and fell in huge clouds of sandy dust, and into that dust, into the city, from all round it the army went. A victory, a massacre, a wiping out of a city already demoralized with fear and terror. No one was spared except the woman Rahab, who had helped Joshua's spies, and her family. Joshua, like Moses his teacher, did not forget promises.

The Hard Way

Joshua, as we have seen, did not forget promises. Neither did he forget that his wildly excited, victorious people were the sons and daughters of a horde of slaves freed from Egypt by God, as famous for their ingratitude and disobedience as for their miracle-laden delivery. Joshua had seen enough of that disobedience and he was a wise and mature man. He called the people together. 'No looting *at all,*' he told them, 'not by anyone. God was very clear on this. The gold and the silver and the bronze is to be collected and put into the holy treasury. It belongs to God who gave us this day and this victory.'

But people are people. God may make us; when we're babies, we are cute; but families develop some nasty habits. And pass them down. So a little private looting went on, and the stuff was hidden, and the parties concerned felt a bit clever.

Hidden? From *God?* Many times in the past Moses had softened God's anger, but now God didn't even consult Joshua. The next battle – a small one – the people lost. And were shocked. None more than Joshua. He prayed and wept and asked why. Then God told him. 'So tomorrow morning,' said God, 'gather the whole people in their tribes and I will show you which tribe, then which family, then which son of that family, stole from me and you will take him and all who share his guilt and the people will stone them and then burn them and raise a great heap of stones over them. The amount stolen was small but the lesson must be huge and remembered – as a big trouble. And the place shall be known from now on as the Valley of Trouble.' And it is. To this day.

Then Joshua had a think about the recent defeat and being a well-trained soldier and a good general he let it teach him. So he took a small force, started a battle outside the city he was trying to take, made like he was running away, then, as the whole city poured out after him, he led them all into a splendid great ambush and the other part of his army finished the job. No survivors. The name of that city was Ai.

This time the people *asked* what they could take.

'Normal spoils of war,' said Joshua, 'and all cattle and livestock.'

Then, to finish the lesson, he gathered the people together in front of the priests and the holy Ark and he read them every commandment and law that God had given Moses. It took time. He didn't hurry.

Gibeon

Well, Jericho and Ai gave the children of Israel a fearsome reputation. But, reputation aside, even after those victories the people were only about twenty miles in. The next place in was called Gibeon. A crafty lot who'd heard about the children of Israel and their all-powerful God and they'd no intention of fighting. But also they'd heard of Joshua's 'no prisoners, wipe-'em-all-out rule. So what they did was they all disguised themselves as foreigners from a far-off land with worn-out sandals and old patched clothes and tired ragged donkeys and dry mouldy bread and they went to meet Joshua to make a 'spare-our-lives' pact. He, a practical man, needing every ally he could get and seeing no saboteurs in this ragged lot, agreed. When he found out the fraud he didn't go back on his word but said that from now on they, the Gibeonites, would be 'hewers of wood and drawers of water' for the people, and for ever.

This place Gibeon was the cause of a happening, a miracle, a favour by God to Joshua, which ought to be as famous as Jericho. A group of kings of various parts of the land were very annoyed at Gibeon surrendering to Joshua, so they decided to band together and all attack at once. Five of them. Joshua didn't mind his enemies coming to him instead of his having to beat the kings one by one. So he prepared. And he and his army went out to meet them. They marched all night and their sudden appearance next morning was a shock. A panic started and the battle became a hunt. God told Joshua he would help with some showers of great hailstones and if he, Joshua, wanted anything else he should ask. Joshua, having chased the five enemy armies into a great valley, was pretty certain he could manage just with the hailstones. But suddenly, at tea-time, it struck him that darkness would certainly help the enemy, a great many of whom were still alive. So Joshua looked at the sun and said, 'Stand still!'

And God arranged it. The sun stood still for about one day – and all the work was done. Never before; never since.

What's in a Name?

You know, it always seems to me a shame that Joshua is most famous for his easiest job. Jericho. A bit of marching, a lot of trumpeting and shouting, down came the walls, and that was it. Yet Joshua, and this is less well-known, was a first-class leader and soldier who fought dozens of great battles and virtually cleared the Promised Land for the children of Israel. He conquered it, and shared it out among the tribes, and settled them in. A great leader. Successor to Moses and close to God. Who liked him, and helped him a lot. You might say, 'Yes, but the Land was *promised*.' True, but the people weren't just *given* it. They had to deserve it, and *fight* for it. And Joshua showed them how. One of the great loyal servants of God. He brought a people from a wilderness and gave them the dignity of a nation and of a belief. An under-rated man. His name, Joshua, means roughly, 'God saves'. And God did save the nation through Joshua. The people have had other Joshuas since. One, the most famous, lived when Greek was the common language of Europe and the Middle East. Now the Greek alphabet has no letter 'h'; and Hebrew didn't write its vowels at all. Which means that if you take a Hebrew name, write it in Greek letters, and then pronounce it in English, some funny things can happen. Take Joshua for instance; some Roman Catholic Bibles call him Jeshua; and everybody calls his later namesake Jesus.

Gideon Receives Orders

After Moses Joshua. Both great leaders. But after Joshua no great leader of the nation for many years. Only local leaders. Judges. The part of the Bible about them is called Judges. Their work wasn't easy. The Israelites had been a pretty well united people when they were fighting for the Promised Land. But, once settled there in the various parts allotted by Joshua to the various tribes, they drew apart and their enemies lost their fear of this God-protected people. Also, as so often before, the Israelites forgot what God had done and began to worship other gods. So God who had protected them for so long didn't always bother. Nearly two hundred years of this uneasy occupation of the land passed. Long peaceful periods and then new enemies and war and persecution and death. Things don't change much really, do they?

So. Now the enemy are the Midianites and they are a vicious, cruel people and the Israelites are having a bad time. Not surprising; once again they were worshipping idols and breaking their word to God. The bad time had gone on for seven years. Many of the people were living in caves and raid shelters, for the Midianites with their countless fast camels were terrible raiders and laid waste everything they couldn't take away. The people were miserable, oppressed, poor. No leader; there hadn't even been a judge for some time. Enter, much to his own surprise, Gideon.

He was the youngest son of an elderly man called Joash and lived with his wife and family at a place called Ophrah. A bad place to live, surrounded by the enemy and quite cut off from the other larger tribes of Israel. Gideon's tribe was Manasseh, descended from one of Joseph's two sons; a half-tribe really, one of the lesser ones. So. A son of an unimportant family in a not very strong tribe in occupied and oppressed territory. Gideon was a careful, cautious sort of man who did what the others did. He grew food in secret, hid it, stayed out of trouble and really was not very brave. Old Joash his father would have no truck with idols though, and was rather a fine man. He was very fond of Gideon.

One day, Gideon, rather miserable, was at the back of the house putting away some wheat in a secret place. He felt very humble, very much the youngest son, and very depressed. Very much alone. Then a voice said, 'You are not alone. God is with you, you mighty man of valour.'

Gideon looked round. He was certain he hadn't spoken out loud. Sitting on the ground with his back comfortably against the oak tree was a tall, rather handsome man with very blue eyes. He was smiling. He looked as though he smiled often. Gideon was certain also that the man hadn't been there a minute before.

'I didn't hear you,' said Gideon nervously.

'You didn't hear me arrive, or you didn't hear what I said?' the man answered.

'I didn't hear you arrive,' said Gideon. 'I heard what you said.' And then, as the man smiled again, 'I didn't think it was very funny.'

'Funny?' said the man.

'Calling me a mighty man of valour,' said Gideon.

'I wasn't joking,' said the man. 'Someone has got to lead the resistance and it might just as well be you. You are big and strong and no fool. And the enemy, the Midianites, have had it too good for long enough. Nasty lot, but only men. Get rid of 'em!'

'Me?' said Gideon.

'Well, you with a few others and a bit of help from my department,' said the man.

'But there are thousands and thousands of them,' said Gideon, 'they're everywhere; they're in control, and the tribes of Israel are scattered and apart.'

'They are waiting for a leader,' said the man, 'to pull them together. You,' said the man. 'You are a mighty man of – '

'No, I'm *not*,' said Gideon. 'I don't even know how to start. Even in this town, in Ophrah, they tell us what to do. And they've got that great idol there in the market that they pray to. Baal. One or two of our people pray to it, too, I might tell you. Disgusting.'

'Ah,' said the man, and got to his feet. He was a handsome man with very blue eyes. Unusual. He smiled. 'Ah,' he said. 'The idol. Baal. Start with that.'

'And another thing,' said Gideon, 'the – eh? Start with what?'

'The idol,' said the man. 'Get a few of your friends and one of your father's two bulls and go and harness the bull to the idol and pull it down and smash it up.'

'Just a minute,' said Gideon.

'Next to Baal is the idol of Asherah his wife. Very ugly. It's of wood. Pull that one down too and chop it up for firewood,' said the man.

'Firewood?' said Gideon.

'Yes,' said the man, 'for a sacrifice to God. The sacrifice will be your father's second bull. Your father won't mind. He'll be proud of you.'

Gideon stood still and looked into the man's very clear blue eyes. 'I won't deny,' he said carefully, 'that I've often longed to do what you've just suggested – you seem to know my mind – and I won't deny you probably have some special authority. Would you think me rude if I asked you for some proof?'

'Not at all,' said the man. 'Go into the house and bring out the meat pie and the pot of stew on the stove. And some bread.'

'I'm so sorry,' said Gideon. 'I should have offered – '

'It's not to eat,' said the man.

Gideon did as he was told and put the meat and bread on a flat stone and then, without question, poured the stew over both.

'Stand back,' said the man and gently touched the wet mess with his staff.

There was a great roar and a flash of flame and everything, including the man, disappeared. Gideon was blinded for a moment, then stood looking at the spot where the man had been. He rather missed him.

When the man spoke again from just behind him Gideon jumped.

'All right?' said the man.

'How many men will I need?' asked Gideon.

'Ten,' said the man. 'Strong ropes and the seven-year-old bull. The younger bull is for the sacrifice. Any questions?'

'Look,' said Gideon, 'I'm not used to doing brave things and I'm not really afraid for myself. But what about my father and mother and my own family? Would it be all right if I did the job at night? Less chance of the Midianites knowing who did it. Do you mind?'

'Good idea,' said the man. 'Do it tonight. See you tomorrow.'

Resistance Leader

Well, Gideon had done it. He'd done everything the blue-eyed man had said. He had gathered ten of his friends and taken ropes and one of his father's two fine bulls and they had gone into the market place at dead of night and tied the bull to the great idol of Baal and pulled it down and smashed it to bits. Then they'd done the same to the other wooden idol of Asherah, the female, wife of Baal; they had chopped it up and used the wood for a sacrificial fire to God, using the other fine bull as a burnt offering. Even in that the man had been right; Joash, Gideon's father hadn't been cross, he'd been proud of his youngest son. He was a brave and God-fearing man was Joash and, if his Gideon wanted to be a resistance leader against the enemy occupying forces, good luck to him.

But now, the next morning, Gideon wasn't so sure. The Midianites were no fools and could put two and two together and in every occupied town there are informers and very soon there was a banging on the door and a crowd of Midianites and idol-worshipping townspeople were shouting for Joash to bring out his son. Gideon saw that the thing he'd feared, that his whole family might be wiped out, now looked very possible. He wished that the blue-eyed man were there.

And suddenly he was. 'Leave it to your father,' he said. 'He's being looked after. As you are. Same department.'

Old Joash went out to the mob. They surged forward but the old man was still and calm and they stopped.

'If,' said Joash, 'the god Baal is so powerful, no doubt he will destroy utterly the people who destroyed his image. How can Gideon escape if he is guilty? Baal will kill him and everyone else who helped smash the idols. How dare *you*,' the old man said to the now silent crowd, 'how dare *you* presume to take over the revenge of a *god*? Let us all be quiet for a minute or two while Baal strikes dead the guilty ones.'

Then the old man stood for a few moments and as the crowd, looking rather sheepish, faded away he went back inside. He expressed no surprise upon seeing the blue-eyed man, whom Gideon now knew to be an angel, and they sat down at the table.

'Right,' said the man. 'Now listen. The Midianites and their friends the Amalekites are massing not far from here for a big new offensive against Israel. Gideon, I want you to send messengers from this tribe to at least three other tribes to gather for a meeting. I will see that this business of the idol is much talked about and the tribes will take heart.'

Gideon, by no means accustomed to being a leader of men, found that people listened to him and got on with it. He, the youngest son, the quiet one, began to feel full of strength and quite soon about thirty thousand people had answered his call. The more the better, he thought. But the blue-eyed man said no.

'God is not all that pleased with the children of Israel,' he told Gideon. 'This last few years there's been quite a bit of backsliding and worshipping of other gods and rubbish and if this big crowd have any success they'll think they did it all themselves. No,' said the man, 'we'll do the impossible, then God's hand will be seen in it.'

So Gideon sent away two-thirds of them. 'Be prepared,' he told them. 'Everyone has a part to play.'

'Still too many,' said the blue-eyed man, 'ten thousand is still too many. Tell each man to bring his oil jar and all those who have them to carry trumpets of ramshorn or of brass and we are going down to the stream in the valley. Tell the men it is a sort of selection board. It's a fair distance and a hot day and by the time we get there they'll all be thirsty. The men will go down to the stream in platoons and you will appoint watchers. Those men who lie flat and lick the water you can send home; those who kneel and scoop the water into the hand and then drink from the hand are the ones we want. These are not times for the children of Israel to lie on their bellies looking into water, these are times for a non-stop all-round lookout; times to use one hand to eat and the other to fight.'

Gideon got the point but, when only three hundred men remained with him, he was a bit unhappy. There was a huge job to be done. The defeat of a large occupying force in order to start off a great resistance movement throughout the whole land.

'Don't worry,' said the angel. 'You are not alone, any of you. Did you remember to ask the homegoers to leave their oil jars and trumpets?'

'Yes I did,' said Gideon.

'Good,' said the angel. 'When it gets dark I want you to take one man and go down into the next valley where the Midianites and the Amalekites are camped. Thousands of them. A valley full of your enemies. Great opportunity. Take no action. Disguise yourselves, get in, and walk about and listen. You'll be surprised.'

The angel was no fool. He knew that Gideon had almost no experience as a leader and lacked confidence. He sat and waited and at about midnight Gideon got back. The angel smiled; Gideon looked, he thought, a little bigger, a little stronger. 'All well?' he said.

'I was astonished,' said Gideon. 'That whole camp is full of fear. Everybody seems to know there's an uprising beginning. I heard them talking of God. Not *their* god, Baal, whose idol I pulled down, but our God, and how he's on our side. I even heard them talking about *me!*'

'*Did* you,' said the angel. 'About destroying the idol and being a man of God and being what I once called you, a mighty man of valour?'

'Well, yes,' said Gideon.

'Right,' said the angel and got to his feet. 'Do it tonight. There's no moon.'

He gave no more orders and left it to Gideon, who went and woke his three hundred men.

'Divide into three companies,' he said. 'Each man will carry a trumpet and some oil jars. We will form a ring above the camp. Watch me. When I smash my jar and set light to the oil, do the same. Then blow the trumpets and shout the words, "For the Lord and for Gideon". Light the jars and roll them, throw them. Fire, noise, confusion, that's what we're after. In the dark they will fight each other in terror. Then they'll run. Let 'em. Thousands of our men from other tribes are waiting for them. I'm not going to ask for any questions. I know it sounds impossible but nearly everything that God does is.'

Gideon turned to the blue-eyed man. 'Did you wish to add anything?' he said politely.

The angel looked at Gideon with great affection. 'Not a word,' he said.

And it all came to pass. A quiet camp in darkness; then, from high above, unearthly trumpeting, shouts of God and Gideon, and rolling, bouncing balls of fire. Panic; pandemonium; men filled with madness and blind, superstitious fear. A headlong retreat into waiting ambushes. Massacre. Victory. As so many times in the past, God had raised a leader when the children of Israel badly needed one, and freed them from bondage.

But still the children of Israel were far from a united people.

Even while the great battle was on and the enemy were in full flight, when Gideon and his small band of guerrillas pursuing them had arrived exhausted at two villages, they had been refused food by their fellow Israelites 'until,' said the people, 'the kings of the enemy are actually caught!'

Gideon had straightened up and wiped the sweat from his eyes. 'When I have the two kings,' he said, 'I shall come back to this place and also to the place over the hill who also refused us food and I shall teach both of you a lesson you will never forget.'

And he did. He never questioned the feeling in him that he was guided by God. A sometimes very angry God with many times good reason to be angry with his chosen people. God had picked Gideon, and was making a leader, and a leader had to know how to punish as well as how to reward. The people of both places were shocked at the hard justice of Gideon's punishments. In one place a terrible scourging of seventy men with whips made of briar and thorn twigs. In the other a tearing down of buildings and a mass execution. But the people, seeing a new Gideon, saw in him also the sort of leader they knew they needed.

When the trial of the two kings took place for their crimes against humanity – their oppression and tyranny had been about as long as the last war – the place was packed with the elders and heads of houses sent to see how Gideon would handle things. The evidence was heard and among that evidence was proof that Gideon's own brothers had been slaughtered on the orders of the two kings. Not as an act of war; as an act of murder. The people waited, quiet. Gideon looked at the two kings. Dark, powerful, cynical men with much more experience in cruelty than he had. 'Had you spared my brothers,' he said, 'I should have spared you. I am a man of peace and killing does not come as easy to me as to you. But here in this place you will die as you lived, by the sword.'

The kings showed no fear and in the silence they sensed how the people were judging Gideon. The elder of the two kings smiled. 'Do it yourself, Gideon,' he said. 'Stand up, take your sword, and *you* kill us.' He looked round at the people with contempt. 'You have to *show* them what you are, how strong. So do it yourself,' he said. 'For as the man is, so is his strength.'

And Gideon, recognizing yet another lesson, did so.

Then the people said to Gideon, 'Rule over us, and after you your son and his son too, for you delivered us.'

But Gideon said, 'No, God delivered you,' he said, 'and God will rule you.'

He was a modest man was Gideon and no fool, though the ideal of being ruled by God doesn't always work out so ideally!

In the Bible the whole story of Gideon takes up less than three chapters. Perhaps he'd have been wiser to accept leadership for himself and his family. Anyhow, the way he obeyed God with unquestioning faith gave the people of Israel forty years of peace.

Samson Takes a Wife

'Never took *any* notice of his parents, got into some terrible scrapes, never shaved, wouldn't have his hair cut, had a terrible temper – and was an absolute fool with women! Came to a sticky end.'

If you heard anything like that in the bus or the tavern or the supermarket, you might think it was some middle-aged person talking about one of his neighbours' teenage sons. But before you jump in and take sides, it's as well to remember that the fellow might be talking about one of the so-called judges of Israel. More a resistance leader than a judge really this one. Name of Samson. And what a tearaway! If he lived today, he'd never be out of the papers. Or the courts. 'No visible means of support, my Lord, a number of cases of assault. Also of grievous bodily harm, insulting words and behaviour, arson, larceny and quite a lot of manslaughter.' Yes, Samson's parents had a *real* handful.

He was their firstborn. Rather a surprise, for they'd tried many times to have a child but with no success. His mother was beginning to get used to being childless. But one day her husband got home from work and as she gave him a drink before his dinner he looked at her.

'Not drinking?' he said. 'Anything wrong? You look a bit odd.'

'I'm not sure,' she said, 'but I won't drink with you. Not wine or alcohol, this man said I shouldn't.'

'Man?' said her husband.

His wife went a bit dreamy. 'Yes,' she said. 'Wonderful-looking fellow. I don't know where he came from; he wouldn't say – nor what his name was. We weren't together long. When he left me he said I would have a baby.'

Her husband put down his drink. 'Oh yes?' he said.

'Yes,' said his wife. 'It will be a boy and belong to God all his life and no wine or alcohol for me till I've had him.'

'I see,' said her husband whose name was Manoah. 'Yes. Well if he turns up again, dear, this fellow, I'd like to have a word with him.'

And God understood and sent the angel again. Again in civvies. Manoah listened to him carefully. Prophets and medicine men were no strangers in that town. Neither were seducers. His wife was virtuous but this was a marvellous-looking man. Magnetic.

'Wonderful thing to look forward to,' said Manoah to the angel, 'having a son. Always wanted a boy of my own. Offered lots of sacrifices to God in the past. We pray every night. Burnt offerings, the lot.'

'You don't really believe,' said the angel. 'Prepare, while I'm here, one *more* small burnt offering to God. A baby goat.'

Manoah and his wife prepared the gift and the man stood quietly. As the smoke rose it turned pure white and the man walked forward into the smoke and gently, with the smoke, went back up to heaven. Then Manoah believed and was frightened, for he'd had bad thoughts both about an angel of God and about his God-chosen wife.

She listened to his wailing and praying for a fair time and then got fed up. Like any pregnant lady she was very practical. 'Do stop,' she said. 'Nothing's going to happen to *you*. We're going to have a son. We've been allowed to see wonderful things' – she touched her hair – 'and meet a wonderful man. I feel in my heart,' she said, 'that our son will be special. Different from other boys.'

Poor soul, she was right. But that was later. Meanwhile she believed and trusted, and everything that the angel had told her came true. She obeyed his instructions to the letter. No alcohol, careful diet, plenty of rest. And when her time came she gave birth to a fine boy. She, whom the town had long given up as one of the barren ones, now had a real prize-winner. She called him Samson and brought him up carefully. As the angel had said, she made him a Nazirite, a member of a special sect who never cut their hair or beards. But Nazirite or not, God-given or not, pretty soon it was evident that he was going to be a handful. Physically, God gave him everything. Great good looks, a superb physique and the strength of a horse. But he had quite a lot of devil in him too. He had a terrible temper and a great fondness for rough company. He attracted trouble like a magnet and got into one scrape after another.

Apart from anything else they and all the other tribes of Israel were under the domination of the Philistines, who, as the occupying force, kept a tight rein. Samson was quite without fear – as foolish people often are. He was thoughtless and head-strong. Gave his mother a lot of sleepless nights.

'If only he would get married,' she would say to her husband, 'find a nice girl, settle down; if not a girl from our own tribe, from one of the others, a respectable Hebrew girl.' *Very* often she'd say that to her husband and when Samson got home from Timnah one night she'd just finished saying it again.

'We were just talking about you,' she said. 'I'm pleased you're back.' (Timnah was a Philistine place and there'd been a lot of trouble. She was always worried when he went there.) 'Do you want some food?' she asked him. 'Something to drink? Anything you want just tell me.'

Samson looked down at her. 'I want to get married,' he said.

His mother closed her eyes a moment. A prayer answered.

God is good. 'A girl of our tribe?' she said. 'Do we know her family?'

'I don't think so,' said Samson the Nazirite, member of a holy Jewish sect. 'She's a Philistine.'

Well, you can imagine. The questions, the arguments, the tears. But mixed marriages have worked before, so Samson's parents, heavy-hearted, agreed to go with him to Timnah to meet the girl's family. Off they went, the parents walking ahead, rather quiet, with not much to say to each other, and some way behind, Samson. They came to the vineyard on the edge of town and, as Samson walked through the trees, a lion roared.

Samson stopped and waited and soon he saw it. He had no weapon but had wrestled in the past with opponents as big as the lion. He had this mad sort of logic, had Samson. And also, remember, he had great strength and a terrible temper. He killed the lion and left it and walked on and caught up with his parents. He was out of breath a little and his robe was torn but they, rather preoccupied, didn't remark upon it so neither did he. Mind you, if your mother asked *you* how you got your jacket torn you *also* might think twice about saying you'd just killed a lion with your bare hands.

But that lion was to make more trouble for Samson dead than it had done alive. Oh yes.

Well, the parents settled all the details and the date was set for the wedding week. (Weddings at that time lasted a week. Big feasting, house guests, happy holiday.) The time came and off went Samson to his bride's town to get married. Once again he and his parents walked through the vineyards on the edge of town, they by tradition ahead, he some way behind. By himself. He came to the spot where he'd fought and killed the lion. There was little left of it; hungry birds, vultures. But there, in among the dried bones, was a nest of bees. A rare thing; and Samson loved honey. He waited till the bees swarmed elsewhere and took a handful of the comb and walked on. A huge bearded handsome man going to his wedding eating candy.

After the ceremony the guests settled down to their week of fun and games. One of the games was the asking of riddles, and Samson, who liked the game – and also liked to gamble – said, 'I've got a riddle. I bet you all thirty weekday suits and thirty Sunday suits that you won't find the answer in the seven days of the wedding.' He chose the number thirty because there were thirty young men at the party. 'All right?' he said.

They agreed and asked for the riddle. So Samson, remembering the dead lion and the honey, said:

'Out of the eater came something to eat.
Out of the strong came something sweet.'

Well, everybody laughed and tried this answer and that but no one got near it – and the bet was huge. Three days went by and the young men no longer thought it funny. Very little is still funny on the fourth day of *any* party. They went to the bride.

'We did not come to your darned wedding to be made fools of,' they said. 'Or to be made poor! You get the answer to the riddle from that Hebrew giant you've married or we'll burn this house down with you in it – and we're not joking!' And they weren't and she knew it.

Well, she *did* wheedle the answer out of Samson – ladies have their little ways – and she told the young men, who gathered round Samson on the evening on the seventh day and in unison jeered at him:

'What is sweeter than honey?
What is stronger than a lion?'

Samson looked at the ring of Philistine faces and, never a good loser, went mad. He went on a rampage worse than ever before and his rages were famous. Next day he delivered the suits of the bet to the young men but they were the clothes of other young men he'd killed. They, terrified, took the shroud garments and fled. He, Samson wouldn't look at his new bride and went back home to his parents.

Exit Samson

As the weeks passed and the time of the harvest came Samson's anger went away and he decided to go to see his wife. When he arrived at her father's house, the dark cynical Philistine smiled up at the huge Hebrew. 'I thought you hated her,' he said. 'I gave her to someone else. Her younger sister is unmarried though, have her.' Samson walked away and looked across at the fields of wheat ready for harvest. He looked at the olive groves too, and decided to burn the lot. And did.

And, as always, bad breeds worse. The Philistine authorities, hunting Samson, burned his wife and her father as a reprisal. Then Samson, in a red rage that made his earlier killing seem like a tea-party, went on a berserk bloodbath that turned him into a dreaded mad-eyed slaughterer. Then he disappeared and turned up again living in a cave high up in the cleft of a mountain.

The Philistines now saw that this wild man, who seemingly couldn't be caught or hurt, was a danger by his example. The Hebrews saw him as a sort of symbol, something to copy. A bad thing. So the Philistines made a plan to have Samson's own people capture him. Not very clever. As we shall see.

The plan was that some of the tribe of Judah, Hebrews like Samson, would go and get him and hand him over. If they didn't, the Philistines said, there would be some killing of Hebrews for a change.

So the men of Judah went to Samson and he listened to them. 'Are you mad?' they said to him. 'The Philistines are the rulers in the land. Because of you many of our people may die.'

Samson got to his feet. 'Swear to me,' he said, 'that you yourselves will in no way injure me. Tie me up with strong ropes and deliver me – which is your part of the bargain with the Philistines – but do not harm me.'

The men promised and Samson let himself be bound and taken from his cave and down to where the force of Philistines were waiting. The men of Judah moved away and Samson stood

alone. Tied up. With a great gang of Philistines charging up
the slope to kill him.

But God stood with Samson and Samson, with a little help
from God, burst the ropes that bound him and looked around
for a weapon. Nearby was the vulture-cleaned skeleton of an
ass. Samson took the sickle-like jawbone from the skull and
proceeded, as so many times before, to lose his temper and kill
Philistines. A great many. And, as before, he got away. To this
day that place is called Jawbone Hill.

And so time passed and although the Philistines remained in
control always there was Samson, the wild man, who lived in
caves and always got away, and was a sort of symbol of courage
to the Hebrews.

Now although a Nazirite, a man of God, Samson was, as we
have seen, an undisciplined character and a bit of a fool with
women. Once he was visiting a lady friend in Gaza – after all,
caves get lonely – and the Philistine police heard about it. Quick
conference; orders given; men stationed here and there; informers; spies; the lot. Knowing Samson they were pretty certain he'd
stay the night. 'Tomorrow morning,' they said, 'when he leaves
her house a bit sleepy and tired, we'll kill him. Tell the men.
We'll do it by the city gates.'

So at dawn the next day they met as planned. By the city
gates. Which weren't there. Samson had left at midnight and
taken them with him! As always with Samson, the larger-than-
life gesture, the over-acted bit.

But enemies in charge are not fools. They never are. They had
quite a file on Samson and one thing went like a thread right
through it; he was a bit of a fool with women.

All right. The top brass held a meeting. 'There is a woman,' said
the man at the top of the table, 'who lives in the valley of Sorek.
She has done one or two little spy jobs for us in the past. Very
good-looking woman. Expensive tastes. She met Samson once
and is prepared to go to a bit of trouble to meet him again. She
charges a lot but, if anyone can give that madman to us, she can.'

'Splendid,' said one of the others. 'What's her name?'

'Delilah,' said the man.

Well, the Philistine chiefs of staff went to Delilah and the deal was made. 'We've nearly had him time and time again,' they told her. 'But this Samson apart from being a giant with the strength of ten men is also obviously protected by some god or other. We are not telling you to kill him, it may not be possible, but fix it so that we can catch him and lock him up and we'll pay well.'

Well, it didn't take long. Samson was soon in love and visiting often. Often too she would bring up the subject of his great strength which so many times had saved him and prevented his capture. She was not just making conversation. If she could find out what magic made him so strong, she could maybe break the magic and make him weak, and the men in the next room could rush in and cart him off, and she'd get her money.

Samson would tease her and show off. 'If I'm tied with new bow strings,' he'd say, 'or new ropes never used.' And she would. And he'd burst out of them as though they were cotton.

So she started to nag and withhold a few favours and generally drive him up the wall. And at last he told her. 'I'm a Nazirite,' he said. 'We are special people protected by God. Every hair of my head is my covenant with God, never broken, never cut. If I cut my hair, my promise to God would be broken and his protection of me would stop. My strength is from God.'

And that was it. Delilah drugged his wine and cut off his hair and called in the men. They chained him and they blinded him and they locked him up in a prison and worked him like a mule.

Now, the Philistines made a big thing out of capturing Samson. 'See,' they crowed, 'no superman. Just a man. Broke a promise to his God and became weak. His God was his strength.' So true. And not only of Samson.

They put him on show. A prisoner; blind, weak, with a shaven head. A sight made easy for us to imagine by something not long ago called Belsen. People queued to look at him. National holiday. To be celebrated every year. Samson Day.

The next year, the first anniversary, the celebration took place in a great hall not long built. Much talked about. The only place with a balcony, boxes and gallery. *Very* new. Everything supported by beautiful marble pillars.

The place was packed to the roof. Splendid show. Songs, brave poems, a little play all about how Samson was captured – with a very famous actress playing Delilah. Interval for refreshment and then the main attraction. Personal appearance of Samson himself! Brought from prison by a young guard. No longer bald, still the same huge physique, hollow eyesockets, walking like a king. They stood him where everyone could see him between the two main pillars of the building and they screamed and jeered and threw rotten fruit. Great sport.

Samson stood and seemed to be talking. He was. To God. 'Give me back, O Lord,' he said, 'just this once more, the strength I had. Just once more. Let me pay them back for blinding me. Please.'

And God listened and guided Samson's hands, his left to one pillar, his right to the other. And God helped Samson, the main attraction of the evening, to bring the house down. Hundreds were killed. Samson too. The man who all his life had loved big flamboyant gestures had been allowed by God to make the biggest exit of all.

Ruth and Naomi

Between the great chronicle of the Judges of Israel and the four mighty books of the Kings, which begin with Samuel the King-maker and go on to Saul and David and Solomon and all the rest – between the Judges and the Kings comes a quiet little story, the story of two famous women and only four short chapters in the Bible, but with a title of their own, 'The Book of Ruth'. The book, as I said, is called Ruth. She gets top billing. But for me her mother-in-law is the one. A completely unselfish, shrewd, big-hearted woman who saw great tragedy. A mother bereft, a wife widowed. Did God perhaps foresee all the terrible jokes that were going to be made about mothers-in-law and arrange for the story of this one mother-in-law to be written down? Naomi, the mother-in-law of Ruth.

The story begins where another more famous story began. In Bethlehem. In a time of famine. The story moves away to another land across the Dead Sea and then moves back to Bethlehem. Do you know that in the Dead Sea the water is so full of various salts that you can't sink? A person becomes unsinkable; like Naomi.

Naomi and her husband and two sons were of the tribe of Judah descended from Jacob's son. They didn't have much money but they didn't need much. 'With two sons like I've got,' Naomi used to say, 'who needs money?' Fine, handsome young men. Both single, both devoted to Mum, both worried, as was Dad, about this famine – which seemed to go on and on. Living was very hard indeed.

One night at supper, a very poor sort of supper, one of those all-the-family-we've-got-to-face-it discussions took place and Naomi's husband, a good man called Elimelech, said, 'Well, we've just got to face it, people are starving here. And not only here. It seems from what I hear that the whole land is barren.'

The two young men said nothing. They knew their father. If he'd decided something it must be after careful thought.

'We will move out of this land,' said Elimelech, 'across the salt sea to Moab. Our two countries are friendly, and I'm told things are better there. We won't be the first. We'll start tomorrow.' He looked at his wife. 'It'll be a wrench for me too,' he said, 'but what else can we do?'

Naomi got up. 'You are right,' she said and smiled at her three handsome men. 'What can I lose?'

Poor Naomi; in not all that long she was to lose the three of them. It all started so well too. They liked their new home and the people of Moab were kind and the men found work and they managed. Then one day Elimelech came home saying he felt unwell and two days later was dead. A dreadful shock. Naomi was stunned. He'd never been ill, and he wasn't old, a strong man, a loving good man. She thought she would die too. She felt very far from home indeed. As they were. Her sons were wonderful to her and she didn't waste time mourning. They stayed in Moab.

One day she said to her sons, 'Now look,' she said, 'I've been thinking. You are both old enough to get married and we all like this town. I want you to know that if you want to marry Moabite girls it's all right with me. These are good people.'

Her elder son smiled. 'In that case,' he said, 'I'd like you to meet someone. Tomorrow. Her name is Ruth.'

Well, the girl was beautiful. Tall, slim, with lovely hair and eyes and the quietest, gentlest smile Naomi had ever seen.

Naomi and Ruth were friends in five minutes. Naomi's younger son wasted no time either. It wasn't long before he also came home with a local girl for his Mum to meet.

'Mother,' he said, 'this is Orpah.'

And soon the boys were both married and Naomi, who'd thought she would never smile again after her husband died, found great happiness in her fine sons and her daughters-in-law, and the girls found in their mother-in-law a wonderful wise friend. They all lived in the same house; the girls insisted. They wouldn't hear of Naomi living alone or moving from one to the other.

The years passed. Happy years. Life was easy and smooth. At least for the three women; the men were mine workers; hard work, but they made a good living. Naomi used to tease her daughters-in-law about her 'sad lack of grandchildren'. But the two couples were young and there was no hurry. There was plenty of time, they would say.

Then one day Naomi woke up with those words in her mind. 'There's plenty of time.' Something was nagging at her. She remembered that two days before her husband had died he'd said that. Two days before. Big, strong, perfectly fit. 'This is a good country,' he'd said, 'and there's plenty of time.' And two days later he was gone.

Naomi couldn't rest. When her two sons left for the mine that morning she was tense, ill-at-ease. 'Be careful,' she said, 'be extra careful.' The two men and their wives joked with her, tried to break her mood, but she couldn't smile. 'Take every care,' she said, 'every care.'

She was by herself when they brought the news. The two wives were in the market. 'An accident,' they said. 'Awful. Unforeseeable. Despite all precautions. Dreadful thing. Both men killed outright. Instantaneous. No pain.'

No pain. Naomi sat like a stone. Hands in lap. Eyes dry. As the men turned to go, the girls came in, running. They were pale, they'd heard a rumour, the women in the market were saying ... Then Naomi stood up and screamed. Just once; like an animal. Hoarse, from the heart, from the broken heart.

For a second no one moved, then as the girls went forward to comfort her she opened her arms to comfort them. Three widows; all childless.

Back to Bethlehem

After the funeral there seemed to Naomi little reason for staying in Moab in this sad town. So she made plans to return to Bethlehem in Judah. She was silent and very bitter. She didn't pray. 'Go back to your mothers,' she told the girls. 'You are young – and better wives no man could find. May you find husbands that deserve you.'

The girls wept and implored her to stay – or that they could go with her – but she was adamant. First she kissed Orpah goodbye and watched her go, then she turned to Ruth. The tall lovely girl looked into her mother-in-law's eyes. 'Don't ask me to leave you again,' she said. 'I won't. Wherever you go, wherever you live, I want to be with you. Your God will be my God, your people mine.'

'All right,' said Naomi. 'I won't argue.'

They left the next morning. A long journey, and it took them several weeks.

They didn't talk much. At each place they stopped, people were curious but stayed away. Curious to see two women travelling alone: one good-looking, though she never smiled; the other, the younger, very beautiful.

When they arrived in Bethlehem, Naomi had been away ten years. She had left during a famine to try a new land. Now on every side she could see a good harvest. She had left with a husband and two fine sons. Now she was back with one daughter-in-law. Naomi, as she walked with Ruth through familiar streets, streets full of memories, was very sad. But she was grateful for the younger woman's quiet understanding and unselfish sympathy.

They came to the market area near to where Naomi had lived. A woman walked by; stopped; came back. Soon others. 'It is *you* Naomi? You seem different. How long is it? How was it in Moab? We missed you. How's your husband? And your two fine sons?'

Naomi told her old friends the story of the last ten years. They listened with tears in their eyes.

'And this is your daughter-in-law?' they said.

Naomi put her arm round Ruth. 'No. My daughter,' she said. 'No husband, no sons – a daughter. All I have left.'

Her friends, who remembered a smiling happy Naomi, wept and sighed at this sad-eyed grey woman. 'Oh Naomi, oh Naomi,' they said.

'You should change my name,' said Naomi, 'change it to Mara, which means bitter, which by God I am.'

Ruth looked into her beloved mother-in-law's eyes. 'And Naomi means pleasant,' she said, 'which by God you are. Everything, you once taught me, is by God.'

And Naomi, always practical and level, was a little ashamed.

Boaz

In no time at all the whole town knew Naomi's terrible story and people were kind as much as they were able. Ruth and Naomi were poor and not keen on accepting charity. One day Naomi said, 'Ruth dear, on the outskirts of town there's a biggish farm owned by a man called Boaz. My husband was related to him. You never met him. At this time of year, at harvest, there is a custom in Israel that poor people may follow the reapers and glean the corn and barley which is missed. What do you think?'

'I'll start today,' said Ruth, and off she went.

The people at the farm, when she told them who she was, were friendly and she joined the other poor people who walked behind the reapers. Towards the end of the morning the owner of the farm happened to notice her as he toured his fields. Boaz was not a young man. He was a good-hearted, much-liked person.

'Who is that?' he said.

They told him. He'd heard the story of the two widows and he was moved. He called her over.

'Go to no other farm,' he said. 'Glean here every day all day. At midday eat and drink with the workers. Orders will be given that no young man will molest you in any way.'

Ruth felt the tears begin to come.

'I've heard of your faithfulness and devotion to your mother-in-law,' said Boaz, 'and God will bless you for it. It seems to me,' said Boaz, looking at the beautiful Ruth, 'that you are a rare person.'

Well, Naomi was glad to see Ruth safely home that night. It was the first time for a long while that they'd spent so many hours apart. She thought her lovely daughter-in-law looked a bit flushed, and she noticed the size of the bag of wheat and barley she was carrying. Also a little parcel of food. But she asked no questions. She knew that Ruth would tell her everything. When the young woman had washed and tidied herself and they were eating she did.

'I met him,' said Ruth.

'Who?' said Naomi, although she knew.

'Your kinsman,' said Ruth, 'Boaz. You said he was old, he's not old, he's sort of mature, distinguished, adult. We spoke together. He knew about us and how I came back with you from Moab when poor Mahlon died and I became like you, a widow. He asked if I felt homesick for my own land and did I miss my mother and I said you were my mother and that seemed to please him.'

'It pleases me too,' said Naomi. 'Did he say it was all right to glean in his fields?'

'He said more,' said Ruth. 'He said I was to glean nowhere else, and I heard him tell the reapers to tie the bundles carelessly so that there will always be enough for both me and my mother. He asked me to join him for the midday meal and gave me too much and insisted I brought the food I couldn't eat home. Said that all this was the least he could do for a kinswoman. I suppose he meant you.'

'Not altogether,' said Naomi and felt a long-dead match-making urge begin in her for her beautiful steadfast daughter-in-law. 'Not altogether. Here in Israel the laws of kin and family are clear and strict. The land belonging to my husband, his inheritance, also as it were includes me and, as the widow of my son, you too. So my relatives are also yours in a way.'

Ruth smiled. 'So I'm sort of related to that man,' she said. 'That's nice.'

Naomi began to gather dishes. 'Yes,' she said. 'That's nice.'

Harvest Home

Every day Ruth went to the fields and worked hard and one night when the harvesting was nearly done she came home rather excited. 'Tomorrow night,' she told Naomi, 'there's to be an end-of-harvesting party for the workers and although I'm only a gleaner I've been invited.'

'By Boaz?' asked Naomi.

'I'm not sure,' said Ruth. 'I don't see him often. Is it all right to go?'

'Yes,' said Naomi, 'it is. Be home early tomorrow.'

The next evening Naomi had a cool bath waiting for her daughter-in-law and helped her to dress and do her hair. They dipped in boxes and found a little jewellery and some good perfume. When the job was done Ruth was a sight to see.

'Now listen,' said Naomi, practical. 'A while back I told you a bit about family custom here in Israel. Widows like us can ask a kinsman to buy the inheritance of our dead husbands and we go with the property. The man gets land plus goods plus, if he wants, a wife or extra woman of his house. Some fine marriages have come out of such deals. Boaz is a close relative, I think next-of-kin in this law. Tonight, ask him his advice on this matter.'

Ruth, rather shy of the rich Boaz, waited till late in the party and then stumblingly spoke to him. He, knowing the laws better than she, told her that another man was of closer kin and that he would ask him if he wanted to take over the inheritance of the two women.

'If he does, well and good,' said Boaz. 'If not, as the Lord lives, I will do the part of next-of-kin for you. You have honoured me by asking me. The whole town knows you to be a woman of worth. You are not of Israel, yet you are an example to us all.'

And there they sat, Ruth and Boaz, and they talked long into the night and found much to say. When Ruth got home Naomi was awake and when the girl had finished pouring it all out Naomi said, 'I know Boaz. He will settle this matter. Tomorrow.'

And he did. He was now sure that he loved this girl from Maob, this beautiful girl Ruth. But he knew that he could still lose her. So he felt a bit tense as he took his seat, accompanied by ten elders of the community, at the town gate, the traditional place of open-air discussion. Together they waited for the man whom he'd spoken of to Ruth to come by.

Before long the man came down the road. As he was about

to pass, Boaz said correctly, 'Turn aside, friend. Sit down here.' The man did.

Boaz began. 'Naomi,' he said, 'kinswoman to us both, has, as you know, now returned from Moab with her widowed daughter-in-law. Her other son also is dead and also Elimelech her husband. She offers for sale the parcel of land belonging to her dead husband and sons. By family law you are the next-of-kin and have first option.'

The man pondered. 'I'll buy,' he said.

'If you buy,' said Boaz, 'understand that by the family law of Israel you also buy Ruth of Moab, widow of the firstborn, thus restoring the name of the dead to his inheritance.'

The man pondered again and Boaz could hear his own heart beating.

'No,' said the man. 'I won't buy. The arrangement impairs my own inheritance. I pass my right to the next closest of kin. Is that you?'

Boaz smiled. 'Yes,' he said.

Then with all due ceremony, with the elders as witnesses, he bought the parcel of land. The transaction, by tradition, was sealed by the giving of a sandal by the party of the first part to the party of the second part. All was correctly done and when the day of the wedding came the whole town turned out and the good wishes were genuine.

Boaz was a generous man and it was a great party. Naomi, mother-in-law extraordinary, moved among the guests and many remarked how she looked as she did ten or so years before when her menfolk were all alive. Naomi cried a little – mothers do at weddings – and turned often to look at Ruth and Boaz standing together in a glow of happiness.

The months passed and one day Ruth went to Naomi. 'You once joked with me about your sad lack of grandchildren,' she said. 'Well, I'm attending to it.'

When the baby was born, Naomi became its nurse, grannie, sitter-in, taker-out for walks, the lot. Ruth didn't mind; in

Naomi's hands *she* had been safe. The baby, beloved grandson
of Naomi, was named Obed. Obed who was the father of Jesse,
who was the father of – But before we go on to Jesse and his
sons, one of whom was to be King of Israel, we must become
acquainted with the last of Israel's judges, the great prophet
Samuel. Samuel, the Kingmaker, who gives his name to the first
two books of Israel's Kings.

Birth of a Kingmaker

As with the stories of Isaac and Jacob and Joseph and Moses
and Samson, we begin the story of Samuel at the beginning –
with our hero's birth.

Samuel's father lived at a place called Ramah, not far from
Jerusalem. His name was Elkanah and he had two wives – most
men of his income-bracket did. Their names were Peninnah,
who had lots of children, and Hannah, who had none. And not
for want of trying, it was just hard luck. She longed for a child.
Her husband Elkanah, who loved her, used to say to her, 'Why
weep? Why be sad, and go off your food? Am I not more to
you than ten sons?'(Nearly as tactless as me whose firstborn
came into the world on May 1st. 'Ah,' I said to my wife about
two hours after she'd had him, 'Ah, Labour Day!')

Poor Hannah. Very much Number Two wife. And Number One
wife, Peninnah, made certain she remembered it, especially each
year when the whole family went to Shiloh for thanksgiving.
Shiloh, where the holy Ark was kept and the sacrificing and
praying went on for days. All in charge of old Eli, High Priest and
one of the leaders of the people. The leaders called *Judges* in the
Bible.

At Shiloh each year Hannah was very sad. Year after year
she prayed and hoped, but no baby. Only a lot of nasty remarks
from Number One wife. Hannah would fast and grow faint and
would look unsteady and sick. She would sway and rock back
and forth and in a low voice implore God to make her a mother.
And one year old Eli noticed this dazed-looking woman who

looked so pale and who muttered and wept. 'You drink too much,' he said, 'you should try to give it up. Be strong.' Nearly as tactful as me!

Hannah explained to the old priest. She poured it all out. 'I told God,' she said, 'that if he gave me a son I would give him back to serve God all his life.'

Old Eli was moved. This was a good woman and this was true love of God. 'Go in peace,' he said to her. 'I also will pray for you and God will answer your prayer. You shall have a son.'

And it all came true.

Hannah had waited so long, prayed so hard, hoped so much, and now she had a fine baby boy. 'I shall call him Samuel,' she said. 'God promised and kept his word. And I shall keep my word to God,' she told her husband. 'Samuel will serve God all his life. In a year or two I shall take him back to Eli and he will be the smallest, youngest helper in the house of God. Each year I shall visit him and I shall take him new clothes. Each year a bit bigger. He will live in the sanctuary and become a priest like good Eli.'

Elkanah didn't argue. He had other children by his other wife and also he felt that this God-granted son might well be a sort of special person. He wasn't wrong.

So the day came and Hannah took little Samuel and gave him over into the kindly hands of Eli. Who was very pleased to have him. You see Eli had two grown-up sons of his own who worked with him in the sanctuary, but they were no good. Violent, dishonest men. Great sadness to Eli who knew he'd been rather weak with them. But in Samuel Eli found great joy. The boy learned quickly and was sensible and good-mannered and he showed the old priest great love and respect. God did not leave Hannah lonely. She had other children; but every year she went to Shiloh, to the sanctuary, to see Samuel her firstborn.

The years passed. Samuel was very observant and he saw and understood many things. He saw how Eli's two sons used the service and sacrifices offered to God to commit every kind of sin. They ignored their father, who *was* rather old. He in turn drew closer to Samuel. Once he said to his wicked sons, 'If a man sins against a man, God can help. But, if men sin against God as you do, who then can help?' But they still ignored him.

Then one day a man called on Eli. The old priest knew the type right away. Gaunt, poorly dressed, eyes with an oddly unfocussed look; the visionary, the bringer of messages, the holy man. The man refused both food and drink and delivered his message. From God. About Eli's two sons and their evil practices – and their punishment to come. 'They will die,' said the man. 'Both on the same day. And your house, the house of Eli, will grow weak. Poverty will come, poor health, early death, sadness. For in allowing your sons' wickedness you have shared in it, and will share their punishment.'

Poor Eli was shocked.

'And,' said the man, 'God will raise up for himself a faithful priest who will be strong and will *not* permit wrongdoing, and a time will come when the remnants of your house will go to his house to beg for a crust, a job.'

Poor Eli. He seemed to lose heart after that. His eyesight, not good for a long time, grew worse. A big man, he seemed to shrink a little, to sag. He looked a bit lost. And leaned more and more on his young helper Samuel to whom he told everything. 'All will come to pass,' said the old priest. 'It was the word of God. How rarely in this land is God's voice heard any more. I do not hear or see visions, nor does anybody else.' Eli looked at Samuel. Handsome, clear-eyed, quiet. 'Perhaps *you* will hear the voice and see the way,' he said. 'You were given by God, perhaps *you* are to be his faithful priest.'

The old man was not far wrong.

Samuel Takes Over

Meanwhile Samuel looked after old Eli with great care. Stayed near him; even slept near him, in a little room just across the passage.

One night Samuel had seen the old man to bed and tucked him in and had gone to his own bed. He had prayed as usual and had settled down. He was tired. He'd had a long day. He dozed off.

Suddenly he was awake, wide awake. He ran in to Eli. 'Here I am,' he said. 'What do you want, father?'

The old priest said, 'I did not call you my son, go back to bed.'

Samuel did and lay still. It was very silent.

Then again the voice, 'Samuel,' it said, 'Samuel.'

Again Samuel went in to Eli who again said he had not called. The old man, nearly blind, sensed a strangeness in the night. 'Go back to your bed,' he said gently, and he waited.

Sure enough, Samuel came in a third time. 'Here I am, father,' he said. 'Are you playing a game?'

Eli was now sure. 'The voice you heard,' he said carefully, 'was not mine but God's. Go back again to your bed and when the Lord calls you again, answer, *Speak, Lord; your servant hears.*'

Samuel did as he was told and the voice did call again and spoke clearly and at some length into his mind. The voice told him many things, all of the future. Samuel, boy priest, was now a boy prophet. Chosen by God.

His life did not change much. He grew into a fine young man and took over many of the duties of the sanctuary. He preached and people listened. He became famous from one end of the country to the other. Man of God, prophet, leader. A leader however whom not all the people followed. Many still worshipped idols and forgot God. So some years later, when the Philistines attacked, God didn't help. Even though the people took the holy Ark to the battlefield and prayed extra hard, they lost. And worse, the Philistines captured the Ark itself and took it away.

The people of Israel were shocked, forsaken. Many thousands were killed in the battle. Among them Eli's two sons. On the same day, as was foretold. A dreadful day. The old priest, who had not wanted the holy Ark to leave Shiloh and his care, was deeply anxious and ill-at-ease all day. He sat on a seat by the road waiting for news. He could not see but could hear and feel the defeat all round him. And when the messenger came from the battle and told the awful news of the loss of the Ark, poor Eli felt that God was lost to him too.

The messenger poured out his news and then stopped in the middle of a sentence. Eli sat still. Poor Eli. He was nearly a hundred years old. 'And what of my sons?' he said.

And the messenger told him.

The old man closed his blind eyes and toppled backwards like a tree falling. His neck snapped. Old Eli, teacher and father to Samuel was dead. All foreseen; all told to Samuel by God. Samuel who now took over the reins.

The Ark of God

Samuel's beloved teacher was dead; his beloved Shiloh without its Ark. Now, you might say, 'Well, the Ark of God didn't win the battle for Israel, it didn't do them much good, did it?' True, but for some time, remember, Israel hadn't been very true to God.

Mind you, it didn't do the Philistines much good either. They took it first to a place called Ashdod, and the five Philistine lords met and decided they would put it in the great temple of Dagon, their Number One god. Half man, half fish. Huge stone statue in the middle of the floor. They put the Ark next to it. Next day, the huge victory ceremony. Prayers outside, then a song or two, then the great temple doors were opened and the people poured in. Dagon was flat on his face with a chipped nose!

Volunteers were asked for and they stood him up again and postponed the second half of the ceremony till next day. Next day they found him flat on his face with his head and arms broken off.

And that wasn't the end of it. No, quite soon a plague of boils and awful tumours began. Thousands were afflicted, people died. Then a plague of mice started that ate everything in sight.

Millions of them.

The five lords called an emergency meeting. 'It's the holy Ark,' they said. 'Powerful magic. Belongs to a God who once used *ten* plagues. Who can part seas and rivers. He must hate Dagon. Get the Ark away from Ashdod, take it inland to Gath.'

It was done and in no time at all the tumours and mice were all over Gath too.

The lords met again. 'All right,' they said, 'up to Ekron with it.'

But the people of Ekron had heard all about it and were full of panic at the thought of receiving the great honour of having the Ark in their city. They refused. It didn't help. At Akron the plagues arrived before the Ark. Even worse.

That was it. 'Send it back to Israel,' the lords decided, and called the magicians and soothsayers in as to how best to do it.

'On a specially-made cart,' the magic men said, 'and by its side a box full of golden statues.'

'What of?' said the lords.

'Tumours and mice,' said the magicians.

One or two of the lords started to object.

'Don't be stupid,' said the wise men. 'What do you want, the full set of ten plagues? Do you want to be clever like Pharaoh of Egypt? Let the cart be drawn by cows, not oxen, cows with new calves, but lock the calves away. Then send off the cart. Let it go where it will. No driver. If the Israelite God is in this, the cows will forget their new calves and go straight to Bethshemesh. That's the nearest town within Israel's borders. The people will be out in the fields harvesting. So they can't miss seeing it coming. They'll know what to do with it.'

And it was done. The cows, against nature, undriven, looking neither to right nor left, took the Ark of God straight back home. The Philistines had had it for seven months and they wished they'd never set eyes on it.

Samuel in Command

In Israel the rejoicing went on for days when the Ark of God came home. Samuel watched everything and listened to God. He knew that a great lesson was starting.

You know, when God chooses a man to speak for him, to prophesy, to lead a people, he chooses very carefully. Abraham, Moses, Joshua, all of them special men. Men who could think big and learn from the past the lessons of the future, and Samuel was no different.

Of all the leaders of the people of Israel, the leaders called *Judges* in the Bible, Samuel was the last, and in many ways the greatest. He had grown up serving God in the sanctuary of Shiloh where the Ark was. A priest, but very much of the people. He knew about people. He knew that the people of Israel were as big enemies to themselves as the ever-present Philistines. Saved by God, protected by God time and time again, often they forgot God and raised up other gods and idols. They always suffered for it but didn't learn.

So Samuel called the people together at a place called Mizpeh. 'There is one God only,' he said, 'only one. If you throw away all the other idols and rubbish and if you all return to the one God to whom you owe so much, and serve him only, you will live free, not in fear of the Philistines, all your lives. You will defeat the Philistines.'

The great meeting went on a long time. But spies are everywhere and soon the Philistines knew all about this vast multitude, many unarmed, ready for slaughter, ready for a surprise attack, a massacre.

Samuel led the people in long services of prayer, in fasting, in sacrifice. The Philistines gathered and drew near. As Samuel was preparing a burnt offering, one of the far-off lookouts saw the approaching Philistine armies and the word spread like a bushfire. The people began to panic. Samuel went on calmly with his duties. Then against the skyline, all round, the enemy appeared.

Samuel looked up and spoke to God.

The Philistines began to descend the slopes, then they stopped. Then a great noise came from the sky; it roared like endless thunder. To the people it was not loud; to the Philistines it was an unbearable head-splitting vibration that brought chaos and confusion. The noise could not be kept out, it was *in* the head. They staggered and stumbled into each other. The people went up the slopes at their enemies and it was a rout, a great victory, a sign of forgiveness, a promise from God. A promise kept. Never again during Samuel's lifetime did the Philistines win. All they had taken was won back. They were subdued, they stayed away. So did other enemies.

The people looked up to Samuel, paid him great respect. He wasn't too much impressed. He knew this people well. Neither did he stay in one place, a great figure that people went to. He went to them. Place to place, a regular tour. The first circuit-judge in history. Often he thought back to his beloved teacher so long dead. Old Eli – and his two bad sons. Samuel would smile rather sadly to himself at those moments. He too had bad sons. He didn't know it but neither would succeed him. No more judges. From then on, kings. He, Samuel, would anoint two. And that must be our next story.

The Lord's Anointed

Samuel, when he was old, was one day sitting in his garden and thinking yet again what a great disappointment his two sons had been to him. Maybe they'd had in him too much to live up to but certainly they weren't much good. Like him they were judges but they were not honest men. They took bribes. And yesterday's visit from the elders of the people hadn't helped either. 'Your sons are no good,' they'd said, 'and you, Samuel, are old. So give us a king to govern us. No more judges. A king like other nations.'

Samuel closed his eyes and told it all quietly to God and after a while God replied. 'First of all,' said God, 'understand that the people are not rejecting *you*. No, as so many times before, they are rejecting me. To have *me* for king would be enough, you'd think, but no. All right,' said God, 'let them have a king, but tell them first what having a king entails. They will be his soldiers and servants and factory workers. Their best farms and cattle and possessions will be his by right. Anything he wants they will have to give him. He will have power over life and death. They will be hit hardest where it hurts most. In the pocket. To have a king is very expensive. Tell them.' And Samuel did tell them.

But the people refused to listen, so Samuel went where God led him and chose a young man who was tall and broad and handsome and anointed him king. His name was Saul. As a king he turned out to be no great bargain. And that's why Samuel was out looking for a replacement fairly soon, and that's where this story really begins. It begins, like the story of Ruth, in Bethlehem, where another story, more famous than either of them, began. It begins about a thousand years before that other story. One thousand years BC. It begins with a rather puzzled man, Ruth's grandson Jesse, a farmer, now middle-aged and with eight sons. It was to his eldest son, a soldier called Eliab, that Jesse was speaking.

'It's all very puzzling,' he said. 'Out of the blue there comes to Bethlehem the prophet Samuel, whom we haven't seen since we all went to Mizpeh for the crowning of King Saul and you got excited and joined the King's army.'

'I know,' said Eliab. 'I'd heard that Samuel had retired or gone into exile or something. Seems that he was very cross with Saul after that battle with the Amalekites and regretted making him king. The story was that Saul disobeyed the rules given by God to Samuel for kings to follow. I don't know the details,' said Eliab, 'but we did win the battle. Saul knows how to fight even if he does break rules.'

Jesse hadn't really been listening to his son. 'Samuel comes to Bethlehem,' he said, 'to make a sacrifice to God. He even brings a young heifer with him for the offering. He is met by the elders who are nervous of him and no wonder. Samuel the great judge, the prophet, the king-maker. Then the sacrifice is arranged to take place in our big field and *we* are invited. "Jesse and all his sons," Samuel said. One or two of the elders were a bit jealous, I'm told. Ah well,' said Jesse, 'let's get cleaned up. It's quite an honour really. A special day.'

It was indeed. At noon the field was full of people and the elders had got everything ready. A lot of noise and excitement for this was the great prophet Samuel, chosen by God while still a child. Maybe some great prophetic announcement was to take place.

Well it did, but quietly, in Jesse's own home, later. Jesse never forgot it. He was an observant man was Jesse and when Samuel had arrived for the sacrifice and the crowd became silent he'd noticed the great horn of oil at the prophet's belt. Chased with silver with a golden lid and handle. It was the anointing horn used by Samuel at Saul's coronation. A *special* sacrifice, thought Jesse? But the horn stayed, unused, at Samuel's belt.

After the service Samuel turned and walked over to Jesse, who was a bit over-awed by this bearded patriarch with the shrewd eyes. 'Come, Jesse,' said Samuel, 'let us sit awhile in your garden and let me meet your sons and then we can eat a little food.'

Jesse sat next to Samuel under a tree and introduced his sons one by one. He felt a great tension and stillness in the prophet.

'Eliab, my eldest,' said Jesse. 'Next, Abinadab; next Shammah.' And so on.

The young men came forward and bowed. Samuel looked into each face intently and his head was tilted as though listening. The seventh son stepped back from Samuel and joined his six brothers.

The prophet turned to Jesse. 'Are these all your sons?' he said.

Jesse said, 'No. One more, David the youngest. He is with the sheep.'

'Send for him,' said Samuel and did not raise his eyes till the boy stood before him, a handsome well-built boy with a friendly smile.

Samuel looked into the boy's eyes and again seemed to listen. Then he rose to his feet and took the great horn from his belt. 'Jesse,' he said, 'this boy, David the shepherd, your youngest son, will be the next King of Israel. A great king, greater than Saul, who will reign many years yet. But after him; David. Who will know great love and great danger, but God will protect him because,' said Samuel, 'God has chosen him.'

Then Samuel anointed David, and David, who didn't much like oil on his hair, went back to his sheep. And Samuel went back home, leaving poor Jesse very puzzled indeed.

Giant Killer

The weeks passed and one supper time Jesse looked across the table at his youngest son and again tried to work it out. This boy, David, was one day to be King of Israel. All by order of God, Samuel had said. Jesse was very fond of his youngest son but quite honestly couldn't see anything very kingly or even princely about him. Certainly a very good-looking boy; beautiful eyes, like his mother. Her love of music too; good singing voice. Made up songs; poems too. Could play the small harp very well. Surely, thought Jesse, a king needs a bit more than that.

Then the old man remembered that on a number of occasions, to protect the flock of sheep he looked after, the boy had shown himself quite fearless. No songs or poems then. A fighter strong and swift, and a dead shot with a sling. Many wild animal skins to prove it.

David looked up from his food. 'Any news about the battle, father?' he asked.

Jesse came back with a bump to his other worries and his other sons. 'No,' he said, 'I know nothing; only rumours. So tomorrow morning early I want you to go again to Azekah where your three brothers are stationed and take food for them.'

'What rumours?' said David.

'Oh, a crazy story,' said Jesse, 'that the Philistines have a great giant in armour who stands on their side of the valley and roars in a great voice for King Saul to go and fight him – or choose someone to do it for him. No battle going on at all, I'm told. Just the two armies face to face and all our lot rather scared of the giant.'

'What a marvellous story,' said David. 'I hope it's true, I've never seen a giant.'

It was true. When David had given over the food to his eldest brother Eliab, the big soldier took him down to the valley. 'He makes his challenge every hour,' said Eliab. 'You'll see him in about ten minutes.' While they waited, he told David that King Saul had offered a huge reward and his daughter in marriage to any man who would kill the giant.

Then there was a great brutish roaring and a clanking of armour and there was the giant. Huge. Marvellous sight. Covered in bronze from head to foot. 'One man,' he roared. 'If he kills me, the Philistines shall serve Israel; if I kill him, Israel will be *our* servants.'

David looked up at Eliab. 'He's only big,' he said. 'Take me to the King.'

Eliab, very much the elder brother, told him not to be big-headed and to go back to his sheep. But David went to the King. And there was something about this handsome boy who called the giant 'an uncircumcised Philistine' and Saul's soldiers 'the army of God'.

'All right,' said Saul. 'Try it. No one else has offered. Use my armour and my sword and shield.'

They dressed David, who was not very big, in all this stuff and when he went to stride out to do battle he couldn't move. So they took it all off again.

'Look,' said David to Saul, 'with God's help I've killed a number of quite large wild animals. And God's on our side. Also,' said David, no fool, 'between the giant's helmet brim and his nose-piece he is uncovered. I shall challenge him from the narrowest part of the stream in the valley and I'll do it with a stone.'

'A stone?' said Saul.

'Yes,' said David, 'from a sling. I can't throw a spear.'

King Saul looked down at this mighty man of valour. 'And then?' he said. 'What will you do then, my young friend?'

'I shall cut off his head with his own sword,' said David, and walked out. A moment later he came back – 'You needn't worry about the reward,' he said. 'And I'm too young to get married.'

Saul watched the whole thing. The calm small figure of the boy, the stone slung like a bullet, the great metallic crash as the giant fell, and the beheading with the absurdly large sword that the boy could hardly lift. Then the terror of the Philistine army and the quick victory for Israel.

That was the first time that David and Saul met. In some ways, battle or not, giant or not, it was their happiest meeting. And they were to see a great deal of each other.

David and Saul

After David had killed the giant his life changed completely. He stopped being a shepherd and went to live in the King's household and was treated almost like a son by King Saul who was very grateful to him. One of the King's sons was called Jonathan; he and David took to each other at sight and as the years passed they became like brothers. And, as the years passed, David the boy who killed the giant became David the soldier who killed *many* of the King's enemies. In the ceaseless battles with Philistines David's skill and complete lack of fear soon made him noticed and Saul made him commander-in-chief.

Saul was a strange man. Very moody. Emotional. Unbalanced. Given to sudden rages and dreadful fits of depression. As David grew to manhood he came to know this dark side of the King very well, for often Saul would allow no one but David near him during his times of what the court doctors called the evil spirits. The King would send for David, who could play upon the small harp and who could make up songs, and David would sit sometimes for hours making music to calm the King.

But as I say, as David became a man, he became a great soldier, and was often away when the King's evil spirits attacked him. It was noticed at court that news of a victory for David would first please the King and then bring on a great rage and deep depression. David, famous since a boy as the giant killer, was now, as a handsome broad man in bronze armour, the hero and champion of all Israel. They made up songs about him and Saul heard them and the dark moods changed their character. He became convinced that David was trying to steal the throne from him. He began to plot ways to kill David. He would send him on dangerous missions with too few men, he would put paid assassins among David's troops. But God, who had chosen David for a special purpose, looked after everything. Saul was right; the next king *would* be David. But David would not need to steal the throne, he would be put on it by God. Much later, though; meanwhile Saul plotted and was filled with jealousy and fear.

Not all the time; when he was normal Saul treated David as a son, heaped honours upon him, gave him, as he had promised, one of his daughters in marriage. But it was an atmosphere that could not continue. On two occasions when David was playing upon the lyre Saul, far from being soothed by it, had suddenly hurled a spear. David's reactions were fast as a cat and both times he'd ducked, but it had been close.

One day Jonathan went to David and told him that Saul was scheming yet again. 'Take my sister Michal, your wife,' said Jonathan, 'and find a house. Live away from the palace and the King. It's safer.'

David took the advice and things were a bit easier for a while. He lived quietly, when not away with the army, and gave orders that he wanted no parades or banner-waving or conquering-hero stuff as it only annoyed Saul. He behaved, as always, in a loyal and principled way. But he was dealing with a man not quite sane.

One night he got home and Michal looked very worried indeed. 'Jonathan was here,' she said. 'Father has given orders that you are to be arrested in the middle of the night and charged with treason and killed tomorrow morning. No trial. By the King's order.'

David stood still. He had the feeling that a new chapter was beginning.

Michal looked up into his face. 'My father has spies everywhere,' she said. 'I've made a sort of dummy and put it in your bed. It's got a goat's-hair wig. We'll have supper and retire early. We'll leave a dim light in the bedroom and the dummy will fool anyone looking in. When the house is quiet you can escape through the garden. Don't worry about me,' she said. 'My father will be angry but he will not harm his own daughter.'

David looked into his wife's eyes. 'I shall go to see Samuel,' he said. 'He is old now but he is God's prophet. He will know what God wants of us all.'

And Samuel did, though it was some days before David found the old prophet.

Samuel told him, 'All this was foreseen. King you shall be and Saul now knows this, but the path to your throne will be hard. Assassins sent by Saul have already followed you here but were made powerless and dazed by God. Saul too came and fell into a fit and tore off his clothes and lay for a day and a night like a beggar under a tree.'

David felt sad. He was a simple good man and felt himself to be surrounded by great forces. Also he knew the other Saul, who was generous and good company – and indeed his father-in-law. 'What of Michal my wife who helped me escape?' he said.

Samuel paused. 'She has been sent to Gallim by Saul and made wife to a man called Phaltiel. One day you will get her back. Not yet. Now you must go from here. To my friend Ahimelech in the town of Nob. He will give you shelter and also the great sword of Goliath the giant. It is yours by right. Go then to the cave of Adullam, where I will see to it that your seven brothers and your parents will join you. Also others. Four hundred. They will be your first force. Go now.'

David did as the old man said and all this came to pass and he felt better. Then he heard that Saul had killed Ahimelech for helping him and had wiped out the town of Nob in revenge.

David now saw that Israel must be split into two, those for him and those for Saul. He knew it to be a bad thing, for Israel had enemies enough without civil war. But it had to be. Now he and his four hundred were outlaws. Soon they were six hundred. David trained his men and they lived off the land. Saul hunted and hounded them without rest. There was one fantastic occasion when Saul, tired at the end of a fruitless day of searching, took shelter in a cave and went to sleep. Further back in the cave were David and a small band of his men. They wanted to kill Saul, but David stopped them. 'He was like a father to me,' he said, 'and he was anointed king by Samuel. Anointed by a prophet of God.'

Then David quietly cut off part of Saul's robe and he and his men left the cave. When Saul awoke and came out into the open David called to him from across the valley and told him how near he had been to death. 'But not by my hand,' he said. 'You hunt me to kill me but I will not harm a hair of your head. See I cut only your robe – with the sword which could have cut your throat. God will judge between you and me.'

Saul stood still. David watched him and recognized the sign of a calm, sane period in the King.

'David,' said Saul, 'you are better than I am; you have repaid my evil with good where I try only to repay your good with evil. Now I know that you will surely be King of Israel, a strong firm Israel in your hand. I ask only that my descendants and my name shall not be destroyed.' And David swore it.

The Last of Samuel

David knew better than to think that the King's sanity would last, or that the war was over between them. And when, a few

months later, news came to him that Samuel was dead –
Samuel, the great prophet of God, who had anointed both Saul
and himself with holy oil – David knew that nowhere in Israel
was he any longer safe from Saul. There was one place, though,
where Saul might not follow him. David and his six hundred
men went to the city of Gath, where the giant had come from.
The city was deep in Philistine country, enemy country to Saul.
David went to the prince of Gath, who, Philistine or not had
a high regard for David the fighter, the soldier, the leader. David
was frank and asked for refuge as now he too, like the prince,
was an enemy of Saul. The prince gave David some land and
he and his men settled in. The prince, rather crafty, had chosen
land on the Israelite border, knowing that David's men would
live by plunder, and hoping to increase the enmity between
David and Saul. But David, just as crafty, plundered the
Amalekites to the south of Judah leaving no survivors to point
out the difference. Over a year passed and Saul stayed well away.
The prince of Gath, believing that David was now a firm enemy
of Israel, made him his bodyguard, but his generals who were
preparing for a big battle with Saul did not trust David and on
the day of the battle sent him and his men back behind the
lines.

Saul had heard of these battle preparations and he too had
made ready. When he saw the huge Philistine army he was
shocked and scared and sadly missed David who had been his
commander-in-chief and a great soldier. Saul asked God for
advice but God, who was not very pleased with Saul, wouldn't
answer. So Saul did something that pleased God even less. He
went to see a witch. The witch of Endor. He went disguised but
witches know and she recognized him. She was frightened, for
Saul had forbidden all mediums and wizards and witches. But
he told her that this was a special job.

'Call back from the dead,' he said, 'the prophet Samuel, who
made me king and is a friend of God, who won't talk to me.'

The old witch, who knew her job, got busy with her bits and

pieces and, sure enough, fairly soon there was the spirit of old Samuel. And not very pleased about being disturbed.

'If God won't speak to you,' he told Saul, 'it is because he has turned from you, as I told you he would after you disobeyed him. Israel's next king will be David whom you hunt like an animal.'

'I've somehow known that for a long time,' said Saul, 'but what about the battle?'

Old Samuel paused. 'Israel will suffer a great defeat,' he said, 'the Philistines will live in Israel's cities and many of your soldiers will be killed.' He paused again. 'Your sons will be killed also,' he said, 'and you Saul also will die.'

Saul was terrified and threw himself at the spirit's feet. When he looked up the spirit had gone.

And it came to pass; the defeat, the massacre; the killing of Saul's sons, Jonathan and two of his brothers. Jonathan the great friend of David. And lastly the death of Saul, who, wounded and afraid of capture, had himself killed with his own sword.

When the news was brought to David he wept. He felt again that he was part of a huge design. How God had arranged that he would have no part in the battle, no part in the death of the King he was to replace. The King who had loved him and hated him. Who had honoured him and degraded him. Who had been at first a great king, then mad, now dead. David, great soldier and leader, knew that his own exile would soon end. But for Saul and for Jonathan he wept. All his life a musician and poet, David made a great lament. He addressed it to the mountains of Bilboa beginning, sadly, *The beauty of Israel is slain upon thy high places. How are the mighty fallen.*

Chapter 4

THE KINGDOM OF DAVID

Even after the death of Saul and Jonathan, David did not become King of Israel right away. No, God, who had chosen David to be King of Israel, was going to make quite sure first that Israel would appreciate a good king when they got one. So David first became king of only part of Israel, he became King of Judah, the southern part, where the tribe of Judah lived, to which tribe he belonged by birth. He lived in Hebron as King of Judah for over seven years. The rest of Israel was governed by one of Saul's surviving sons. He was not very good at it, but he had a good commander-in-chief, a sensible man called Abner, and he it was who finally brought the civil war to an end and united all the tribes under one king, David. Another thing he did was to restore David's first wife to him. Michal, daughter of Saul. Mind you, when she came back David had a few other wives, as was the way then (Multiply, God had said), and a fair-sized family. But she was made very welcome.

So: Israel was now united, and David, more experienced now in kingship, took over and made Jerusalem his capital. The years of tribal war seemed now at an end. One of the saddest of the last incidents was the ill-judged murder by one of David's men of Abner, who had done so much. David, a wise man, made the funeral a great lesson in the stupidity of war and strife.

Then David decided to bring the Ark of God, the scrolls and tablets of the laws and commandments, to Jerusalem. For twenty years or more the Ark had been looked after in a small village not far from Jerusalem. David made it a great day of joy. A great feast. The people danced and sang, and none more than David. Michal, who hadn't been too happy about all the other wives and children was rather sour about David's dancing and singing in the streets till all hours. 'So *vulgar,*' she said. 'I am a king's daughter, and your prancing, I assure you, is not very kingly.'

David pointed out without anger that he was not trying to be kingly, he was paying homage to God's word. 'God,' he said, 'who chose me above your father.'

God listened and decided that perhaps Michal should stay childless. And she did.

The Ark stood, as always since the time of Moses, in a decorated and beautiful sort of tent. And David, who lived in a handsome palace of stone and cedar and gold and silver, was bothered by this. He felt that the Ark should have a palace too, a great temple, a house to live in. He spoke of this to a prophet called Nathan, an elderly and respected man.

The next day Nathan went to David with words given to him by God in a dream. 'God said he understands your feelings,' said Nathan. 'But the tent will do for the time being. Certainly a great temple will be built for the Ark but by your son, not by you.'

'Which son?' said David. 'I've got lots.'

'God didn't say,' said Nathan, 'although I rather gathered he isn't born yet. He will be wise and a credit to you. If you like,' said Nathan, 'you can start gathering building-materials but don't start work.'

David listened, prayed his thanks to God, and started gathering. Another thing he did round about this time was rather fine, bearing in mind he was a rather busy king. He found out that Saul's son Jonathan, his own great friend, had left a child, a boy in his teens, with crippled feet. The boy lived far off with an old servant. David had them both brought to Jerusalem and to live in the palace. 'Your father was like a brother to me,' he told the boy, 'and you shall be like my son.'

A Real Big Sin

Very human man, David. A man of principle, a brave man, a man blessed by God, and indeed chosen by God, as we've heard. But a human man, and subject, as we shall hear, to human weaknesses. What is a king after all but a man? A man who sits in a rather more fancy chair than the rest of us. Kings have burnt cakes, and tried to stop the tide coming in, and abdicated for love; they have been fools and gamblers and great sinners. And King David also was a great sinner. Not regularly, just once. But a real big sin. He was punished by God and forgiven. Poor David, a man in a fancy chair. The fancy chair was on the flat roof of his palace.

David had been King of Israel for some time now and he loved to sit in the evening and look out over the hills and skyline of Jerusalem. He was by himself. Earlier that day the prophet Nathan had come to lunch and they'd talked about things in general and David had been pleased at Nathan's approval of his careful leadership of the nation. The people loved him and Israel was united as never before. The Ammonites were the enemy now and many battles took place, indeed there was one going on now, but in general things were going well. David got to his feet and stretched. Joab his commander-in-chief could handle this battle, he thought; capable fellow, Joab. David strolled to the handsome balustrade of the roof and looked down. And that was it. In a small roof-garden of the house next door, glowing in the pink light of the evening sun, a beautiful woman was rising gracefully from a white marble bath.

Now David was not a boy, middle forties; and not a fool. He was married to a number of wives and had a fair-sized family. But it was bonnet over the windmill. He was a very handsome and virile man and the lady got carried away too. Her name was Bathsheba and her husband was an officer in David's army and away at the war. Convenient. But quite soon she was pregnant and it was months since she had seen her husband.

David had him sent home on leave for a few days but the gallant officer had foresworn all women till the battle was won. He wouldn't go near his wife. David tried everything; gave him presents, got him drunk, had the dancing girls in, sexy music. Nothing. The officer went back to war.

Then the whole thing went really bad. David told Joab his commander-in-chief to put the officer in the sort of danger that would kill him. And it did. Bathsheba mourned for her husband and then went and lived in David's house and he married her. Weeks passed and it was nearly time for her baby to be born. Then Nathan the prophet went to David. No approval this time. No, a strange-faced Nathan with an odd question. 'Ponder,' he said, 'a rich man with many sheep who steals the only sheep of a poor man, for pleasure's sake. Does he sin?'

'He most certainly does,' said David, 'and shall be punished for it. Who is the man?'

'You are the man,' said Nathan, 'and you are to be punished by God. In a number of ways.'

Then Nathan left and David prayed for forgiveness, and when the baby was born weak and sickly he prayed for its life. But the baby died and Bathsheba wept. She was not a bad woman any more than David was bad. Such things happen. But there are rules. Called commandments. Given to Moses by God. They hadn't been out all that long and God wanted them obeyed, especially by the man he had chosen to be an example to others.

Absalom, my Son

David in his comforting of Bathsheba gave and found great love in her and when she again told him she was going to have a child he prayed differently. For *her*. That *she* should have joy. And God was pleased and sent a message again through Nathan the prophet. 'It will be a son,' said Nathan, 'and he will be king after you, and he will be gentle and have great wisdom. His name will be Solomon which means Peaceful. And God will be his friend.' Nathan paused. 'I must tell you however that your punishment is not complete,' he said. 'As one son shall bring you joy so is another to give you grief. And God will raise up evil against you out of your own house.'

As the years passed and David and Bathsheba enjoyed the growing up of their son Solomon, old Nathan's words were almost forgotten. Then the thing began.

Apart from Bathsheba David had, as we've seen, a number of other wives, all of whom he'd met and married before Bathsheba. And by them he'd had quite a large family. His first-born was a young man called Amnon who fell in love with his half-sister called Tamar. He behaved very badly and her brother, called Absalom, swore revenge and waited his chance. He waited two years and then killed Amnon. And fled. King David, who loved his fine family and handsome sons, grieved terribly. He wept both for the death of Amnon and for the loss of Absalom, the most handsome of them all.

Then Joab, David's commander-in-chief and old friend, saw that the King's heart was not really in the banishment of Absalom and he found a way for David to forgive and Absalom to return. But after his son's return to Jerusalem, for two full years David wouldn't see him and this set up in Absalom, already an arrogant and ambitious young man, a great bitterness. He began to plot and scheme to win the affection of the people. It wasn't hard. He was the King's son, and in line for the throne, well known, one of the best-looking men in all Israel. He created a whole network of spies and supporters and the conspiracy grew strong and dangerous.

Four years passed by and David, who was no fool, put some twos and twos together and decided to abdicate and he and his family and household left Jerusalem and Absalom moved in. But it was not that simple; it never is. Not everyone wanted a new king, and David was much loved, and as he walked into exile many thousands decided to walk by his side.

David now saw Israel was divided and vulnerable. A country at war with itself is anybody's prey and Israel had no lack of enemies. Surrounded by them; like today. So David mustered the thousands with him into an army and, as so often in the past, Joab and his brother Abishai commanded them.

Soon all the espionage and counter-espionage and preparation for the big showdown began, though David gave strict orders that Absalom was on no account to be killed. Not that Absalom had any such scruples. He had the throne and many spies and a huge force of trained men and no feelings at all about killing his father. He tried a number of times but David got away, warned by *his* spies.

And the day came. A terrible day – when tribe fought tribe and Israel killed some of its finest sons. A great many. Twenty thousand men died that day. The battle was won, if such a battle can be won, by David's army.

And Absalom died that day in a way that was almost farcical. He'd fought all day and watched his men and his hopes beaten into the dust. All was lost. He turned his horse and made for the nearby forest of Ephraim. As he entered the forest he was snatched from his horse by the forked branch of a great tree and there he hung, by the neck, helpless, wounded, dazed. Soon along the same track came some of David's men and recognizing Absalom they told Joab. He, who less than five years before had arranged the forgiving of Absalom by his father, now ordered – he valued the rough justice of those times more highly even than the King's command – that Absalom be killed as a traitor. So Absalom was speared to death as he hung, and his body taken down and buried in the forest. The last death of that terrible day.

The news was brought to David and the people saw no triumph, no elation, just a heartbroken man who'd lost a son. 'O Absalom,' they heard him say. 'Would to God, I had died instead of you. O Absalom, my son, my son.'

Choosing a Successor

But soon David put aside his grief and got busy. There was much to do. Tribes had to be made friendly again; the army, split in half, had to be completely re-organized. He knew that this civil war, begun by one of his sons, was part of the punishment God was giving him. 'Out of your own house shall come evil,' God had said. And more was to come too. Later, another son was to try to steal the throne, and there was to be famine, and pestilence. Poor David, who sinned for love and killed for love, was to suffer much. But Bathsheba, for whom he sinned and killed, was worth it. She became his favourite wife and a loyal and splendid mother to their son Solomon.

The son who tried to steal the throne the second time was called Adonijah. Like Absalom his brother he was in line to be king anyway but, as David grew to be rather old, Adonijah got impatient and started to undo all the careful unity that his father had built up in Israel. He talked some of the higher-ups of the army and religion into joining him and held a sort of 'I-hereby-crown-me-king' ceremony. Word came to old Nathan the prophet, now *very* old, and he told Bathsheba. Who went to see David. 'Once you promised me,' she said, 'that our son would be *King* Solomon. Now I hear that Adonijah has declared himself your successor. Solomon is much liked by the people and the city is full of rumours and confusion. All Israel waits to be told the real truth.'

David wasted no time, he sent for the prophet Nathan and gave clear orders. 'Go to Gihon,' he said, 'and take Solomon, who shall ride upon my horse and wear my crown. And take also Zadok the priest; at Gihon you shall anoint Solomon king. You and Zadok. Then the great trumpets are to be blown so that Adonijah will know by hearing them that Solomon is the new King of Israel and not he. Let there be no rumours and confusion, only joy, for Solomon is God's choice as well as mine.'

All this was done and the people were pleased. It was done at roughly the same time as Adonijah was having a big party to celebrate *his* taking over. Very big affair. He had many sup-porters, who thought they were onto a good thing. But when all these guests and friends found out what all the excitement in the streets and all the trumpeting and music meant, they got up and one by one made excuses to leave early. Not because they were at the wrong party. They'd backed the wrong horse. Eventually their host was all by himself. Packing. He didn't live very long, that one. Rough justice in those days.

But David's story ends on a quiet note. It ends, as many old men's lives end, with the old man passing on some advice and a few thoughts to his son. The handing over of the reins. David was about seventy when he died and his mind was clear to the last. Early in his reign when he had wanted to build a great temple to God, God had said it would be built by his son but that David could prepare the plans. So David gave to Solomon to the last detail the plans for the Temple, and told him where the great stores of precious metals and rare woods and fine marbles were waiting in readiness.

'God has chosen you to do it,' he said. 'A great task; but be strong and of good courage. Fear not, be not dismayed, for God is with you.'

Then there was a great ceremony where David gave into the temple building fund his great personal fortune; and all the tribal leaders and the heads of houses and anybody else who wanted followed suit, freewill. And David, who was a great king, because he could put things simply, said to God, 'All this that we give you, you first gave to us.'

And David died, the Bible says, *in a good old age full of days, riches and honour. And Solomon his son reigned.*

The Wisdom of Solomon

Now, when King Solomon took over the throne of his father, King David, he wasn't after all very old. Early twenties. He had a good head on him and a good education. He was interested in everything and possessed a marvellous memory. Strong-minded; like his mother, Bathsheba. He was remarkable and rare. More sophisticated than his father, who'd begun life, you remember, as a shepherd-boy. Solomon for *all* his life had been the son of a *king*, the first great King of Israel, and maybe, even counting Solomon, the greatest.

The most important gift left to Solomon by David was a united and peaceful people. The twelve tribes close and happy together as never before. Missing their beloved King David but seeing in Solomon a new David. And Solomon was aware of the huge responsibility but not daunted by it. It's no fun being the son of a great man. People compare.

But Solomon, as I said, was a different sort of thinker. He was a planner. Enormous breadth of mind. He sat down and looked at the country and people he was to rule. He saw clearly and with admiration what his father had done but was not over-impressed. Very little did impress the young King. He saw a largely peasant people with not many skills. Happy to be at peace and willing to work to remain so. They were proud of him and trusted him. He also knew the value of peace, especially with the old enemy, Egypt.

So the young King, who was a great realist, decided to test the people's trust in his judgment. He announced that he would take as his number one wife the daughter of Pharaoh, King of Egypt! The Elders were shocked, but then saw Solomon's good sense. In one blow the enemy was now a father-in-law, and import-export could begin. Solomon was to marry into other countries many times in his forty-year reign. It made for trouble eventually but that was later.

Not long after Solomon became King, during a big religious meeting, God appeared to him in a dream. A sort of vision-dream, and God asked Solomon how he could help. Solomon was honest and told God how very much aware he was of his young shoulders and that he could do with a really wise head on them. 'An understanding mind,' he said. 'Clear knowledge of good and evil. This is a huge people. I don't know much.'

God was pleased. The humility and modesty pleased him. It always does. 'Right,' he told Solomon, 'you shall have wisdom and discernment as no one before you and as none who come after you. Also you shall have things you didn't ask for, riches and honour and possessions. Great power, and peace.' And it was almost from the next day that Solomon began to be called 'the wise'.

Part of his new God-given wisdom was a great knowledge of people and how they think. One day two women were brought before him for judgment. A nasty case. One woman accused the other of swapping her dead baby for her, the accuser's, live one. In the night. Both babies only days old.

Solomon listened. Both ladies very upset. Lot of screaming and crying. 'Bring a sword,' said Solomon. 'Cut the live baby in two. Each lady to have half.'

Silence. Then the real mother begged it not to be done. 'Give her the baby,' she said. 'Don't kill my son!'

Solomon did nothing of the kind. 'Keep your son,' he said. 'Next case.'

This judgment went through the land like lightning. Everything the King did or said was news. His laws for full employment. His division of the country into equal tax and supply areas. The people were involved, interested, alive. Solomon had big plans for them; the building of the great Temple in Jerusalem. His father David had begun to collect materials and left detailed instructions. Now it was time to put those plans into execution. It was a holy, special task.

The Building of the Temple

For nearly five hundred years, the Ark of the Lord had travelled and wandered wherever the people of Israel had travelled and wandered. Now they had a King and a King's capital city. And in that city, Jerusalem, the Ark was to have a permanent home. The foundations were dug in the fourth year of Solomon's reign. He supervised every detail. Only the best was good enough. And if the best was not obtainable in Israel, then he would import it. The timber for the great Temple was a good example. The local stuff wasn't good enough so Solomon asked a great friend of his father's called Hiram to help. He'd known this Hiram all his life, almost an uncle, but his deal was businesslike. So much timber plus so many skilled wood-men per year in return for wheat, oil, foodstuffs, and some land. Hiram agreed to everything gladly. He'd loved David and saw in Solomon all that was best in his old friend. His forests were in Tyre, north of Israel, on the coast. A long way to go, but they worked it out and the cutting began. Great rafts of the finest cedars and cypresses of Lebanon were brought down the coast and then inland by camel-train. Thousands of men were put to quarrying stone and thousands more to dressing it into squared blocks – a very new thing in those days. Joiners and carvers and metalworkers were brought from other lands. Every kind of expert. Time and money did not matter. It was gorgeous. Whole rooms were lined with pure gold. Fine marbles and precious stones were everywhere. Beautiful winged figures of cherubim stood against exquisite tapestries. All the work in gold and silver and bronze, in stone and wood, and the weaving and dyeing was in charge of one man called Hiram – yes, same name as David's old friend Hiram, King of Tyre, who supplied the wood from Lebanon; probably named after him. And loaned by that Hiram. Rather confusing.

This Hiram was the son of a widowed Jewish mother who had married a craftsman in Tyre. Both he and his master, the King of Tyre, were dead keen on the building of the Temple. All right, you'll say, both were well paid. So were all the other workers. But this wanting to join in the great work was remarkable. Like David before him Solomon had this drive, this ability to get people going. A marvellous, unique man. Yes, Hiram, the genius, could *work* in copper and bronze, but it was Solomon who created the huge mining and smelting plant far south in the hot, windy desert. He even *used* the hot wind and built his furnaces in its path. Blast-furnaces three thousand years ago! Metal was cast in moulds made of local clay and taken north for Hiram to finish and build in.

The Temple took seven years to build. It employed thousands and developed many new crafts and techniques which Solomon noted and used in other ways. He learned from everything. In any age he would have stood out. A genius, vastly gifted, and a dynamic human being.

Solomon in his Glory

But one thing Solomon was not. He was not 'the man of the people' his father, King David, was. The people were staggered by Solomon. Impressed, overawed, overpowered. But no *love*. David they had loved. He'd had the 'common touch', the warmth. Not Solomon.

Solomon performed miracles of planning, created great buildings, works of art, gardens, vineyards, huge business deals. But forced labour was known in the land. No choice. One month in three many, many thousands of workers left their farms and homes in what was a sort of draft call-up. It rankled. One leaves home to fight for it, not to be reminded of the slavery of one's forbears in Egypt.

And then there were the taxes and the vast supplies demanded by the court and the army. Full-size army kept up; Solomon took no chances. Indeed he created a chariot corps that was huge. Housed in stables of a size and magnificence never known before. Famous, talked about. As Solomon meant them to be.

Jerusalem became, under Solomon, the centre of a vast import-export organization. Solomon had a fleet that included ships able to go on trading trips lasting three years. And the things they would bring back! Apes, peacocks, ivory, the rarest woods, gold, silver. Mind you, silver during Solomon's reign was not counted very valuable. Rather common. Solomon wouldn't have it in the palace. He preferred gold. He drank out of it, ate off it, sat on it, and slept on it. No statesman or prince or King visited without bringing valuable presents. Always including gold. No vanity on Solomon's part. A currency backed by gold is no new idea. These days we bury it in mountains or forts or banks. The only difference is, he let you *see* it.

Solomon was so *intelligent*. Even having so many wives had good sense behind it. He married into the ruling families of many nations who might otherwise have got jealous or unfriendly. Every King for miles around was an in-law! No raiding parties, just parties. Why go to war with Solomon if you could go for the weekend? Especially if your weekend might show you wonders you'd never seen before. The glorious Temple like a great golden jewel. The palaces with their fountains and gardens. The great camel-trains that went off in every direction. Heavy-laden, valuable, important.

This building of a huge freight service using camels was pure Solomon. These especially bred and tamed beasts that could ignore the water-holes which mules and asses absolutely depend on. Far down into Arabia they went, these trains; into the Yemen; even to Sheba, nearly fifteen hundred miles. Their drivers spoke of King Solomon. So did the seamen of Solomon's fleet who brought ashore the rare goods and fine cargoes from Solomon's land.

The ruler of Sheba was a Queen. She ruled well. Shrewd, logical, a good Queen. But also a woman. And curious. She listened to the stories, allowed for the boasting and exaggeration, and was still left with something that, being a woman, she really had to go and see for herself.

So she went. Fifteen hundred miles. With a tremendous retinue of servants in gorgeous array. Camels weighed down with gifts of every description. Not only gold and precious stones but vast quantities of rare spices and perfumes – which were the riches of *her* country. Nothing was forgotten. She was prepared to be impressed but, womanlike, she also intended to do a little impressing herself.

Well, she made an impression. But what she saw and heard at the court of Solomon left her speechless. There were no secrets. Solomon answered her every question and showed her everything. The way the court was run, the various ministries, the religious life and, most impressive of all, the frequent conventions, where thinkers from many lands would sit together to talk – and to listen to Solomon who seemed to be able to speak with knowledge about everything. Kings and princes would travel long distances just to talk to him. She was staggered and said so. And when it was time to go back home to Sheba, Solomon matched her gift for gift, and anything else she desired was freely given. Not marriage – he normally married princesses not queens! Not even romance, as far as I can make out from the Bible. With seven hundred wives it's maybe a little difficult to find room for romance. Some of these wives, mind you, Solomon had married for political reasons, as we've seen. Good thinking. But seven *hundred?* And three hundred *concubines.* He needed to be rich.

Idols at Court

Solomon was a civilized man. These women were of many different beliefs and he didn't insist that they should give up their religions. He built them idols, told them to bring their gods and other rubbish with them. Gave them incense-accounts and sacrifice-allowances. And, I'm sorry to say, as he got older and not so wise, got rather interested himself. Eventually he built a huge sacrifice-stadium to some of these gods not far from Jerusalem. Within sight of the Temple.

Well, that was it! God was angry. There are too many commandments forgotten for 'political reasons'.

'For the sake of your father David,' God told Solomon, 'your kingdom will remain intact till you die. Then it will be broken in two. Part will be given to your son and the rest to your servant.'

God didn't name the servant and Solomon didn't ask. He knew that all the rest God said about not keeping faith and so on was true. And Solomon, because he was a man of vast

knowledge and achievement, knew that for the people of Israel
the party was over. The forty years of peace, the prosperity, the
unity as a nation was at an end. He also knew, special God-
gifted person though he might be, that it was his fault.

This perhaps is the less well-known part of the Solomon
story. How the wonderful gifts of wisdom and wealth from God
gave him the sort of absolute power which corrupts. Solomon
was after all human, and you've got to be very careful with great
power; Solomon wasn't careful enough.

The Kingdom Divided

When God told Solomon that one of his servants was to rule
over part of what had been Solomon's kingdom, he didn't mean
one of the grooms or the footmen. But a very able man with
a high position in Government called Jeroboam. He was told he
was to be a king by an old prophet who met him one day on
a country road. The old prophet showed Jeroboam the new order
of things in a rather costly way. He tore up his new coat. Into
twelve pieces. Then the old man, in his shirtsleeves, told
Jeroboam his fate. 'The twelve pieces,' he said, 'are the twelve
tribes. You are to be king of ten. God said so.'

When Solomon got to know, he tried to kill Jeroboam.
Understandable. So Jeroboam fled to Egypt and didn't come
back till Solomon was dead and his son was on the throne. A
very stupid man, this son of Solomon. Often the way; clever
men have stupid sons. He had grown up knowing that one of
the least popular laws his father had made was the one about
forced labour. The people for a certain period of each year had
no choice; and they hated it. Solomon was a realist, and hard,
and the law got many things done, but the people hated it. So
when this stupid son, after his father died, had a chance to
remove the law, to 'lighten the yoke' – and he was advised to –
he did the opposite. And with no tact either. 'My father
chastised you with whips,' he told the people, '*I* will chastise you
with scorpions! A *heavier* yoke,' he yelled.

Idiot! An immediate general strike. The Minister of Forced Labour was killed. And the people all went quietly home. 'To your tents O Israel,' was the slogan. 'This is not what King David meant for us.'

God looked on. Sadly. But it had to be, and soon Jeroboam was back from Egypt and the old prophet's words all came to pass. The ten tribes in the north of Israel asked him to be their king and he said yes. And almost overnight the people, whom King David had unified for his son Solomon to rule as one nation, broke into two. The north, the ten tribes, kept the name Israel; the south, mainly of the large tribe of Judah, called itself Judah. (The other tribe in the south was Benjamin, descendants of Joseph's younger brother.) Stupid son reigned over the south. Stupid son had a name; it was Rehoboam. So similar to Jeroboam that I have purposely avoided using it. It seemed less confusing to be rude to him. But that idiot reigned seventeen years, the Bible says, going downhill the whole time. Other books say seven; quite long enough in my opinion. Anyway, he and his kingdom went to the bad. Idol worship worse than ever and shocking decadence of every kind.

Jeroboam's ten tribes up north were a bit better but not much. He started well. He was shrewd and was soon aware that his people were going to miss Jerusalem and the great Temple, the centre of their religious life, the house of God's Ark. Jerusalem was now in Judah, the 'other country'. So Jeroboam got busy. He chose two places in the north, both of them rather holy places in the minds of his people, and he built at each site an altar, a place of worship. Good idea. But he got rather carried away. He appointed his own priests, invented services, and even created new feast days.

'I will even give you,' he told his people, 'in each place, a feature as good as the great Temple.' D'you know what he put up? Golden calves. Honestly, people never learn. It would be comic, if it weren't so sad. A tragic sequel to the greatness of Solomon and David. But one thing they had done. They'd left

Israel with a picture of the greatness that might be hers – a happy people, powerful, prosperous and united; at the centre of it all, the great Temple of God in the Holy City of Jerusalem. They would hang on to that picture through all the years that followed. So much trouble was to follow. As we shall see.

Chapter 5

PROPHETS, PRIESTS AND KINGS

Well, king followed king in the two kingdoms of Israel and Judah. None of them much good in those early years. Some good prophets, though. The first were Elijah and Elisha, who did a great deal to keep up faith in God among the people of the north. They needed to. For we are now to meet a new King of Israel. Ahab, son of Omri, an army commander, who had come out on top after another army commander had wiped out Jeroboam's grandson and his family. This Ahab was a real stinker. Who did evil, so the Bible says, more than all who went before him. And as if this wasn't enough, says the Bible, he took for wife one Jezebel who was worse than he was! They both of them just ignored God and worshipped Baal and built idols and temples to him. And not only the King and Queen but all the court too. The corruption spread down from the top and the whole people rather went to the bad.

Right. God had now had enough and as before looked around for someone to speak for him. He chose a man from a place called Tishbe, a Tishbite, gave him certain instructions, and sent him to see King Ahab. The Tishbite's name was Elijah.

Always a bit cross was Elijah. Mind you, he always wore a shirt woven of camel's hair, which couldn't have helped much. Anyway he went to see Ahab and came straight to the point. 'No more rain,' he said, 'until further notice. Goodbye.'

Well, the weather started to get a bit dry, so God thought Elijah had better go where Ahab couldn't find him. 'Go east,' said God, 'to the brook of Cherith. Very barren, but the water is pure.'

'Any food?' said Elijah, who didn't eat much but liked a little.

'Food will be brought to you morning and evening,' said God.

'Won't the bringers be able to tell Ahab where I am?' said Elijah.

'Not these bringers,' said God, 'they will be birds. Ravens.'

So off went Elijah and settled in and twice a day, sure enough, the food arrived; bread, meat, all he needed.

Then the brook began to dry up (no rain, you see) and God moved him again. 'North,' said God, 'I've arranged your food.'

'More birds?' said Elijah, who'd come to like his beautiful blue-black friends.

'No,' said God, 'a poor widow.'

Elijah found the place – it was a little town just outside Ahab's kingdom. Just as he came to the gate he saw a poorly-dressed woman gathering sticks and somehow knew that she was his new landlady. He sat down on a stone. 'I am tired and very dry,' he said. 'Could you bring me a little water and perhaps some bread?'

'I will bring the water with pleasure,' she said, 'but I've no bread. No food at all except a little flour in a bowl and a little oil in a jar. And that's all. I suppose,' she said, 'you could say we are starving.'

Elijah got up. 'I will gather some sticks for your oven,' he said, 'and I will live in your house and, until God sends us back the rain, there will always be flour in the bowl and oil in the jar.'

She started to say something.

'God said so,' said Elijah.

And it was so. The poor widow was a very puzzled woman.

Then one day her son became ill, and got worse, and then died. She said to Elijah, 'What have I done? What have you against me? You say you are a man of God. Did he send you into my house to kill my son? He's all I've got.'

Elijah knew her to be a good woman and he himself was puzzled. 'Give me the boy,' he said, and took the child up to his room. He laid the body on his bed. Then he talked to God.

'I know, Lord,' he said, 'that there are many wicked people in Israel and that Ahab and his awful wife Jezebel have got to be punished for all the idol-worship and so on and that's why you've stopped the rain. And I know, Lord,' said Elijah, 'that you are very busy. But I'm sure you didn't mean this poor woman to suffer such a blow.'

He looked down at the body. A good-looking boy whom he'd been very fond of. He knelt beside him and laid his own head on the boy's chest.

'Lord,' he said, 'make his heart beat again. Such a cheerful little spirit. Give it back.'

The body remained lifeless.

'Give it back,' said Elijah, his head still pressing on the boy's chest.

And then again, 'Give it back, Lord, please.'

And the heart began to beat.

Soon the boy opened his eyes and looked into Elijah's face. 'Hullo,' he said, 'I'm hungry.'

'So you should be,' said Elijah. 'It's supper time.'

And they went downstairs.

Elijah versus Ahab

Well, Elijah lived just over Israel's northern border with the poor widow and her son for about two and a half years until one day God told him to go down and see King Ahab.

At roughly the same moment King Ahab was talking to his chamberlain, a good man called Obadiah who was rather afraid of the wicked King and of his wife Queen Jezebel who was worse.

'This famine is all that prophet's fault,' said the King, 'that Elijah in his hair shirt! Ever since he turned up over two years ago and said, "No rain", there's been none. People are dying like flies. We've had to cut the palace banquets down to five a week! The Queen's livid. My race-horses are losing weight! Obadiah,' said the King, 'go and see whether there are any springs or grassy valleys we may have overlooked.'

So off went Obadiah and was soon back with bigger news. 'I met Elijah,' he told the King. 'He wants you to go and meet him.'

'We've had this nonsense before,' said the King. 'Hoaxes. I've searched this country top to bottom for him. I've even sent messages to all the neighbouring kings. He's disappeared off the face of the earth!'

'It's not a hoax,' said Obadiah. 'I *know* him. And he *will* be there. It's about bringing the rain back.'

When Ahab saw Elijah, he found it a bit difficult to meet the prophet's hard unforgiving eyes. So he started to blame *him* for the drought and famine and Israel's trouble.

'Not me,' said Elijah. 'You and your false gods Baal and Asherah, and your wicked ways. All right,' said Elijah, 'the rain is to come back, but on condition that all the hundreds of priests of Baal and Asherah meet me up on top of Mount Carmel and all the people are there to see the meeting. Don't argue,' said Elijah, 'you have no choice.' And it was done.

Elijah looked down at the thousands of silent people. 'How much longer,' he asked them, 'are you going to limp along with two opinions? Either Baal is the true god or God is.'

The people were silent; listening.

'I say that God is,' said Elijah, 'and here are four hundred and fifty priests who say that Baal is. So let us both, they and I, prepare a fine bull for sacrifice, on dry wood. Then let us both call upon our gods to send down the fire to light the wood. They can go first. Is it fair?'

And the people said yes. And it was done.

Well, the priests of Baal nearly went berserk. They prayed and shouted and walked round and round and cut themselves with sharp knives and went into fits and frothed and raved until nearly tea-time. Not a word. Not a spark. The meat started to go off a bit. Hot day.

Elijah rather enjoyed it. He even rubbed their noses in it. 'No one at home?' he asked them. 'Perhaps he's out the back, or upstairs asleep, or maybe,' he shouted, 'like always, there's no one there at all! All right,' he said to them. 'Get yourselves bandaged up. It's my turn.'

He turned to the people. 'Come nearer,' he said. The great multitude surged up the slope. Then Elijah drenched the meat and wood with water and then did it twice more. Then, in silence, alone, he prayed. One voice. 'Show them Lord. They need miracles. They always have.'

There was a pause and then a great roar of flame and the soaking mass went up like a firework. Nothing was left. Not even the great stones of the altar. Marvellous sight. The people fell back and then prayed to the one and only God. Fervently. Elijah watched them, not too impressed. He knew about mobs, did Elijah.

He raised his voice and pointed at the priests of Baal. 'See that they do not escape,' he said, 'for they are wicked and led you wrong.'

King Ahab looked at Elijah with no affection at all. 'I ought to kill you,' he said. 'Two years ago you walked in, said that there would be no more rain and then disappeared. Today you turn up and do this trick of burning up a sacrifice without making a fire and everybody's impressed and the people are all now going to believe in your God for five minutes as they've done before so many times. Also you've let the people loose on nearly five hundred of my wife's holy men. They're sure to kill the lot and my name will be mud. Jolly good day's work! I hope you're satisfied.

'Well, my old enemy,' said the King. 'I'm not impressed. If you want to impress *me*, bring back the rain.'

Elijah straightened up. He tilted his head as though listening. 'I hear a sound,' he said, 'like the falling rain. Come, we will go back up the mountain and you shall eat a little meal and by the time you've finished the rain will have begun.'

The King looked up at the absolutely clear sky. There hadn't been rain or a cloud in that sky for over two years. Drought and famine. 'Right,' he said.

When they got to the top the King's servant fixed him a snack and Elijah's servant waited for orders. Elijah sat down and lowered his head between his knees. The servant waited. The King chewed a date.

'Go,' said Elijah, 'to the very top and look toward the sea.'

The servant did and came back. 'Nothing,' he said.

Elijah didn't raise his head. 'Go again,' he said, 'and again. Seven times.'

By the seventh time the King was at the toothpick stage.

'There is a cloud,' said the servant, 'small, no bigger than a man's hand.'

Elijah got up and he smiled. A rare thing. 'Get in your chariot,' he said to the King, 'and go and don't stop till you get home. Because there's going to be the biggest rainstorm you ever saw.'

'Want a lift?' said the King.

'No,' said Elijah, and hitched his robe up to his knees, 'I'm going to run. I haven't run down a hill since I was at school.'

'Horses are faster,' said the King.

'Not this time,' said Elijah, 'I shall beat you all the way back to the Palace.'

And he did. About thirty miles. Not bad for an old prophet! Mind you, for that sort of performance you *need* to be a friend of God.

The Still Small Voice

King Ahab got home drenched. As soon as he'd changed he told Queen Jezebel all about it. 'Really?' she said. 'So Elijah killed nearly five hundred of my holy men. Well, you send a little message to that filthy old prophet to say that by this time tomorrow he'll be where they are!' Terrible woman. Scared everybody. Elijah too. Friend of God or not he was only human.

He cleared out that night. South to Beersheba and then into the desert. Very depressed and exhausted. 'Lord,' he said, 'it's all too much. I'd be better off dead.' And he fell asleep.

When he awoke he was parched and hungry. 'Ready to eat?' said a voice and Elijah was aware suddenly of a wonderful smell of hot bread. He turned and there it was. On hot stones with a glowing fire below them, and a jug of sweet water near his hand. In charge, a friendly-faced youngish man in white.

'I'm staggered,' said Elijah. 'No one knew I was here.'

'Well, God knew,' said the young man. 'Please help yourself.'

Elijah was starving and ate well. It seemed a special sort of bread. Wonderful taste. Elijah reached for the water, smiled at the young man and took a good drink. When he lowered the jug he was alone. Under a single tree in the middle of a desert. He lay down, much comforted, and slept all day.

He woke after dark. 'Ready to eat?' said the voice.

Elijah sat up.

'Eat a lot,' said the young man, 'for you have a long journey ahead of you and you'll need all your strength.'

And it was a long journey. Forty days and forty nights. To the mountain called Horeb, where Moses saw the burning bush and received his orders from God about freeing the Egyptian slaves. Well, God had sent for Elijah to tell *him* a few things too. Also God knew that Elijah was feeling low. Always rather cross, remember, and just now he had some cause to be. He'd done miracles for the people and preached and healed the sick and the people still worshipped idols and were wicked. Elijah felt that as a prophet of God he was a failure, that he still walked alone.

Well, the days passed and at last he was on the mountain. He'd told it all to God and now he waited for God to speak. Which God did, but not right away. First Elijah was given a sort of show. A great wind began, which moved huge boulders as if they were cotton-wool and lifted mighty trees out of the ground. Then the mountain heaved and split and a great crack ran along the valley like a tear. Then every tree and bush burst into flame with a great roar. In the middle, quite safe, Elijah. The noise was tremendous, deafening, yet suddenly, in his mind, quite clearly, Elijah heard a still small voice, which spoke quietly and told him many of God's plans for the future including the news that quite soon he, Elijah, was to have an assistant who would take over from him when he died. There was nothing vague or mystical about the message. God supplied Elijah with the full name and address. The name, Elisha. Rather like his own, easy to remember. The place, a village near the Jordan not far from his own home town. Elijah went there right away.

He found his new assistant in a ploughed field. Elisha was a ploughman. Middle-aged, strong-looking man. Elijah talked with him and then formally put his cape for a moment across Elisha's shoulders. A bit sadly, for he knew how hard a prophet's life is. Far harder than a ploughman's. Elisha said his goodbyes and off they went. Two men of God.

Naboth's Vineyard

Now you might say, what does a prophet *do?* What sort of life did Elijah – and after him Elisha – live? Did they sit around and prophesy all day long? Five-day week? Working hours?

Well, no. They travelled around a lot; they were judges; they had wide knowledge of the great list of laws given by God to Moses – upon which all law is based. A sort of unofficial theocratic government over against the government of Israel's idol-worshipping kings. They gave advice; were healers; were respected, held in awe. They were 'men of God' and had devoted disciples.

Meanwhile the King and Queen and Israel went on with their nasty ways. Next door to the palace lived a man called Naboth; quiet-living man, who was a farmer and specialist in wine-grapes. Naboth's vineyard was famous. One day the King decided he wanted that vineyard next door for a vegetable garden so he told Naboth he would offer him either money, or another vineyard as good elsewhere. Reasonable.

But Naboth refused. 'The God *I* believe in,' he said, 'the *only* God, gave us a law which forbids the selling of an inheritance.'

The King, who hated to be crossed in anything, was made even more angry by Naboth saying 'the only God'. He and the Queen spent a fortune on other gods. The palace was *littered* with idols. So he swore at Naboth and went home very put out. Went off his food. Told the Queen all about it.

'Poor darling,' said his wife, 'just you leave it to your little Jezebel. She'll get your vineyard for you.' Terrible woman. She got busy and wrote lying letters on palace notepaper, and used the royal seal, and bribed and corrupted and threatened and brought false witness. In the end poor Naboth was accused of treason and sacrilege on a trumped-up charge in front of dishonest judges and he was found guilty and taken outside the city and stoned to death. Disgraceful business.

Jezebel went to the King. 'Naboth is dead,' she said. 'You wanted his vineyard. You're the King. Go and take it.' So Ahab had his supper, his appetite fully restored, and went next door to the vineyard. Very satisfied with himself and his clever little wife.

First person he met was Elijah, sent by God with one or two messages. 'I won't stay long,' said Elijah. 'This vineyard. To steal it you broke just about every commandment in the Book.' It was nearing dark and the prophet seemed to grow taller. 'I am instructed to tell you,' he said, 'you know who by, that where Naboth died, there shall your blood flow. Evil will come upon you and your family and nothing can stop it. It will be arranged that nobody belonging to you will get a funeral. Jackals and vultures will eat their bodies.'

The King was now terrified. 'It wasn't me,' he said, 'it was Jezebel.'

'Jezebel,' said Elijah, 'will die by violence and her body also will be eaten by wild dogs. Goodbye. We won't meet again.'

It all came true, of course. In God's good time.

In fact the first part, the death of King Ahab, happened very soon.

He and the King of Judah had struck up an alliance against the King of Syria. But after what Elijah had told him he didn't go into battle without special precautions. Had the King of Judah go into battle in the royal chariot while he, Ahab, was disguised as an ordinary soldier. A lot of good it did him! You may think that the phrase 'If it's got your name on it' is modern. King Ahab, in disguise, in the middle of a great army, was killed by an arrow shot by an enemy archer who, as the Bible puts it, *'drew his bow at a venture'*. An arrow which found a chink in Ahab's armour. It had his name on it all right. Meanwhile the King had built new stables in what had been Naboth's vineyard. And it was there that they washed down the chariot in which the King had bled to death. God has his ways of doing things. Some sooner. Some later.

Elijah's Mantle

Meanwhile there came a day when Elijah told Elisha that he had to go on a journey. It would be his last journey and he knew it. He didn't tell Elisha. But Elisha knew. Prophets do. So did the sons of the prophets in all the townships of Israel, through which they went together. 'You stay here,' said Elijah in one town after another. 'You stay here while I go on to such and such a place.'

'Not me,' said Elisha. 'That's a long way. I wouldn't rest. I'll come too. How *can* I leave you?'

They came at last to Jericho where they were met by fifty young men, all of them from god-fearing families who revered Elijah. The old man was tired.

'Here?' said Elisha. 'Have we come far enough?'

'No,' said Elijah, 'further east, over Jordan. You stay here.'

'Not on your life!' said Elisha. 'Take my arm. I *can't* leave you. We'll *all* go.'

It was meant. God meant the young men to be witnesses. Not of everything but of enough. They saw the two prophets go down to the river. Then Elijah took off his sleeveless coat, his mantle, and he struck the water with it. The water parted and he and Elisha walked across the dry riverbed. As they reached the other side the water came down again. The young men were goggle-eyed.

The prophets walked on till out of sight. They stopped. 'Here,' said Elijah, 'I am to be taken from you.' Elisha looked sad. 'What shall I do for you?'

'For years,' said Elisha, 'I've known I am to follow you. To wear your mantle. I've known I'm to have a share of your spirit. It will be hard to take your place. Give me a double share. I shall need it.'

Elijah understood. His eyes took on that unfocussed visionary look that Elisha knew so well. 'I am to be taken from you in a special way,' he said. 'If you *see* this miracle you will know you are in my place, with double share. If not, not.'

Then he walked away a little. Elisha saw everything. And it was a sight to see. A sort of glow began high in the sky above Elijah's head. It began to descend, turning, swirling. It was white and gold, shimmering. It hurt the eyes. Warmth came from it. Then it took shape and became a chariot and six white horses, all incandescent like white heat. It circled, coming down. Then Elijah was in the chariot and it circled, going up. And up. The noise of a whirlwind began and grew louder, then died away. The chariot and horses became again just a glow. The glow faded.

Elisha was alone. A bit lonely. He turned and at his feet was Elijah's mantle. He picked it up and walked back to the river. The young men hadn't moved. Elisha felt a bit nervous. 'Oh well,' he said to himself, 'I can only try. And I did see the miracle.' And he banged the water with the mantle. It stopped and parted and he walked across and up the other bank and as he passed through the young men they all bowed their heads to him. They had witnessed; now they knew. And through them soon the whole nation would know that Elijah the great prophet was dead. Dead and gone; leaving nothing behind except his cloak, his mantle. And Elisha, the young men would say, chosen by God, now wore that mantle. Also, as time went on, they would learn that he was just as blunt and honest as his master, and just as fearless.

Elisha in Shunem

Elisha in his work travelled a *great* deal and with his servant, a much younger man named Gehazi, came one day to a place called Shunem. First time. They stopped at a rather fine house to ask the way. The woman of the house, without knowing who her tired dusty poorly-dressed callers were, had them in, showed them where to clean up, and gave them a good meal. Gehazi wanted to tell her who his master was, but Elisha, rather amused, wouldn't let him. 'I – er – travel,' he told her, 'a teacher of Law, a sort of judge.' When they had finished, she made them promise to call any time they were passing. And they did.

One day when they arrived she said to Elisha, 'I hope you won't think it a liberty but we've built a sort of bed/living-room for you to use when you come. It's given me great pleasure to do, and my husband too. We knew you to be a man of God before we found out your name and we are much honoured that you eat at our table.'

Elisha was touched. The little room was charming. She was a wealthy woman and had good taste. As time went on, he found out that the one sadness in her life was that she had no children. She'd married late and her husband was quite an old man, much older than she was.

So one day Elisha had a word with her. He'd come to admire and like this sensible friendly woman. 'One way and another,' he said, 'you've gone to a lot of trouble. I've been thinking of how I can repay you in some way. As you now know, my work brings me into contact with some very important people and I only have to ask. But I've often heard you say you need nothing. That you are content. This is rare, and good. However,' he said, 'one thing you do not have is a son. Build another room. A nursery. He will be born a year from today.'

And he was. And grew into a handsome boy with all his mother's gentleness. He loved to be among the workers on his father's large farm. A fit strong boy. Never a day's illness. But one terrible morning he complained of a bad headache and by lunchtime he was dead. His mother was frantic and rushed to Elisha who was at Mount Carmel about twenty miles away. She was distraught, beside herself, sobbing, hardly making sense. She threw herself at Elisha's feet, clutched his robe, Gehazi moved forward. Elisha waved him away. He was shocked. Stood still. Waited.

She looked up. 'Did I *ask* you for a son?' she said. 'You *gave* him.'

'God told me to,' said Elisha.

'Has God told you that he is dead?' said the woman.

Elisha helped her to her feet. 'No,' he said. 'Come on.'

The boy's body was on Elisha's own bed in the room the woman had built. Small body, pale, cold. Elisha was tense. His beloved master Elijah had once given back life to a child, but could he? He took the boy's hands and put his mouth to the boy's mouth. Nothing.

He got up, walked about, prayed, *demanded* God's attention for a minute, and tried again. Time passed. The child's hands became warm, then his lips. Elisha sat back. The boy's eyes remained closed. And then, into this holy silence of a miracle, the boy sneezed. He sneezed seven times. By the seventh his mother was at the door with a hankie.

An Unprofitable Servant

Now, when Elisha took over Elijah's mantle he also took over fifty disciples, you remember. The fifty young men who witnessed. As the years went by they became a hundred. It was a good life; even in famine. If there was nothing for the soup but wild roots, bitter, maybe poisonous, Elisha was there to put in a pinch of flour and it would taste marvellous. He could make a little food go a *very* long way. If you were chopping firewood and your iron axe-head flew off into the river, the Master would make it float back to you. A good life. But you learned not to take advantage, or you were in *real* trouble. Like Gehazi, Elisha's servant. It happened like this.

The King of Syria had recently won a big battle against Israel – who didn't win them all by a long way. And he was very pleased with his C-in-C, a man called Naaman, who deserved it. But Naaman, poor chap, was a leper. Early stages, but positive. Rather unsightly. One day his wife said to him, 'My little maid, who was one of the prisoners brought back from this last war with Israel, tells me that there's a prophet there who she's sure could help you. She's a nice truthful girl. Nothing to lose. Go and see the King.'

Naaman did and the King said, 'Right, I'll give you a letter to the King of Israel asking him to arrange your cure. You go and pack your bag and take a nice present.'

So off went Naaman with a few servants and when the King of Israel read the letter, he – the King, that is – got very bothered. He thought it was a plot to start up the battle again.

'Am I *God?*' he said to his Prime Minister. 'Can I perform miracles? How can *I* cure leprosy? I can't even win a *war*.' He went on and on.

Now the Prime Minister was no fool and he went and told it all to Elisha. 'Tell the King to calm down,' said the prophet, 'and send Naaman round to my house.'

When Naaman arrived with his servants and chariots Elisha didn't invite him in, or go out to him. He sent Gehazi out. 'My master says go down to the Jordan,' said Gehazi, 'and wash yourself all over seven times and you'll be cured.' And went back inside.

Naamen felt like a brush-salesman, and lost his temper. 'I didn't come all this way to be told to go and wash myself,' he shouted at his servants. 'The least he could have done was to have come out to me himself. Done a bit of praying to this God of his. A burnt offering or two. Bit of magic; laying on of the hands; all that stuff. If I'd wanted to wash in a river I could have stayed at home in Syria. Our rivers are a damn sight better than any here in Israel. Come on,' he said, 'I'm fed up.'

But his oldest servant said to him, 'Why not try? If Elisha had asked you to do something complicated and costly, you would have done it without question. As Mrs Naaman said, what can you lose?'

So Naaman did. Seven times. Obedient as a child. And by the seventh time his skin was as clear as a child's. He went back to Elisha, who this time was waiting for him outside the house. 'Your God is the true God,' said the soldier. 'I'd like to change to him. Is it too late?'

'Never too late,' said Elisha and when Naaman offered payment for the cure he wouldn't take a penny.

But Gehazi was greedy and when Naaman and his party left he went after them and caught them up. 'My master sent me to say,' he told Naaman, 'that he does after all have a use for some of those bags of silver and so on.'

'Delighted!' said Naaman and lent him a couple of men to carry it all.

Gehazi hid it. Didn't do him much good. 'I know all about it,' said Elisha. 'The soldier was to be shown God, not a liar and thief. So, Gehazi,' said the prophet, 'as you've taken over a fair amount of Naaman's property, you'd better take over his leprosy too. As from now.'

Man of War

Now, it might seem to you that Elisha was a bit hard on his servant Gehazi. But, make no mistake about it, Elisha *was* hard. He had to be. You might think that because a man is a prophet of God, he must therefore be a man of peace. Not a bit. Elisha was a very useful man to have on your side in time of war. And in Israel at that time the war never seemed to stop. Syria was the main enemy just now and the King of Syria used to get in a terrible state. His most secret plans seemed to be known to Israel almost before he finished writing them down. 'Elisha, the prophet,' he was told. 'Special powers.' So he sent a large army marching off to kill him. Elisha met them, made them all blind, kept them marching right into captivity, gave them back their sight and a good feed and sent them all home. After this the Syrian king got rather discouraged for a while. Understandable.

Then he tried a new idea. A siege. A huge army, with supplies and equipment enough for a year, went and surrounded the city of Samaria, capital of Israel. No one went in or out. Before very long things were very bad indeed. People would eat anything, eventually even each other. Such things happen. The King of Israel would walk along the ramparts of his besieged capital and look out, and to every side he could see the enemy and their mouth-watering heaps of stores. His name was Joram and he was the son of the wicked King Ahab. Joram was a bit better than his father but not much and Elisha didn't have too much time for him. Or he for the prophet.

So, when the people cried out to the King to deliver them, he blamed God for the siege, and soon was blaming Elisha, God's representative. Then he decided to kill Elisha. He screamed and shouted at the old man about what people were forced to eat and the huge prices that were being charged for almost any kind of food – even corpses. 'A man is worth more dead than alive,' he yelled and he wasn't joking.

Elisha got up. 'Keep quiet,' he said, 'and hear the word of the Lord. By this time tomorrow every kind of food will be on sale in the city and at the right price.'

The King nearly frothed at the mouth but decided to delay Elisha's execution for a day or two. He'd been made to look silly before, had the King, and in addition he was hungry.

Well, Elisha prayed and God arranged it. He arranged it that evening just as it was getting dark. Suddenly the Syrian army, camped round the city, began to hear from all around them the full sound-effect of a much larger army. Chariots by the thousand, a million marching feet, bands, horses, the lot. Nothing to be seen.

'Reinforcements for Israel,' someone said, and in five minutes a mad panic was under way and the Syrians dropped everything and just ran.

Into that deserted camp later that night wandered four lepers from the city. They were starving and had worked out that they had nothing to lose by going over to the Syrians. They couldn't believe their eyes. To every side piles and heaps and boxes and sacks of everything. They went mad. They ate and drank and sang and looted and hid things and dressed themselves up in finery and armour. And then calmed down. 'This is not right,' said one of them. 'This is a day of good news. Let's go and tell the King.' And they did.

The King at first thought it was a trap to entice the people out of the city, so he sent out scouts on some of the last few horses and they followed the trail of stuff abandoned by the Syrian army right to the Jordan. They reported back and the people left the city and gathered up every single thing. A wonderful day!

During that afternoon Elisha went down to the main market where it was business as usual. Crowded. Very cheerful. He bought one or two things and as he turned he met the King.

'Shops seem well stocked,' said Elisha politely. 'How are the prices?'

'Normal,' said the King – and could have bitten his tongue. But he came to a bad end. Like his father. He was one of Ahab's sons remember.

Elisha the Kingmaker

Let us go back for a moment to the day when old Elijah was told about his new assistant, Elisha, on Horeb, the mount of God. He was told other things too. About happenings and changes that would take place among the ruling families in Israel and Syria. New kings to be anointed for both places. Also, soon after that, you remember, Elijah told Ahab what he and his family could expect after the way they'd behaved over Naboth's vineyard. 'Where Naboth died, there shall your blood flow,'

Elijah had said. 'And your wife Jezebel and all your male descendants will be wiped out. Not one of them will get a funeral. Jackals and wild dogs will eat their bodies.'

Ahab had died soon after that, remember. Killed by 'a bow drawn at a venture' in one of Israel's many battles against Syria. Now it is time for the rest of those prophecies to be fulfilled. Not by Elijah himself, of course, but by Elisha.

The King of Syria, we've noticed, in spite of the fact that their two countries were nearly always at war, was not above sending messages to the man of God in Israel. This time the man he sent was called Hazael, and his errand was to enquire whether his master, the King of Syria, would recover from a sickness which had laid him low.

Elisha looked at the King's messenger. 'Your master will recover,' he said. 'But God has shown me that he will never have a chance to do so. That he will die soon.'

Elisha looked unseeingly, unblinkingly into Hazael's eyes until the younger man felt very uncomfortable. Then Hazael saw a great sadness come into the prophet's face and the unblinking eyes fill with tears. He felt himself in the presence of huge forces.

'Why do you weep, my Lord?' he said.

'Because,' said Elisha, 'God has shown me also that *you* are to be King of Syria and that you will bring death and destruction to the people of Israel.'

It all came true. The Bible tells us little of Hazael, but the day after he got back and gave the King the message about his certain recovery he killed him and took over the throne. And he *did* become a terrible enemy to Israel for all the long years of Elisha's life. Fifty more years nearly.

Well, now that they had a common enemy, the kingdoms of Israel and Judah had begun to draw together a bit. Also King Ahab and Queen Jezebel had married their daughter to a prince of Judah and one of *their* sons was the reigning King of Judah and nephew, of course, of the reigning King of Israel.

And now it was the turn of the King of Israel to be sick, and his nephew the King of Judah was visiting him. Well, the King of Israel, Ahab's son, had an officer called Jehu, who one day was in the mess with a crowd of his brother officers when a messenger from Elisha asked to see him outside.

The messenger was brief. 'I am to anoint you King of Israel,' he told Jehu, 'and you are to clean things up generally. Also you are to wipe out every last one of the family of Ahab including his widow Jezebel, the worst of the lot.' Then he anointed Jehu and left.

Jehu went in and told the mess and rather to his surprise they believed him and joined him. Off they all went to find the King. As I told you, he was poorly and the King of Judah was visiting him. So Jehu paid his respects and killed them both. Both of them descendants of Ahab, remember.

Then Jehu went to attend to Queen Jezebel. 'Driving furiously,' the Bible says. Apparently it was a habit of his. Anyway by the time he arrived at the Palace, Jezebel was waiting for him. Painted and powdered and dressed to kill. She looked down at him from a high window screaming insults. Behind her were two or three of her eunuchs. Now these fellows were no fools and they could see that Jehu was the new man. So when he invited them to throw Jezebel down to him they did. Very nasty mess indeed.

Jehu then attended to her entire family, to all the idol-worshipping priests, and everything else on Elisha's list. Needless to say, not one of Ahab's family was given burial. Jackals and vultures, as Elijah had prophesied. All, as I said, in God's good time.

Elisha lived a long time. Right through the thirty years of Jehu's reign, and the seventeen years his son ruled after him. He made many prophecies and performed many miracles. Even on his deathbed he told a rather worried King of Israel, Jehu's grandson, that the next three wars against Syria were going to be all right. Even *after* he died, he helped to bring a dead man back to life.

'A double portion of your spirit,' he had asked from his master Elijah. Certainly he seems to have had it.

Another Kingmaker

We heard how after Solomon the children of Israel split into two kingdoms. Israel in the north and Judah in the south. And we have heard about Elijah and Elisha and how they stood out against the wickedness of King Ahab and his family. Now, all these happenings took place in the northern kingdom, Israel. So it's time we had a look at the southern kingdom of Judah and the city of Jerusalem, where David had set up his capital and where Solomon had built the great Temple for the Ark of the Law.

King had followed King, as in the north. None of them particularly good, but none so bad as Ahab. One other difference, though. None of this throne-stealing by other families which was such a feature of the north. Jeroboam, then Omri (Ahab's father), then Jehu, were army commanders who had seized the throne of Israel. In Judah the family of David still reigned. There had been bloodshed, though. Most of it arising out of the marriage of Joram, prince of Judah, with Athaliah, the daughter of Ahab and Jezebel. Tried to bring her parents' idolatrous ways to Jerusalem with her. And her husband, who ought to have known better, didn't. This Joram was an ugly customer. As soon as he came to the throne, he killed off all his own brothers – and anybody else who might be expected to cause trouble. But he didn't last long. He died of a horrible disease. And not before the Philistines, those old enemies of the Israelites, had invaded the country and killed all *his* sons except the youngest. It was this youngest son, now King of Judah, who was killed by Jehu together with his uncle, the King of Israel, on the day that Jezebel and her sons and grandsons were put to death.

Well, when the news of all this came to Jerusalem and Athaliah, now an old woman, heard that her only surviving son was dead, she decided to kill all *his* sons and reign herself. Odd sort of grandmother. Mind you, the death of her own sons may perhaps have turned her mind. Anyway, she was Jezebel's daughter and she arranged it.

But *her* daughter was a God-fearing woman and married to the high-priest of the time, Jehoiada, and she managed to steal the baby of the family away. And she and her husband hid him in the Temple, where they brought him up carefully and kept him out of sight.

For six years Queen Athaliah reigned and then Jehoiada could stand it no longer. He called the Temple and Palace guards together and introduced them to the real King who was now seven years old. 'Get your coronation drill brushed up,' he told them. 'We've had a mad old Queen long enough.' He issued to them the spears and shields that had been King David's and set the day and it was a splendid ceremony.

The old Queen, when she saw the boy with his crown on and the guards at attention and the trumpets blowing and the happy rejoicing people, screamed, 'Treason! Treason!' But the people remembered murder, murder, and Jehoiada thought it best that she were put to death. 'Not in public,' he said, 'nor here in the Temple, but at home.'

Jehoiada had great wisdom and gave that wisdom to the teaching of the boy King. The boy's name was Joash, and the high-priest taught him everything. Above all, a love for God and a love for God's great Temple where, after all, he had spent all his early childhood. He grew into a fine young man and indeed not since his ancestor Solomon had Judah had a king who cared so much for the Temple and its worship.

When King Joash was about thirty years old he said to his old foster-father the high-priest, 'A great deal of money comes into the Temple one way and another, yet not a penny gets spent on repairs or maintenance. I know that the priests have to live off the money that they are given, but the place is looking very shabby. I've spoken to the priests but they won't cooperate. Any ideas?' The high-priest had a think and invented what we now know as the collection box. The priests got some, but less. The box was by the door and when it was full it was emptied by the King's Secretary. He used most of the money to pay for a crowd of carpenters and stonemasons who soon had the beautiful Temple built by King Solomon looking spick and span again. Joash and the high-priest were determined practical men. They knew that the people had to be involved; that if your religion costs you a little you appreciate it more. Like anything else.

Never Kill a Prophet

Joash, brought up and taught by Jehoiada, was a sound practical ruler. But Jehoiada died when Joash was about forty. The middle years, when a certain silliness is known, even in the wisest. The old priest was buried like a king. Among kings. He deserved it. People remembered him – and his words. Pity they didn't take more notice of them. The rot began to set in right away.

After the funeral ceremonies came the entertaining by Joash of all the various powerful men who ruled the rest of his country for him. Not quite so well brought-up as he'd been. But persuasive; and as I said, powerful. In no time at all the restored Temple was being ignored. Idol-worship began. There were men who stood fast in their love of God, the only God, but there were plenty of the other kind. It would be pleasant to say that Joash, bred and taught by a man of God, emerged as a hero and brought his straying people back to the Law. Well, he didn't. There *was* a man; not unexpectedly the son of Jehoiada. He and Joash had known each other all their lives. He was called Zachariah, and it was to him, not to Joash, that God spoke when things had really got rather bad.

The next day Zachariah went to the Temple and climbed up till he was high above the people. He was known and a vast crowd gathered. Someone went and fetched Joash. Zachariah stood silent, looking down. His eyes were glowing, odd, unfocussed. He raised his arms and the noise of the huge mob died away.

'From the time of our fathers' fathers,' he shouted, not loud but every word could be heard, 'from the time that great Moses gave us the Law of God, we have known that to keep that Law was *right*, and that, if we did right, we, God's people, would grow and prosper. It was promised, spoken, written on stone. If we break the Law we are punished. If you forsake God, he will forsake you. Prepare then for punishment; you have forsaken God, now he has forsaken you.'

No one moved. Deathly quiet. To the idol-worshippers, the Temple-forgetters, this was the enemy. One of them bent down, picked up a stone. 'Does he think he is an angel of God?' he shouted. 'Stone him!' And the mob went mad – as mobs do. Zachariah was dragged down and beaten and the mob stoned him to death in front of the Temple doors.

Now Joash could have stopped it, but he didn't. He let the son of the man who'd been a father to him be killed for telling the truth. His own brother, near enough. After the stoning, the mob drew back and the King went forward to the battered, bloody body. As Joash halted, Zachariah's eyes opened. Joash was transfixed. It was like looking into the eyes of Jehoiada who'd taught him all he'd forgotten about honour.

Zachariah's bruised and broken mouth moved. 'May the Lord see,' he said, 'and avenge.'

The Lord did. Quite soon too. Before a year was out the country had been invaded by the Syrians and all the powerful, persuasive rulers were dead. King Joash, wounded in battle, was killed in his bed by servants who remembered Jehoiada, the priest buried among kings. But not before he'd given away most of the gorgeous treasures of the Temple to try to buy off the Syrian king. Sensible, you might think? Practical? A king who'd spent all his childhood in the Temple should have known better. Joash was not even buried among priests. He wasn't good enough. He was only forty-seven. Nothing sadder than when a promising man goes to the bad.

'The Rod of God's Anger'

King Joash was succeeded by his son. Twenty-five years old. Rather like his dad. Bit weak. Allowed the old trouble, the idol-worship, to continue; took no account of the value of God's help and thought he could do it all himself, just because he was a king. He thought that a king makes gods. Wrong. God makes kings. And everything else. Anyway, the new King of Judah made a big army. You might have thought he'd get his own back on the Syrians but instead he decided to take on the other kingdom of Israel in the north. The King of Israel wasn't keen but had no choice really. This was the king whom Elisha had encouraged on his deathbed to make war against Syria. And so he did. But here he was attacking Jerusalem, breaking its walls, and taking reparations from the Temple treasure. Surprising Elisha didn't turn in his new grave.

Anyway king followed king in both kingdoms. As the kings were, so were their subjects. Always the way. For a time Syria continued hostile, as Elisha had prophesied, and attacked both Israel and Judah many times. (Still is a bit troublesome, by all accounts!) But Hazael was dead now and Syria soon had troubles of her own from the north – the new and terrible empire of Assyria based on Nineveh. A much more powerful and sophisticated enemy this – in spite of the way one of their kings is said to have repented at the preaching of Jonah! Hard, cruel, unstoppable. Soon, having disposed of Syria, the King of Assyria was looking on past it to the divided nation of Israel with its two kingdoms and beginning to lick his lips. 'The rod of God's anger,' as the prophet Isaiah would soon be calling him.

He set to work on the northern kingdom of Israel first and demanded a crippling amount of gold and silver to stay away. It was collected by heavy taxation and paid. But this taxation bred a discontent, then a sort of revolution, and over the next few years the country nearly destroyed itself. Then the Assyrians, like a great cloud of locusts, swept down and the kingdom of the north was no more. Ten of the twelve tribes of Israel lived in the north and they were taken away in their tens of thousands. Slaves, prisoners of war, refugees, displaced persons. And they'd had so many warnings. Been given so many chances.

Samaria, the capital of the north, fell after a brave fight and its story was the same as the rest of the country. It was depopulated; its people captured and taken away. The Assyrians knew about killing resistance. They moved other people into Samaria. Beaten people, captives from other conquered lands. Many cultures, many religions, many idols worshipped in many tongues. The city, once great and important, became the place of discouraged and demoralized people. People with no status, no position, no standards. Eventually despised. The word Samaritans was coined for this motley lot. A term of abuse. Excuse my dwelling on this, but it makes the practical charity shown by a later 'good Samaritan' an even more valuable story.

Enter Isaiah

Well, the people of Judah had not always been on the best of terms with their fellow-Israelites of the northern kingdom. We've noticed that. But never can they have wished them a fate like this. Besides, there seemed every prospect that Jerusalem and its lovely Temple would go the same way as Samaria.

It is twenty years now since Samaria fell. And the King of Judah, like his father before him, has become accustomed to doing much as the Assyrians tell him. He pays huge tribute, shows respect, does as he's told. His name is Hezekiah. A sensible good man. At present rather worried. He had been led into joining a coalition of armies to try and stop the Assyrians and it had gone wrong. He'd done all this against the advice of a man who'd always counselled him well. A man called Isaiah. A shrewd careful man whom today we call 'the prophet Isaiah'. Who now stood before him, listening carefully.

'They demanded a fortune in gold and silver as a sort of punishment tribute,' said the King. 'I even had to strip the gold facings from the Temple doors. All the lovely silver things from inside the Temple too.' Isaiah said nothing. He was not the sort of man to say, I told you so.

'And now that I've paid it and apologized,' said the King, 'it's all for nothing. There's a tremendous army massing outside the city walls. Jerusalem will fall and it's all my fault.'

'It will not fall,' said Isaiah. 'I've told you dozens of times. This is God's city. Where the Tablets of Moses are kept. Where the Ark lives, where the Temple stands. I tell you again. Have confidence.'

But the great armies settled down all round the city. The King of Assyria sent high officers who told the frightened people lining the great walls in their own language exactly what they could expect. 'And forget your God,' they shouted, 'this Lord you think will help you. Did he help the north? Did he help all the tens of thousands of your brethren?'

King Hezekiah was worried sick. He went and talked to Isaiah. Described the huge forces, the thousands of archers, the great battering rams.

'Not one arrow will come into the city,' said the prophet. 'No soldier, no shield; no siege will happen. The Assyrians will go back the way they came. God said so. God will defend this city. It is his. God, and the Angel of Death who helped that time in Egypt.'

And it was so. The next morning nearly two hundred thousand of the Assyrians were dead. The great camps were silent. Cemeteries. The survivors were soon gone. They didn't come back. Jerusalem was left alone.

But good Hezekiah was succeeded by a son who was as evil as his father had been good. A terrible fellow. He even built idols *in the Temple.* God had him taken by the Assyrians, in chains, and brought near to death for a while. That taught him. He changed his ways quite a lot. But during his wicked time Isaiah grew very worried that the true ways of God would be forgotten entirely. Not many books in those days; even the Law of Moses handed down by word of mouth. So Isaiah and his disciples started to collect the Law in a book. Jews, and Christians too, have been people of that book almost ever since.

Jeremiah and the Fall of Jerusalem

We have seen how Isaiah and his disciples collected God's Law in a book, and with it a prophecy of the disaster that was in store for the people if it were neglected.

Nobody knew of this book at the time. It was found nearly seventy years later when a very good king was on the throne – Josiah, grandson of the wicked one. He was busy restoring the rather neglected and shabby Temple, and this old book turned up in an odd corner. It was like a bombshell. Josiah saw it as a sort of message from God and he began a clearing out of every idol, image and false god in the whole country. The people loved him and gladly turned again to the true God.

Well, as might be expected, God was pleased at this turn of events. And so was one of God's prophets. A man called Jeremiah. A wise shrewd man, Jeremiah. He knew that the things that had happened to the children of Israel were, to a large extent, their own fault. The old trouble. Idol-worshipping; God-forgetting.

'Good,' said Jeremiah to the people. 'Pay tribute to the Assyrians, and busy yourselves finding God again. The enemy is strong. Don't depend on miracles; you haven't deserved a miracle for some time.'

But Josiah, when he was about forty, decided to have a go. He was killed in battle. A sad loss. The people felt more than ever surrounded by their enemies. Like today.

Then, among these enemies, over the next few years huge shifts of power took place. New nations grew, the Medes, the Babylonians. Great battles raged around Judah. Egypt and Assyria joined forces and were both crushed. Assyria's great city of Nineveh, where Jonah went, was utterly destroyed. The Medes and the Babylonians shared the spoils. Judah became subject to Babylon. Left alone and at peace, so long as she kept up the payments.

'And so you should,' said Jeremiah. 'The new King of Babylon, Nebuchadnezzar, is not soft. Live as God said you should. Obey his laws. Babylon is a punishment. Do *not* revolt.'

But the King, Josiah's son, made the same mistake as his father. His attempt failed too.

Nebuchadnezzar took heavy toll. 'All the nobility to be taken to Babylon,' he said, 'all the artisans and skilled workers, and all the soldiers. *I'll* choose Judah's new king. Josiah's second-born. And I'll name him too. Call him Zedekiah. Easy work for a twenty-one-year-old. Very few people left to rule.' Then he left, with his huge army and the thousands of prisoners.

Jeremiah stayed by Zedekiah. Gave the same advice. 'Do not oppose,' he said over and over again. 'You can lose everything.' And for nine years the young King took heed.

Then, having raised and trained a few fighting men, he barricaded Jerusalem and shouted a defiance. It was a walled city and withstood the Babylonian siege a long time. But the time came when people were starving, so Zedekiah and his men went at night through the wall and made for Jordan and help. They were captured. Zedekiah was tried by Nebuchadnezzar and his punishment was dreadful.

His sons were killed one by one before his eyes: then he was blinded and led away to Babylon together with nearly everyone else left in Jerusalem. Then the Babylonian army moved in and smashed down the walls. Then they pulled down the great Temple. It was the end. Or so it seemed. The end of the Temple, of Judah, of the nation.

So sad. Mountains of rubble, which glowed golden when the sun went down. So sad. And odd. For the Babylonians were a people from Ur of the Chaldees, where Abraham came from. Where it all began. And where the people of Judah were soon to experience a new beginning.

Ezekiel Foretells the Return

In Babylon the two tribes which had formed the country of Judah were given a new name. It took too long to say 'People from Judah' or 'Judahites', so they were called 'Jews'. Their religion, which they took with them and were allowed to practise, Judaism. Nebuchadnezzar, King of Babylon, allowed his thousands of Jews more than their religion. He was no fool the King. They had many skills, these Jews, many scholars, many fine families. They were a valuable addition to any empire. They could show him much.

Mind you, Babylon had plenty to show the Jews. They were goggle-eyed. A wonder of the world. The great hanging gardens, the gorgeous buildings with their towering bronze gates, the wide avenues, the endless riverside embankments with their palaces and villas. The wonderful bridge over the Euphrates, and, even more fantastic, the Tower of Babel, heard of since the oldest times and now restored by the King. A great wedding cake of brick and stone in seven tiers nearly three hundred feet high. A wondrous magical city. Department stores, banks, huge markets, hundreds of temples and chapels and altars to every kind of god and goddess.

So the Jews remembered what Jeremiah the prophet had taught them. He had stayed on in Jerusalem and wept over it. But not for long. 'Don't weep,' he had said, 'don't look back. Establish yourselves, put down roots, make the best of it. Ignore their gods; you have your own religion; practise it.'

And the people did make the best of it. Very few doors were closed to them. Business, the law, industry, even the court – as the story of Daniel shows us. A boy from a good family in Jerusalem who rose to be right hand to the King of Babylon. And translated some writing on the wall for that King's successor which pleased him not at all. *And* all came true. We shall come to that story later.

Well, the years passed. Another prophet appeared among the people. Younger, harder than Jeremiah. Ezekiel. He had made the seven hundred mile trek from Jerusalem to Babylon and his eye was clear. He knew that the Jews now had to find God within themselves; not look for signs, portents, miracles. They'd had those, and turned away to other gods so many times. Now they had no Promised Land, no kings, no leaders. Only their religion and one, the only, God.

The people were discouraged, they felt forsaken. They thought that God lived in Jerusalem, in the Temple. Well, the Temple was now destroyed. Even if God still lived there, it was a long way for him to come. Ezekiel didn't rest. He had to teach that God is everywhere, that the exile was only a lesson, it would end one day but when didn't matter. 'God is here in exile with us,' he taught. He was a visionary and a magnetic preacher. And the people listened. They made a new life, they prospered, they turned out to be the good investment that Nebuchadnezzar meant them to be. But more important, their faith grew strong. In exile, far from the Promised Land, surrounded by every kind of idol and belief, they stopped the nonsense that had gone on for so long and brought them so much trouble, they served one God, and God was pleased.

Now Ezekiel began to prophesy a return. God granted him a vision and he translated it for the people. 'If you think of yourselves,' he told them, 'as a dead nation, a dried and scattered skeleton, a pile of dry bones, then hear the word of the Lord. Each bone will be connected to another bone . . .' There's a lovely negro spiritual about it.

And of course it all came true.

Home Again

Now, let us for a while move our story from Babylon, where the Jews have been in exile for nearly fifty years, to Persia. And let us meet a remarkable man called Cyrus. He was the son of a King. A King who ruled over a small place. Cyrus was what today we might call a princeling. I suppose people called him that in those days too, when he was young! They were sorry. For Cyrus was not only a highly competent man with ideas of government far ahead of his time, but he was also ambitious. First he took the huge Median Empire from his own grandfather, then he moved north and west, conquering a vast area, the whole of Asia Minor near enough. Everywhere he brought a firm, humane rule. He removed one cruel despot after another and put his own men in. Even the King of Lydia, called Croesus, whose name still means untold wealth, was conquered and removed by Cyrus. He created new laws everywhere and gave the word law a different meaning – 'the laws of the Medes and Persians, which alter not'.

Then Cyrus, who created the Empire of the Medes and Persians, looked south, at the Babylonian Empire. Nebuchadnezzar, who'd taken the Jews into exile, had been dead for twenty years now and Babylon was ruled by a much weaker man, Belshazzar, who'd allowed his country rather to go to seed. He was the man who saw the writing on the wall and had Daniel in to tell him what it meant. Well, what it meant, Daniel told him, was that Babylon would fall to the Medes and Persians. And it did. Mind you, you didn't have to be too much of a Daniel to see that it probably would. After all, the great armies of Cyrus had been digging this huge trench right round the city for months.

The people, led by Belshazzar, had laughed at first. Theirs was the most important city in the world; mighty Babylon, with food stocks for twenty years of siege. The soldiers in the trenches would starve first. Their city, on the great River Euphrates, was protected by superb fortifications. It would last for ever. Also, they'd heard a story about Cyrus taking revenge on a *river* for drowning his favourite horse! He'd spent a whole summer cutting the river into nearly four hundred channels. The Babylonians laughed even more. 'All this power's gone to his head,' they said. 'Gone a bit mad. Trying to teach a river a lesson!'

Well, not quite. Maybe, as it worked out, Cyrus was trying to teach *himself* a lesson, about rivers. For when he took

Babylon, on the night of the writing on the wall, he did it by diverting the Euphrates into the great trench, and he and his army went into the city along the river bed. They broke down the city walls here and there from the *inside*. And the overflow from the trench created havoc and confusion. Special man, Cyrus. In no time at all he got the river put back and the place dried out and some good government going.

The people were staggered. No killings, no marching-off of herds of captives, no interference even with the various religions and Babylonian idols. Cyrus, an Emperor, thought in terms of a commonwealth. With everyone benefiting by peaceful trade and shared knowledge.

Cyrus then looked at all the various peoples of Babylon, captives from so many lands. 'If you want to,' he said, 'you can all go back home. Government grants. Cheap fares.'

Well, this meant the Jews too, who had become very much a part of Babylon. Fifty years is a long time. Very few of the original captives still alive. New generations, new ways. Not everyone wanted to return to the Promised Land; where living, by all accounts, was much harder than in prosperous Babylon. But the Jews themselves were now different. Their *religion* called them back to Jerusalem. Their belief in God was strong. Isaiah and Jeremiah and Ezekiel had all been right; the exile was to punish and to teach. Now they had begun to learn, they were forgiven, and God's Temple must be rebuilt. In David's city, in Jerusalem.

So thousands gathered together and a great caravan of horses and mules and camels. Cyrus was generous. He gave the Jews all the vast treasure of gold and silver that Nebuchadnezzar had taken from the Temple so long before. Everything to the last bowl and chalice and candlestick.

It was a long way. With detours for water places, nearly nine hundred miles. It took a long time. Once back in the Promised Land people went off in all directions to try to trace family, but the Temple was begun. A simple altar, and regular sacrifice to God. The first big gathering of the people was the Feast of Tabernacles. Very apt. It was at Tabernacles, the Harvest Festival, that Solomon had dedicated the first Temple.

The Second Temple

The rebuilding began well enough. A good feeling everywhere. The returned exiles with their new strong belief in God, their careful practice of his Law, put their brains and their money together and chose their priests and their builders and got the work started. But then a lot of the local people, people descended from the various nations brought to Israel by the Assyrians as captives in the past, asked if they could join in. 'We believe in the same God,' they said. 'We have done since our fathers and grandfathers were brought here from other lands. All right, we may have intermarried a bit and have some different customs, we may not be the pure Jews you are, but still.'

It was a chance for a tolerance, an integration. But the exiles said no. They were jealous of their new letter-of-the-law Judaism and maybe afraid a bit also to let outsiders in. Anyway, the people not allowed to help decided to hinder, and there were a lot of them. The exiles built houses for themselves, schools, factories, even some synagogues, but no Temple. The building got no further than foundation level. Whenever the Jews attempted to return to it there were threats and trouble.

The years passed. Cyrus, founder of the Empire of Medes and Persians, died. Good Cyrus, by whose edict the exiles had returned to build their Temple and put back in it the glories and treasures that Cyrus had given back to them. Cyrus had even promised them, in the same edict, money and supplies. A witnessed document. An emperor's order. But now he was dead. So was his successor, his son. Now there was a new emperor, Darius, whose low opinion of the power of God had been radically changed when Daniel, now rather old, had walked, unharmed, out of the lion's den.

Enter now, as so often before, a prophet. In fact two. Haggai and Zechariah. They'd got rather tired of seeing that unfinished Temple and began a sort of What-have-we-got-to-be-afraid-of campaign. They prophesied that all would be well. They pulled up their sleeves and started work themselves. Soon there were others.

Well, the trouble-makers were soon busy and the Governor of the province turned up. 'By whose order are you building?' he said. 'What are the names of the people in charge? Whose servants are you?'

The elders of the Jews were polite. 'We are the servants of God,' they said, 'and we build to honour our God, and by edict of Cyrus. A witnessed document.'

Well, the Governor asked them to stop the work till he could write and get a reply from King Darius, but the elders said gently that they thought God would like them to continue. 'But write anyway,' they said. 'We don't tell lies.'

So a report was sent and Darius looked through the files and sure enough he found the document. He wrote back right away. 'Leave them alone,' he told the Governor. 'The edict is of the Medes and Persians, it must be honoured. We pay the full cost of the work and all sacrificial supplies. Everything from the meats to the wine and oil.' He then added some unpleasant details of what would happen to anyone who interfered. And signed his name.

It took about four years. Not as beautiful as the first Temple (which after all had had Solomon, a great connoisseur of the arts, in charge) but a splendid and nobly-appointed place of worship. About seventy years from the destruction of the first Temple to the dedication of the second. Almost exactly as foreseen by Isaiah and Jeremiah and Ezekiel. The voices of the prophets go through the Bible like a golden seam of common sense.

The Temple was finished in time to celebrate the Passover. When Jews remember their freedom from slavery in Egypt. It was a wonderful, heart-warming, emotional occasion. All the exiles and those of the land who'd joined them in their new, true Judaism made the eight days of the festival a joyous happy time. Among the huge sacrifices of bulls and rams and lambs was a smaller offering of twelve goats, to recall the scattered twelve tribes. A sad reminder of how fortunes can change for people. Now though, with their new Temple, the Jews felt that all was well. Their small country, Judah, was not their own; it was a province of the mighty Persian Empire, but their ruler, King Darius, was an enlightened and tolerant man. After the years of exile and the hardships that marked the first few years of their return, it seemed that a new age had dawned.

Ezra and Nehemiah

With the rebuilding of the Temple it seemed that a new age had dawned for the returned Jewish exiles. But it wasn't to last. Kings die. Time passes. Things change. After Darius, his son called Xerxes, or in the Bible Ahasuerus. This was the King with the rather bad temper who got rid of his first wife because she didn't like his boozy parties. And set up a sort of beauty competition to get a new Queen. He was lucky; he got Esther. Who managed to stop the mass-murder of countless Jews at the last minute. We could have used an Esther during the War. Marvellous story, Esther. We will have it a little later. Meanwhile, let us stay with the fact that Esther was a Jewess. The King didn't know it when he married her, but didn't mind when he found out. Wise king; labels don't matter, it's the person. The point is, there were a great *many* Jews in Babylon and Persia. Not all had wanted to go back to the Promised Land. The Jews had suffered *many* invasions and occupations. They were scattered now across *many* countries.

Well, Esther's husband died and his third son became King. Another odd name, Artaxerxes, sometimes called Longimanus or 'longhanded'. Complicated, isn't it? We'll call him 'the King'. He took over a huge empire and a magnificent court. The leaders of the various peoples living in Persia made their visits of homage and their oaths of loyalty. Soon the various sects and factions came with petitions to the new King.

The Jews sent one of their leading priests, a man called Ezra. He'd heard things about the Jews living in far-off Jerusalem he wasn't happy about. 'Also,' Ezra told the King, 'quite a number of your Jews here in Persia *would* like to return to the land of their ancestors.' Well, Ezra nagged at the King and at his flock, and eventually, about seven years later, the King let him lead about seventeen hundred Jews back to Jerusalem. He had the King's authority to examine affairs at all levels, both civil and religious.

Ezra wasn't pleased at some of the religious backsliding he found in Jerusalem, and said so forcibly. His reports to the King were clear, strong, to the point. He spoke of intermarriage and various other bad lapses among the people of Judah. He was a powerful preacher, Ezra, and he shook the place up. Eventually called a vast meeting in Temple Square and, whilst the thousands stood chilled to the bone in heavy winter rain, Ezra took his time and showed them the error of their ways.

The years passed and the King used often to mention at dinner to his guests the nagging he used to get from Ezra. He respected loyalty and single-mindedness, did the King. And such people he would raise to high office. He was no fool. One such person was Nehemiah, an important and trusted official of the court and cupbearer to the King. He saw the King at every meal. The King was used to him, and liked him. So, when for a day or two Nehemiah seemed a bit sad, the King asked him why. 'You're not ill,' said the King. 'What's troubling you?'

Nehemiah began to tell him and the King decided he would avoid, if possible, another nagging. He listened carefully. '. . . so you see,' said Nehemiah, 'the city of my fathers, Jerusalem, stands among rubble. The walls and gates broken down by your predecessor Nebuchadnezzar have never been repaired. They remind my people all the time that they are a conquered people.

A fine city, with a loyal populace, a splendid Temple, surrounded by a waste of smashed stone and brick . . .' He went on a while.

'Right,' said the King not wasting any time. 'Go to it. You can have letters of authority, requisition-forms for materials, and an escort of cavalry. Try not to take too long. Good cupbearers are hard to find.'

When Nehemiah arrived in Jerusalem, he could see that the reports were not exaggerated. There was much to be done. Also he saw right away that there would be trouble with the Governor of the province.

In those days a walled city was an *important* city and the Governor of the province, a Persian Empire man, did not want a lessening of his own authority, either by the upgrading of one of his cities or by Nehemiah, who had arrived from the Persian court with powers equal to his own. Nehemiah didn't waste too much time with him. He surveyed the work to be done, at night, in secret. Then he called a big meeting, took over the governorship of the city and told the people his plan. His enthusiasm caught on. Volunteers and donations poured in. The work started.

Neighbouring gentile tribesmen, egged on by the deposed Governor, did their best to hamper the work, first by jeers and derision and then, as the walls began to grow, in more violent and threatening ways. Nehemiah was a realist. 'The work will continue,' he told the people. 'But every builder and labourer will be protected by an armed man. In one hand a tool,' he said to them, 'in the other a weapon.' Much of today's Israel has been built in the same way.

The people, reassured and protected, worked with a will. They knew from Nehemiah that *God* wanted this work done – and they did the whole job in fifty-two days! There was a great ceremony of thanksgiving. With their grand new Governor himself a Jew, and with Ezra the priest to declare and interpret God's Law to them, they had indeed a great deal to be thankful for. Advised by Ezra, Nehemiah made many good laws, carried out many reforms, especially concerning the financing of the

Temple and the conduct of its worship. The people practised their religion, kept themselves to themselves and hoped the neighbouring countries would stop molesting them. And they did. For almost three hundred years. A happy ending to this section of our story.

IN FOREIGN LANDS

Jonah the Prophet

Now once or twice in the last few pages, I've found myself mentioning stories which needed to be told at some length but which we hadn't time to stop for if we were to get a proper picture of Jewish history. The Bible doesn't stop for them either. It tells them separately. The first of them, Jonah, is to be found among the books of the prophets. Not that Jonah wanted to be a prophet. He wasn't even very good at being a prophet, and was very cross about having to be one. Mind you, some of the things that happened to Jonah would have made anybody cross.

Jonah was quite an ordinary man. Not rich; not poor. Rather inclined to argue – with anybody. Hard-headed, obstinate sort of man. Even when he received a message direct from God he argued. Suddenly, straight into Jonah's mind God had spoken. Unmistakably God; and there was no mistaking the message either. God spoke clearly. 'Jonah,' he said, 'I have an errand for you. I want you to go to Assyria, to the great city of Nineveh, and tell them that I know how wicked they've all become and that in forty days from your arrival the city will be destroyed and the people will perish.'

Jonah thought for a minute and then decided to argue. 'Look, God,' he said, 'Nineveh is a long way and it's not the time of the year for long journeys – it's too hot. But the main point is I don't want to be made to look foolish. Look,' he said, 'you're not the kind of God that destroys cities and wipes out thousands of people. You're gracious and kind and slow to anger

and merciful, and everyone knows it. I'll go all that way, make
a lot of speeches and nothing will happen, and I'll look silly.'

There was a little pause and then God, who was rather used
to people like Jonah said, 'Leave first thing in the morning.' And
Jonah knew that he'd better shut up.

The next morning, very bad-tempered, he packed a few things
together and started the long hot walk to Nineveh. He was cross
when he set off and by the time he got to Jaffa he was even *more*
cross.

Now the fact that Jaffa was a port gave him an idea. He said
to himself, 'I won't go to Nineveh at all. I'll get a ship and go
to Tarshish – in Spain. I'll hide. Who wants to be a prophet, and
be made to look daft?' He found a ship that was going to
Tarshish, bought his ticket and went aboard. Very silly. As he
was soon to find out. He went below and very tired from his
long walk he dropped into a deep sleep. The captain ordered the
anchor lifted and they set sail. A hot calm day with a slight
breeze. Very pleasant. Jonah slept on.

Now God, who was a little surprised at Jonah's disobedience,
decided to take a hand. The skies became grey and leaden. The
breeze stopped. Everything grew still and close. And then,
suddenly, from nowhere, the hurricane struck! Panic was
everywhere. Passengers and crew screamed and shouted and
were full of fear. Jonah, below in a corner of the hold, slept
on. The captain ordered everyone to pray to their various gods
to find out which one was cross. Vows were made, sacrifices
were promised. But of course nothing happened. The great
roaring wind did not lessen one bit.

Then the captain came upon Jonah fast asleep and woke him
roughly. 'Ah,' said Jonah, 'are we there?'

'*There!*' said the captain. 'The only place we're likely to be
is at the bottom of the sea. Never known a storm like it. Sea's
gone mad! Come on,' he said, 'up on deck. I've got everyone
praying to their different gods to try and stop it. Up you go,'
he said, 'get started.'

When Jonah came out on deck into the screaming wind and among the weeping, praying people, he knew at once what was up. He took the captain to one side. 'Look,' he said. 'It's my God. I'm a Hebrew and we only have one. There is only one. And he looks after everything. I've done something I shouldn't have – or rather I haven't done something I should have and this hurricane is all *my* fault.'

'Well,' the captain said, 'do something about it. Start praying.'

Jonah said, 'I don't think it would do any good. If I were you I'd have me tossed overboard. I've got a very strong feeling that's the only solution.'

The captain said: 'Have you tossed . . . I couldn't do a thing like that! Had my own ship thirty years and never lost a passenger yet. I can't go tossin' – it's against the regulations! Besides it may not work and in these seas I couldn't guarantee to fish you out again. Also, quite frankly, I don't really believe there is only one God. Seems a lot of work for just one. Try praying. I'll come back.'

But the storm grew worse and somehow the word got round among the terrified people that it was all Jonah's fault. So, when the captain came back followed by the crew and passengers, Jonah got to his feet, apologized to the captain, and allowed himself to be dropped over the side.

Immediately the sea became calm and the hurricane died away and the sun came out and the sky became blue. As Jonah floated away from the ship he could hear the captain leading prayers to the one and only God.

A Second Chance

Time passed and now Jonah was all alone. Calm blue sea. Clear blue sky. Silence. He floated on his back, looking up to heaven and thinking, 'Now what?' Suddenly he was aware of being caught in a current. He turned over and looked ahead. He saw an odd sort of small island. It had no trees and seemed quite smooth. The current was swifter now and was carrying him towards what seemed to be a cave. As he drew nearer, he looked up. Above the cave, at either side, were small bad-tempered eyes. It was a whale! As Jonah opened his mouth to yell, the whale shut *his* mouth with a snap with Jonah inside. He was cold, wet, very frightened and he didn't like the dark and never had. There he sat inside the whale, he didn't even know what he was sitting on, and started to have a think about things.

'All right,' he said to himself, and his voice sounded echoey and spooky, 'all right, I disobeyed, but God could have sent someone else. *I'm* nobody. The message could have been given to someone important, a priest or a prince or something, not to me, I'm nobody.' And the words 'I'm nobody' went on echoing and ringing round the great vaulted inside of the whale for far longer than the other words until Jonah's head was banging. And then suddenly all was deathly quiet. Jonah was now looking at himself very honestly and seeing himself very clearly – as of course you can when it's pitch dark – and he saw that he was really at a very low point, the lowest ever, lost, alone, very unhappy – and all really his own fault. Maybe this down-into-the-depths-and-then-being-saved is what the Jonah and the whale story really means. But let's not get too theological. We must get on with saving Jonah. He now felt very humble and very wretched. He asked God to give him another chance. He promised to do as he was told. He remembered, and was grateful for, all the good things in his life given to him by God and spoke quietly and sadly into the vast listening silence for quite a while. When he'd finished he felt better. Of course!

Well, nothing happened for a time. And then, far off, Jonah began to see a golden glow. After the darkness it hurt his eyes a bit. It got no bigger. Jonah got up, stretched his cramped legs and walked forward. The glowing shining spot grew larger. Jonah walked faster and along the whale's tongue and out through the whale's open mouth and on to dry land! The glow was God's sunshine and the gold was the yellow sand.

Jonah stood and wept with relief and joy. As his clothes dried in the hot sun they began to smell a bit fishy, but he kept his mouth tight shut about it. He offered up a heartfelt prayer of thanks and waited for God to speak. He waited quite a while. Not a word. So Jonah thought that perhaps the subject ought to be broached by him. 'Er – God,' he said, 'I haven't forgotten the message. Not a word. You said I was to go to Nineveh and tell them that you know all about their wickedness and that in forty days after I get there the city will be destroyed and the people will perish. That's what you said. I was to go and tell them. And God,' he said, 'I'll go right away.' And he did. Straight from that empty beach to Nineveh. His steps were guided and his journey safe.

In Nineveh

Very impressive place Nineveh. For those days a big city. A hundred and twenty thousand people lived there. And God was right. The people *were* wicked and cruel and they *had* forgotten him. At first they all laughed at Jonah and were rather rude, but there was something about this cross little man and eventually Jonah was brought before the King. The King told him to stop shouting and to tell his story quietly. Which Jonah did. The King listened in silence and realized that it was all true. He *had* ruled badly and the people *had* all gone to the bad. He had a long serious talk with his government and then issued a great proclamation. He said, 'Everyone is to fast; you are to pray to God for forgiveness; you are to dress in sackcloth and you are to stop the violence and evil ways.' Then the King himself dressed in sackcloth and began *his* fast.

Jonah watched all this without saying much. He'd told his story and delivered the message. If this huge city had got themselves into this highly dangerous position it was their lookout. Mind you, in his heart of hearts Jonah didn't really believe that God would do it, but he said nothing.

In the course of a few days he saw a whole city change its ways. The gambling and the debauchery and the cruelty and the evil and the selfishness disappeared. The people walked in fear of the Lord, silent, fasting, praying. One day the King, who was now very pale and thin and wasn't a bad chap really, said to

Jonah, 'Who knows,' he said, 'who knows, Jonah? Perhaps God may yet forgive us all. Perhaps he will lose his fierce anger and change his mind so that we don't all perish. Who knows?'

Jonah had, as we've seen, his own ideas as to how likely the all-merciful God was to wipe out a hundred and twenty thousand people. 'Ah,' he said, 'who knows?'

Now the time was nearly up. The people were hollow-cheeked and weary. Even the most hardened evildoers had mended their ways. There was no gossip, no rumours, no lies, no slander, no raised voices. Truth and honesty had come. People rediscovered simple values and they blamed only themselves and repented and prayed, from the heart, for forgiveness.

And of course God did forgive them. You cannot imagine such joy. It was like V-day and New Year's Eve and a great noisy wedding rolled into one. Every single person was filled with joy. Except one. Jonah. Jonah, who all the time had been pretty certain it wouldn't happen, when it didn't happen, went very strange indeed. He was so cross, so angry, that he rushed out of the city and sat on a stone in the hot sun and sulked. Meanwhile the city went mad with joy and God smiled down upon them. It was some time before God noticed that Jonah was not among the dancing, happy people and asked him what was wrong.

'Well,' said Jonah, who was now right back to his old argumentative self. 'Well, I was *right!* When you spoke to me at home about coming all this way with that all-wiped-out-in-forty-days message, I knew you wouldn't do it. I *know* you. You're *not* vengeful. You forgive people. I told you then that I didn't want to come and be made to look silly. That was why I disobeyed you and caught a ship to Tarshish instead. And all that business with the hurricane and that great smelly whale! I've frightened a lot of people half to death and I've had some very nasty experiences and all for *nothing*. So, if you don't mind, I'm going to sit here in the hot sun till I *die*.'

God said gently, 'Do you think you are *right* to be angry?'

But Jonah refused to answer and by nightfall poor Jonah was feeling very unwell.

During the night God made a large tree come up suddenly and all next day Jonah sat in its shade and began to feel better. During the next night God caused the tree to wither and die, and the next day Jonah, as the sun burned down again on his head, again told God he wished only to die. He felt very miserable and mistreated and, what with the heat and dust and a very nasty east wind which had started up, he began to feel a bit odd in the head too.

'After doing all those things to me,' he muttered to himself, 'the shipwreck and the whale and the long walk and the waiting around in Nineveh for forty days, the least he could have done was to keep his word and wipe 'em all out. The *least*.'

The sun grew hotter and the dust worse. Poor Jonah slept for a while. When God asked him again if he still wanted only to die he said wearily, 'Yes, Lord, I really think I'd be better off dead. I've had enough. Oh, one more thing before I finish,' he said. 'I want you to know I appreciated the tree. It was a nice thought. But, as you can see, the poor thing's withered away. Shame. Beautiful tree. Oh well.'

There was a sound which might have been the wind but which sounded like a loving chuckle. Then God spoke. '*Poor thing?*' he said. 'You feel *sorry* for the tree, Jonah? You think it a *shame?*'

'Well, yes,' said Jonah.

'Well Jonah,' said God, 'if you feel sorry for the tree which cost you nothing, which you didn't plant or tend, which gave you no trouble, should I not feel sorry for Nineveh? Should I not spare a hundred and twenty thousand people – over whom I've taken a great *deal* of trouble? They may be foolish and slow to learn right from wrong, but should I not spare them?'

And Jonah, at last, got the point. Have you?

Poor Blind Tobit

And now another story of Nineveh. You may not find it in your Bible. Or you may find it tucked away in a sort of appendix of later books called 'The Apocrypha'. But it's a Jewish story and a good one. And it begins, as I said, in Nineveh in the days when Nineveh had been taken over by the Medes and Persians and when Jews were to be found in all the main cities of the east.

In a very poor part of Nineveh, in what was little more than a mud-hut, lived an elderly couple and their son, a youngish man, the child of their later years, the child they'd waited a long time for. Maybe because of this they'd over-protected him and maybe that was why he, Tobias, was rather timid. Pleasant, certainly, but a bit weak and with not much push in him. Very fond of his little dog called Toby – although I think we'd better rename the dog Sam. Otherwise it's going to be confusing for us all. I'll tell you why. Tobias's father's name was Tobit. Dad called Tobit, son called Tobias, dog called Toby. No; the dog henceforth shall be known as Sam. Tobias's dad, Tobit, was about sixty, maybe a little more. Marvellous old man. Truly humble, do anything for anybody; give away his last penny. Which his wife, old Anna, used to say he'd just about done. And, mind you, she had a case. They hadn't always been poor, in fact they'd been pretty rich. Tobit had been a merchant, who supplied the court and sold to the people at the same prices and with the same fairness and honesty. His door was always open to travellers who were tired or brethren who were hungry. Anna never knew how many she was catering for. She used to get cross sometimes. Very practical sort of woman Anna was. 'Some of your so-called brethren,' she'd say, 'are just a lot of hangers-on and spongers!'

'Ah yes,' Tobit would say, 'but some are not, and all men *are* my brothers. God said so. Anna dear,' he would say, 'if we are well off, it is God's will; if we are able to help other people, it is God's will.' Mind you, Anna believed in God, too – but a good nag helps sometimes.

But one day – a dreadful day – Tobit went blind. He was marvellous about it, a bit puzzled, very patient. Kept on saying, 'It must be God's will.' No nagging from Anna during *that* time. Nor during the time which followed, when misfortune followed misfortune. They lost everything. People did not rush to help. They forgot their debts to blind Tobit who'd never asked for either thanks or receipts. New people at the court at first looked greedily and then confiscated the old Jew's business. Such things happen. And, let's face it, son and heir Tobias, was no *strong* man.

So, here we are. Blind Tobit, Anna and Tobias – oh and Sam the dog – in their mud-hut. Nothing in the place to eat. Suddenly, Sam's tail went between his legs and his hair stood on end and he seemed terrified. The light in the doorway was blocked by a tall broad man carrying a large heavy-laden basket. The sunlight behind his head gave him a sort of halo, thought Anna for a second. Then she said, 'Hallo indeed! What do you want, young man?'

The tall man lowered the basket. 'I want nothing. In the basket is food. Meat, bread, wine, fruit. A fair amount of each. Er – it is a gift. The message is, "peace to Tobit, Tobias and to you Anna". Goodbye.'

'Just a minute, just a minute,' said Anna. 'Gift, message, all our names . . . who *from,* the gift – God knows we need it – who *sent* the message – and who are *you?*'

The tall stranger, who hadn't moved, said, 'Yes, God knew you needed it – er – who am I? Er – my name is Azarias – the son of Ananias of Nephtha.'

'Ananias of Nephtha!' said old Tobit. 'I knew your father very well. Anna,' he said – (and she knew what was coming) – 'our friend will stay to dinner!' And the tall man did.

Although it must have been obvious to him that, for Tobit and his family, this was the first decent meal they'd had for weeks, Azarias gave them no sign of it. He helped unpack the big basket and get the food ready and at the dining table he was polite and pleasant, ate little and spread a sort of calmness round him. Tobias's little dog, Sam, however, was not calm. There was something about this tall stranger that Sam couldn't fathom. And neither could Anna. Like many old ladies, she got 'funny feelings' about people and she had a funny feeling about Azarias. Tobit, enjoying the food and the company, noticed nothing, nor did Tobias. But Anna and Sam the dog were right. This *was* no ordinary traveller – and his name was not Azarias either. It was Raphael. And he was an angel. An archangel, in fact. Special one. On a special mission. And the badly needed gift of food was only a tiny part of the mission.

Azarias – or Raphael if you like – smiled at Anna gently and said, 'I've been admiring your seven-branched candlestick and that lovely brass and leather chest in the corner. Beautiful.'

Anna was pleased. 'Yes,' she said, 'our only two nice things. All that's left. We had a lovely home once. Servants and comfort and everything. A candlestick and a box full of rubbish! All that's left.'

Tobit reached out his hand. Blind people know quicker than others when someone's upset. 'Not rubbish, Anna dear. Your wedding veil and my prayer shawl and the little painting of Tobias as a child, and some other little things. Not rubbish, my dear. Show our guest the little painting.'

Anna went to the chest and rummaged around. After a moment she came back. Not with the painting but with a small parchment. 'This is odd,' she said, 'I don't remember seeing this before. It's a receipt for a loan of ten talents of silver you lent to Raguel. Who's Raguel?'

'Raguel?' said Tobit. 'Oh yes. Oh, a nice man. Yes, I remember. Wanted to move his business to Persia. He was in carpets. Thought he'd do better there. Nice man.'

'I've no doubt of that,' said Anna, 'but did he ever pay you back?'

'Well,' said Tobit, 'if we still have his IOU . . .'

'Ten talents is a lot of money,' said Anna, 'and we need it. Where does he live in Persia?'

'I've no idea,' said Tobit.

'Ecbatana,' said Azarias.

'I *beg* your pardon,' said Anna.

'How do *you* know?' said Tobias.

Azarias said, 'Er – yes, well, it may not be the right one but there *is* a firm called Raguel Carpets in Ecbatana. I – er – travel a lot and I was in Ecbatana only recently. This Raguel, I am told, comes from those parts.'

'That's him,' said Tobit, 'unusual name, carpets – and it *was* to Ecbatana he went, it's just come back to me. We'll get in touch with him. Splendid!'

'How?' said Anna. 'Send a paid messenger? We haven't a bean!'

'Send Tobias perhaps?' said Azarias.

'Tobias!' said Anna. 'He's never been further than the city gates! He'd be lost in half a day!'

'What,' said the angel, 'if I went with him? I – er – have to go roughly in that direction tomorrow. Good experience for him. Company for me.' He turned to Tobias. 'What do you say, eh? Chance to help your parents. Chance to show your Mum you're a big boy now.'

Tobias, who quite honestly was not a very adventurous young man, suddenly felt full of strength and courage. 'I'll go,' he said. 'We'll leave first thing in the morning!'

Anna, who was not used to her only chick rushing off into the unknown, started to say a lot of things against the trip but Azarias stopped her. 'Don't worry, Mother,' he said, 'your son is in good hands.' And of course, he was.

Tobias Falls in Love

By midday next day Azarias and Tobias were well on their way. They'd been walking since before dawn. It was now very hot and poor Tobias was feeling it. He wasn't used to such an open air life. And his companion, who showed no sign of heat or fatigue, was keeping up a fast pace.

'Do you think,' said Tobias, 'we could stop for a breather? I'm puffed.'

'In about twenty minutes,' said the angel, 'we come to a river. We'll stop and you can have a swim. All right?'

Sure enough in twenty minutes they came to the river and sat down. 'Coming in?' said Tobias.

'Er – no,' said Azarias, 'I'll watch the things.'

'And me too, please,' said Tobias. 'I'm not a very good swimmer.' And in he went. He didn't go too far out but he splashed about and was having a great time. 'Come on, Azarias,' he yelled, 'it's marvellous in, what are you afraid of? I'm a rotten swimmer and I'm not – Help! A shark – a whale – it's *huge* – save me!' Azarias stood up. 'Take the fish by the gills,' he called, quite calm, 'and hold its head out of the water. Don't be a coward and we'll have *it* for *our* supper.'

Well, there was a great noise and yelling and splashing and then Tobias appeared dragging rather proudly a very big fish indeed. No shark; no whale; but very big.

'Well, Azarias,' said Tobias, 'what about timid Tobias now, eh? I fought him with my bare hands and beat him! And look at the size of him!'

Azarias smiled. '*He* is tremendous and *you* are brave beyond words. Get your knife. We'll have a splendid fish supper, but first, listen carefully, cut out his liver and his gall and put them carefully away in your bag.'

Tobias couldn't see the point of this but did as he was told. They slept well that night and the next day continued their journey.

At last they came to Ecbatana in Persia and to the house of Raguel who made Tobias and his servant (as he took Azarias to be) very welcome. 'How wonderful to hear again of my old friend Tobit,' he said. 'Sad to hear he's gone blind though. Very sad. Poor Tobit. Of course you shall have the money – *and* all the interest over these years, whether your father likes it or not. Eat first, then when you've rested and cleaned up you'll meet Sara my daughter who'll be home later.'

When Tobias and Azarias had eaten they went to their rooms. Tobias was so travel-weary he hardly remembered bathing or anything else. Later that evening he was awakened by Azarias who was sitting on his bed.

When Tobias was sitting up, Azarias said, 'Listen carefully, this is about Sara, Raguel's daughter. She's very beautiful and quite young. Are you listening?'

'Yes,' said Tobias still rather sleepy.

'Well,' said Azarias, 'some time ago a demon fell in love with her – '

'A what?' said Tobias.

'A demon,' said the angel, 'and as demons can't marry young ladies (and what young lady would want to anyway?) the demon said, 'Well, if I can't no one else will.' Mind you, one or two young men have tried. Seven in fact. Poor Sara has been married seven times, and seven times on her wedding night her new husband has been strangled by the demon.'

Tobias was now fully awake. 'What a fantastic story,' he said, 'seven husbands!'

'And,' said the angle, '*and,* unless I am very much mistaken, you, Tobias, are going to be her eighth.'

Tobias sat up in bed and looked in absolute astonishment at Azarias. 'Do you calmly sit there,' said Tobias, 'and tell me that I'm to be the eighth husband of a lady I've not yet met, whose previous seven husbands were all strangled to death on their wedding nights by a demon who's in love with the lady? A *demon?*'

'Yes,' said Azarias, 'his name is Asmodeus; very ugly; tail like a dragon and very nasty breath.'

Tobias jumped out of bed. 'You're crazy,' he said. 'I thought so when you made me keep the liver and gall of that great fish and now I'm certain of it!' He crossed to the window, very angry. 'Anyway, I didn't come here to get married. I came here to collect the money Raguel owes my Dad. I didn't come here to marry Raguel's daughter Sara.' He looked down into the garden.

'Sara's seven husbands and her demon are *her* business and – oh, Azarias, that is the most lovely girl I've ever seen.' He was transfixed. 'Azarias,' said Tobias, 'do you believe in love at first sight?'

Azarias crossed to the window. 'Tobias,' he said gently, 'that is Sara.'

Raguel, Sara's father, tried to put Tobias off. 'Your father, my old friend Tobit, was good to me when I needed help. I can't put you, his son, in danger. It's not fair. Also I'm tired of digging graves for Sara's bridegrooms. Makes me ache for days. Don't do it, son.'

But Tobias, who now was sure that Sara loved him as dearly as he loved her, had made up his mind. 'It may be,' he said to Sara, 'that to marry you means to die but not to marry you won't be really living either.' So Raguel gave his consent and the eighth wedding feast was prepared.

On the day of the wedding Azarias took Tobias to one side. 'Now listen,' he said, 'and do what I say without question. When you and Sara go to your room tonight, light a small brazier outside your door and on it put the fish-liver I told you to keep. Not the gall; that's for something else; the liver. It will make a bad smell, but you'll be on the other side of the door. No, not a word. I promised your fine old Dad I'd look after you and this is my way. Trust me. All will be well.'

And of course it was. It wasn't Azarias making a bad smell. It was the archangel Raphael dealing with a demon and bringing a lot of previous experience to the job. Between you and me, he rather enjoyed it. When the demon arrived at the door of the bridal chamber, there was a bit of burning liver and it stopped him dead in his tracks. He got very mad and was going to try something even nastier – when Raphael stepped out of the shadows. And the fight was on.

They were evenly matched. Wing-tip to wing-tip there was nothing in it. The demon, of course, had his great tail but the angel was in better condition through cleaner living. They fought it out high in the sky and it took most of the night. As Raphael flew down to earth again, tired but happy, all the birds, who had been silenced long before by the demon, burst into song. Poor Raguel who'd spent most of the night digging the eighth grave was helped next morning by a very-much-alive Tobias to fill it in. Sara was radiant. Happiness was everywhere.

Raguel, when his back stopped aching, got busy. It was to be the richest, largest, longest wedding party ever known. Nothing was too good for his lovely daughter and his fine son-in-law. 'In addition to the money I owe your father,' he told Tobias, 'there's Sara's dowry plus half of all I possess – and I'm the biggest carpet man in Persia. It'll take a little time to work out and gather together, so go and enjoy the party.'

Happy Ever After

Well, the wedding party went on for about *three weeks!* People came from far and wide – for the story of the demon and the seven husbands was well known in Persia. Tobias and Sara lived in a cloud of tenderness and love. But one day Tobias said to Azarias, 'Look, I think I'm being a bit selfish. My Mum and Dad must be worried sick about me and I've been far too long at this shindig. Sara agrees. We go home tomorrow.'

Azarias smiled down at this new rather decisive Tobias. 'Right,' he said. 'Don't forget to pack the gall of that fish I told you to keep.'

Tobias was right. His parents were worried sick about him. So let us go back to where this story began, to Nineveh. Outside their mud-hut sit Tobias' parents, blind Tobit and Anna his wife. They'd seen a lot of trouble but this was the worst of all. 'He should never have gone,' said Anna for the thousandth time, 'our only child. I must have been mad. My poor Tobias! Never been further than the city gates and I send him all the way to Persia just to collect a debt – and with a complete stranger too.' Then, as people in distress sometimes do, she looked for someone to blame. 'If *you* hadn't lent or given money to everybody who asked you in the old days, he wouldn't have needed to have gone! Three months!' she wept, 'Not a word. Not a sign. That man Azarias has robbed him or killed him or sold him or something. As soon as I saw that man I wasn't happy. Something odd about him.'

Tobit lifted his tired old head. He said, 'I *never* saw him, I'm blind, but I knew that Tobias would be safe with him. There *was* something different about Azarias, but it was a good something.' Suddenly Tobit stopped. 'Listen!' he said, 'camel bells.'

'There are *always* camel bells,' said Anna crossly.

'No,' said Tobit, 'these are silver bells – and there is gay music; weddingy sort of music. Far off!'

Anna got to her feet. She was trembling. At first in the glare of the sun she saw nothing; and then it was a sight to see! Raguel had kept his word. A huge procession of camels, asses, servants, the bride and groom, and gifts and riches beyond description. And the joy and the kissings and the happiness and the wonder and the overflowing love can't be described either. You can guess what went on.

Azarias, tall, handsome, stood quietly by and watched old Tobit wiping tears of joy from his blind eyes. As Tobias passed he grabbed him. 'Tobias,' he said, 'listen carefully. Go and get the gall of the great fish which you caught. Rub it on a new silk handkerchief and give it to your Dad. He's old and very happy so he's crying a lot. Be quick.'

Old Tobit took the clean hankie. 'Thank you, Tobias,' he said, 'very thoughtful, a long time since I had a silk handkerchief.' He wiped his eyes. 'So silly to cry so much – but only for joy. Wonderful sort of handkerchief, and such a pretty design too . . . Tobias, I can see!' And he could.

Well, the next half hour I won't describe either. Tobias, later, said suddenly, 'Where's Azarias?'

And Tobit said, 'Yes, I want to thank him – and see him too with my new eyes – and, Tobias, we must give him a most generous gift.'

Then, oddly, there was a sort of hush, and, oddly, there was Azarias, a little way off.

'He's changed his clothes,' said Tobias softly, 'looks *bigger*.'

Azarias looked at them one by one with great affection. 'I can't accept gifts,' he said to Tobit. 'Tipping's not allowed in my job. *Doing* the job is enough.' A sort of glow came from him. 'Tobit,' he said, 'my name is not Azarias. It is Raphael and I am an archangel.' He smiled. 'Always sounds so silly to say it out loud. Tobit,' he said, 'all your life you have *given* – which, where I come from, is regarded very highly. Because of this,' he said rather formally but with a twinkle, 'I am instructed to tell you that you and yours will live happily ever after.' And they did.

The Beauty Queen – Esther

We come next to the Book of Esther, ten short chapters, in my Bible only seven pages. Esther who won a beauty contest and got a King of Persia for a prize! The one with a funny name, you remember, Ahasuerus. But in this story we'll just call him the King.

The story begins in the royal palace at Susa, where the King is giving an enormous party for all his chiefs-of-staff and nobles and governors of provinces. Gorgeous marquees in the garden. All the royal cutlery and crockery on show. Most of it solid gold. Every kind of food and drink served. First class cabaret. And all this to go on for a week. In another part of the Palace, the Queen was giving a party too. For all the women. Rather quieter affair. She was beautiful, the Queen, and that, I suppose, was the start of all the trouble.

By the seventh day of these parties the King was rather drunk. Not surprising. 'Bring my seven chamberlains,' he said. And when they were all before him he said, 'Go to the Queen and tell her to put on her best crown and so on and to come to my party because I want to show her off.' But the Queen didn't want to be shown off and said no and that was it.

The King felt pretty stupid and was very cross and sent for his wise men. They listened and then the wisest one spoke. 'Very serious,' he said. 'The palace is buzzing with talk and gossip. Tomorrow all the guests go home and the word will spread and soon *all* the wives will start disobeying.'

'What shall I do?' said the King.

'An announcement,' they said. 'Right away. That the Queen is fired and all her goods and so on will go to the new Queen who will be chosen soon. Thus,' said the wise men, 'wives will know their place and in every home the man will be king.'

'Let it be done,' said the King. 'Good sense. That'll show 'em. When do I get the new Queen?'

Well, the chamberlains got busy and the great competition was announced. All entrants had to be young and beautiful. There would be heats and the finalists would live in the Palace for grooming for one year. Applications poured in.

Now, in one of the back streets of Susa lived an elderly Jew. (The Jews, you remember, had been carried off to Babylon some seventy or eighty years before, and colonies of them were now to be found in most of the cities of the east.) His name was Mordecai, of the tribe of Benjamin, and with him lived a young cousin whom he'd brought up after she'd been orphaned. A quiet, wise old man was Mordecai, and this girl Esther was his pupil, his daughter, his life. And she was beautiful. 'You are a special sort of daughter to me,' he told her, 'and you would be a special sort of Queen too. You must enter the competition.'

'Do you think I've any chance?' she said.

The old man looked at his lovely, graceful daughter with the quiet eyes and gentle wit. 'How can you lose?' he said. 'Do as they tell you but say nothing of me or of your religion. I have a feeling that God, our God, the God of the Jews, is guiding me and he will tell us when to reveal that you are a Jewess.'

So Esther entered her name and things seemed to go well for her right from the start. She just walked through the first heats and when the finalists moved into the Palace for the beautifying and grooming year, she quickly became popular. People just liked her. Especially the two men in charge of the whole thing. Hegai and Shashgaz, the King's eunuchs. They gave her good advice, extra lessons, taught her how to give orders quietly, to remember that all people have dignity, to show respect, to be a Queen. When Esther was declared the winner, Hegai and Shashgaz wept with joy. There was a great crowning ceremony and a national holiday and certain tax reliefs were announced and the King was very happy and very generous. He loved his new Queen at first sight and she was worth it. Old Mordecai was right, she *was* special.

The King's Vizier

Not long after Esther became Queen, Mordecai told her he had heard two of the King's chamberlains plotting to kill the King. She told the King and the two men were arrested, tried and hanged. 'Write all this down,' said the King, 'and don't forget to put down the name of Esther's loyal friend, who gave us the warning.' After this the 'counsel of chamberlains' method was looked at and the King decided that he would appoint a Grand Vizier over all the chamberlains and princes and nobles of the court and he did. But he wasn't much of a judge of character, the King, and he gave the job to a chap called Haman, who not only had great ambition but also great cunning and cruelty.

Well, the new Vizier lost no time in making his presence felt. He had a throne made and sat always by the King's right hand. He treated people like dirt and made laws regarding his own importance. 'Everyone will show the Vizier great respect,' he had posted up. 'Everyone will kneel or bow as he walks by.' And everyone did. Except one. Old Mordecai, who was not young, and saw Haman for what he was, and was quite unafraid anyway. 'Also,' he would say calmly, maddeningly, 'I am a Jew, and we save our kneeling and bowing for God.'

Well, all this made Haman very angry indeed and he decided

to destroy not only Esther's father but every single Jew in all the provinces ruled over by the King. He took his time and made plans and spoke often to the King of a 'strange people' scattered throughout the vast lands with 'their own laws and practices.' He hinted at disloyalty, rebellion, disturbance, sabotage, all the age-old reasons for mass murder. Having got the King thoroughly flustered and worried, he then put forward a brilliant plan for the final solution, the extermination of every single one. 'All on one day,' he said. 'Every one of 'em. At my expense.' He went on and on and the King, dizzy with it all, signed the orders and the notices went out. You can imagine.

Well, Mordecai heard about these arrangements for mass murder. When he told Esther, she was shocked. 'I don't know what to do,' she said. 'When the King fired the last Queen for disobedience, new rules were made. To go to him without being asked is absolutely forbidden. If anyone approaches the King without being summoned it means death unless the King points his sceptre.'

'Points his sceptre?' said Mordecai.

'Yes,' said Esther. 'If he does you live. If not, you die. Even me. I haven't seen the King for a month,' she said sadly. 'He's locked up with Haman from morning till night.'

Mordecai looked at his beautiful daughter. 'With God's help,' he said, 'you became a Queen. It may be that if you do nothing you will escape death. You will not die. Except,' said Mordecai, 'of shame.'

Esther stood up. 'Beloved father,' she said, 'gather your friends and let them fast and pray for me. I and my women will do the same and in three days' time I will go, unbidden, to the King. And if I perish, I perish.'

On the third day, Esther got up early. She'd hardly slept and felt rather weak from lack of food. She dressed carefully and wore no jewellery. She did her hair simply. Only a very little make-up. Her ladies-in-waiting, normally a talkative happy crowd, were silent. This could be the last time they would ever see their beloved mistress. One by one they came forward and kissed Esther on the cheek. Then they walked with her to the flower garden that separated the King's apartments from the Queen's. They stopped and Esther walked on alone.

It was quiet. The murmur of a fountain. A little birdsong, not much. The soft steady sound of her own feet. She came to the first door and, as she went into the cool corridor, she felt cold.

She walked on. Four more doors to the innermost private sanctum where the King sat with Haman.

One, two, three, four. Esther stood in the doorway. She was pale, quiet, still.

Then the King looked up. 'Hello darling,' he said. 'How nice to see you.' Then he pointed his sceptre. 'That's a nice dress,' he said. 'I like it.'

Esther let out a long fluttery breath and walked forward.

'You look a bit upset,' said the King. 'We can't have that, can we? Let me give you a nice present. Something *very* nice. You can have anything you want. Anything at all. Just ask.'

Esther looked into the King's smiling face, then at Haman, who seemed just lately to be more powerful than the King. She closed her eyes and asked God if this was the moment and God said not yet.

The King leaned forward and kissed her. 'Had a think?' he said. 'Well, what would you like?' She smiled. 'What I should *really* like,' she said, 'is for you to come home for dinner tonight.' She looked at Haman. 'You come too,' she said. And they did.

It was a splendid dinner and at the liqueur stage the King again told Esther she could have anything she desired and again she asked only that he should take an evening off. 'Tomorrow,' she said.

'Come to dinner again?' said the King.

'Yes,' said Esther.

'Me too?' said Haman.

'Yes,' said Esther.

Well, Haman went home that night and told his wife everything. 'Dinner with the Queen tomorrow *too!*' he crowed. 'Two days *running!* Just her, the King and *me.* Equal to the King I am! *Great* honour. I'm a great expert on honouring.' He went on and on and then stopped. 'And *still* that old man won't bow or kneel to me,' he said.

'I know what,' said his wife. 'Don't wait till your special kill-'em-all day, attend to the old man right away. Get some carpenters and have a gallows built, a nice one, near the Palace, and tomorrow tell the King you're going to hang the old man as a sort of before-dinner entertainment.'

Haman looked at his wife with great affection. 'You're a very clever girl,' he said, and he gave the orders right away. Then he went to bed and slept like a baby. Very happy.

The Tables Turned

But at the Palace the King couldn't sleep. So he asked to be read to. 'Bring the Book of Memorable Deeds,' he said. 'Read to me from that.' So the King's Night Reader was sent for and the King lay and listened. The Reader began with the most recent deeds and soon was telling how Mordecai had saved the King's life by discovering the plot by the two chamberlains.

'How was he rewarded?' asked the King, who had not even bothered to enquire the name at the time. Simply had it written in the book.

'In no way,' he was told. 'Nothing was ever done.'

'Disgraceful oversight,' said the King. 'Send for Haman.' So they went and woke him up and he came over.

Haman didn't mind. It would be a good opportunity to talk to the King about hanging Mordecai.

But the King was the first to speak. 'You're an expert on honouring,' he said. 'Tell me a really big honour for someone I'll be delighted to honour.'

Haman smiled to himself. 'He means me,' he thought. 'For my kill-'em-all plan.'

'For such a man,' he said to the King, 'only the best. Let him be dressed in a robe of the King's; let him ride on the King's horse. Let the horse be led through the city by one of the King's most noble princes who shall call out, "This is the man the King delights to honour".'

'Marvellous,' said the King. 'You be the noble prince and go and do all this for an old man who saved my life.' He picked up the book. 'Here's his name and address.'

Well, what could Haman do? It was the worst day of his life and made much worse by the modesty and lack of malice in old Mordecai who seemed to be looking up to heaven and smiling all the time.

When they arrived back at the Palace, it was time for Esther's second dinner party. Even better than the first and the King said so. Also he said again, 'Esther dear, I think you want to ask me something. What is it? Anything. I would give you half my kingdom.'

Esther stood up. She was a bit white but very beautiful and composed. 'I am to be killed,' she said. 'I and the people to whom I belong. Orders have been given and it is to be done quite soon. I ask the King,' she said formally, 'to spare my people and thus spare my life also.'

The King could hardly speak. 'Orders!' he roared. 'Orders? What orders? Whose orders?'

Esther pointed at Haman. '*His* orders,' she said. 'Haman's orders. Sealed with your ring,' she added gently.

The King got up. He was trembling with rage and shame. Haman was just trembling. The King went out into the garden and walked around to cool down a bit. He saw what he had nearly done. When he came back into the Palace, Haman, now terrified, was pawing and clawing at Esther as she sat, imploring that she save his life.

That was the last straw. 'Take your filthy hands off my wife!' roared the King. 'You're not fit to be in the same room with her!'

And that was the end of Haman. The gallows he'd had built was ready. He'd paid for it, it was his, it seemed a waste not to use it, so they hanged him on it. Then because the time now seemed right, Esther had Mordecai brought in and told the King that he was her father. The King was delighted to be related to such a wise and good man and offered his father-in-law Haman's job which the old man accepted. He called a meeting right away, borrowed the King's seal-ring and cancelled all Haman's orders. And so a lot of Jewish lives were saved. As I said when I mentioned this story before, we could have done with an Esther in Hitler's Germany.

Daniel and his Friends

After the Book of Esther in the Bible come the Wisdom books – the Psalms of David, the Proverbs of Solomon, the Song of Solomon, and the sayings of other wise men – not forgetting Job, who suffered so terribly – the loss of his property, his children, his health; unhelpful advice from his wife and his friends; and finally something of a telling-off from God himself, who after wards made it all up to him. But these are not stories; we must pass them over. As also the books of the prophets – Isaiah, Jeremiah, Ezekiel. We've already seen the place of these great prophets in Jewish history. But the next book, the Book of Daniel, is different. Full of stories. He was a prophet, yes. But in Jewish Bibles his book is placed not among the prophets but among the histories. Straight after Esther in fact, though the stories it tells must have happened some forty years earlier, not in Persia but in Babylon, where the Jews had been taken into captivity by King Nebuchadnezzar.

Well, Nebuchadnezzar, King of Babylon, was no fool. He had use in his large empire for many skills and knew all about finding the right young people and training them. And now he had in his kingdom thousands of these highly civilized people from Judah. Valuable people who could enrich his nation.

So one day he sent for the head of his household, an old

friend called Ashpenaz. 'These Jews,' he said, 'they are now of Babylon and their noble and royal families are as old or older than ours. Among them are many youngsters of a very good type. Go through them carefully. Select the best. Not too many. They will live in the Palace, learn our language and customs and at the end of three years I'll hold exams and they'll join the staff.'

Ashpenaz was careful. He knew the King had high standards. Eventually he sifted down his selections to the final group. He lined them up. Roll call. Given new names, by the King's order. The last four to be renamed stood together. Obviously close friends. They answered with their old names and Ashpenaz gave them their new ones. 'Shadrach,' he said to the first; 'Meshach' to the second; 'Abednego' to the third. Then he turned to the fourth. Handsome boy. Steady clear eyes. A gentle smile. Ashpenaz had marked him from the first. He returned the boy's smile. 'And what's your name?' he asked, although he knew. 'Daniel,' came the reply. And Daniel we shall call him in this story. His new name doesn't matter.

Then Ashpenaz issued all the other orders. Subjects to be studied, homework, lesson times, recreations, games, mealtimes. And food. 'The best food,' he said, 'from the King's own kitchens, and wine from the Royal Cellars. As much as you want. You are to be kept in perfect condition, and the King believes in good food.'

The boys looked pleased and Ashpenaz dismissed them. But Daniel and his three friends hung back. 'May I speak to you a moment sir?' he said. 'It is important.'

Ashpenaz nodded; this was not a boy to waste his time.

'It's the food and wine,' said Daniel. 'All four of us come from orthodox families and have never eaten certain foods because our religion forbids them. Neither do we drink wine. Do you think,' said Daniel, 'we might have fruit and vegetables and plain water instead?'

Ashpenaz was stunned. This was right outside his experience. He knew about eccentrics and cranks, the court was full of them, but these were quiet, well-behaved youths with a sort of dignity. He was flustered. 'It's very difficult,' he said. 'You see, it's not me, I don't make the orders. The King does. I only carry them out. To the letter. Good food means good condition. The King said so. If I do differently, if I go against him, I could lose my *head*. I'm not joking!'

'We don't mean to be difficult,' said Daniel, 'or to get you into trouble. Will you let us eat what we ask for ten days? Then compare our condition with the others. Then, whatever you say, we shall do.'

Ashpenaz was about to speak when Daniel added, 'We don't make the laws. God does. We only carry them out.'

And the old servant knew that the boy was not being funny. 'All right,' he said. 'Ten days. Keep it to yourselves. I'm not sure whether all that rich food and wine is good for the King either.'

And of course at the end of ten days Daniel and his friends were in great shape. Even heavier. Ashpenaz was convinced, and made all arrangements. He was very fond of 'the quartet' as he called them and they showed him great respect. As the months turned into years he saw his quartet sweep the board at every prize-giving. They worked hard and were always cheerful. They were much liked and bred no jealousy among the other young men. As the end of the third year approached, the schooling changed its character rather. These were to be young men of the court, of the government, of the ministries, a certain polishing began. Particular talents began to emerge. Diplomacy, directness, leadership, oratory. Daniel possessed all of these and something else too. He discovered in himself the ability to interpret dreams, to understand visions. An extra sense. Special. God-given.

So. End of term. End of school. Passing-out parade. Diploma day. Ashpenaz sad but rather proud. 'I shall miss you four,' he said. 'You've passed out top. But now you're on your own.' So

Daniel and his three friends entered the royal service.

They soon saw that the King's power was absolute, his every wish was a command. 'They are young,' said the King, 'but already men and wise. And that will be their job. Wise men. I want them near me at all times.'

But Nebuchadnezzar was no tyrant. Quite a human sort of person really. Bit of a worrier, often had bad dreams and would look pale and tense for a day or two until the soothsayers had soothed and the magicians and enchanters had cooked up for him a lot of rather flattering interpretations of his nasty dreams.

Daniel would listen and say nothing. Like his distant ancestor Joseph he had a true gift for reading the meanings of dreams and visions and he knew it. But he was a new boy and kept quiet.

One day, though, it was different. Daniel wasn't there, and neither was Shadrach, Meshach or Abednego. The King had got up in a shocking state and had demanded a full muster of all the magicians and sorcerers and dream-readers. They filled the Great Hall. Trumpets sounded, gongs banged and the King was helped to his throne. He looked awful. Pale and trembly.

They waited. Then the Chief Wise Man stepped forward. 'Tell us the dream, O Lord,' he said, 'and we will tell the meaning.'

The King looked up. 'I can't remember the dream,' he said, 'that's just it. I only know how it's left me feeling. Worse than ever before. It must be important. Tell me what it was. And be quick.'

The wise men blinked. 'We can tell you what it *meant* – ' began one of them.

'I know you can,' said the King. 'This time that's not enough. First tell me what the dream *was* – and *then* tell me what it meant!' The King looked very bothered indeed and a bit mad.

The great crowd of magic-doers were thunderstruck. They began to play for time, to make speeches, to try to calm the King. The flattery began.

He stood it for a while, then got to his feet, white with fury.

'Send for Arioch the Captain of the Guard,' he said. 'A special job. The killing of every so-called wise man on the payroll.' Then he left.

Absolute pandemonium. Arioch posted up the notices, sent the message, drew up lists. Efficient man. He went himself to Daniel, whom he liked. Told him regretfully that as he, Daniel, now had the honour to be one of the King's wise men he was to be killed too.

'Arioch,' said Daniel, 'make an appointment for me to see the King. Don't kill anyone. I think I can help the King.' Then he and his friends prayed and God, who had arranged the whole thing, gave him the answers and Daniel told the King first the dream and then its meaning. Not flattery, not nonsense, but a logical-sounding prophecy.

The King, deeply impressed and comforted, then heaped honours upon Daniel and his three friends and forgave the rest of the wise men. Who however did not forgive Daniel *or* his friends who were soon made by the King rulers over whole provinces. Daniel himself the King kept by his side. Second-in-command, no less.

Nebuchadnezzar Humbled

Now, although the King had said some nice things about this God of Daniel's who'd helped with the dream business, it didn't stop him making a great golden idol over ninety feet tall and arranging a huge ceremony of dedication. Officials and delegates from every part of the Empire were invited. Special music was written for huge orchestras and this music was played at certain times and strict orders were given that when the music played all the people had to do a sort of all-fall-down and worship the great idol. If you didn't you would be thrown into a pit of fire, a fiery furnace. The idol was the *real* god, because it was the *biggest* – and of *gold,* so no praying to any *other* gods. If you did, the furnace.

The sorcerers and magicians and soothsayers kept watch and

in no time were telling tales on Shadrach, Meshach and Abednego. 'Rulers of provinces,' they told the King, 'whom *you* honoured, who ignore the orders and pray only to their own Jewish God.'

The King who should have known better, especially after the dream business, lost his temper, and when Daniel's three friends flatly refused to all fall down he was even more foolish. 'Make the furnace seven times hotter,' he bellowed. 'Tie 'em up and let strong men carry them right to the flames and throw 'em in.'

All was done and the strong men were burnt to a cinder. The flames roared: white hot. In the middle, Shadrach, Meshach and Abednego, having a quite stroll in conversation with a visiting angel whom God had sent to keep them company! You can imagine the state the King was in. He'd thrown in three and he could see *four*. And when the angel disappeared and the three Jews came out there was not even a smell of burning on their clothes. Not a hair was singed. Only the ropes and chains which had bound them had gone. Completely. They walked free.

The King then made a lot of speeches and issued statements saying that the God who could do what they'd all just witnessed must be a special God. *Very* special, and that anyone who said anything different would get into serious trouble.

The King was too proud to say that he himself believed in the Jewish God and God noticed his pride. So God prepared another lesson. Rather harder one, but maybe God was remembering that the King had destroyed the beautiful Temple in Jerusalem. Anyway it took the form of another dream. Not forgotten this time, recalled in every worrying detail by the King. Who sent for his friend and right-hand man, Daniel.

Daniel listened carefully and then looked very worried for he liked the King.

'Is it bad?' asked the King. 'Never mind, I must know.'

Daniel said that he wished that what he had to say was about the King's enemies, for it *was* bad. Then he went on to give the meaning of the dream, which was that the King, the great and powerful King, would one day live away from men – in the open like an animal. He would eat grass and have long matted hair and claws. He would live wet and cold and naked. But the kingdom would be safe for his change-back, which would depend on how truly he believed.

All this took a long time to tell and the King was silent. What could he say?

'The dream doesn't say when,' said Daniel. 'Maybe if you change your ways a bit it might not happen. Be righteous, show more mercy, be less proud and so on.'

But it did happen. A year later, right in the middle of a rather boastful speech in which the King was telling of his great power and majesty. It happened exactly as foretold, to the last detail. A great king was changed into a strange creature, neither man nor beast. Set apart. Dumb, with no place. But time passed – twelve whole years – and a day came and the King changed back and there were other changes in him too. He was more humble and thus a better king. More simple in his way of life. Had no more doubts as to who the true God was. (No more bad dreams either.) And his new faith made him happy till he died.

Belshazzar's Feast

Now five years after Nebuchadnezzar died his son was deposed by one of his most ambitious subjects. So ambitious that he moved on into Arabia to do a bit more empire-building, leaving his son Belshazzar on the throne of Babylon. Meanwhile Cyrus of Persia was the coming man and Belshazzar had to pay tribute to him. That no doubt made Belshazzar all the more particular to assert his royal dignity in Babylon. Even made a point of speaking of Nebuchadnezzar as his father. But he had no use for Nebuchadnezzar's new-found faith in the God of the Jews. Daniel soon faded into the background. Until the day when King Belshazzar threw his biggest dinner-party – and his parties were famous.

Belshazzar always tried to have a moment at each of these great gatherings when he would give his guests something to remember. A very special exotic dish, a unique cabaret, a costly gift for everyone, a moment. Well, he certainly gave them a moment on this occasion. Unforgettable indeed. The party was already at its height. Then a great clash of gongs and a silence. Up got Belshazzar. 'A special wine!' he shouted. 'Superb. And you shall all drink it out of very special cups. The vessels and goblets that my father, King Nebuchadnezzar, took from the Temple of Jerusalem. Let's see whether the wine tastes different in *holy* glasses! We'll toast all *our* gods!' he roared. 'Every one of 'em – from the god of wood to the god of stone!'

Out came the beautiful cups and goblets and bowls, all in gold and silver, and the wine was poured. As the King took the first sip there was an odd change in the light. The wall at the end of the great hall began to glow and shimmer. The laughter and shouting died away. Then, before everyone's eyes, a man's hand, just the hand, grew out of the air and with one finger wrote words on the wall and then faded away. The hand faded; the words remained.

The King was white and scared. The magicians and sorcerers and astrologers were sent for. Huge rewards were offered. Prime ministerships were promised. Nothing. Nobody could either read the strange writing *or* tell its meaning. No one.

But the Queen Mother, Nebuchadnezzar's widow, remembered something. 'Stop trembling,' she said to the King. There *is* someone. Daniel. In my husband's time he was the top man over all this lot. He interpreted dreams, explained riddles and read signs time and time again. Never wrong.'

So Daniel was sent for and the vast rewards and gifts were offered to him. The King made the offer himself. He was impressed by Daniel.

It wasn't mutual. 'Keep your gifts,' said Daniel. 'The meaning won't please you. Your father, as you call him, was taught by God, my God, the only God, that pride is a sin. When he was at the height of his power everything was taken from him and he was changed for a while into a creature neither man nor beast, with no place. The lesson he learned then – that *God* decides the fate of men and must be honoured – you seem to have ignored. You have used God's holy vessels to toast and praise idols that are nothing. As you are nothing; other than what God allows you to be.' Daniel paused. 'God has decided to end your kingdom,' he said. 'He has considered it carefully but you are not worthy. Babylon will fall to the Medes and Persians. And that,' said Daniel, 'is the meaning of the writing on the wall.'

All came to pass. That very night the King was killed. We don't know how. And Babylon was occupied by the Persians.

The Lion's Den

The King of Persia, Darius the Great, put in now governors of his provinces, a hundred and twenty of them, all answerable to three Presidents. He had heard of Daniel and made him one of those three top men of his kingdom. It mattered little to Darius that Daniel was not of Babylon but was really an exile from Judah, a Jew. It mattered a lot to the other top men though, *and* to all the governors and councillors who had to answer to Daniel. They hated him. And the more Darius trusted Daniel the more jealous they became. So they did a little plotting. Daniel was an incorruptible man, an absolutely honest man, a loyal man. Difficult to discredit or destroy such a man. So the plotters, knowing that Daniel was deeply religious and that he prayed every day to his God, three times a day, and had no time at all for their idols and images, decided to get at him *that* way. They prepared an order, a law dealing with a short period, called an *interdict,* which said that anyone making petition or request to any power but the King's within the next thirty days would be cast into the palace den of lions. They presented it to King Darius with so many heretofores and howsoevers and suitable legal language that he, poor chap, didn't know what he was signing.

Within the week they were back with lots of witnesses to say how President Daniel just ignored the new law and petitioned and requested and prayed to his God. Three times a *day*. 'And the law is of the Medes and Persians,' they shouted, 'and cannot be revoked.'

Poor Darius! He knew what he'd done and tried every way allowable to undo it, but it was impossible. He had established a law and it could not be set aside, not even for a friend. Daniel also knew how he had been betrayed but said nothing, just prayed as usual, three times a day.

Well, the plotters brought the order for Daniel's death and the King signed it and he and Daniel went down to the palace zoo together. 'You have served me with the same devotion you serve your God,' said the King, 'and I have killed you. May your God treat you better than I have.'

They shook hands and Darius could not see for his own tears. The cave of lions was sealed with a great stone and then with the seals of the King and court. Darius went to his Palace and mourned for his friend. He would eat no food and could not sleep a wink.

As dawn broke the King went back to the cave. He didn't know why, a wild hope, maybe Daniel's God could do even this thing? Daniel was quite unharmed. The lions had shown no interest in him at all though they had been starved by the plotters for days. When Daniel had lain down among them for warmth, they'd made room!

Darius was overjoyed. And when not one word of reproach came from Daniel, the King saw clearly who served him best and gave a few orders regarding the plotters and the lions didn't go hungry after all!

Then Darius made a great proclamation in all the languages of his great Empire that Daniel's God, the God of the Jews, was the living God, everlasting. A God who creates signs and wondrous things – 'and who saved my friend Daniel,' wrote the King, 'from the lions.'

Chapter 7

THE NEW JERUSALEM

'Abomination of Desolation'

The second half of the Book of Daniel is taken up with dreams and visions. Dreams and visions concerning the various empires that would rise and fall. And their various rulers, some good, some bad, until the reign of a really terrible man. A man who claimed to be a god. That's what the second of his two names implies. Antiochus Epiphanes. Set up his own statue in God's Temple at Jerusalem. 'The abomination of desolation,' Daniel called it, 'standing where it should not.' But not for long.

Well, we left Jerusalem, you remember, under a Jewish governor, Nehemiah, its Temple newly rebuilt and rededicated and its people happy and united, left at peace by their neighbours, a semi-independent territory within the vast empire of the Medes and Persians. But soon the changes dreamed of by Daniel began and they were to be huge. The mighty Persian Empire had spread and reached out even as far west as Greece. Athens was burned. But when the Persian Empire fell, it fell to a Greek. To Alexander the Great, warrior extraordinary, a regent at sixteen, educated by Aristotle. A king at twenty. A conqueror. Stopped only by his own death, at thirty-two, of a fever, in bed. A remarkable, rare man. Every land from Egypt to India he took and, having taken, ruled with justice and without blood. After he died, a group of his army commanders cut up the vast Empire between them. They fought among themselves for years, like dogs over a bone.

One of these commanders, a man much trusted by Alexander, was named Ptolemy, and he ruled Egypt and Libya and Cyrene. He was an educated man and made Alexandria, named after Alexander, a great seat of learning. Over the years many Jews have made their home there, soon speaking only Greek. Legend has it that Ptolemy arranged the translation of the Law and Holy Books of the Jews because *he* wanted to read them. Seventy scholars, so it is said, did the work in seventy days. On a small island near to Alexandria. This version, the Septuagint, was of great use to the Greek-speaking Jews.

This Ptolemy founded a dynasty of Egyptian kings. Not all as good or enlightened as he, but all called Ptolemy. Another of Alexander's generals, Antiochus, founded a similar dynasty in Syria. Jerusalem was now part of what was called, till a few years ago, Palestine. As Ptolemy succeeded Ptolemy in Egypt and Antiochus Antiochus in Syria, Palestine changed hands between them many times. But in the main the people, with their careful Judaism, their religious way of life, were left alone.

Until this man who called himself Antiochus Epiphanes. Put on the throne of Syria by the Romans, who were the new great Empire, he decided that *he* wanted, throughout his domain, which included Palestine, a new order. No more Judaism, no more God of the Jews. Jupiter was to be worshipped and himself as an incarnation of Jupiter. The Jews protested but he was an absolute monarch, a Hitler, with storm-troopers and special police. They robbed the great Temple and in the inner sanctum, the Holy of Holies, they put up an idol of Jupiter. There was burning of all holy books. All Jewish festivals, including the Sabbath, were forbidden. So was the circumcision of boy babies. The full terrors of religious persecution descended like a black cloud on the whole of Palestine. A crushing taxation began. Confiscation of property, rape, murder, slavery, concentration camps. Nothing is new.

The people were dazed. It seemed the end. But there was more to come.

Two years after the first great pogrom there was another. Whole streets were pulled down, whole families wiped out. Mass executions. Jerusalem, the golden city, became a rubble-piled waste area where half-starved people scratched a living. To be a Jew, to observe in any way, was to die. It was the law. On every side there were idols and pagan chapels. Once a month, right through the weeping land, there was a sacrifice day, and these were days of terror. On those days were slaughtered all Jews who had dared to practise their religion. Young mothers who'd had their baby sons circumcised died with their dead babies hung round their necks. Old men, too old to change their ways, fell with the blood running into their beards. Once a month a murder day!

In Jerusalem itself, as month followed month, very few Jews remained. Heathen, lawless men lived there, put there by the King, to further desecrate and despoil the city of David and its Temple. The nightmare went on and on. In every town and city of Judaea the storm-troopers would see that only heathen sacrifices and profane services were observed. There were many spies and informers, many who had given up the fight, gone over to pagan ways, to stay alive. In every public place, town square, crossroads, altars and idols. Sacrifice and prayer were compulsory. It was the law. If you broke the law, merciless whipping and torture. Slow death. A terrible, terrible time.

A New Resistance Movement

Just north-west of sad Jerusalem, about fifteen miles away, was a town called Modin. Not a big place. The people of the town had heard of the dreadful happenings all over Judaea but had not themselves suffered a great deal. Not like some places. But there was rumour that there was to be a shake-up; that a huge idolatrous altar was to be built in the square and that the King's special officers were coming to hold the first big sacrifice-meetings. It was true. The hard-faced men arrived and notices were posted up and the ceremonial altar built. The officer-in-charge knew his job; he'd done it many times before. He knew that there was always a top man whom a town looked up to.

A leader of opinion whom people would follow. He knew also that most people had a price.

In Modin one of the elders of the community was a man called Mattathias. He was a Jewish priest, a religion whose practice meant death. He was an elderly man, too old he would say, to learn new ways, and a great worry to his five sons. 'Not that I am so old,' he would say. 'But the old ways are better. They are God's ways.' Often, though, his sons would see him weep for the broken Temple and its profaned altars. 'What point,' Mattathias would say, 'is there in living?' His sons, who were muscular, handsome men, were not too much upset by their father's low moods. They had inherited not only strength from their father but bravery also, and knew him to be quite fearless and of great resilience of spirit.

When the day of the first sacrifice-meeting came, a messenger arrived from the officer-in-charge. Polite invitation; no threats. The five sons waited. Mattathias rose to his feet. Tall, powerful shoulders still, silver hair and beard. 'Come,' he said to his sons. 'This, I feel is to be a special day.'

When they arrived the square was packed with people. By the new altar, near the new idols, were the animals prepared for sacrifice. Mattathias and his five sons walked forward to where the officer-in-charge stood on a small platform. He looked down at them cynically. He wasn't impressed. He'd killed many priests in his time, many sons of priests. It was just a job; get it over with. He spoke only to Mattathias.

'You are a leader in this town,' he said, 'with sons, and of a large and distinguished family. I have dealt with many such, and many have obeyed the King's order without argument. The others are dead. Now come, you show your people the way, you be the first, and they will follow. Make the first sacrifice, and the King will be your friend. He will reward you.'

Mattathias looked straight into the officer's cynical eyes.

'You ask me to be the first,' said Mattathias, 'to make the first sacrifice to an idol. A graven image. Because I lead the community and am a priest of God,' he paused and raised his voice a little, 'the only true God.'

The officer and his men stiffened. The five sons moved a touch closer to their father.

'If the whole country – and every other country under the King's rule,' said Mattathias, 'obeys these terrible orders to give up our covenant with God, my sons and I will not. Not one step will we take from the path of our belief. Neither to the right nor to the left.'

The officer sighed. These old priests were a bore. As if it mattered which God. 'Please yourself,' he said. 'We'll deal with you later.'

He turned to the crowd. 'All right,' he said, 'who's first?' There was a pause, then a man stepped forward. It surprised few people that he was the first. He bowed to the officer and his bow had a scrape in it too.

Mattathias was a priest, bred on the commandments, a mild man. But he felt an anger begin in him like heat. And a strength and power that he knew was from God. He moved forward, every sinew taut, springy as a dancer. He and the man reached the altar together. They were much of a size but Mattathias picked him up and broke him like a stick. It took a second. One scream, and the man was dead.

Then everything happened at once. Mattathias left the troopers to his five sons, who were already upon them. He himself turned, without hurry, to meet the officer, now pale, with a short sword in his hand. Mattathias caught the wrist as the sword came down and turned it as though it were putty. He looked into the officer's eyes, standing close, the point of the sword under the man's chin, the handle still in the man's hand. Mattathias reached up his other hand and put it on the officer's head like a blessing. He bowed the head and helped the officer to kill himself.

He looked around. His sons had coped very well. 'Come,' he said to them, and to the crowd of townspeople he spoke louder.

'We go, my sons and I, to the mountains, to hide and to plan, for this is not the end, it is the beginning. We are Jews and will not break the covenant. Let all who think the same, do the same.' Some came forward right away, and in half a day, leaving everything, they were gone.

Indeed it was not the end of the matter. The news of the revolt soon reached Jerusalem, where the occupation forces had their headquarters. Together with news almost as unbelievable; that after Mattathias and his sons and friends had gone to the mountains, no less than a thousand men, women and children with their sheep and cattle had left the town and were hiding away in the desert scrubland. Soon where they were was known (there are always informers) and a large heavily-armed force set out.

The troops found the people on a Saturday morning. The officer-in-charge knew his job. 'Make no resistance,' he told the people, 'give up your religion as the King says, and you will live.'

'We will not give up our religion,' said the people, 'nor will we offer resistance. It would profane the Sabbath. Which is today.' And they did not resist. The soldiers went in among them and slaughtered every living thing. Men, women, children, cattle and sheep.

When the news was brought to Mattathias in the mountains, he wept. Then he gathered his sons and his friends round him.

'For over two years,' said the silver-bearded Mattathias, 'our country has lived in terror, in blood. Thousands have been killed, thousands more imprisoned, robbed, maimed; our beloved Temple in Jerusalem has been stripped and defiled.' He paused. 'In the inner sanctum an idol now stands. And to it *pigs* are sacrificed. All this you know. And now, another thousand of our neighbours have been massacred. The soldiers found them yesterday and they would not fight back because it was the Sabbath. So they were massacred. Everyone. Men, women and children. Even their sheep and cattle.' He straightened. '*We* will fight on the Sabbath,' he said. 'We will fight every day, in every way. To keep alive the Law of God we have for a while to break it. He knows and is with us. We have many Jews to avenge. We are few, but I have sent word to many. Come,' he said, 'let us fortify this place, our new home in the mountains, let us plan, and harden ourselves.'

Before a week was out their numbers had doubled, trebled. Every kind of man from pale young priests to mighty warriors skilled in the use of arms. A hard discipline began. They were outlaws, wanted men, revolutionaries. Soon they made their first raids, a highly trained, highly mobile guerilla corps. They would descend upon a town without warning. They would pull down every idol and image and wreck every altar. Every profiteer and informer would be punished. They took an eye for an eye, a tooth for a tooth. Their numbers grew, they seemed in ten places at once. They were a clarion call to the people.

The Temple Lives Again

It was a hard life, and sadly one of the first great losses was Mattathias himself. After about a year. As he lay on his death-bed, he asked to be propped up a little the better to look into the faces of his five sons. They drew nearer.

'My sons,' said the old priest, 'we live now in a time of ruin and fury. I die for God and am happy to do so. Show zeal for his Law. Give your lives, if need be. Keep faith. You will be in good company. Father Abraham never wavered. Nor did Joseph, nor Joshua, nor David, nor Elijah, nor Daniel and his three friends. So many, so many.'

No one spoke.

Mattathias began again, his voice firmer. 'Now listen carefully,' he said, 'for upon you, my five sons, rests a huge responsibility. Of you all Simeon is wisest in counsel. He shall take my place. Judas has been a mighty warrior since a youth –' he turned his head, and Judas leaned forward. They were a bit alike. Lean, wide-shouldered men, deep-set eyes, wide resolute mouths. The old man smiled. 'Judas the Hammer,' he said,

'Judas Maccabaeus. You shall command the army, and your brothers will be your spear and your sword. Observe the Law, avenge wrong. Pay back in full both good and evil.'

Then he blessed them and died.

Soon all Israel knew, and mourned, and soon the army of Judas Maccabaeus grew in numbers again. The old priest's call to show 'zeal for God' made a new name for the army. 'Zealots' they were called.

Judas was a fearless man. A born leader and a master of tactics. He created a vast information system throughout the land. He was always forewarned. And he knew the value of surprise and the effect of shock upon the enemy. The enemy now was huge. The whole army of occupation, controlled from Rome, was against him. An order arrived for the attention of Apollonius, who controlled Samaria, north of Judaea. Destroy Judas Maccabaeus and his rabble, it said. Apollonius gathered a large force and went out to do so. Judas, as always, was aware and prepared. He met Apollonius halfway, tore his army to pieces and took everything except prisoners. Apollonius was no coward and, when he came face to face with Judas, fought fiercely. Well matched. Judas killed him and took his sword. And used that sword in battle for the rest of his life. Many battles.

Antiochus was beside himself with fury. 'Two of my armies *beaten!*' he roared. 'By a lot of blasted Jews. I'll do the job myself!' So he gathered all his own personal army, which was huge – including the latest heavy stuff, elephants – and gave every man a year's pay in advance. Then he found himself a bit short of money. Not surprising. So he called in his Prime Minister, a man called Lysias. 'Look,' he said, 'you do it. Take half the army and the elephants and go and wipe Jewry off the map. I'll take the other half of the army and go east and raise some money. The tribute to Rome is about due.'

The battle took place not far from where Judas and his brothers came from. They knew the orders given to Lysias; all Israel knew. And before the battle they and all Israel prayed. And

God looked after the whole thing. Even allowing for the do-or-die part, and the first-class tactics, it was still impossible that the Jewish army should win. But they did. And they took vast plunder, elephants as well. And when, next year, Lysias tried again with even more troops, the Jews won again. Lysias had never seen people fight like that before. He was, the Bible says, perplexed and discouraged. I should think so.

Judas called his army together. 'Our enemies,' he told them, 'for the time being, are crushed. Now let us stop fighting for a while and give thanks to God in the best way I know. Let us go to Jerusalem and make it clean and holy again. We will clear out the thieves and wicked men put there by Antiochus and we will cleanse our beloved Temple from top to bottom.' And they did.

Jerusalem, city of David, broke their hearts when they saw it. And when they came to the Temple they wept. Neglected, desolate, dirty, the beautiful gates burned and smashed. Empty of all its lovely furnishings. All its gold and silver vessels and lamps looted and stolen. The gardens overgrown, the altars filthy with the remains of pig-sacrifice. Idols and images everywhere. The people wept. And then went to work. They smashed down the idols and the defiled altar and built a new altar of rough stone. They restored and renovated and rebuilt and scrubbed and swept and wove cloth and beat metal and made lamps and found oil and sweet herbs.

And the day came. It was the same day of the month on which, three years before, the Temple had been profaned. Three years to the day. The Temple was rededicated with songs and music and happy tears. It glowed with light and was fragrant and spotless. The celebration lasted eight days. And on the last day Judas told the people that the rededication would be celebrated every year from then on. And it is. To this day. It is called Hanukkah, when the branched candlestick is used. A happy festival. A festival of joy and light.

THE NEW

THE BOOK OF WITNESSES

David Kossoff was born in London in 1919. After a short career as a furniture designer he began to devote his full time to acting, and soon became established as a familiar character actor. He has appeared in many films and has a British Academy Award.

A chance reading on the BBC of his version of a Bible story proved an astounding success, resulting in a series and his first book, *Bible Stories*. Subsequently he began a new radio series, From *The Book of Witnesses*, and requests came streaming in for copies of a book that was not yet written. *The Book of Witnesses* was an instant success in hardback and then in paperback.

This book is for my father, who died long ago. Once, when I was small, about eight, I was with my father, who was a loving man, in a narrow street in the East End. A huge labourer suddenly roared down at us that we had killed Jesus. My father asked him why he was so unhappy, and the fist lowered and the shouting stopped and he began to cry. We took him with us to my aunt for tea. This book is for my father, who was a loving man.

CONTENTS

INTRODUCTION

How, you might ask, does a Jewish actor come to be writing a book all about Jesus? Not a very devout or scholarly or deeply-observing Jew; more a 'well-known' , 'known to be' , 'he's never denied it' sort of Jew. An occasional writer-and-teller-of-Bible-stories Jew. *Old* Testament stories. Of course.

Well, we live in many-media times. Occasional little stories become series; on radio and television. They become records, and short films – and are published. And an actor who wrote a little as a second string finds himself the author of a best-seller.

The bestseller contained all his stories but one. That one, from the New Testament, was an early, toe-in-the-water effort to solve a problem, to see how it came out. The problem was to find a format that would give him the same 'at home and at ease' feeling in the New as in the Old Testament. The little story told of three donkeys in Heaven reminiscing about their lives, in Jerusalem and Nazareth, long ago. What they saw, what they witnessed. Witnesses; there at that time.

Bestsellers, as in the way of things, demand sequels – and what other sequel can there be to the Old Testament but the New? The actor's reaction was as expected: 'But I am Jewish!' He became expert at evasive conversation on the subject. Promises were at last extracted from him that 'thinking about it' would take place. The thinking had a familiar shape. How to find a formula that would allow the same 'easy-walking' feel of the bestselling collection. A lot of reading was done; a lot of tryout writing; a lot of talking to priests. A trip to Galilee; a lot of walking and thinking in Nazareth. A problem, a problem.

The solution was right under his nose. The three donkeys. Witnesses. There at the time. But not donkeys, people. Faces in the crowd. People who were there; who *must* have been there.

The worry stopped, the imagination raced, the pen flew. *The Book of Witnesses* was born.

As with the Old so with the New. From the first work on the book, a short radio series: *From the Book of Witnesses*. And from the first broadcast, no further doubts. The letters poured in, all wanting to know more about a book that did not yet exist.

Here is the book. A little description of each Witness heads each story. If, good reader, the description does not seem to match the way of the words, then make up your own description, attach a different person. No offence will be taken; the speakers are long dead.

Alternatively, if the way of the words bothers you, the way the Witnesses 'say it', do not be too concerned. Truth is not lessened by being spoken in translation.

Lastly, if it distresses you that the Witnesses of the book are fictional – and it cannot be denied – take comfort. At least that of which they speak is true. It is Gospel.

Chapter 1

THE BABY

Simon

Ex-Temple worker. Now much engaged in youth welfare work.
Middle fifties. Heavily built, with a ruddy complexion and greying
hair. Blue eyes, rather bald. A smiling, pleasant man. A warm, kindly
voice.

I was very fond of Zacharias. He was quite a bit older than
me. When I was first taken on at the Temple he'd been there
many years. The Great Temple in Jerusalem employed hundreds.
All sorts of people, but for the jobs and duties connected with
services and the inner holy rooms and courts they were very
selective. You had to be of a priestly family. And old Zacharias
was. His family went right back to Abyah, a priest appointed
by King David himself. The direct line of Aaron. Zacharias's
wife, old Elizabeth, was also of that line. She was as nice and
as kind to me as he was. I saw her often, and him every day.
For a time I lived with them, they treated me like a son. They'd
never had children of their own, it was their one sadness. So
I sort of filled a gap. They loved children. Elizabeth used to help
at the children's Scripture school, and when she used to tell the
story of Abraham's wife, old Sarah, who laughed when the angel
told her she would be a mother, Elizabeth would laugh too,
rather sadly.

But when she became a mother, like old Sarah, in old age, she
didn't laugh. She was full of gratitude. 'Simon,' she said to me,

'God is very kind. I was always a bit ashamed of being childless – and people used to say some very thoughtless and humiliating things – but now all that's over. My son is from God.'

'From God,' was true. Although poor Zacharias was stricken dumb for nearly a year. A most remarkable time altogether. I remember very well when the dumbness began. We were in the Temple, during a service, and Zacharias had to go into the inner room where the incense altar was. The preparing and lighting of incense was one of his jobs. He was gone longer than usual and I went to see if anything was wrong. As I got to the door he came out. He was pale and trembling and couldn't speak. He kept making signs that no one could understand. I took him home and Elizabeth made him go to bed. When he was calmer he wrote it all down for us. He'd seen a vision, an angel, Gabriel himself, who'd told him that Elizabeth would have a son, who would be special and holy and a prophet, and who would prepare the way for the coming of the Lord – although we didn't know what the last bit meant till years after. 'And,' wrote poor Zacharias, 'when Gabriel had told me all this I expressed some doubts, so Gabriel said I'd better not say another word till it had all come true. And he made sure I couldn't.'

Poor Zacharias. But Elizabeth had no doubts at all. Soon she was pregnant. She didn't go out. She became calm and quiet, and sort of beautiful. She was far from young but she'd always been good-looking and she became beautiful. Zacharias looked at her with wonder in his eyes. Quite dumb he was. Not a sound. He was very gentle and thoughtful to her. He asked me to find a young woman to take over the housework and be company for Elizabeth and I wrote to my mother who found Ruth in the next village and she came down and took over my room. And me. She's my wife, and she can add to this story, if you want. It is, after all, rather a woman's story, and she has a remarkable memory, has Ruth.

Where was I? Yes, Zacharias. Well, dumb or not, father-to-be or not, his life didn't change much. He was not ill or anything and was back at work no more than a week after losing his voice. I was his assistant, he'd trained me, and we did not need words. The time passed very quickly. In a way, I think Zacharias got used to being dumb.

He got his speech back in a nice way. When Elizabeth's time came she had a fine, healthy boy, with no trouble. She and Zacharias were much liked, and the crowds of friends and relatives made it a joyous occasion. I got carried away and proposed to Ruth. So did she, and accepted me. On the eighth day, as the child was fit and well, he was circumcised and given his name. It was pretty well understood by everybody that the boy would be called Zacharias, after his father. But at the moment in the ceremony when the name is given, Elizabeth said, 'No! He is to be called John.' Great disturbance; for there were no Johns in either family. Then they asked Zacharias, who asked for a writing-tablet. He stood next to Elizabeth and looked into her eyes. Two old people. Then he wrote: 'John is his name.' Everybody was very surprised. Nearly a family row. Then Zacharias *said* loudly and clearly, 'John is his name.' Nice moment. He was a remarkable child, that John. He became a preacher who believed in purification by water. In baptism. He became famous. He was called John the Baptist. I'll go and call Ruth.

Ruth

Rather like her husband. Big-boned and handsome. Black hair and eyes. Early fifties. A relaxed, easy person, quick to smile, and of great charm. Down-to-earth, sensible.

Of course, it's all a long time ago now and Jesus is dead, poor soul, and so is John. People are inclined, I think, to forget the parents of famous men. John's parents have both been dead for many years and hardly anybody ever mentions them. They only had John, and he never married, so they are forgotten. Not by me, they were two of the loveliest people I shall ever know. Kindness itself. John was a present from God, and God doesn't give presents to just anybody.

You know, when I tell people about them, I rather gloss over the fact that old Elizabeth, bless her sweet memory, had a baby at an age that everyone knows is out of the question for having babies. But she did, I assure you. I was there when the child was christened and called John – and Zacharias got his speech back. A remarkable occasion in every way. As Simon no doubt told you. I always thought that it was a bit harsh for the Angel Gabriel to strike the old man dumb, just because he couldn't quite believe the news that he was going to be a father. Maybe Gabriel didn't want Zacharias to go telling everyone.

You know, there was a happening during Elizabeth's pregnancy that stays in my mind most clearly. I was living with the old couple. My own home was far to the north, and, shortly after I'd joined them, they found a little house up in the hills so that Elizabeth could be quiet and secluded and hide herself away a bit. She was a bit shy about the whole thing. Very nice house it was, practical and pleasant. They'd no children and I was made very welcome. It was rough on Zacharias to be made dumb, for he liked to talk. But he could write and we managed. Elizabeth passed her days in a sort of dreamy happiness. She would tell me over and over again of how Gabriel had appeared to Zacharias in the Temple and told him about the son he was going to have. A holy, special son, beloved of God. She never tired of telling the story and I never tired of listening to her. She was full of wonder, like a child. 'Ruth,' she would say to me, 'imagine! I am picked out, chosen, blessed among women!'

Well, when she was about half-way through her pregnancy or perhaps a little more, we had a visit from a young relative of Elizabeth's. A young woman from Nazareth. I'd heard her spoken of but had never seen her. She was unmarried but engaged to a carpenter. He was not with her; she came alone. Elizabeth was pleased to see her, she'd seen almost no one since the baby had begun. The young woman's name was Mary, a quietly-spoken, friendly-faced person. We'd had no message that she was coming and Elizabeth was curious to see the young woman's reaction to her old aunt's rather surprising condition. But Mary had her own surprise. 'I know about it,' she said, 'the Angel Gabriel told me!' And she went on to tell us that the angel had told her that she, too, was to have a special, holy baby. When she'd pointed out modestly that she was not even married the angel had said that her husband-to-be, Joseph, would not have anything to do with the matter. God would be the father. The baby, a boy, was to be called Jesus and he would be a great man and his name would live for ever.

When Mary had finished telling all this, Elizabeth became very excited. She laughed and cried and seemed full of joy. For the younger woman and also for herself. As she had perfect faith in her own promised child, she had the same faith in Mary's. She recalled that Gabriel had told her that her baby would be a prophet, to 'prepare the way', he'd said, 'for the coming of the Lord.' Neither she nor Zacharias had really understood that part but now she did. 'Ruth,' she said to me, 'Mary's baby is the Lord! I'm certain of it!' She was full of humility. She felt honoured that the mother chosen for the Lord should come to see *her*. Very typical of Elizabeth, that was. 'Ruth,' she said, 'even the baby inside me is full of joy at the news. He kicks and leaps and moves!' She made Mary and me feel, and it was true. We put our hands on her and she put her hands on ours. 'Be friends,' she said, 'love each other.' And we did. Mary and I are the same age. Then we were both girls in the middle of remarkable happenings. We became like sisters. Mary stayed about three months. She shared my room. We kept in touch for years.

John was a lovely baby. Good as gold. I looked after him until my own babies started to come. A lovely time in my life. I often think of it. Of Mary, and old Elizabeth, and of the love and happiness, and of their holy, special sons given by God, special men, born in glory, who died so terribly. Jesus and John the Baptist. One crucified and one beheaded. In their thirties. It's a great puzzle.

Seth

About seventy. A weather-beaten, ruddy, lined face. A still, patient man. Bent, but still wiry and active-looking. Blue eyes, of a sharp intelligence, but kindly and interested. A deep countryman's voice.

My father and my grandfather were shepherds. It is a thing that runs in families. My sons own their own farms and their own sheep, but that is progress. I always looked after other people's sheep. Mind you, my sons are both clever, and quick in the mind, like my wife. She's always been rather a scholar. A good thing, for I can hardly read or write, but that was not unusual when I was younger. We were looked down on, I suppose, for often we had to work every day, ignoring the Sabbath, and with so many priests among the people, we were often told we were breaking the law. Though where the priests would have got their perfect lambs for sacrifice without us, I don't know. They could be very rude, the priests. Especially the young, silly ones. It's the same today. And not just with priests. People speak before they think. That's one good thing about looking after sheep. You get into the habit of keeping quiet. If you have to use words, you take your time to get them right. Words are important.

People often tell me that mine was a dull life. Well, maybe. Looking after sheep *is* much the same each day. But many people have never seen the lambs play and leap, have never sat quiet on a hill and watched the sun. Or the moon. I like to watch the night sky, the moon and the stars. Once I saw, at night, a sight that very few have seen. Just once, but once was enough for any man. If a priest is rude to me, I always say to myself, 'It doesn't matter, I had that night and you didn't.'

I was about nineteen at the time, and, although it's now about fifty years ago, I remember it like yesterday. I lived with my parents, not far from Jerusalem, and I was one of a group of shepherds who looked after the sheep owned by the Temple. As I said, the sheep for the Temple services have to be perfect, and a great many are bred for food, too. We, our group, usually worked at night. On this night I'm talking about, we'd met up where we usually did, on the side of quite a big hill. We'd had a bite to eat and drink and were sitting talking. Around us, our hundreds of sheep. All normal and usual and quiet. Very restful and pleasant, those talks at night. It was a dark night.

Then there was a sort of stillness and a feeling of change, of difference. We all felt it. I had a friend called Simon, and he first noticed what the change was. It was the light. There was a sort of paleness. It was a dark night but suddenly it wasn't so dark. We began to see each other's faces very clearly in a sort of silvery shimmering light. We seemed surrounded and enclosed in a great glow. It was the purest light I ever saw. The sheep were white as snow. Then, as our eyes began to ache with it, just farther up the hill from us the glow seemed to intensify and take shape, and we saw a man. Like us but not like us. Taller, stiller. Though we were still enough, God knows.

He looked at us and we looked at him. We waited for him to speak. It didn't seem right (we all felt it) for any of us to speak first. He took his time – as though to find the right words – and then he began to tell us what he called good news of great joy. Of a new-born baby, born in David's town. A baby sent by God, to save the world, to change things, to make things better. He told us where to go and find the baby and how to recognize him. And to tell other people the good news. His own pleasure in telling us filled us with joy, too. We shared his pleasure – if you follow me. Then he stopped speaking and became two. Then four, then eight, and in a second there seemed to be a million like him. Right up the hill and on up into the sky. A million. And they sang to us. 'Glory to God,' they sang, 'and on earth peace to all men.' It was wonderful. It came to an end and then they were gone. Every single one, and we felt lonely and lost.

Then Samuel, who was the eldest of us, said, 'Come, let us go and find the baby. David's town the angel said; Bethlehem. In a manger. In swaddling clothes.' And off we went. We ran, we sang, we shouted, we were important, we'd been chosen. We were special. We were on a search, we had to find a baby.

And we did find him. We were led there. There was no 'searching'. We were led, and we saw for ourselves. Not much to see, perhaps. A young mother and her husband and her newly born baby. Born in a stable because all the inns were full. Poor people they were. The man was a carpenter.

Well, we did as we'd been told, we spread the word, and people did get excited. But not for long. Nothing lasts. We shepherds were heroes for a while, but then everyone knew the story. It was old news. Soon we were just shepherds again. Doing a dull job. But we were different from all the rest. We'd had that night. I don't talk about it much any more. But it keeps me warm. I was there.

Jethro

Over seventy. Of medium height and rather spare. The face is arresting. Very pale and thin-skinned with a gentle, almost saintly, expression, but with alert, bright brown eyes. The hair and beard are pure white and fine in texture. The voice is silvery, clear, precise. The hand gestures are graceful, small.

Sometimes people tell me that my life spent inside the Temple somehow has shut me off from the world outside. I explain that this is not so; that the world *outside*, as it were, comes *in*. Neither is the world *inside* an unchanging one, any more than the outside world is; many changes, many.

When Herod died and Archelaus was King, the terrible riots

and massacres were *in Temple precincts.* When the Roman procurators came to Jerusalem, one after the other, always in the Temple we felt change! The tempo of life changed. Thirty, thirty-five years ago, life in the Temple was easier somehow. Just as orthodox, just as strict in the observances, but softer.

It was like a small town, a village. Very high walls, as somebody once said, but many gates. A wonderful feeling of shelter, of safety. A haven. As people grew old, they would try to live close to the Temple, and they would spend all their days within the walls. They had their place. They were honoured, shown great respect. At that time, just before Herod died, most of my work was in the part of the Temple where the old people sat, near the Inner Court where the babies were brought for the ceremony of Presentation to the Lord and the Blessing. It was pleasant to see the young parents and their babies and our 'old residents', as we called them, all together sharing the joy. Some of these were grand occasions, with large families bringing huge offerings of animals for sacrifice and gifts of every kind, but the kind I liked best were the poor people, who were allowed by the Law to bring as their gift a pair of young pigeons, or turtledoves. Always shy, such young people, always overawed. And nearly always put at their ease by one or other of our 'old residents'.

Some of these old ones were famous. Two I remember very well. One, Anna, was said to be a prophetess. Very old indeed, very devout. She lived in the court of women. She had married young but had been widowed after only seven years. She gave her life to God soon after. When I first met her she must have been nearly eighty. A great quality of stillness, of repose. It was easy to believe that she could see into the future, that she knew more than others. But she was not remote. She was kind, and of a sympathetic nature. People confided in her. She was interested. A good listener. She knew all about her old friends; she'd been there longer than any of them. She knew them well. Often we would talk of another favourite of mine, Simeon, another very old resident. Like Anna, also surrounded by legend, also 'famous'. He, it was said, had been told by God that he would not die until he had seen and touched the Messiah, the saviour of Israel, the one given by God. Simeon was regarded as a bit of a joke by some of the other old ones, but not by Anna. 'Simeon is very old,' she said to me once, 'but he is close to God, and God knows him well. I sleep little,' she said, 'but lately I dream, and I think that soon I will lose my old friend Simeon.'

She would say no more, and I tried to put it from my mind, but I found I was making it my business to be near Simeon whenever I could. He liked to sit in the sun, 'looking at the people go by,' as he put it. I don't know quite what I expected. It could be anybody. He spoke to many, a friendly man. Apart from the young fathers, all sorts of people. Holy men and soothsayers and seers and prophets were no strangers in the Temple. All sorts of learned close-to-God teachers and preachers were constantly passing through.

So I watched carefully. Who Simeon met, and how he reacted. Well, I was there when it happened. When he met the one that would allow him to die happy. I shall never forget his face. The moment had come, the sign so long awaited. And yet, it was strange, when it came, it was at once astonishing and ordinary. You will understand better what I mean, if I tell you a little more about Simeon, and about myself, too.

I have worked in the Temple all my life. As my father did, and his father. I began when I was fifteen, and finishing my education within the Temple. The elders and teachers in the Temple were men of vast knowledge. My first duties were all to do with ritual, with the services and festivals. People came from all over the world to Jerusalem, to see Great Herod's Temple. A pilgrimage, a wonder. But soon I began to know the regulars, the members of the congregation who never missed. Every Sabbath, every feast, every fast. The devout.

And Simeon was one. I was about twenty when we first met. About fifty years ago. And he was elderly then. He was kind to me. I had much to learn, and he knew all the services by heart.

He was a very highly respected man, and when we first met, much involved in community and charity work. He did less as the years passed, and spent more and more time in prayer and with the Scriptures. It was a great part of his life to join in the ceaseless discussion among the elders and the teachers on the hidden meanings in the great history books of the people. The writings of the prophets, the written-down visions of the sages and seers of long ago. He would meditate for hours, almost in a state of mystical trance – often during a long fast. As the years passed, he confided in me more and more. And one day – and this must be nearly forty years ago – he told me he was now sure that a saviour of Israel was expected. 'It is written,' he said, 'it is shown in the books. One will come anointed by God. A Messiah. A leader.' He was lit up by the thought. Well, he wasn't the first to express such wish-thoughts. At that time there was a great hunger in people for a new, simple way. A kinder way. Great Herod was a hard king. Life was harsh; full of rules and regulations which had crept into God's Laws, too. So I listened to Simeon and gave him respect, but he wasn't finished. 'It has also been shown to me,' he said, 'that I will not die until I have seen the one sent by God.' He said it quite simply. He had not been very well, and he was quite old, but there was a sort of positive strength in him. From then on he lived in a state of expectancy, waiting. At first he spoke only to me about this conviction he had, but then others heard of it and some thought that Simeon was now senile as well as old.

But one morning, about five or six years after his vision, he was in the Temple earlier than usual. It was about a month after Anna had spoken of her dreams. 'Today,' he said. 'It will be today. I have been told and I am ready.' He sat in his usual seat. Near the Inner Court where the parents brought their babies for the Presentation to the Lord ceremony. A weekly thing; part of my job. I watched carefully. Many of the young fathers and their brothers or friends were fine Godly-looking men. But Simeon sat on. Then a poorly dressed couple approached. The woman rather younger than the man and carrying her baby son. The man carrying the most modest offering allowed by the Laws of Moses. A pair of doves. Simeon got to his feet. He was trembling, and I went nearer in case he should need help. He went forward, not as I thought to bow low to the man, but gently to take the baby in his arms. He stood and lifted his face and spoke to God, as to a loving friend who'd kept a promise. He blessed God, and thanked him. 'Now I can die in peace,' he said. 'I have seen him – and held him in my arms.' He spoke on, of salvation, of a truth for all people, of a standard too high for many, of one who would see into men's hearts, and bring to many a great joy. Then he stopped and looked into the face of the young mother. 'But not you,' he said, and tears came into his eyes, 'for you a sword, to pierce your very soul.' The young woman was transfixed, amazed. I don't think she'd understood most of what he'd said. Neither had I.

Simeon blessed them all and they went away. Back to Bethlehem. Simeon died soon after. I missed him.

Nezzar

Of Babylon. Dark, smooth-skinned, with curled beard. About sixty, of a learned manner but without pedantry. A gentle, soft voice. A habit of smiling at the recollection before speaking of it. Graceful, well-kept hands.

I never liked to travel much. One of my brothers was a merchant and he travelled all his life. It was his livelihood, his work. He had no choice. I think perhaps that this place, where I was born and have always lived, has something to do with my dislike of travelling. Babylon, on the mighty Euphrates, has everything a man needs. I had no need to travel. But once, only once, I went on a remarkable journey. A long journey, a search. It is a long time ago, but I remember it as clear as if it were yesterday.

I was about thirty at the time, and I lived and worked in the home of a man nearly twice my age. I was a scribe, and had a certain skill with figures. My master was a scholar and astrologer. He had spent his life in the study of the planets and stars. It was part of his religion, of mine, too. He was famous. His family was old and among his forebears had been sooth-sayers to the Persian court, lawmakers to the Medes, men of prophecy and divination. He was a silent, large man – with deep-sunk eyes. Often he would not speak for days and then would dictate to me, or just talk, as though to think out loud; to sort the mind. For about three years, he had been studying the Scriptures and the religion of the Jews of Israel, far to the west. He admired them. 'A remarkable people,' he would say, 'with a remarkable history, all written down. A history full of prophets and prophecies. A people who seem to be waiting. For a saviour, a leader, a Messiah.' My master was in close touch with other scholars and astrologers like himself. He and they were of the tribe called Magi, or wise men. Philosophers, thinkers, men of influence. Teachers, they were, and priests.

Well, one day my master seemed rather excited. A friend of his from a place up north on the Tigris had been staying with us, and they had been deep in study and discussion for days. And up most of the nights studying the stars. 'Something is happening,' said my master, 'something big. A whole series of signs and prophecies seem to be forming a pattern. We have worked sep-arately and apart – and our conclusions agree. In two days' time we will have a third opinion. Have a room prepared.' And in two days a third friend arrived. I knew him well. A big, friendly man. I met him at the gate. 'Hallo,' he said, 'where are they? There's something big going on. Don't unpack my bags, pack theirs. We have to stop looking at stars, we have to start following one!'

We started the very next night. There was a lot to arrange but the three of them were energetic and lively as schoolboys. They pointed out the star. 'A new one,' they said, with wonder, 'and it moves and gets brighter and we have found words and prophecies. We have to go and find a king and speak to him of another king greater than he, and we have to take for the greater king worthy presents. Gold and frankincense and myrrh. As the Queen of Sheba long ago took gifts to King Solomon, so we, too, have to go to Israel with gifts for a king!'

The caravan was big. Servants to put up tents, to cook, to look after the camels, and to guard the gifts – which were gorgeous. The purified resins of the frankincense and myrrh were in priceless caskets covered with jewels. I had never been outside the city, and suddenly I was faced with a journey of hundreds of miles across desert. I had duties. I was in charge of the gifts, the astrological tables, the books – and the Magi also. For wise men are notoriously bad at looking after themselves.

We went from East to West and by the time we got to Jerusalem my three wise men had worked it all out. The king we were looking for was not Great Herod, but a baby, a little child, recently born. And not a king of a country, but 'King of the Jews'.

Jerusalem was beautiful – and the Great Temple breathtaking. Equal to, if not better than, anything we had at home in Babylon. We began our inquiries and soon were aware of a strange atmosphere. The Magi were right, people did seem to be waiting for a leader, a king, an Anointed One, a Messiah. A feeling of expectancy, a hope, a waiting. In all kinds of people. But the people of Jerusalem were very careful in their replies.

'A new king?' they said. 'We have a king. Herod. And he has sons. And,' they said, 'Herod has murdered many to protect his throne, to ensure the succession.' 'Be cautious,' said an old priest, 'Herod is old and ill, and as sick in the mind as in the body. Be cautious, his people are everywhere.' And very soon, some of Herod's 'people' came, with an invitation from the King. I was nervous, but the Magi were not. 'The King was on our list of people to ask,' they said. 'We are not beggars. We are a tribe of priests, of teachers. In Persia we teach kings their job.'

And indeed Herod showed us great courtesy. I accompanied my master, the eldest of the three, as secretary and aide. The King asked many questions and seemed interested and helpful. He told us that his own priests and scribes had found in the Scriptures a prophecy that pointed to Bethlehem as the place where we would find the child. 'Go,' said Herod, 'find the child and send me news. So that I, too, can come and pay my respects.'

Bethlehem was not far, and that very night the great glowing star, which had led us all the way from Babylon, led us to a small house in a narrow street and we saw the child. A young mother, with a rather older husband. Poor people. I could see nothing remarkable, but my master and the other two Magi wept and prayed and handed over the gorgeous presents of gold and incense they had brought. The parents seemed rather stunned. The child slept. It was difficult to get the three wise men back to the inn and to bed. They were like excited children. In the middle of the night, my master woke me. His face was serious. 'Get up,' he said, 'rouse everyone. Pack everything and load the camels. All three of us have had the same dream. A clear message from God that we must not return to Herod but must go back to the East at once, by a different route. There is great danger. Come, hurry.' 'What about the child and his parents?' I said. 'If God goes to such trouble for us,' he said, 'three elderly Magi, we can be fairly certain that he will look after the little family. That is no ordinary child.'

Well, we escaped. We went back to Babylon. I don't know what happened to the little family. Herod died soon after and his sons reigned as part-kings under the Romans. And I never left Babylon again. And we never saw the great star again.

Shem

Late sixties, or early seventies. A tall, lean, sinewy man. Deep-set eyes, which are dark and alive. Clean-shaven, with close-cropped hair. The face is strong, the skin weather-wrinkled and tanned. Big, worker's hands.

I'm not a religious man, you understand, and I didn't have much in the way of an education, but I'm not young and I've travelled a lot and listened a lot and you learn, you know, you learn. I was born in Samaria in the same year that Herod became King. Herod the Great he was called. Well, maybe he was great. He didn't do much for us in Samaria. All right, we are a mixed lot but we are not lepers. Our law is based on the same rules as the rest of Israel. The Law of Moses. One of those Laws is that the children shouldn't suffer for the sins of the fathers. That's a joke. All my life I've suffered for some nonsense generations ago about my people wanting to help in the rebuilding of the Great Temple and being refused because our religion wasn't holy enough. You'd have thought a few extra gods and idols would have made it *more* religious. And Samaritans are good builders. My family have been joiners and carpenters for a long time. I think that's what first drew me to Joseph.

I'm a journeyman; I work anywhere. My tools are my luggage. When I first met Joseph and his little family in Bethlehem it was the first time I'd ever been there – and I've worked all over; Phoenicia, Syria, Parthia, Egypt. Not a big place, Bethlehem. One big inn, a decent synagogue, a meeting hall. Anyway, this inn had been damaged by some sort of religious demonstration. There'd been crowds of people who'd broken things off for souvenirs. A lot of the timber in the stables needed replacing. I heard about it and was taken on. I found a room on the edge of the town. And met Joseph, who lived next door. When he told me he was also a joiner, I told him about the inn and he smiled and said he'd like to help with the repairs. So I put in a word for him and we worked together.

Very quiet man he was. His wife was younger. Her name was Mary. They had a baby boy. When I met them, they'd just come back from taking the baby to the Temple in Jerusalem for his blessing by the priests. Joseph and I worked together for some weeks before I told him I was a Samaritan. 'Oh,' he said, 'I've never been in Samaria. Will you eat with us this evening?'

Well, I forget now how long we worked at the inn but we got it done and I was working on a barn north of the town. I'd kept my room on and one night I got back very late. It was pay night and I like a drink. The street was quiet and dark. As I got ready for bed, Joseph knocked on my door. 'Can you help us?' he said, 'We have to leave right away.' We went next door. Mary was packing and the baby was fast asleep in his crib. On the table were three caskets. They were gorgeous. Gold they were, worth a fortune. 'Gold, frankincense, and myrrh,' said Joseph, 'gifts for the baby. They can bring death to us all. We have been told by God to go down to Egypt. Right away. Tonight. We know nothing of long journeys. Please help us.'

I went next door and packed my tools. We were out of the place in an hour. We borrowed a donkey for Mary to ride on with the baby and we joined a trade caravan of merchants and we kept ourselves to ourselves. If people got too inquisitive I used rough talk and said loudly I was a Samaritan. That got rid of them. Sins of the fathers can be very useful sometimes.

Now you might ask why did I go with them. Well, there was nothing heroic in it. I've moved around working in different places all my life. And Joseph had hardly been out of his town. Also we were both joiners, and carpenters can pick up work anywhere if you know the way. Another thing, as I told you, I'm a Samaritan, which at that time, thirty-five years ago, just before Great Herod died, was the same as being a leper nearly. No one had a good word for you. You walked by yourself. Well, Joseph was an orthodox Jew and he accepted me like a brother – and so did Mary. Even the baby liked me. I was one of the family. Of course I went with them. I looked after them.

It took us a long time to do the journey. We had a donkey for Mary and the baby, but Joseph and I walked. We stayed with no one long, for Joseph and Mary were afraid. My gentle friend, who never raised his voice, was a wanted man. Mad King Herod himself was after him. Well, not him so much as the baby. I don't know all the ins and outs of it even now, but somehow or other Joseph and Mary had got an early warning that Herod was going to kill all the baby boys under two in Bethlehem. They were not hysterical people, and when they went I went with them, but I didn't really believe such a thing would happen. But it did. We heard about it. Mary wept for days, and Joseph was quieter even than usual.

We didn't go deep into Egypt. We stayed this side of the great delta of the Nile and found a little house in a village. There was enough work round about and the village people were used to travellers. We weren't too far from the coast and a main trade route. I've made a point all my life not to ask too many questions. If people want to tell me something, they will. Joseph never spoke much. Once, when I said I'd no idea how he knew about the order to kill the babies, he said, 'I didn't know. I was told in a dream by an angel of God to leave immediately. My little son was given to Mary by God. I did as I was told.' He was quite serious. I made a sort of joke, I remember. I said, 'Well, when the angel tells us to go back home, let me know. I'm not too fond of Egypt.' Joseph laughed.

I forget now exactly how long we lived in the village but one morning I came down and Joseph had the little boy on his knee. Mary was by the stove, Joseph smiled. 'Good morning,' he said, 'we can go home.' 'Another angel?' I said. 'Same one,' said Joseph 'Herod is dead. It is safe now.' Well, it wasn't so safe really. Herod's son, Archelaus, was now King and was more hated and more cruel than his father. There'd been riots and disturbances and mass executions, so when we'd gone up the coast as far as Gaza, Joseph decided that he would not go back to Bethlehem, where little Jesus had been born, but farther north to Galilee, where it was more peaceful. He knew Galilee, he came from Nazareth, and that is where we finished up. I went with them and helped them find a place and get it fixed up, but then I moved on. Nazareth was a very religious, very orthodox place. Joseph fitted in well, me not at all. I was sorry to go. I saw them from time to time. The last time I saw them, the eldest lad, Jesus, was getting ready to go to the Temple in Jerusalem for his confirmation. He was twelve or thirteen. Fine boy. Then I worked in Syria and Cyprus for a long time and lost touch. But I think of that time often.

Sylvanus

Over seventy. A thin, pale, acid man. The skin of the face very fine and wrinkled, the eyes hooded, many-folded. The voice is meticulous, slow, rather high. The impression of frailty is physical only; the strength of mind is apparent immediately.

It may be that, when we have conversed for a little while, you will form the opinion that I am a cynic, or a sceptic. It is an opinion that you may well carry away with you. You will not be the first, and if we meet again, it may well prevent us being friends. Well, I shall understand. I have very few friends. As I get older (if getting much older is even possible in my case), I find I can do with fewer.

However, as to my being a cynic, or a sceptic, you must remember that I have spent my whole life at court. I have seen black proved white and miracles made commonplace. I have seen slaughter blessed by holy men and sanctity made a crime. I have seen prophets and men of God murdered with not a word from the God they represent. I have seen wickedness prevail and virtue made meaningless. I have watched vanity lift a man to heights where humility is unknown. So you will readily understand (I hope) that in such a world detachment can become an art; cynicism a protective shield; scepticism the only intelligent attitude.

My world was the world of Herod. King Herod. Herod the Great. And great he was. People, I find, when remembering others, remember the bad and forget the good. They remember Herod's senseless murders and forget his loving rebuilding of the Great Temple. They remember the stupidities at the end of his life and forget the far-sighted good sense at the beginning. He was a Jew who knew how to be a Roman and the Romans recognized his worth. Antony himself made Herod King. And Octavian, great Augustus Caesar, agreed.

You might say to me that Herod was mad. Possibly. But it was not a time of sanity and a certain madness is not unknown in great men. Also, it should be remembered, although it is difficult to believe, that Herod, Great Herod, never, ever, felt secure. He was suspicious, often rightly so, of everyone round him. Certainly he had little joy of his wife, the exquisite Mariamne. She was like ice. Admittedly, her life was, to say the least, difficult. When her younger brother, whom Herod had made a high priest, became popular, Herod had him drowned, in his bath. Her grandfather, of eighty-seven, was put to death. Her sons were killed. Handsome, well-liked young men, with their mother's looks. There was so much death. Even Mariamne herself was killed. Tragedy, tragedy. It almost turns into bizarre comedy the ghastly edict made by Herod that all boy babies under the age of two in Bethlehem should die to make certain that one particular baby was destroyed. This special baby that everybody seemed to be talking about.

Herod, being as I say a morbidly suspicious man, had built up, over the years, a very efficient informer system. At court we knew everything that went on in Judea. We knew about the crowd of shepherds looking for a baby born in a stable the morning after it had happened. We knew exactly how long the excitement would last; we'd had glad tidings from angels before. We'd had Messiahs by the dozen – and had regulations about how to get rid of them. Holy men and healers and miracle-makers and magicians were thick upon the ground.

A report was given to Herod about the baby in the stable but I don't think he even read it. He was quite ill at the time, and very unbalanced. He was full of disease, bloated, disgusting. He was in pain, living on drugs, but hardly sleeping at all. He was afraid of the dreams, I think. He looked awful.

He was nearly seventy and looked a hundred. He had ruled in one way or another since he was fifteen. He had killed without mercy. Enemies; friends; his own flesh and blood. His hands were red. It was said at court that remorse, about

Mariamne and his dead sons, was destroying his mind. His periods of lucidity were infrequent. Reports about shepherds and special babies were unlikely to be read.

But not long after the shepherds, wise men from far-off places came to him, talking of a baby. Of a baby that was to be, so they said, 'King of the Jews'. They had seen signs, they said, a bright star, they said. And Great Herod, mighty king, was filled with a mad fear of a poor baby born in a stable, who was going to steal his kingdom. With a heavy and transparent cunning he told the wise men to find the child and bring him news so that he could do homage, prepare the way, make ready the throne.

He never saw the wise men again and he never found the baby. So he made the terrible order: 'Kill *all* the babies!' he said. 'All boy babies under two.' It was almost the last order he made. He was dead soon after. And never another word of the baby.

It is nearly forty years ago. Indeed I am old. I saw many changes after Herod, many. The country was divided among such sons as were still alive. Men of cruelty and folly and weakness. The worst, Archelaus, banished by the Romans after ten years, who would have no more kings of Judea. From then on, the country was run by procurators, who were Roman. I knew many. The one I remember most clearly was Pilate. Pontius Pilate.

———

Here Sylvanus stopped, saying he was tired, having been unwell recently. He said he would be happy to speak again another time. He kept his promise. On page 370.

Chapter 2

THE GROWING UP

Ezra

About sixty. Small, silvery. A lined, intelligent face, with deep-sunk rather piercing eyes. An impression of neatness in both appearance and posture. A contained, still man. A clear, educated voice.

Although, as you say, Damascus is an important place on a main trade route, which means that Damascus knows quickly what has happened elsewhere, it does not necessarily follow that all who live here in Damascus are quite so well informed. The high wall enclosing this garden is no accident. Neither is the rather secluded position of my little house. I work at my own speed, in gold and silver and precious stones. I do not need the world shouting its news in my ear. I am not fond of the world, which shouts obscenities and is cruel. My friends are poets and painters and musicians, who call me, to my intense pleasure, artist. Not metalworker, or craftsman, but artist.

So, if you sit and tell me that a Galilean preacher, executed by crucifixion nearly a year ago, was the youngster I knew twenty years ago in Nazareth, I must believe you. You seem an honest man, and certainly the matter of the caskets is convincing.

I lived in Nazareth for about three years in all. I've lived in many places. My main repute for many years was as a restorer, a repairer, of jewellery and articles of gold and silver. I still do. To make things new again gives me as much pleasure as to make new things. So I could live anywhere, in small towns or great cities, fairly sure of making a good living.

My house in Nazareth was small but adequate for my needs. I never married, and am well able to look after myself. The house was south of the market, in a street where a number of metalworkers lived. It was one of them, Samuel, who found me my house. It was also Samuel who brought me the casket. Samuel worked in iron and brass. Large work.

One day, not long after I'd moved in and set up my workshop, he visited me. We drank some wine and talked of this and that. Then he told me that a casket made of gold, inset with precious stones, had been brought to him for repair. Not his kind of work at all. He had explained to the woman and she had taken it away again.

'Woman?' I said. Samuel then went on to explain that the way the woman was dressed, simply, like a workman's wife, had also made him unwilling to touch the casket. 'Which was gorgeous,' he told me, 'Babylonian, or Armenian work. Superb, beyond price.'

I was curious. I sensed a mystery. I told Samuel to send the woman to me. He promised to do so if he saw her again, for she'd left no name. A week or two passed and then he told me he had been fitting a wrought screen in a house and the joiner doing the cupboards and windows was one day brought his lunch by the woman, who was his wife. Samuel had greeted her and mentioned my name.

Two or three days later she came to my house – with the casket. She had with her a boy, of about eleven years old. Her eldest son, she told me. He was good-looking, as she was. He resembled her. She carried the casket wrapped thickly in cloth. When I took off the cloth, it took my breath away. Quite superb. Worth a fortune. The woman listened to my rapture calmly. She was a calm, quiet person, with a look of great candour.

'Very few people have seen the box,' she told me. 'It was given to my son' (she put her hand on the boy's arm) 'shortly after he was born. By a wise man from far away who seemed to be very rich. There were three.'

'Three wise men?' I said.

'Yes,' she said, 'and three boxes. This one contains as you see small blocks of pure frankincense resin.'

It did, too. Quite full. The purest, whitest, I'd ever seen. I asked her about the other boxes, as she called them.

'One is of pure gold, without jewels,' she said, 'and contains gold. The other is like this one and also contains blocks of resin. Of myrrh.' Then she paused. I remember it so clearly. 'Myrrh,' she said, 'which is used in the purification of women and the anointing of kings. It is used in wine to deaden pain. It is used in the preparation of the dead for the grave, and in the ointment of embalming.'

It was said strangely. Not to inform, to show knowledge, but in an even flat voice. Then, with more animation, she told me what she wanted done. To repair and make new again. The work I love. The workmanship of the casket was wondrous. I knew that, in putting right the damage here and there and in its renovation, I would learn much, and I made that my excuse for promising to do the work at a very low price. The woman, her name was Mary, I recall, told me that they had little money anyway, and that her plan was that her husband Joseph would pay me in work. He was a skilled carpenter, she told me, and they often paid bills that way. Also, she said, the boy would give his services in any useful way.

I found her honesty and simplicity most attractive, and agreed. And so it was. I worked on all three caskets and was paid in benches and shelves and cupboards – and a beautiful hardwood workbench, which I use to this day. And when the family took the boy to Jerusalem to be confirmed at the age of thirteen, I looked after the boxes for them.

He was a pleasant boy. We became good friends. I would see him nearly every day. He would call in to see me if I needed anything and I grew to trust him completely. A steady lad, with good sense, and initiative. His father was teaching him to work in wood and I added a few lessons in metalwork. He was quick and dexterous. He enjoyed the company of older people, I think. He always seemed a little apart with boys of his own age. He was a good reader and loved the Scriptures, as I do, so we had lots in common.

I left Nazareth about nine months after his confirmation in Jerusalem. I was sad to leave. I made him a belt buckle in silver and bronze with his name, Jesus, engraved on it. I went far away to the North, and later to the East, and I lost touch with the family. Pity.

It is very sad to think that a pleasant boy like that should have come to such an end. He could have been no more than thirty-three or -four. Awful. I wonder if Mary somehow knew (women, I'm told, are remarkable in such things); I wonder if she knew in some way that her pleasant son would die young, and have myrrh, the gift of his birth, used in the anointment of his death. Poor Mary. Sad, sad indeed.

Eshtol

Early fifties. Tall, well-built, with a rather serious, scholarly expression. Grey hair and beard. The forefinger used much in speech, tutor-like. A warm voice, and strong.

I was born here in Jerusalem, and have always lived here. I've never wanted to live anywhere else. My father used to say – well, he still does – 'Why leave Jerusalem to see the world? The world comes here to Jerusalem!' It's true. It is a place of infinite variety, a different mood each day, a different colour. The Jerusalemite can be cruel and kind, warm and cold, stubborn and easily led – like the people of a major city anywhere. The city has much to be proud of – and some things of which it may be ashamed.

Last year's business with the Galilean preacher, Jesus of

Nazareth, is a happening many people would like to forget. I heard him preach a number of times. Remarkable. And in no way dangerous to law and order, I would have said. I was told he was a healer; he could cure disease and make the blind see. Certainly his followers work very hard to keep his memory and lessons alive. They will, I fear, get into the same trouble as their leader.

A friend of mine, a lawyer, told me that the preacher seemed to go out of his way to provoke the authorities, to make them angry, to make them look foolish. He gave offence, he ruffled feathers, he pricked pomposity in high places, he showed no respect for the Establishment. My friend says no wonder they killed him. And Jerusalem wept. And jeered. And stayed at home. And went in their thousands to the execution. Like people everywhere.

Perhaps, in its 'infinite variety', Jerusalem is best at the times of fast and feast. The festivals. Looking back – and I have played a small part in a great many such celebrations – I think I am right. I have always loved festival time. Passover, perhaps, more than all others.

Passover in Jerusalem was always, for me, full of beauty. I think the Temple had a lot to do with it. The gorgeous restoration by King Herod was one of the wonders of the world, and during the festivals a lot of extra people were taken on to help handle the huge crowds of extra worshippers and tourists. My family are of a priestly tribe and so I was eligible for these duties. But although of a priestly tribe, we were not priests, my father and I. We were both schoolteachers, but at Passover time, more than at any of the other festivals, we *felt* like priests. We looked forward to it.

Such a happy festival, with the wonderful stories of Great Moses leading the slaves out of Egypt, and the miracles of the parted sea and food from Heaven and the sweet water from the rock. And the plagues and the terrible visit to Egypt of the Angel of Death, who passed over the Jewish homes. The passing over of the Angel. The Passover. Every year in the Great Temple the youngsters' eyes used to grow wide at the story of the Angel. There were always a lot of youngsters. And always among them boys of twelve or thirteen brought by their parents to be made 'a son of the Law', a man. A lovely part of the service. I taught boys of that age, and I knew what terrors they could be, but during that day in their lives they were angels. Spotless, obedient, glowing with pride.

It was part of my job to see that when each family left the Temple they paid a courtesy visit to Solomon's Colonnade, in the great courtyard, where the elders and teachers held their open-air discussions. The boys and their parents would listen dutifully for a while to the rabbis and theologians and then go away to their celebrations and more interesting things. All quite understood and allowed for. These discussions, on the fine points of the Scriptures and the Laws and the sayings of the prophets, were *not* of much interest to the children. It was grown-up talk.

Occasionally a boy, well prepared by his father or teacher, would ask a question, and listen, rather dizzily, to the learned answers, and then go away. But there was one boy, I remember, who didn't go away for nearly a week! It's about twenty years ago, but he stays in the mind, that boy. Nearly a week. My father and I and the old teachers and rabbis became fascinated by him. He was a good-looking well-built boy. He'd come as usual, after his confirmation, with his parents, to watch and listen. One of a number of families, all from Nazareth. They all left, but, not long after, the boy came back. He sat and listened, with great respect, which was usual, but with a remarkable comprehension, which was not. Even in grown-ups. You sort of felt this deep understanding, and when he asked a question, it showed. He would listen to the answer – and then discuss it! Which was unheard of! Boys *listened* to their elders; they did not *discuss!* And many of the old teachers on these occasions were rather lordly and conceited. But there was something about this boy. All day, every day, he was there. The old men looked forward to seeing him, they shared their food with him, enjoyed him. 'Little Rabbi' they called him; 'the Teacher from Nazareth'. The boy's knowledge of the Scriptures and of all the 'Messiah prophecies' was truly astonishing. He was articulate and his voice was pleasant on the ear. He had none of the awkwardness, or sullenness, or shyness that most boys of that age have with adults. He seemed almost to prefer grown-ups to youngsters of his own age. He had a very pleasant smile, and his laugh was infectious. I arranged for him to sleep at night in one of the junior students' hostels.

After about five or six days his parents came for him. We thought they'd known where he was, but it seems they hadn't. They'd searched everywhere. They'd left the city with all the other families of their party, and had nearly arrived back in Nazareth before they'd noticed that our boy was not among all the other lads. His mother was very upset and worried – and told him so. Very out-of-character behaviour on his part, we gathered. She and the boy were obviously very close. Quite a young woman, I remember. The father was a good bit older.

The boy listened to his mother and took his telling-off well. With dignity. He apologized, to both his parents, correctly. Then he said, rather oddly, I thought, 'Didn't you know I'd be here? In the Temple? In my Father's house?' Then he said goodbye to us and went away. The old men missed him, and were sharp and cross with each other for a day or two.

My father, who is quite old, but of unimpaired memory, is given much to what he calls 'conjecture thinking'. For about a month he has been convinced that the Galilean, Jesus, and our boy were the same person. It may be because Passover is coming round again – and we always recall the boy – or it may, in fact, be so. It would be dangerous, I think, at this time, to start to ask questions – and to no purpose. If it is so, as I said to my father, more's the pity.

Zirim

About forty. A tall, graceful man. Clean-shaven, with dark, luxuriant hair and delicate features. Finely shaped eyebrows and large, expressive eyes. The mouth and hands are feminine, the voice musical, and soft. Clothes, jewellery, and perfume, of great taste.

Since Jesus was crucified, six years ago, a hundred legends and stories have grown up round him. Vast exaggerations and 'eye-witness accounts' by people who never laid eyes on him. A whole fellowship of followers and believers exists. To every side, people who knew him and loved him.

I knew him. And loved him. And will do so till I die. Which, believe me, is not so common here in Nazareth, where he grew up. He was right; no man is a prophet in his own town.

Most of the Fellowship, his followers and believers and disciples, knew him for about three years. From the start of his preaching and healing till his death. I knew him all his life. We were the same age. We lived near each other. We were boys together. At least, I say boys. Until I was about six I didn't know what I was. I was an only child, and my mother really wanted a girl, I think. So she dressed me like a girl, and made my hair pretty and so on, and kept me indoors, or in the garden. About the only outings I had were to synagogue.

I hated going to synagogue. The children knew I was a boy and they were very cruel. Not all of them. Not Jesus. One day Jesus's father came to our house to do some joinery. To make a cupboard in my bedroom. He thought I had a sister. When I told him the room and the clothes and pretty things were mine, he was surprised.

The next day he brought Jesus with him and we played in the garden. Jesus was my first friend. He never laughed at me, or called me names, or was cruel. The most elaborate and detailed stories are told today of his tolerance and love for others. Of his acceptance of people, no matter who they were, whatever they'd done. Well, let me tell you he had those qualities when he was six years old! Don't laugh at me, friend, I tell the truth. There *are* such children, full of love, and Jesus was one. Remember, I was a girl-boy, accepted by neither girls nor boys. I needed someone to be my friend – and to get me out of that garden – and to get my mother to change my way of dress! Jesus did all three. He was my only friend. Such 'boy' things as I did, I did with him.

My father had little time for me. He was a sport, an athlete. He wanted a son like himself, but was not strong enough to stop my mother's wanting me to be her daughter. He used to sneer and shout and bully. I hated him. He died of a seizure when I was nearly fourteen, about a year after Jesus and I had been to the Great Temple for our confirmation. To be made 'men in the eyes of God' as my old teacher used to put it. A poor joke in my case. I'm more woman than man – in anybody's eyes.

My father, as I said, died about a year later, and in the following year, at Passover time, Jesus asked me whether I would like to go with him to his aunt in Capernaum, on the Sea of Galilee, for a fishing and sailing holiday. My mother, who was still treating me like a child, wasn't keen, but Jesus's mother, Mary, talked her round.

It was the best holiday I ever had. We lived in the open. I don't know whether Jesus had told his aunt and uncle and cousins about me, but I was one of the family in about ten minutes. My clothes were too light, too gaily coloured (my mother to her dying day did not lose the habit), so I was given old stuff belonging to the cousins James and John. Jesus's aunt, Salome, told me to get as dirty and untidy as I liked, and stay that way – and then I'd be like *her* sons! She was marvellous to me. When I asked how I should address her husband, she said, 'Like everybody else does, just call him Zebedee!'

I got very brown and fit. James was a bit older than Jesus and I, and John a bit younger. They had just started in their father's fishing business, and Zebedee took Jesus and me on as extra hands, 'for bed, marvellous board, and not much money!' I can still hear him saying it.

There are few times in my life when I've felt like other men (most of the time I haven't wanted to), but I did on that holiday. I rose early, worked hard – and ate enough for three. After supper we would sing and drink wine till we were nearly asleep. Then to bed. A wonderful time. Wonderful.

I suppose, thinking about it, that on that holiday I became an adult, or whatever it's called. On that holiday James fell in love with a girl called Sara and later married her. On that holiday I fell in love too, I suppose. With Jesus. I don't know how else to put it. It was strange. For nearly ten years he had been my friend. My first and closest friend. My brother, my twin. I knew everything about him, as he did about me. Indeed, about my realization that I was more girl than boy, he alone knew.

I remember the moment. It is like a picture in my mind, a painting. We were about a mile off shore, in the smaller boat of the two Zebedee owned. It was a calm and beautiful day. We'd put our nets down and we were finishing our midday meal. There were just the four of us, and James was extolling the beauty and brains of his Sara. John was making ribald remarks, as brothers do, and Jesus and I were getting rather bored. Then James, who had little humour, got tongue-twisted and said something meaning quite the opposite of what he'd intended. I forget now what it was but we exploded. We lay back and we roared. James threatened us with a bucket of water but it made no difference. Then he looked at Jesus and began to laugh himself. Which was puzzling, for James hated to be laughed at. Well, it's difficult to explain, but Jesus was not laughing *at* James – John and I were laughing *at* him – Jesus was laughing, as freely as a child, because it was *funny.* His head was thrown back, his eyes were half closed against the sun, and his whole being was full of joy and happiness. He was naked to the waist, as we all were, and his skin was brown and smooth. His hair was long and untidy. I could draw how he looked.

The boat was full of laughter. Only I was silent. I wanted the moment to go on for ever. What is there like first love? I could hardly breathe. I was at once happier and more sad than ever in my life, before or since.

The moment passed, and everything was the same, and different. The holiday ended, and Jesus and I went back to Nazareth. I think my mother knew something had happened to me, we have always been very close, but I said nothing to anyone, certainly not to Jesus. I did not languish, or pine, or die for love. I saw my loved one nearly every day. He did not need to know. He had love for everyone, I loved only him. I was content. I did not have to disguise or change my ways, I was always affectionate and demonstrative, I had always admired him, had always said so.

The years passed, and when we were of an age to marry and neither of us did, the gossip started. I was by that time quite used to being called the various names for those of my kind. It was of no importance, there are many of us, but I did not want Jesus to be hurt in any way because we were friends. So my mother and I moved to Jerusalem. She raised no objection, indeed she was pleased to have her little boy to herself again. She never remarried, and we lived together until she died, about a year before Jesus did.

If you care for irony I can supply it. I am by profession an historian and teacher of history. At the time of Jesus's arrest and death I was teaching at the Pharisaical College and was also official recorder to Pilate. So, at the so-called trial of my childhood friend, I wore the badges of both Pharisee *and* Roman.

When Jesus died, I moved back here to Nazareth, to the house I grew up in. I have memories to last me a lifetime. I go for holidays to Capernaum. I have a little house there. And a boat.

Reuben

Elderly, slight. A slow speaker, looking often for the right word. Educated and widely read. Born in Perea, living for most of his life in Jerusalem and, later, Nazareth. A bachelor, slightly spinsterish in his ways, but open and friendly.

It is difficult for me to believe, even after nearly two years, that Jesus is dead. Or that he brought about his own execution, or that he created such violent upheavals and disturbances. I knew him well, he was a pupil of mine. I taught him Scripture. Not when he was a child. When I came to live in Nazareth he would have been about thirteen or fourteen. He was the eldest of five brothers and two sisters, and a very responsible boy indeed. He had to be. A big family and not a great deal of money coming in. His father Joseph was a fine joiner, a good careful craftsman, but a one-man business. In busy times he would hire another pair of hands, but not often. He made all the furniture in this house, Joseph did, and the doors and cupboards, too. He married late. Mary was much younger than he was. She is still only in her middle years, although I hear she has aged a lot since Jesus died. They were very close always, she and Jesus.

I was a scribe and legal clerk for most of my working life, and taught Scripture in my spare time. Not so much for the money, but because I like children, and I come of a family of scholars. My father and grandfather were rabbis, and many of my uncles were teachers. But I have never had very good health, and neither the altitude nor the tempo of Jerusalem really suited me, so I gave up my legal work and moved my home here to Nazareth. Nearly twenty years ago now. I have never married and my needs are few, and, once I was accepted by the town, they found a place for me. I became a teacher in my own pleasant house, which, as you see, is only two doors away from where Jesus and his family lived. He and I studied Scripture together until he was a grown man, until he left Nazareth.

They've all gone now. I miss them. An agreeable lot of people.

When Joseph died, Jesus was about eighteen or nineteen. He had been his father's right hand for some time, and took over as head of the family and bread winner. People liked him. He was practical and straightforward but no more ambitious than his father had been. As his brothers grew up, he taught them the skills of the trade as he had been taught by Joseph. Slowly, with patience. A born teacher. I once said that to him and he replied that he wanted his brothers to stay in the trade and know their craft because he had a feeling he would not always be a carpenter. Odd, that. For he did not say what he thought he would be – certainly not a preacher. His brother James, who came after Jesus, was the one with the preacher in him. Indeed, I hear that he is now very active in carrying on the work that Jesus began.

The family left here not long after Jesus left. They live in and around Capernaum. The two girls are married and I'm not sure where they live.

Mary is an interesting woman. Very quiet. A marvellous mother. One of those women born to be a mother. Very calm, very placid. A quiet voice. She ruled her brood with love, and no doubt still does. Judah, the youngest, was a very naughty boy, of violent temper, but she could calm him without raising her voice, almost without words. She has a quality of innocence, of being young. She has never lost the ability to be delighted, like a girl, by simple things. I miss her the most.

When we first heard about John the Baptizer here in Nazareth, Mary came in to see me. She told me that John could be related to her. She wasn't sure. She told me that just before Jesus was born she went to Jerusalem to visit an old couple who were cousins, or possibly her aunt and uncle, I can't remember. Her aunt, or cousin, told her that she, too, was pregnant and that the child was to be given to God to be brought up as a Nazarite, far away in the desert, to prepare him to do God's work. To 'prepare the way for one greater than he'. Mary said,

'So the Baptizer could be that baby. His parents died long ago.' She was quite excited. I said. 'It could be. Who is "the one greater than he", then?' The question had the strangest effect on her. She went very pale and I thought she was going to faint. I made her sit down. She was silent, looking into the distance as though she had just remembered something. Then she began to cry. She made no sound. She was like an unhappy child. Her eyes filled and the tears ran down.

Then Jesus walked in and went straight to her as if she'd called him. He knelt down and she rested her head against his shoulder like a tired little girl. He dried her eyes and they stood up. It is difficult to describe how they looked. Very still, very alone, separate. Apart, different, special in some way. Then Mary smiled and Jesus thanked me for looking after her and the moment passed.

It was only a few days after that, that Jesus told me he was going south to find John and be baptized. I was curious, for, since Joseph had died, Jesus had led the family in the same orthodox Jewishness always observed by Joseph. 'As a memorial,' he told me once, 'and because the religion is beautiful. My father loved beauty.' I was puzzled by this pleasant, hard-working carpenter's desire for baptism, which symbolizes cleansing, rebirth, repentance – none of which he seemed to need. I said so.

'You are an orthodox Jew,' I told him, 'and a good man. You do no one harm, and in your own way do a fair bit of good. You have a great knowledge and love of the Scriptures, for which I claim a modest credit, and you have an unblemished reputation both as a man and a craftsman. It seems a needless journey.'

He said, 'I have no choice, my teacher. My love and knowledge of the Scriptures indeed I owe to you. The meanings and prophecies I find in them are my own.'

It was oddly said. In no way abrupt, or rude. More as a statement of fact. I have thought about it often since his death. I think now that he meant that the prophecies and their meanings were about *him*, they were his *own*, it was *him* they meant. A frightening thought. The more so from a levelheaded, well-read young man. Certainly he had great knowledge of the words of the prophets. Often when we were discussing the inner meanings of this or that prophecy – a favourite intellectual exercise of mine – he would show surprise at my gropings and theories, and would say simply and with great certainty what was meant, especially by the prophecies telling of the coming of a Messiah. It was disturbing, for opinion upon such matters is usually offered only by our oldest sages – and then with hushed reverence, and tentatively.

I never checked him in this way of speaking, for usually there were just the two of us, and I did not mind. But, not long after he'd been baptized by John, he came back and preached in the synagogue here in much the same way. It gave great offence and nearly caused a riot. It was very ugly. The crowd threw him out of the synagogue and right out of the town. He never came back. I didn't blame him. In the middle of all the shouting that day in the synagogue he said, 'No man is special in the eyes of his family or neighbours.' It was quietly said, with some humour. Not many of us heard it.

I didn't see him again. Since he died, two years ago, I've heard a hundred stories about him. As a healer, as a miracle-worker, as a great preacher, as a prophet. Who knows what to believe? Perhaps his name will live on, who can tell?

Sarah

A large, fat, jolly woman, with a most infectious laugh, and a chuckling way of speaking. A great love for, and shrewdness about, people. Middle fifties.

When I first heard you were coming to see me, I thought you were a client – as my husband likes to call the people I work for – but I thought about it and I didn't see how you could be. People I find husbands or wives for don't just turn up, they are sent by people I know. Or they are relatives or friends of people I've arranged marriages for in the past. I suppose I'm the best-known matchmaker in this part of Galilee. Not just here in Nazareth, as far away as Nain and Cana! It's all recommendations, you know, I don't advertise. My husband says I'm good at making marriages because I'm nosey and a gossip and I know everybody's business. Well, maybe, but I *like* nearly everybody, too – and it's not that I'm so nosey (I am a bit), it's that people tell me things. Everybody talks to Sarah – and I listen more than I talk, believe me. I can be trusted, and people know it.

I'm not a clever woman, but I seem to be clever at putting people together. I don't think I've ever made a bad match. I'm not always successful, mind you. After all, *both* parties have to be willing. It's not only the girl's parents who come to me first, you know. Men are shyer than girls in most cases. Oh yes, positively. I won't deny I make a good living, but I don't do it only for the money. I get great happiness and satisfaction as well. I have ten thousand friends.

I was an only child and I know about loneliness. Sometimes I've seen someone and I've known at a glance that that person is lonely. Not sad, or unhappy – might be well known, have lots of friends – but I know that he or she is walking alone. What I call 'an apart person'. Now, to find a wife or husband for *that* person is a real happiness, a blessing from God – for God invented marrying.

Jesus was like that, you know. An apart person. Everybody liked him, and he was a friendly easy chap, with a nice voice and good manners. And good-looking, too. As things turned out, with him getting into so much terrible trouble and being executed, it would have been bad for any young woman I'd found for him. Great shame, he'd have made a good husband – and a wonderful father. You can take my word, I'm never wrong.

I'll be quite honest, I did try. About nine or ten years ago. He's been dead about a year and he left the town about three years before that, when he was about thirty. Yes, about nine years ago, when he was about twenty-four or -five. His father Joseph had been dead for some time and Jesus was head of the family and running a small joinery business with two of his brothers. I knew the family well, indeed Jesus did a number of jobs in this house. And I loved his mother, Mary, like a sister. I miss her very much, although I do see her from time to time. But it's not like her living round the corner, as she did for so many years. But she and the family were right to move away. Nazareth didn't deserve Jesus, who *was* a bit special. Still, it's over.

Well, as I say, I tried to find a nice wife for my carpenter. He wasn't a great catch really, a small-time woodworker of poor family. But he was hard-working and a good Jew. He knew his religion and observed it. And he was quite learned, too, you know.

Well, although Mary and her sons and daughters had exchanged many jokes with me, I'd done no business with them, as you might say. I always know when to stay away. But Jesus bothered me – and so did my middle daughter, Leah. Another apart person, another lone walker.

Now, I'm inclined to work by instinct. I trust my instinct – believe me, with good reason. But with Leah, who is precious to me, and with Jesus, I went slowly. I thought and thought. And I decided that I wanted him for my Leah. I wanted him in the family. He and Leah knew each other well. And that, you know, is the most difficult, to make old friends into sweethearts – and my Leah is no fool. She'd seen me at work too many times to be taken in by my little games. So I trod gently – a thing I'm not famous for – I went slowly. I found all sorts of woodwork that needed doing. I found lots of little messages for Leah to take round.

Well, I kept up this careful business for over two years and it didn't work. Although now, I think, Leah will love him till she dies. She is in Jerusalem with the Fellowship. When Jesus preached in the synagogue here, right at the start of his work, and the elders threw him out, Leah became his follower. One of the first. She came home and I knew at a glance she was in love. A shame, for I'd long given up hope. Oddly enough, and I've never told this to anyone before, my conviction that it was a lost cause as far as Jesus was concerned came from Mary. Truly. About two years *before* the synagogue business. You see, there's always a time when you bring the mothers together. A psychological moment, to talk in a different way.

Well, the mothers were Mary and me. And in five minutes I knew she wasn't making the right noises. Very strange. Never before. I'll never forger it. She told me she loved Leah like her own, and that she could want nobody better for Jesus, but that it would be wrong and cruel to offer brief happiness and great sorrow to so fine a girl. I was speechless. Was Jesus ill with some terrible disease? Was he a bad man who would ill-treat my daughter? What could Mary mean?

Then Mary, who was weeping, looked up. She looked heart-broken.

'Don't ask me too much,' she said, 'I can't answer in any way that makes sense. But, before Jesus was born, and in the Great Temple at his circumcision, I was told things that meant that my splendid son, who gives me so much happiness, will one day give me sadness like a sword piercing my very soul. I feel it will all come true, and not long from now. I cannot help being 'the woman of grief' in my son's life. I am his mother. You must protect Leah, my old friend, from such grief. She deserves better. Not a better man, there is no better, but a better life.'

Well, what could I do? Although, to be truthful, at that time they were not really closer than at any other time. There had always been a loving warmth. Jesus was a loving, warm person, like Mary. So I comforted Mary and told her there was nothing really to stop, it wasn't working anyway.

Odd how it's all come true. Leah will never marry, I don't think. But neither is she what Mary called 'a woman of grief'. She followed my carpenter to the end – and she saw that terrible end. Now she is with the Fellowship – and in her own way is one of the happiest people I know.

Chapter 3

THE START OF THE WORK

Yuri

Rather plump, with dark, curly hair and black, lively eyes. Rather sunburned and healthy-looking. A strong, cheerful voice. Good clothes. Well-furnished home.

I was very sad when the news came that John the Baptist was dead. That was what we heard first; that he was dead. It was quite some time after, that we heard how he died, how he was murdered in the prison at Machaerus. Terrible business, but that Herodias was a terrible woman. Not that Salome is much better. What a thing for the Tetrarch to do – on his birthday, too. Although he's not a tetrarch now, of course. He's nothing; an exile in Gaul. Herod Antipas, banished by the Romans, by Caligula. I hope he never comes back. Over ten years since John died. Nine since Jesus. Antipas could have helped spare both, but he did nothing. A weakling; a fool. As the sons of strong men often are. His father, Herod, was not called 'the Great' for nothing.

John and Jesus. Marvellous characters, both. Neither of them was on the scene for very long but they certainly made their presence felt. I miss them both. How different they were – although I'm told they were related to each other. Jesus made you calm, and sort of happy. John frightened the life out of you! Do you know, I was there when they met for the first time? I will never forget it. It was not very far from here, where the Jordan meets the Salt Sea.

I made a sort of living out of John. He, right from the first, attracted huge crowds, and crowds get hungry, and food has been my family's business for generations. We grow it, we store it, we preserve it, we pickle it – and when John drew the crowds we would go out and *cook* it – on the spot! We are famous for it. Not that John ever sampled any of our goods. He never seemed to eat or drink anything. He was a Nazarite – and there's no harder way to live. Never to own anything, never to drink wine, or cut the hair or beard, endless prayer, to always be separate, alone, close to God. To drive yourself all the time. John lived in the desert, in the dry heat. He went barefoot, and wore a robe of woven camel hair and a heavy leather belt. The Scriptures say that Elijah dressed like that – and was a similar sort of man. Some say John was Elijah reborn. I don't know about such things. Food is my business.

John would stand on a little hillock or on a rock and the crowds would gather. Hundreds, from all over. He would stand still, waiting. He had strange eyes, which, until he began to speak would be without light, looking inwards almost. His voice was powerful, rather hoarse, full of energy – and doom! He gave little comfort. 'Repent!' he would roar. 'Change! Alter your ways! Wash away your sins!' Then he would lead the way to the river, or a stream, and walk in chest-high, and the people would line up and go to him and he would pray and duck their heads for a moment. People would come out of the water and dry themselves in the sun or go and change. They always looked happier.

Well, it was at the end of one of these days. A lot of the people had gone. John looked very tired. I was nearby, clearing up. One or two of John's followers were near him. Suddenly there was a sort of hush and I looked up. John was face to face with a man who seemed as relaxed as John was tense. They were of similar build. The man was of fairer complexion. 'I have come to be baptized,' he said. 'Do you want my name?' 'I know who you are,' said John, 'I have preached of your coming since I began to baptize. I preach and baptize people to prepare them for you. It's for them, not you.' John went on and on, almost refusing. But Jesus insisted, and a most beautiful moment took place. I saw it.

It doesn't seem like all those years ago. People sometimes get cross with me – or jealous. 'You weren't there to be baptized,' they say. 'You weren't a follower, or disciple – of John *or* Jesus. You were a food-seller to the crowds! How come *you* were so close and saw so much?' Well, I wasn't a follower *then*, quite true. And I was close because a lot of the crowd had left and the Baptizer knew me. I fed his flocks. I cleared up after his flocks. He preached to them, and frightened them, and led them into the water and baptized them, and I sold them food and tidied up after them.

It was the end of the day. Late afternoon. The crowds had been huge. They usually were for John. He'd spoken in his usual doom-laden way, telling the people they must repent and change their lives; that they must *deserve* salvation. That being, as he put it, 'related to Abraham' carried no privileges. Powerful, sensible stuff. But also that day John had come back a number of times to the fact that he was only a 'messenger', to bring news of the coming of 'a great one'. 'I am nothing,' he shouted, in that hoarse, powerful voice, 'compared to him. I'm not fit to tie his shoe.' Many of the crowd that day were country folk, people of the land, and John used word-pictures they would understand. He always did; a marvellous man. 'The Great One will sort the chaff from the corn,' he told them. 'The chaff will be burnt. The rubbish on the threshing-floor will be cleaned away!' And so on. You must understand that at that time there was a great desire in people's hearts for a Messiah to come, a great hunger for a sort of new start. Everything had got so complicated; the simplicity had gone. The simple, great rules of Father Moses had become a vast rulebook that it seemed only the scribes and priests understood. John was simple. He made sense.

Anyway, as the sun was going down, there, suddenly, was Jesus. Asking to be baptized, in a simple, natural way. As I said, John was rather off balance. He didn't think it right. But Jesus insisted, and they went down to the river together. About fifty yards away. Some of John's followers went with them. I did, too. At the river bank John paused, but Jesus looked into his eyes and smiled and they walked into the water. The water looked lovely, catching the late sun. John didn't say much. Probably couldn't think of the right words in this special case. Understandable. When Jesus lowered his head beneath the water so did John. As the two dripping heads came up there was a change in the light. It was very odd. I looked up. We all did. Right across the sky, from the sun right across above us, there was a great band of light, as though we were looking up through an opening. Up into Heaven. Not a sunbeam; a gap. It was very quiet. No wind, no birdsong, no river noise, nothing. Then we saw, high up, a tiny, white, shining spot. It descended and became a bird, then, lower, a dove. A perfect beautiful dove. It flew down to Jesus and settled on his wet head. Then we heard a voice. A quiet, loving voice, like a father, which said, 'This is my beloved and only Son.' Now, whether I myself heard it, or whether only John heard it and told his followers and they told me, I'm not sure. It's a long time ago and a lot has happened. But I like to think I heard it, too.

Salome

Mid-sixties. A cheerful, down-to-earth woman, looking younger than her years. Grey, abundant hair. Dark eyes of great liveliness. Solidly built, but not fat. A feeling of strength, and honesty.

———————

Often I think how nice it would be if you could choose what your memory will hold. I've seen things I wish I could forget, and about other things I wish I could remember more. Ah, well!

You are not the first to ask me about when Jesus was a boy.

I like to talk about him, he was my favourite nephew, it's no effort to remember. When he was a young man and his father, my brother-in-law Joseph, died, and he took over the business, I saw him less, and remember less. About his twenties I know little. He and his brothers were running the little joinery and my own sons were giving me grandchildren. From thirty onwards, till his death, he was very much part of our lives here in Capernaum. James and John, my sons, were among the first to follow him. People sometimes say 'Yes, well, they were his cousins,' as though that explains everything. It explains nothing. For a lot of it there is no explanation. Mind you, it is a sort of 'family' story.

John the Baptizer was a second or third cousin. His mother, my Aunt Elizabeth, God rest her sweet soul, was the first person that my sister confided in about Jesus. My sister Mary was always different from me. *I* was the one more likely to get pregnant before I was married! Mary didn't say a word to me when she knew she was going to have a baby – she went to old Aunt Elizabeth. I asked Mary why, not long ago. After all, I was her older sister, I was already married – and a mother! 'Why?' I said, 'why not tell *me*?' She always told me everything. She told me she was 'sent' to Aunt Liz. That, in any case, she didn't think I'd believe that no man was involved. She was right. It's only since Jesus has gone that Mary has told me and one or two others the story of the angel. Now; Mary is a sad, middle-aged woman. A widow, who watched her firstborn – and favourite – son executed like a thief. But she is as sane and level-headed as you and I. An angel, she says.

I don't think too deeply about it. Joseph married her well before Jesus came and it was a good marriage. He was a good man. Older than Mary, quite a lot older, but he was right for her. To this day Mary has a sort of 'young girl' quality, almost virginal. She adored our father. Maybe she found in Joseph a sort of another father. My husband, Zebedee, always said that Joseph was another Heli – our father.

As I say, I remember the early years more clearly than the later ones. Jesus would come and stay for weeks, either alone or with a friend – or one or two of his brothers. This has always been an open house, and it's always easy for a fisherman to feed his guests. And always work for them to help with. The youngsters used to love going out on the boats. They were perhaps the best years, when the boys were becoming men. My two married in their twenties. Happy times.

It was quite a surprise to me when one day James said he was going south to hear John the Baptizer preach. It was an even bigger surprise when he came back and told us he had become a sort of disciple. I didn't take it too seriously. I asked him what was so special about immersion in water. 'You spend half your life immersed in water,' I told him, 'it's your living!' He laughed. And next time he went to hear the Baptizer he took his brother John.

Zebedee and I weren't too worried. They were both grown men and they worked hard on the boats when they were here. No harm. I think now that the Almighty was preparing us for when they both decided to go with cousin Jesus. To go *with* him, to be with him all the time.

It began in this room. Jesus was here on a visit and James had just come back again from John the Baptizer. He was full of it. Jesus listened to every word as though he'd been sort of expecting to hear such things. He found out where the next baptism meeting was to be and made a note of it. Not long after that he and John met and John baptized him. And it began.

You know, it was very difficult for me to see Jesus in a different way. I'd known him all his life pretty well, he was like a son. And then suddenly he was a preacher – and a healer. He cured many round these parts. People I know. A positive gift. Remarkable. A young carpenter from Nazareth. And compared to my James and John, poor. They'd done very well, my two. They and my husband were in partnership with Jonas's sons, Andrew and Simon – although Jesus changed Simon's name to Peter, and changed a great deal else round here, too.

I'll be quite honest, I didn't like it. I've always been ambitious for my sons. The family came first. My Zebedee, bless him, was an energetic and well-liked man and he built a fair-sized business. We lived very comfortably, we lacked for nothing. We have another house in Jerusalem – where Mary now lives, with John and his family. Well, with his family more than John, who's hardly ever at home.

You see, it was so quick. One day the boys came round for supper and said that the Baptizer had called Jesus the 'waited-for Saviour' and, in no time at all, it seemed, Jesus was the most talked-about person in Israel. A marvellous speaker – and a man who seemingly could cure any disease or ailment. People would travel great distances – and wait for hours – just to see him, to hear him, to have him touch them and make them well again. Jesus, my favourite nephew, who used to help his Uncle Zeb to gut fish – and his Aunt Sal to cook them!

I must admit that, when James and John decided to leave the business to become full-time helpers of Jesus, I was against it. When they told me that Andrew and Simon were going to do the same, I thought they were all mad. Oddly, Zebedee accepted it. He somehow knew nothing would change what was to be.

I got very cross with Jesus once. He may not have meant to hurt Mary, but he did. I told him off about it. He hadn't been home to Nazareth for some months, and Mary was missing him. So she came here to Capernaum with her four other sons. They arrived in the evening, and Jesus was holding a big meeting, so I took them round to the hall where he was speaking. We went round to the back and I told them to wait while I went inside and told Jesus they were there.

The place was packed to the doors. He was by himself on a platform. I wrote a little message saying his family were outside waiting to greet him and had it passed to him. He took it, read it, and said to the audience: 'I am told that my family, my mother and brothers, are outside. Who are my family? Who are *really* my family? Anyone who does the will of God is my family.

They are to me mother and brother and sister.'

Yes. Very clever point. But Mary heard it and was very hurt indeed. As I would have been, too. Needless and tactless. I told my miracle-working nephew exactly what I thought of him. He saw my point.

And yet you know, people are funny. I was just as insensitive to him once. Not long before he was executed. I think of it often and I always feel badly about it. Being ambitious for one's children is no excuse.

It was like this. One day James and John were home having a meal with their father and me, a rare thing. As often before, they were trying to explain to me what it was all about. Jesus's mission I mean, his campaign. The Kingdom of God and so on. Well, I got it into my mind that a sort of new order of things was to come on earth, with God's help, and that Jesus was to be in charge. The King. And all the miracles and healings and so on were to show people he was the right man for the post. Well, I thought, my boys were almost his first helpers, so they ought to get good jobs. I'll see to it, I thought, after all, I'm their mother.

So some time after this I heard that Jesus and the Twelve were going up to Jerusalem, and I decided that the time was right to go and talk to Jesus about the good jobs for my James and John. The time could not have been more wrong, but I wasn't to know.

I caught them up just outside Jericho, on the hill road. They were surprised to see me. They all looked rather serious.

Jesus greeted me and asked if he could help me in any way. I knelt down in front of him. I thought it right as he was soon to be a king. He looked rather startled. I said, rather formally, that I had come to ask a favour.

'What is it you want?' he said.

'When you are King,' I said, 'will you grant that these two sons of mine, your cousins and first followers, will sit on either side of you?'

Jesus helped me to my feet. James and John were as embarrassed and put out as the rest of the Twelve. They were all very cross and voices started to rise. Jesus stopped it, and, as often before, put it in simple terms. I think for my benefit. He explained that absolute power, in a heathen way, was not the idea at all. That the new kind of king, or leader, was not one who was served, but who served others. 'As I was telling you just before my aunt arrived,' he told them, 'soon I will be betrayed and condemned to death. I will be ridiculed and flogged and crucified. But through giving *my* life, many others will know a *better* life, will be set free. Thus *I* will serve *them*.'

Can you imagine how I felt? Could I have chosen a worse time to open my stupid mouth? Especially as it all came true.

Jonas

A large, handsome man, rather overweight and of florid colouring. About fifty-five. Greying hair and brown eyes. A humorous, amused expression. A warm, throaty voice, with expansive hand gestures.

When you sent me the message that you were going to pay me a visit so that we could talk about that wedding, I was rather surprised. For two reasons. Firstly, the wedding was quite some time ago. What is it, about six years? And secondly, I have very few visitors, let alone someone who comes a long way specially to see me and listen to me. My company and my conversation are not sought in this little town. Well, I can see their point. Here, in Cana, we have a town genius and a town idiot and a town ladies' man. I suppose I'm the town drunk. Not all the time, but often enough to support my reputation. Ah, well, never mind. Large villages or small towns are all alike, and Cana is no different. You'd think that the fact that the Carpenter was here twice and did magic both times would make a difference, but no.

The first time was at the wedding. I was told it was his first bit of magic anywhere. I was surprised to be asked to the wedding. I'm inclined to get a bit noisy in drink. Not quarrelsome or nasty; noisy. I sing and dance. Well, everybody should at a wedding. Anyway, I was there. The bridegroom was a nephew twice removed or something. The bride was related in some way to the Carpenter. His mother and brothers were there. She is a pleasant woman, Mary. Didn't really deserve all the trouble that came her way. Terrible thing to have a well-educated son put to death like a thief, with thieves. Terrible . . .

Where was I? Oh yes, the wedding. It was a fair-sized affair. The bride's father, whom I'd known a very long time, had done his daughter rather well. Tables inside and outside the house, a master of ceremonies, and plenty to eat and drink. Well, rather more to eat than to drink, I thought, but that I expected. He was worse than me when we were young but he married a strong-minded wife and she tidied him up. Maybe I should have married . . . although I don't know.

Anyway, it was a very happy affair. It was very nice to see Mary. I'd been quite friendly with her husband too, Joseph. He's been dead quite a long time. He was of Nazareth. I'm found of Nazareth, although the people are a bit too straitlaced for me. I remember Mary was quite excited. She hadn't seen Jesus for some time. He'd gone south to see his kinsman, the Baptist, John. Another sad death, that one. Awful.

I'm not sure, but I think Jesus came late. I'm never sure about anything after I've been at a party for an hour or two. But I do remember quite clearly that he didn't arrive alone. He had, I believe, four others with him. Two brothers, who were fishermen, I remember, and Philip and Nathanael from Bethsaida, the other side of Capernaum. I knew *them* both quite well. I was surprised to see Nathanael with the Carpenter, for he had no opinion at all of anything or anyone from Nazareth! But they all seemed very close friends and very ready for a party. Which was a pity, because about five minutes before they arrived the wine had run out! The master of ceremonies was most embarrassed. So was our host, the bride's father. *He* deserved to be. I could hardly keep a straight face. I'd done my share but I wasn't the only one singing and dancing, I can tell you.

Well, I'm not sure exactly what did happen then. There was a sort of discussion between Mary and Jesus and his friends and a running to and fro by servants between the well and the great water jars on the porch. I was in the garden with the master of ceremonies, who was very put out. Very dignified man. An old friend. Then a servant came out with a goblet on a tray. My old friend tasted it and his face lit up. 'Is there more?' he said to the servant. 'Gallons and gallons!' said the servant. My old friend, as was his job, made a graceful speech to the guests pointing out that *this* host, contrary to custom, saved *his* best wine till last. He was right, it was a marvellous wine. Mary told me during the evening that Jesus made it. I told the Carpenter he was in the wrong trade. He thought it was a good joke.

Amos

A heavily built man of about sixty-two or -three. A feeling of wealth and authority. Well-spoken, with some humour. Large, well-shaped hands, used much in speech. A keen-eyed, alert look.

———————————

It's odd, I think, how hearing about someone or something after a long time sets the memory off. All sorts of connected details come to mind. In council this morning someone asked if there was any truth in the rumour that Pontius Pilate had committed suicide, that he couldn't get over his recall in disgrace to Rome and his banishment, and that he'd killed himself. I doubt it. I never liked him and I was pleased to see him go, the new chap is better, but, as I say, mention of Pilate – after, what is it, two years since he went? – sparked off all sorts of memories.

A trip I made to Nazareth came into my mind. With great clarity – and it's at least ten or eleven years ago. My wife said she would like to visit her brother in Nazareth. I was happy to agree. I had always had a sort of sentimental liking for the place. My wife came from Nazareth and we had first met there. I myself was born in Jerusalem, and, when we were married, we made our home in the city. My work, both as a merchant and as a councillor, made it necessary. My work also kept me very busy, and opportunities to go visiting family were few.

But it was the time of year when business was a bit slack and I had a little time. So when she said, 'Amos, let's go to Nazareth,' I said yes. Not that I liked her brother so much – he was rather too strait-laced for me – but because our visit was going to coincide with a visit to the town by this young preacher that people were talking about. Jesus. All sorts of stories were going round about him. How he'd turned water into wine; how he healed people; and did miracles; and was the Messiah – all sorts of stories.

One story I know was true – although it was some time after our trip to Nazareth. He threw all the money changers out of the Temple. Caused a great disturbance. It was discussed in council. A rather foolish action in many ways. Temple dues and offerings had to be paid in the shekels of Judea and people came from everywhere in the world to the Great Temple. The money changers were necessary. Perhaps some were a bit dishonest, but, nevertheless, a foolish action.

Not long after I'd first heard of Jesus, my interest in him was increased by a fellow-councillor's rather odd reaction to something I said. This fellow-councillor's name was Joseph, an old friend of mine. He came from Arimathea, a pleasant place near Jaffa – where Jonah caught the boat to Tarshish. 'Joseph,' I said, 'this Jesus is going to make a lot of enemies.' 'Maybe,' said Joseph, 'maybe. But I would give a great deal to be his friend.' I was surprised. Joseph of Arimathea was not young. He was rich and an orthodox Jew of good family. A level, cultured, worldly man. 'He preaches like no one else,' Joseph said, 'very simply. He teaches. He tells stories to show a point. He gives off a sort of love.' So, when Joseph told me that Jesus was going back to his home town of Nazareth to preach and my wife told me she wanted to see her brother, I made time. Joseph came, too.

Well, the young man did speak well – and caused nearly as big a disturbance as with the money changers! He spoke in the synagogue, on the Sabbath. He read from some of the prophecies of Isaiah and then made the lesson sound as though the prophecies referred to him! Caused quite a commotion. People knew him to be one of the local carpenters, a poor man. They said rude things. The young preacher took it well. 'No man is a prophet in his own town,' he said – and started to develop the point! The people got very angry indeed. They ran him out of town. I found the whole thing rather amusing. 'Still want to be his friend?' I said to Joseph. He was pale. 'More than ever,' he said, 'more than ever. I am a weak man and a coward. And to follow Jesus needs courage; the sort of courage I don't possess. But I will find a way to be his friend. I'll find a way.'

He did, too. And it took plenty of courage. I don't refer to his taking no part in the show of hands when Jesus was sentenced to death – a number of us abstained – but to his going to Pontius Pilate afterwards to ask for the body. Pilate was not only sick to death of the whole affair but he was also a very cruel man with great power. It would have been quite in character for him to have suggested that Joseph join his friend on the cross. Another thing that made the action brave was that the mob, although quieter after the crucifixion, was still unreliable, and could have taken Joseph's request to be proof that he was a disciple. A very dangerous thing to be on that day. All the disciples had gone into hiding. As I say, a brave man, Joseph.

Chapter 4

GREAT HAPPENINGS

Rebekah

Late thirties. Rather plump. Fresh-complexioned, with dark hair and eyes. A relaxed and happy person. A clear voice of low pitch. An expressive face, in repose rather plain.

Simon, whom they now call Peter, is married to my younger sister. Andrew, his brother, is married to my second cousin, also younger than I am. I didn't think I would ever get married. But I am, and to the only man I ever loved, and I owe it all to the Carpenter. Jesus is dead, and gone. It's nearly four years since they killed him and I miss him as much now as I did when I first heard about it. I named my little boy Jesus.

My mother lives with me now. Seven years ago, when Jesus first came to Capernaum, I lived with her, in Simon's house. Not far from the synagogue and nearer to the shore, where the boats were kept. Andrew lived about four streets away. We lived well. Simon and Andrew and the sons of Zebedee made a good living as fishermen. They'd never done anything else. It's difficult to think of them now as preachers and healers. Jesus brought many changes to this family.

I've known my husband Yigal since we were children. We are much the same age.

When I was about sixteen and beginning to think about getting married, Yigal had his first attack. He tore his clothes and ran through the town screaming about death and devils. He frothed at the mouth and was like an animal. He did not harm anyone, although by the time he was cornered and locked up, he himself was scratched and bleeding.

The elders and doctors of the town examined him and then told my father that Yigal was possessed by a demon and that he would be kept locked up for a time. They said that marriage was out of the question, that the Laws of Moses forbade it, and that the Prince of Darkness would use the demon to father devil-children and crippled freaks, who would be blind or have extra limbs.

Yigal was kept locked up for nearly a year. He was calm and normal and remembered nothing of his attack. He was allowed out, and about a month later, when we were alone together in the little park near the jetty, it happened again. He went as white as a sheet and rigid in every limb. His eyes became huge and staring, seeing terrible things. Then he started to scream. I could do nothing with him at all. People came and he was put away again.

And so the years passed. My younger sister married Simon, and I prayed for Yigal. His attacks became more frequent, but, because he never harmed anyone but himself when he fell down or knocked into things, he was not locked away for more than a day or two. He would spend a lot of time in and around the synagogue sweeping and polishing and planting flowers. He knew every word of every service. People got used to him. He was harmless. The town loony, some people called him. Despite the fact that, when he was all right, he was as sane as – and better educated than – most of the people who called him names.

Then my father died, and my mother became ill. She used to feel faint and get a blinding headache and a terrible fever would begin. She would pour with sweat, and shiver. It would last sometimes for days, and would leave her weak and pale for a week or more. Simon was marvellous. He took us both into his house, so that my mother could have both her daughters near her when she was ill. It was practical and kindly. Poor Yigal would come occasionally for a meal, but he was poor company. Over the years he had become silent and frightened of his 'demon' as he called his illness.

Then one day Andrew started talking about the Baptizer, John, who was preaching in the South. Andrew became a follower, and would go to hear John whenever he could. One day he took Simon, and they both came back talking about another person, a kinsman of John called Jesus, from Nazareth, not far from here. It seemed that John himself thought Jesus was very special in some way.

Well, about two months after that, Simon came in very excited and told us that this Jesus had decided to leave his home town of Nazareth and come and live here in Capernaum. My mother and I were a bit worried by the news, for Andrew and Simon – and the Zebedee boys, too, James and John – seemed to talk of nothing else but Jesus, whom hardly anyone had ever heard of. Simon told us that Jesus would arrive that night and stay with Andrew, and the next day, Sabbath, would speak in the synagogue. 'You come, too,' he said to my mother and myself. 'If you are there, Yigal will behave. You know how any sort of excitement sets him off.'

We said we would, but the next morning my poor mother began one of her bad turns, as bad as any she'd ever had. My sister stayed in to look after her and I went alone to the synagogue. Partly to keep an eye on Yigal but mainly to see this Jesus. The synagogue was packed. So was the women's section behind the lattice, which cut down how much I could see, except at the side, where there was a gap. But I was late and the space near the gap was crowded, and no one would move. So I heard more than I saw.

The service was normal up to the part where the rabbi or teacher speaks. Which was to be Jesus. He was the day's rabbi. He had a marvellous voice. Deep and strong, with a Galilean accent, which can be harsh, but in his case wasn't. He spoke simply, and seemed to have a sort of certainty, authority. We listened to it all and understood every word. He made word-pictures that we knew about, of fishermen, and boats, and catches, and working together, and mending nets, and being watchful of the clouds, to look upward often.

When he finished, there was absolute silence. Then Yigal began to scream at the top of his voice. It was absolutely unexpected, and frightened people out of their wits. Then I heard Jesus's voice cut into the screaming like a knife and cut it off. I fought my way through the crowd in the corner and looked through the gap. Yigal had fallen down and Jesus was helping him up. Yigal looked dazed but at peace, and happy. They walked out together, like friends. There was pandemonium. When I caught them up, Simon and Andrew were with them. I took Yigal's hand and he turned his head and looked at me. He looked different, the frightened look had gone. 'No more demons,' he said. 'Jesus said so. I'm cured.' And I knew it was true. I had no doubts at all.

I told Simon about my mother being so unwell, and he told Jesus. When we got home, we went straight through to her room. She was in a terrible state, shivering and flushed and burning hot. Soaked with perspiration.

Jesus stood near her bed and looked down at her. Her head stopped rolling from side to side and her eyes opened and looked into his. The shivering slowly stopped. A shudder went through her once or twice and then she was still. Jesus touched her hand. 'Come,' he said, and he and the men left. My mother got up immediately, and by the time my sister and I had helped her wash and change and do her hair, her high colour had gone and she was bossing us and worrying what to make for lunch.

The stories of my mother and Yigal spread like the wind, and, by the time the sun went down, there were hundreds of people outside the house. Sick people and their friends or families who'd brought them. Jesus put his hand on them one by one and made them better, even those with demons, like Yigal. The elders withdrew their objection and Yigal and I were married in the Spring. Jesus came to the wedding and he and the disciples (there were twelve by then) gave us a gift. It was a little demon, made of copper.

Noach

About forty-two. Lean, strong-looking. In rough-weave robe and sandals. Uncut hair and beard. Lively, intelligent eyes. A friendly man, a warm, genuine smile, a deep voice.

———————

You are not the first to ask me about the time that John the Baptist was in prison at Machaerus. Although it gives me some sadness to recall that time. I am content to do so – even glad – for it helps to keep fresh in my mind many remarkable things. It brings poor John back to life for me. Preaching, his face lifted to the sky, not locked away in Machaerus. Free, a voice. Not a silenced prisoner.

Machaerus. It was a strange place. More a fortress, or a fortified palace, than a prison. By itself. About five miles east of the Salt Sea, the Dead Sea. Enormously thick walls of the black rock common in that area. When Herod Antipas sent John there, six of us went with him. He was locked up. We, his followers, were not. We could come and go.

For John, one of the worst things about Machaerus was being shut away from the desert and the open air. He asked us for nothing; food and drink and comfort meant nothing to him.

'Go,' he would say to us, 'go everywhere. Bring me news of my kinsman Jesus. One of the things that sustains me in this place is the sureness in my mind that he was the one whose coming I was put on earth to announce. The Son of God. Bring me news.' And we would. But, as the time passed, we began to sense in John a doubt. He was no longer so sure in his mind. And one day he said to us, 'Go to Jesus and ask him plainly, for me, if he is the one. Or are we to look for someone else?'

We found Jesus up in the North, in Galilee, just ending one of his great healing meetings. We gave the message. He knew us. He told us to look around, to see for ourselves, to talk to people, and to go back and tell John of the cures, the spreading of God's word, the miracles of healing. 'Tell John,' he said, 'not to lose faith. Tell him his work goes on, his words live. His words were truth – and cannot be imprisoned. His words are free. Tell him I am the one.'

The two eldest of us went back right away to John. My cousin and I stayed behind. Huge crowds. Invalids and cripples and blind people. I spoke to John and James Zebedee, the first two followers of Jesus. We come from the same village in Galilee, we went to school together. They looked exhausted and dazed and spoke of the unbelievable and miraculous things they'd seen. 'Lepers have been cured,' John told me, 'people blind since birth have been made to see, the dead brought back to life.' Now, John and James were just ordinary fishermen. Rough, matter-of-fact men. Not men to be fooled, or easily taken in. I wandered about. I saw big Simon, now called Peter, and Andrew his brother. Matthew the tax-collector was there, looking much the same as before he decided to follow Jesus, but much more at peace. He was busy; they all were, all the disciples. They all seemed to have great skill in organizing the crowds. There was a sense of order, of peace. It is hard to describe.

I met that day Judas Iscariot. I didn't like him. Not a happy man. Hard, ambitious, but with a great belief in Jesus. For Judas, to be a friend of God's Son was important. John the Baptist was to him a fool for getting himself put in prison through being tactless. He said to me, 'If he'd watched his tongue, he could have been here today with us!' When I pointed out that Jesus wasn't too tactful either at times, he shouted, 'It's not the same!' and walked away.

Jesus did not think John a fool. Or anybody. Not even people who were. He finished the great meeting with a long speech all about John. A wonderful speech; it made me proud. 'A true prophet,' he called him, 'and far more than a prophet.' The huge crowd were silent, listening to every word. 'No one greater than John was ever born of man,' said Jesus. 'The man whose coming and purpose was foretold in the Scriptures. A messenger, a bringer of awaited news, a preparer of the way. The new way. Compared to great John,' Jesus told them, 'many people are like children who play in market-places at silly games. Children not old enough to recognize honesty and truth. John, who has lived all his life close to God in the most austere and self-disciplined way, is called by such people "crazy".' Then Jesus touched almost with humour on the dangers of him and his followers being 'normal', like every-one else, enjoying life. 'Then we are called gluttons! Who mix in bad company, who are *too* ordinary!' It was a wonderful speech. I wish John could have been there. The disciples were beaming. Not Judas. He was cross at Jesus for giving all the credit, as he put it, to the Baptist. I was never comfortable with Judas. Strange man.

My cousin and I moved on with Jesus and the disciples. We joined in, we helped, we saw astonishing things. When, a few weeks later, we arrived back at Machaerus, we were elated, full of news for John.

We were too late. Two days before, he had been beheaded, by order of Antipas – and his head passed round and shown to people as though it were a curiosity, a hunting trophy. I was told recently that Antipas has not slept well since; that, for a time, he believed that Jesus got his power from dead John; that, in the death of Jesus the year before last, he thought peace of mind would return. I was told that it has not. It seems just.

Hesseth

About sixty-two years old. Retired palace official, living now in a small villa on the shore of the Sea of Galilee. A quiet, rather sad-faced man, of slim build. Pale-complexioned, with grey eyes. A reader, and gardener.

If Antipas had not married his brother's wife, my son might be alive today. Equally he might not. He was a soldier, and soldiers get killed in the course of their work. But, when Antipas decided to marry his brother's wife, he was married already. To a princess of Arabia – and a beautiful woman. He must have known that her father would see it as a terrible insult, as it was. And her father, King Aretas, took terrible revenge. He sent in an army and absolutely wiped out the army of Antipas, my son included. A bad time, a bad time. My wife will never get over it.

I've known Antipas since he was a boy. He was always jealous of his brother, Philip. Well, half-brother really. Different mothers. King Herod, their father, had ten wives. Vast 'inter-relating'. Not unusual in the great families. When Philip married Herodias, who caused all the trouble, in my opinion, he was marrying his *niece*. As a marriage, it seemed to work all right. They had a daughter, Salome, who, in her own way, was to cause nearly as much trouble as her mother.

When it was rumoured that Herodias was going to leave Philip and marry Antipas, I didn't believe it. I served the court all my life, and always in a personal-guard, close-to-the-throne, man-in-waiting sort of way. We knew everything.

But, apart from what seemed foolishness – and dangerous (as was proved when the army was destroyed) – it was also against Holy Law. Not that Antipas observed very much in the way of law, Holy or otherwise, but it was just not done to marry your brother's wife.

It is forbidden by God. It is written. As I say, I didn't believe it. I didn't believe that Antipas would make such a decision. I remember telling my wife, and her saying, 'Maybe Herodias made the decision that he would marry her. Women often do make up men's minds for them.' My wife was right.

A very strong-minded woman, Herodias. An immoral, cruel woman. But, in her own way, loyal. When Antipas went into exile some years ago, she went with him. An ambitious, hard woman. A good hater, as my wife would say. Certainly she hated John the Baptist. She never forgave him for denouncing her marriage to Antipas – and she arranged a dreadful death for him.

I met John. The day before he was killed. A very special sort of man I think. Quite fearless. Whilst the priests and the court whispered behind their hands about the marriage, he shouted how evil and wrong it was at the top of his voice. Everywhere. Until he was arrested.

They put him in the fort at Machaerus, by the Dead Sea, where only the desert hears a loud voice. I might never have met him, but once a year, on his birthday, Antipas used to move the whole court down to Machaerus for a few days, for a big celebration. A lot of guests, music, dancing, everything.

I did not think it was going to take place that year, because there were already rumours that the King of Arabia was massing his armies to wipe out the insult to his daughter, but the rumours were ignored by Antipas, who was quite besotted by his new wife. She dominated him, and everyone else, too. Frightening woman.

I was curious about John the Baptist. My son had heard him speak a number of times, and had become a sort of follower. Very little impressed my son, who was a regular soldier and a tall, powerful, outdoor sort of man. 'John makes you uncomfortable,' he used to say to me, 'stops you being self-satisfied, and too complacent.' I'd heard how thin and sunburned John was, how he dressed like a beggar-monk, how he had lived most of his life in the desert, in caves or tents.

When I met him he'd been in prison some time. Not so much in a cell or dungeon, as just locked up, to keep him quiet. It was in the afternoon. The King's apartments in the fort are far from the prison block. Machaerus is huge. I was taken down by a young warder. What I didn't expect was the stillness of John. And the remarkable eyes. They burned. They were more open than most people's, and you got the impression that they saw more. My son was right, he made you uncomfortable. I was aware of his own simple integrity, and, by comparison, the whole hill of rubbish in which I crawled. I remember thinking, as I sat down, that the choice of scented oil for my beard that morning had taken me twenty minutes. The curling of my beard by my servant, a half-hour.

I spoke to him about the birthday celebrations, and asked if he needed anything. He said he required nothing. He would not mention either Antipas or Herodias by name and had only contempt for them. Suddenly he asked me about Jesus, of Nazareth. 'My kinsman,' he said, 'a great man, a prophet sent by God. Jesus, whose birth and coming were foretold in the Scriptures.' I told him that I had heard of Jesus, that he was preaching regularly, that he was becoming well known, that he was said to be able to heal the sick and cure disease. He listened to me with his whole attention, without blinking. 'Then I am content,' he said.

The next evening was the great party. The biggest ever. Herodias had a great flair for such things. Every kind of rare food and drink, and between courses the most unusual and exotic entertainers. Drugs and aphrodisiacs were in the food and drink. The most sensual music was played, the heaviest incense perfume was burnt. 'There is no such thing as an orgy,' she used to say, 'only freedom. At my parties no one must wish, or desire, or want. Every wish and desire and want must be gratified.' She was decadence itself, a whore-mistress, a witch – for she knew men's minds. In the main, people, in her company, became as rotten as she was. She could bring out the worst.

Well, you know the story of how the night ended. Salome danced for the guests and Herodias told Antipas that the dance was his gift. She hinted that the dancer, her daughter, might also be his for a while. The company roared, although it was not a joke, and Antipas, who was more drunk and inflamed than his guests, told Salome she could have anything she desired. Then there was a silence, and the girl stood staring at her mother, who looked like a mad sorceress. The girl, I swear, was bewitched. She asked for the head of John. Then Herodias turned her eyes on

Antipas and gestured that an officer swordsman should be sent to do it immediately. Antipas, too drunk with wine and pride to retract, gave the order and the officer left. Some people started to sober up and wanted to leave, but Herodias forbade anyone to go. 'Not until my husband's order has been obeyed!' she screamed. 'Antipas, son of Herod the Great, must be obeyed!'

So we sat and waited. Then the main doors were flung open and the officer came in with four soldiers, marching. He carried in a shallow silver dish the severed head of the Baptist. The eyes were open. The officer strutted round showing the ghastly head to everyone.

People seemed to go mad; to become more crazed than before. They fainted, tore at their clothes, shouted obscenities, struck each other, screamed in fear, covered their eyes, rushed from the place like maddened animals.

John's body was buried by some of his followers. Soon the court moved back to Galilee and Machaerus wasn't mentioned any more. Herodias went on as before. There was a change in Antipas. A change hard to define. Some weeks later I was with him when some of his advisers were reading him reports about Jesus. 'A poor man,' they said, 'an artisan. A carpenter, of Nazareth. A healer, with positive cures, checked and proven. A preacher of some power, with a considerable following.'

Antipas sat silent till all had finished. They waited. Such careful attention was rare. Then he said, 'This Jesus must be John the Baptist. He has risen from the dead. That is why he has the power to work miracles.'

I've never forgotten the way he said it. With absolute certainty. Not long after this happened, the King of Arabia attacked. It was a massacre, and I lost my son. People say to this day that such a total defeat was because Antipas had killed the Baptist. Well, maybe. Doesn't make too much sense. Antipas is still alive and my only son is dead.

Itzhak

Tall, thin, about fifty-three. A pock-marked face with many scars. A missing eyebrow adds to an already hard expression. Thin, white hair, which like his clothes and skin is spotlessly clean. A deep, hoarse voice.

I was a leper. You needn't pull away, I'm not a leper any more. I haven't been for some time. I'm 'clean', as the priests put it. I've got a piece of paper from them to say that I have been examined, that I have made the proper sacrifices, such as I could afford, and that I have said the proper prayers and all the paraphernalia with the lamb's blood and the oil and the flour and the turtledoves has been carried out, and that I'm clean. Not unclean, as before, but clean.

When the priests at last gave me the bit of paper, you'd think it was they who'd cured me. I don't have a great deal of time for priests. Not the Jerusalem lot. Leprosy is important. Not important enough for the authorities to provide a little comfort for the lepers or a decent place for them to live in – or die in. But if you get better, which can happen, or get cured, as I was, it's straight up to head office for all the performance and the bit of paper.

Don't think I'm ungrateful. I thank God every night. And I say a prayer for the man who cured me. The Jerusalem lot looked after him, too. They had him killed. I blame myself a bit. I'm sort of famous. Everyone knows my story, certainly in Galilee. I was one of the first cures that Jesus ever did. Certainly the first leper. I often think to myself that I talked him into it. Convinced him, gave him confidence.

He's been dead about a year, the Carpenter, and he worked as a preacher and a healer for about three years before they killed him. So I've been clean about four years. It seems less, for I was unclean for a lot longer – about thirty years! I was nearly twenty when I caught it. I'd been married about a year and a half. My wife was pregnant. I was seen by the priests, who did all the examining and tests, as it says in Leviticus, and, when it was confirmed, I was sent away to the caves. My wife was passed as clean and, when the baby came, he was 'without blemish', as they say. She came from the North and I sent her back home. I divorced her and never saw the baby. It was best.

There are different kinds of leprosy. Some kill you quick. Others cripple you or make you blind. Another type covers you from head to toe and changes the face of a person with bumps and swellings. It's called lion-head, or, as we called it, 'the ugly'.

That was my kind. I'm not pretty now, but you should have seen me four years ago. Leviticus says you must live away from others, 'with torn clothes and bare head'. It says you must cry 'unclean, unclean' and wear a half-mask. The 'caves' where I lived served a large area of Galilee. We supported ourselves as best we could, and depended on charity. Lepers, in the main, just sit, or lie down. No energy, no strength. I was luckier than most, I was hideous but active, and I grew a little food and herbs. It was a simple life. You knew where you were. You were without hope. Simple. No problems. All in the same boat.

I heard about Jesus from a man who twice a week used to bring us some food. His daughter was one of us. He used to give us what news there was. We'd heard of John the Baptizer and his dipping people in water to make them pure again. A good joke that was, around the caves. We needed more than bloody water.

Anyway, this man told us that Jesus, who came from Nazareth, not far from us, and was a relative of the Baptizer, was getting a name for healing people. Not in Nazareth, his home town, they'd slung him out, but in other places. That bit sounded very genuine to me, so I listened carefully. This Jesus, the man said, had cured a woman of a high fever and made a man full of screaming devils sane again. With a touch, a word. For the woman's son-in-law, he'd arranged a miraculous great catch of fish.

On his next visit, the food man told us that Jesus was on a tour of synagogues, preaching every day, and that he was going to be quite near us, in a small town about four miles away, the next day.

I couldn't sleep, I couldn't rest. It was ridiculous, I'd long ago given up any hope. I was used to it, it was my way of life, a leper with 'the ugly'. But I couldn't rest.

The next morning I got up before anyone else and walked to the edge of the town. It was permitted, for begging purposes. And I waited. I didn't beg. I was never good at it, and if I went too close, my face, even with the bit of rag over half of it, was enough to frighten people to death. I waited till past noon. The sun was full on me, and I dozed off. I woke suddenly and about fifty yards away I saw him. Don't ask me how I knew. He was with other people and yet not with them. He was walking towards me and one or two were trying to stop him – for there was no mistaking what I was, mask or not. He put their hands away and walked on until he was no more than a yard or two away. I was riveted. No one ever came that close.

We looked at each other. His eyes were calm, and compassionate. He stood quite still. I thought he was weighing up the size of the job, so I helped him. I took off the mask. His expression didn't change, except – and I'm not sure about this – to look a little uncertain. A sort of power was coming from him.

I knelt down. 'Cure me,' I said. 'Make me clean.'

He said nothing. I was a bit dizzy in the hot sun. 'Try!' I said. 'Try! I don't ask to be whole again, or handsome! Just *clean!* Make a sign, ask God, say a prayer. *Try!*'

The tiny uncertainty was still in his face. I held out my arms to him. 'You can *do* it! You can make me clean!' I told him, 'You *can!* If you *want* to, you *can!*'

Then he smiled, as though remembering similar words he'd said to others. He came nearer and looked down into my eyes. Then he put his hand on my head.

'Certainly I want to,' he said. 'Be clean.' Then, very lightly, he passed his fingers over my face. I don't know how he could bear to do it.

Then his face became serious. 'Arrange as soon as you can to see the priests,' he said, 'your trial is over. By the time you go before the priests, your blood will be clean and clear of the disease. Your flesh will heal. You will pass all their tests, as written in Leviticus, and they will declare you clean. Make all the offerings and sacrifices laid down by the Law and God bless you.'

I was weeping. I couldn't speak. I felt no different and looked no different, yet I knew I was cured.

'One more thing,' he said, 'the most difficult. Don't tell anybody, not even the priests, how you were cured.'

And then he left me. All he said would happen, did. It took time, but I had no doubts at all. I didn't need to tell anyone, the story spread like wildfire. My cure, you must understand, was impossible. I was rotting away.

So I became a celebrity. A freak show. But I didn't mind. And, as the story was already known – and authenticated by the priests, bless 'em – I never stopped talking about the Carpenter. As things turned out, I may have done him harm. But I think he knew he was going to die young. I know about death. And I think he knew.

Joseph

Tall, rather bony man. Clean-shaven, rather long face, with vigorous grey hair and eyebrows. Steady grey eyes of some kindness. A feeling, however, of great strength and firmness. A deep voice. No hand gestures at all.

It is now about ten years since Jesus died on the cross. So many things have changed. I am glad that Pontius Pilate has gone. He was a cruel man who did not really like his job – or do it particularly well. People sometimes ask me why I didn't go back to tax-collecting after Jesus died. Well, there are a number of reasons, but one of them certainly was that I was happy to have no more dealings with Pilate and his tax department. Mighty Rome took heavy toll. It charged its subject nations high prices for being subject, and ruled, and occupied. The system they had once used was simple and direct – and open to much abuse. They would say, 'For such a district, so much,' and would sell to the highest bidder the collecting rights. As long as they got what they wanted, they would ask no questions about how much the collector had made for himself. Rome knew very well how greed can corrupt.

Over the years, the system was changed but the people's ignorance of how much they had to pay did not. Rome, and the Government, made few announcements, only demands. And the tax-collector, extortioner-turned-civil-servant, was the most hated man in the land. We were feared, and despised. We were welcome nowhere. We mixed with our own. We could not act on a jury, or be a witness, or be part of a congregation. We were sinners. We were called vultures and bloodsuckers and outcasts. But the job had to be done.

I worked for three collectors. The last one was Levi, or Matthew as he was known. He was an honest man – in that profession, a rare thing. He was rich, but you had to be. The treasury and Rome would not wait, but you might have to. Often the tax was a percentage of a man's crop; it could be wine or oil or wool or skins. So many taxes. Income tax; on certain articles a purchase tax; a vehicle tax. There were road tolls and harbour dues, and the markets were taxed. There were import and export duties.

People paid us unwillingly, as always. They lied and made excuses. They were tense and strained with us. Unnatural, full of hate. So you see, my friend, when Jesus came and stood in front of Matthew, quite relaxed, quite natural, steady-eyed, quiet, it stays in the mind. Matthew was not in a good mood, it had been a bad day. 'Name?' he said. 'District? Address?

Goods or money? Occupation?' Jesus said nothing, and Matthew looked up. He recognized the Carpenter. So did I. We had been twice to hear him speak. He was well known as a healer. People believed him to be a miracle-worker. Not us. Tax-collectors as a class don't believe in miracles. We are shown the worst side of people and come to believe it to be the *only* side. We learn cynicism early.

Matthew and Jesus looked at each other without speaking, then Matthew got up. They were much the same in height, although Matthew was broader, older, much more richly dressed. A strong man. Well educated, powerful, realistic, hard-headed. He stood still, his eyes as steady as the Carpenter's. He seemed to be waiting. That morning he and I had been talking of how the sons of Zebedee, James and John, had given up their trade to join Jesus. We knew them. The story was that Jesus had just said, 'Follow me,' and they did. Without question. I waited; like Matthew. Then Jesus made a little gesture that seemed to say, 'This is a *life* for a man? This is to be *rich?*' Then he spoke. 'Follow me,' he said.

And Matthew did. He walked away from his tax-gathering table and never went back to it. No doubts, no hesitation, no looking back. I don't mean that he just got up and left his desk and his office and his staff just like that. He was a senior civil servant, an efficient man; and hard. He had to be. His mind was made up and it seemed that in no time he had arranged everything. Even a replacement for me; for I wanted to follow, too. If Jesus made sense to Matthew, that was good enough for me.

In a way, Matthew and I were close; he talked to me. I knew him well. I thought *very* well, but in the few days following his decision to give up his job, a new sort of Matthew emerged. Very calm but very cheerful. 'I'm going to give a big party,' he said, 'a sort of farewell party – or a start-a-new-life party!' I pointed out as gently as I could that, as tax-collectors, we were outcasts, pariahs, we had no friends; no one would come to the party. 'Pariahs will come!' said Matthew. 'Outcasts, tax-men like us, excise-men, customs-men, duty-collectors. A gathering of the hated, the feared, and the unpopular!' He roared with glee. 'And their wives and children!' Then he was quiet. 'The party will be for Jesus,' he said. 'Guest of honour. If he'll come.'

Of course he came. And with him came his first followers. 'My new workmates,' Matthew called them. The four fishermen, Simon-Peter and his brother Andrew, and John and James, sons of Zebedee. Philip came, and Bartholomew. They were all very different people. And Matthew was different again. I had the feeling that Jesus, village carpenter, chose very carefully.

It was a huge party. Wonderful food and drink – and music and songs. Jesus and his friends mixed easily and joined in everything. Jesus was very well known, a famous healer, a magnetic speaker. I was interested to see that at close quarters, in a noisy, crowded party, he had this same attraction. He spoke simply. You understood. If you spoke to him, he gave you his full attention; you were important.

During the evening, fairly late, when the party was at its height, a group of Pharisees and scribes turned up. These lovers of orthodoxy, these experts in the Laws of Moses, were the Carpenter's bitterest critics. They disapproved of him entirely. They came in, wouldn't sit down, wouldn't eat or drink, just criticized and were unpleasant. People were embarrassed and grew silent. Eventually everyone was listening, as they made their remarks and Jesus replied. He didn't get cross. He answered them with little comparisons and parables. He didn't call them inflexible or shut-minded or stiff or resistant to new ideas. He spoke gently of new wine that needs time to mature, of old garments too far gone to be patched. And, when they compared his followers with the fasting and praying disciples of John the Baptist and their own sects, Jesus paused. It was very quiet. He answered a little sadly; we did not know it was a prophecy. 'They are friends of a bridegroom,' he said. 'Should they not share the feast and joy of the wedding? But the day will come when their friend, the bridegroom, will be gone. *Then* they will fast and pray.' Matthew looked absolutely desolate. Peter, too. I will never forget it.

How well I recall that time. It seemed to me that the change in my life sharpened all my senses. And to make the change had seemed logical and easy – yet to be a 'follower' of someone or something was not really my nature. My brother was the 'devout', the 'believing' one of the family. He joined the Baptizer, John, when he first appeared. We called him 'The Disciple', my brother. I was the worldly one, the tax-man, with the good job in Matthew's office. Yet suddenly, here was I – also a disciple. Listening, being made to think in a new way, a more simple way. Belonging. I was happy and stimulated and proud.

Maybe proud in the wrong way, for, when the day came that Jesus chose his twelve whom he called 'apostles', I was not among them, and I was hurt, for I'd joined when Matthew did. I remember the occasion very well. There was a great crowd of us disciples and, surrounding us, an even greater crowd of people, of every kind. Many of them from far, far away. From all over Judea – from as far north as Tyre and Sidon. Many ill people, many cripples, many blind. We were waiting for Jesus. Tens of thousands of us. On the lower slope of a mountain, and on the plain below. Most of us had waited all night, waiting for Jesus to come down from the top of the mountain, where he'd gone to pray by himself. To be with God. We never disturbed him at these times – we waited.

We waited. We were quiet. It was cold, as always, before dawn. The huge crowd were quiet, too. A sense of something going to happen. Then the sky lightened and, as the sun rose and lit the top of the mountain, we saw Jesus. He came down slowly, thoughtfully, and the sun was on him all the way down. He joined us, and we crowded around. He greeted us with the easy friendliness that was very much his own, and then began to speak to us. To us, his disciples, not to the waiting crowds below on the lower levels of the slope. He said that there were to be twelve what he called apostles.

Matthew told me it was from a Greek word meaning someone who is sent out, an envoy, an ambassador. Then Jesus named the Twelve, and many, like me, were disappointed, although we all felt that Jesus, who knew men, had chosen the best. The last one named was Judas. Judas Iscariot, and as Jesus named him, he looked at him with a sort of sadness. He probably knew what Judas would one day do to him. Odd. I've only just remembered that sad look.

Then the Master walked on down the slope, and we all followed. The sun was now fully up, and it was warmer. The great crowds surged forward, bringing – as always – the sick and maimed to the front, for at that time the whole of Israel was talking about the cures and the healing done by Jesus. And that day he gave off his power like heat – you could feel it. Then he gave his great sermon – which people now call the Sermon on the Mount. Matthew was hypnotized by it – we all were. It seemed to turn every belief and law upside down and make even more sense than before. Matthew could quote the sermon word for word, and used it later in his own ministry. It was full of hope for the poor, the hungry, the sad, the outsiders. Full of love.

Matthew, as I told you, was a rich and sophisticated man – and before Jesus called him, a hard, cynical man. But not long after that sermon, I met him when he returned from one of his first trips as an apostle, and he was completely changed. Even his clothes. He looked like a poor preacher. He carried nothing. No staff, no purse of money, no food or water, nothing. 'As Jesus told us,' he said to me. 'He also told us that we would be able to heal the sick.' Matthew looked at me and smiled, a new, more gentle smile. 'And I can,' he said.

Samuel

Medium height, about sixty. A relaxed man, with a rather quizzical expression. Brown eyes. A large, handsome head. White-haired, but a feeling of vigour, energy. Deep-voiced, articulate.

I remember once asking my schoolteacher whether I had any chance of becoming like my father and grandfather. Absolutely orthodox and devout; obeying every religious rule, never forgetting anything. Fast or feast, prayer or blessing. 'Every chance,' he said, 'if your sense of humour doesn't get in the way!' I was slightly shocked, I remember. I thought he was being flippant. I'd asked a serious question; he'd given me a silly answer.

I told my mother, who laughed, and ruffled my hair and told me not to worry about it. As I grew older, I realized that my teacher had seen before I had that I would be rather like my laughing mother. She saw humour in everything, and it made her happy and popular till the day she died.

I also see humour, am also in my own way happy, although less popular. For the humour I have is an unerring nose for the ridiculous, the idiocy of men, the vanity, the hypocrisy, the whole mad comedy. So today, my father and grandfather safely buried, I am neither orthodox nor devout. I obey few rules, and fast rarely, I offer blessings to no one, and ask for none.

It was not always so. I was an only son and the disciplines of a very strict religious upbringing are hard. For generations my family have been watchdogs of the Law. Religious men, and men of religion. Not priests, but wardens; not spiritual leaders, but keepers of the rule-book. Inquisitors, men beyond reproach, heads of colleges. True Pharisees. Custodians of absolute conformity. Good men; sincere men. Men often in the middle of a forest unable to see the trees . . .

I followed in their footsteps, as expected. Sat in their seats. Took over their duties. Became grave, keeping the irreverent and humorous side of my nature, inherited from my beloved mother, firmly in check. If it all got too much, I would visit her and we would laugh till we cried. I miss her sorely.

A happening, when I was nearly forty, some twenty years ago, a happening sweet in the mind and beyond explanation, finally decided me to live in a way more agreeable to my true self. The self seen so clearly long ago by my teacher.

My mother's elder brother was born sickly, and, by the time he was a young man, had almost entirely lost the use of his legs. He had no belief in doctors at all, having been in their hands since birth. In the family he was known as Uncle Bethesda, which was not his name but where he spent most of his life. At the pools of Bethesda, here in Jerusalem. For years and years he lay on a low bed near to the Fifth Arch, by the smaller pool. He lay with other incurables, believing, as they did, that the first one into the pool 'after the Angel had moved the water' would be cured. An ancient legend. The trouble was that no one knew when the Angel would come – and there were many sufferers both nearer to the water and more active. So, for year after year, he lay there on his back, resigned, cheerful – he had my mother's humour – and pleasant. He was among friends; it was a community.

As I grew up, I used to visit him whenever I could – which was often. And when I left university and joined my father, I continued the habit. Later, when I took over certain religious duties at the Pharisaical College, my office was near the Sheep Gate, not far from the pools. It was no duty; I liked him. He was an interested, enthusiastic man, always encouraging, always proud of his nephew. When I was a little boy, my mother would leave me with him and the other invalids and cripples for hours.

Now, the happening. I was in synagogue one Sabbath. Passover time. The Pharisee Mother-Synagogue. Every part of the service perfect, as written, as laid down. To every side, the serious, stern, righteous faces. The service ended and we were filing out. Suddenly there was an excitement. One of the helpers at the pool came running. He was breathless, hardly able to speak. 'Quick!' he shouted, 'your uncle!' My first thought was that he was dead. I set off at once – it wasn't far – and some of the synagogue elders and my colleagues came too. It was good of them, but I would have preferred to be alone. Grief is a private thing.

As we drew near to the Sheep Gate we saw an amazing sight.

Not what it was, *who* it was. As a sight it was ordinary. A man carrying a narrow bed on his head. Not unusual. A porter; a market carrier. Walking slowly, carefully. A man of about fifty-five, sixty.

It was my uncle. I stopped, my mouth open. I'd never seen him vertical. He saw me, and proceeded at the same pace, watching his feet walking, with a sort of wonder, smiling. He came to a standstill in front of me.

'A man did it,' he said to me, 'a young man. No more than thirty-five. Dressed poorly, with a Galilee accent. He stopped by me and we talked. He was friendly and had not heard the Angel legend. I was telling him how, when the water moved, I always missed it. How, in any case, I could never be first. "Do you really want to walk again?" he said to me. "Then get up! Walk! Get up, pick up your bed, and walk!" And I did. I had no doubts. I got up – I was very wobbly – and then I picked up my bed and I walked. And here I am.'

I felt strange. My uncle, always lying on his back, was part of the order of my life. I felt I was present at a great occasion; beyond my understanding; to do with God, and miracles. My uncle, with his bed on his head, stood smiling at me. Then the most venerable and respected of the elders stepped forward.

'Is it not written,' he said, 'that on the Sabbath it is wrong for a man to carry a burden? Do you not know it is wrong for you to be carrying that bed?'

The other elders lined themselves up by the one who'd just spoken. A jury; a line of silent reproach. My uncle carefully lowered his bed to the ground and looked along the line. Then he looked at me and started to laugh. He put his hands on my shoulders and laughed and laughed, like my mother, till the tears ran down. He hugged me to him, he hung on me, helpless, shaking, the laughter pouring from him like a great delirious wind of joy. Soon, for I put up no resistance, I was helpless as he, as wet with tears, as incapable of speech. The wind of his joy swept away for ever the dustiness of my life.

I picked up his bed and we walked away, not daring to look back at the line of motionless, affronted faces. Once round the corner, he stopped, drew himself up and straightened his features in a parody of the disapproval we had just left. He peered down at me, held it for a moment and then collapsed in hysterics. And so we made our way home, to my mother's, for Sabbath lunch. Two men, carrying an old bed, screaming with laughter, wet-eyed with joy and freedom.

Gideon

Early sixties. A broad, muscular man, with heavy arms and hands. Rather bald, but with vigorous side-hair and beard. A humorous, weather-beaten face, with hazel eyes below big eyebrows. A deep, warm voice, with a rough, Galilee accent.

I have lived all my life here in Capernaum. It suits me. My family have been boatbuilders for generations, and it was my trade too. The lake, or, as some call it, the *Sea* of Galilee, gives a living to many people, certainly to folk who build and repair boats. I've never travelled much. Never been to Jerusalem, or Jericho, or Caesarea. Never seen the Salt Sea – or even the Great Sea, which is nearer. But plenty happens, or has happened over the years, in Capernaum, or nearby. More than people might think. It's not a big place, but it's a market town, a tax-collection centre – and a Roman military post. Plenty goes on.

I suppose what really put us on the map was Jesus. When they threw him out of Nazareth, where he was born, he came here to live. Good lesson; never try to impress your home town. I don't think he would have impressed *us* much (we were never short of preachers), but he began to perform those remarkable cures. You listen in a different way to a man like that.

I knew a number of the people he healed. One of the first, Peter's mother-in-law, was a distant relation of mine. Peter and Andrew and their father before them all used boats made in our yard. Boats take a fair time to build and your customers become your friends. I was at Peter's wedding. Great big fellow and tiny little wife. Lovely little person his wife is. Very capable, very level.

I remember very well when Peter and Andrew and the Zebedee sons joined the Carpenter. Very well. Though it must be nearly ten years. It caused quite a disturbance. Especially in old man Zebedee's life. Unbroken line of fishermen, the Zebedees, for God knows how many generations. Great place for gossip, a boat-yard, you get to hear everything. And I knew all the parties concerned in that first 'joining Jesus' – or the Carpenter, as we called him. I knew the tax-man, Levi – or Matthew, as he's known now. Well, everyone knew the tax-man. He was better than most of them. A hard man, obstinate and unbending. He changed a lot you know, after he gave up his job to follow the Carpenter.

Wonderful speaker the Carpenter was – and he had good, simple things to say – although some of his parables were difficult until he explained. But, as I say, it was the healing, the cures, the making people well again that first made him famous. One of these healings I was a bit involved in. Remarkable business altogether. Because the 'doctor', as it were, never met the patient. Never touched him, or laid eyes on him.

I knew the patient, although not very well. He was house servant to a friend of mine. An army officer. The Roman garrison in Capernaum numbered at that time about two hundred men. Two centuries, as they were called, under two officers, or centurions. My friend was one. He'd been in the town for a long time. A very well respected man indeed. Very good at getting people working together; very philanthropic. We have a fine synagogue in Capernaum that we owe almost entirely to his leadership and energy. And he wasn't a Jew. He was shifted to Cyprus about two years ago, just after Pilate was sent home. I miss him. Not Pilate, my friend. Nobody misses Pilate.

My friend, whose name was Caspius, and I became friends not long after he came to the town. We are much the same age. I learned a lot from him. He was a better-educated man than I – and interested in everything.

We spent a lot of time together. We went together to hear the Carpenter – when he gave his great speech up on the hill. What's called the Sermon on the Mount. My friend was deeply impressed; I thought it very dangerous stuff in parts. For Jesus, I mean. I was right as it turned out. Well, not long after this, Caspius told me his servant was very ill. 'He's been with me a long time,' he said, 'and I'm very fond of him. Nothing seems to do him any good. Do you think the Carpenter would help? Perhaps someone would speak for me.'

Typical remark. Not false modesty; *real* modesty. A rare man.

I went off right away. It wasn't difficult to find people to speak for Caspius. We went as a group and told Jesus about him. How he'd built a synagogue for the town. How fair he was in all his dealings. Jesus listened and said he would come immediately. I ran on ahead and told Caspius, who immediately – and very unexpectedly – became agitated. 'No!' he said. 'Go and tell him I didn't mean him to come *in person,* to go to any trouble. Just to give the order and that will do it. Tell him I know about orders. I'm a soldier, and I've taken orders and given orders all my life. I had to learn authority from men. He has it from God. Quick!' he said, 'go and stop him. Tell him just to give the order. It will be enough.' And he pushed me out of the house.

Jesus was just crossing the market place, now with a big crowd. I gave the message word for word. The Carpenter listened, then he turned to the crowd and repeated it. Then he said, 'I have never met faith like this anywhere.' He seemed full of wonder, and a sort of happiness. He walked back the way he had come and the crowd followed. I went back to Caspius with one or two others. We found him in his servant's room, helping him to get dressed. Although he needed no help. He was a bit pale, but perfectly well and lively. Rather apologetic about neglecting his duties. Caspius smiled and looked at us. He didn't look very surprised.

Shim

Middle forties. A ruddy, open-air kind of man. Sturdy and muscular. Slow-speaking, like a man used to long silences or solitude. Steady, grey eyes. Big, capable hands.

You seem surprised to hear that I've never been across the lake, across the Sea of Galilee. Well, let me tell you that there are many people here in Gerasa who haven't even been out of the town gates. Why should they? How much you travel depends a lot upon what you do for a living, I think. A cousin of mine, who sells cloth, is *always* going across the lake – or round the top of it into Galilee.

Well, I look after pigs. A pigman, a swineherd. I've one or two of my own, but mainly I look after other people's. I've always done it. I know every inch of the country round here that's good for pigs. But not far afield, not far away. Pigs don't go far afield. And the buying and selling, the cattle market, is here in Gerasa.

It's a quiet place, Gerasa. Nothing much happens here, although your mentioning Jesus of Galilee brings back to me a remarkable day, remarkable. I don't often recall it, except with strangers. Most people here in the town remember it as clearly as I do. And, of course, it is some time ago now. About ten or eleven years. Jesus has been gone, how long is it, eight, nine years?

Well, Jesus came here, to Gerasa, just once. And once was enough, believe me. I nearly lost my job because of Jesus – although I must admit that I saw remarkable things because of him, too. I know that since he died he has become very well known, but he wasn't then. He'd just started, and news travels slowly round here. At that time, too, the two sides of the lake were two separate provinces. We were Philip, Galilee was

Antipas. If you count Decapolis, the ten towns, *three* provinces. Many changes since. They're all gone, Antipas, Philip, Pilate, too. And we are part of Syria. I don't change; I go on looking after pigs.

Yes, just once, Jesus came. By boat. He landed just south of the town, where the low cliffs are. I was up on top with the pigs. I saw this fishing boat with about six people in it and it looked as if they were intending to land at the bottom of the graveyard slope. Well, I left the pigs and started to make my way down to tell them not to, for it was dangerous, because of the madman.

He'd lived in the graveyard, in among the tombs and graves, for years, the madman. He was mainly the reason they closed it. People were afraid to go there. He was a tall, skinny man, filthy dirty, naked. His hair and beard were matted and crusty with blood, for he was always falling down and cutting his head on the stones. His eyes were ghastly, wide-staring open and sort of terrified. And he screamed from morning till night. Terrible noise.

I used to leave food for him. For weeks on end there would be only the two of us on that bit of shore, me up on the cliffs and him down among the tombs. I was used to him. If he came too near, I'd throw a stone and he would scream and run away and hide. I don't think he would have hurt me but I wasn't taking any chances. There'd been a time when the authorities used to catch him and chain him up, but then he'd go berserk, like a wild, trapped animal, and seem to have the strength of ten, and he'd break his chains and fetters and cover himself with cuts and bruises and blood. Pitiful.

So eventually they left him alone, poor soul. Left him to rot. A pigman's life is not much, but, when I used to see him, I used to count my blessings, and collect food for him. He became known as 'Shim's Friend'. People used to say to me, 'Shim, how's your friend?' and have a laugh. I didn't mind, if they put some food in the basket for my 'friend'.

But my 'friend' was mad, and full of demons and terror, and

strong enough for ten, strong enough to kill anyone. So, when I saw the men in the boat, I started round the edge of the cliff, shouting. They didn't hear, and beached the boat. The madman was nowhere to be seen, so I decided to risk it and I ran down the slope through the graves towards the boat.

Jesus, although I didn't know it was him then, had landed and was walking up the beach. He waved his hand to me. I was about fifty yards away. Then, suddenly, half-way between us, the madman got to his feet from a clump of dwarf bushes. And began to scream. He had his back to me so I went on, picking up a big rock in case of trouble.

I heard Jesus say something, like a sharp order, a command, and the madman's scream took shape, became words, although I couldn't make them out. He seemed to be asking permission; there was fear in it. Then he was silent. Everything was silent. It was weird. The madman went to Jesus and sat down near him, looking up at him. There was no sound.

Then, suddenly, from the top of the low cliffs, the screaming began again tenfold. It frightened the life out of me. It was the pigs. I started up the slope to them. I thought maybe some wild dogs had got in among them. The screaming got louder and louder. As I reached the top, I was aware of a new noise. A great splashing and thudding. I stopped and looked round. Below me the graveyard sloped down to the Sea. To either side, the cliffs. And from the edge of the cliffs the pigs were jumping, screaming, into the Sea! Many, many more than my herd, hundreds more! Among them, pigmen from miles inland, shouting in despair and rage. It went on and on, and suddenly stopped. No more pigs. Silence. Down below, Jesus, with the naked madman sitting in front of him.

Well, the other pigmen and I rushed off to our farmers. We feared for our jobs. And what could we tell them? Only the truth – which sounded as though we were mad, or drunk! That some strangers had landed and done some magic and filled the pigs with mad demons which made them all jump into the Sea or smash themselves on the rocks below the cliffs! The word went round like a fire and half the town turned out, rushing back to the cliffs and down through the graveyard.

When we got back, the madman at first was not to be seen. Then I realized that the man nearest to Jesus was my 'friend'. Jesus and the fishermen had washed him and found some clothes for him, and there he sat, as calm and sane as I am. As I realized it and recognized my 'friend', so, it seemed, did everybody else. It was somehow more frightening than the pigs. The town elders stepped forward and asked Jesus to go away and not come back, as his magic was powerful – and very costly, for some two thousand pigs were missing. Most of the elders were our pig farmers, and I could see their point.

Jesus didn't argue. He and his friends turned and prepared to push their boat off. The madman went after them, imploring Jesus to take him also, but Jesus said no. Then, when the madman began to cry with gratitude, Jesus stopped him. 'God did it,' he said. 'God can do everything. Go and tell everyone what God has done for you.' And he and his friends sailed away.

Then there was an odd thing. The madman turned and looked up the slope at the people, then came across to me. 'Thank you for all the food,' he said. It came true about him being 'Shim's Friend'. He's more; he's my brother-in-law.

Judith

Middle forties. Dark hair and eyes. A gentle, smiling expression, an inner content. Slim, graceful, quietly dressed. The voice is low and pleasant.

———————

This has been a special day in my life. Of a special sweetness, for my Deborah was married today, and of a special sadness, for the man who made her marriage possible was not with us to celebrate it. He has been dead nearly six years. He didn't deserve the death he suffered. To say that he rose again from the grave is of little comfort really, he is gone. His disciples are remarkable people, but they are not he. God's ways are strange indeed, if such a special young man had to suffer such a terrible death. Nearly six years, and it seems like yesterday. He should have been the Guest of Honour at my Deborah's wedding today. Instead, she and I talked a little of him, and, like women, wept a little.

How easily I say 'my' Deborah. She is related to me in no way (although she always called me Aunt). She is the only child of Jairus, who was the best friend of my late husband, David. They were two of the founders of the synagogue here. Deborah is part of my life. She was born about six months after my husband died. We were married only eight years and we were not blessed with children. Then David became ill and died and my life went dark. Not long after, I myself fell ill and began an internal bleeding, which took away my energy and my colour and my will to live.

Jairus and his wife, Anna, were wonderful to me. They are wonderful people. Anna had a difficult time when she had Deborah, and asked my help. It was just what I needed. To look after a family, to help tend a baby, to have a place, a reason for living. I suspect that Anna purposely stayed 'weak' for much longer than was true because she could see that her weakness was giving me strength – and joy. And what a lovely child my Deborah was.

I learnt to live with my complaint. When it was very bad, I would stay in bed and pray, and go as pale as the sheet, and try a new doctor or a new treatment. They were always bad times, depressing times, but always, too, there was Deborah to cheer me up. A golden-hearted child, a loving child.

The years passed. Deborah was nearly twelve and Anna and I began to plan a big party. We would talk for hours. It would be out of doors, with lanterns. A magician, a ventriloquist, puppets, Deborah's favourite dishes, which I would make.

It was during one of these talks that Anna first mentioned Jesus. 'A woodworker,' she said, 'from Galilee. A poor man, with a gift of healing.' She told me that he had cured a leper, a paralytic, a man's withered arm. He had taken the demons from people's heads and made them sane again. 'And for a widow, like you,' Anna told me, 'he did the greatest miracle. He brought her dead child back to life.'

Now, if you knew Anna, you'd know she is impressed by very little, least of all by magic-talk and hearsay. But she was serious and urgent. 'And he can cure you, too,' she said. 'It is said that if you yourself believe that he can, if you have faith, then he can, and does, in a minute.'

I couldn't sleep. I could think of nothing else. A few days later I heard that the Carpenter, as people called him, was coming here to our district, to hold a meeting. I had no more doubts. I was sure that God had sent him. I told Anna that I was going to the meeting and she said that she would also have liked to have gone but Deborah wasn't too well. Nothing serious.

I went to bed early, and next morning I was up at dawn, for the meeting was some way out of town, and great crowds were expected. I went by myself. I felt trembly and pale, but no more than usual. Someone let me ride a little way on their cart. Then I walked, and the crowds got thicker by the minute. I began to lose hope of getting near to him.

Then there was a great cry and people began to run and I was swept along. Someone took my hand and I looked up. It was Dov, a servant of Jairus. He shouted something about Deborah and let go and I lost him. I began to feel frightened, for I had little reserve of strength and the crowd was rough. I began to feel faint. I concentrated upon keeping my feet, I clutched at people, leaned on them. No one minded, I must have looked ghastly. The noise was deafening.

Suddenly, my part of the crowd slowed down. I pushed on, blindly. Then I fell to my knees. I was at the front. In front of me, a yard or two away, were more of the crowd, facing me, making a path. They were excited, looking to their left, pointing. I looked where they were looking and saw the Carpenter. I knew it was him, don't ask me how. Other men were with him – and by his side, Jairus. It was a surprise.

They moved towards me, the crowd pushing and jostling, closing in behind them. They drew level with me. I was afraid to look up. I was on my hands and knees. I prayed that the Carpenter would stop, and he did. His robe was brown and dusty. I reached forward and touched it. I knew with absolute certainty that touching his robe would be enough. It was. Then someone's knee caught me in the side and I fell over, hurting my elbow. But, as I fell, I knew that I was cured. A feeling of ease and strength came over me.

Jesus and his followers had moved a step or two and had again stopped. There was a sudden hush, for the crowd was more orderly just there, and it was not they who had stopped the Carpenter. He was very still, then he half turned. He was no more than four yards from me.

'Who touched me?' he said. He looked tired and pale. One of his followers, a big man, who I now know was Peter, said, 'Master, the crowds are huge, all around you, pushing and pressing. It could have been anyone.'

'No.' Jesus said, 'not that kind of touch, a touch of faith, in bone, for I felt the power go out of me.' He said it quietly. He looked drained. Then Jairus saw me and came over and helped me to my feet. I took his hand from my arm and I went to Jesus and knelt down and told him it was me. The touch had been mine, in faith, in hope of a cure. I told him I was now sure that I was cured, that the bleeding had stopped and would never occur again.

'That is what cured you,' he said to me, 'your faith. Go in peace.'

At that moment, Dov, the big servant of Jairus, pushed through the crowd. People objected but he ignored them and went to Jairus. I got up. I knew something was wrong.

'Master,' he said to Jairus, 'my mistress says that there is now no need for the healer to come to Deborah. The child is dead.'

I turned to poor Jairus. He stood like stone. I could not believe it. The shock was tremendous, and, following the shock, a feeling of great guilt. In a second I was convinced that I had stolen Deborah's cure for myself. I began to stammer and weep, hardly able to speak. Jairus, kind as always, put his arms around me, told me that Deborah had suddenly become very ill indeed, almost overnight, that she had seemed unable to breathe, beyond help, dying. That his going to the Carpenter had been desperate, the last hope.

'But I believed,' he said to me, 'I believed. I had faith, like you, Judith. Perhaps not enough.'

Then Jesus spoke. 'Go on believing,' he said. 'Have faith. Your daughter will be all right. Come!'

We went as fast as the crowds would allow, straight back to Jairus's house. When we got there, the downstairs rooms were full of noise. Jairus was wealthy, and every professional mourner and wailer and dirge-player for miles around was there, in full voice. The flutes and pipes and death gongs were deafening.

'Stop the noise!' said Jesus. 'No one is dead here. The child is asleep.' The beggars and wailers laughed at him. Jesus told his friends to turn everybody out and they did. Then he took big Peter, John and James, and Jairus showed them up into Deborah's room, where I could hear Anna weeping. I waited down below.

Then there was a silence. Not for long. Then they all came down. Deborah, too, her hand in the Carpenter's. Jairus was supporting Anna, who looked ready to faint. Her eyes were enormous.

'Are you Aunt Judy?' said Jesus. 'Well, Deborah says you know what her favourite dishes are. Make them. She's starving.'

I fed them all. Jesus told us to say nothing to anyone, but the whole town knew before we got up from the table. You can't keep such things quiet.

Aaron

About fifty-eight to sixty years old. Heavily built, muscular, with full beard and thick eyebrows. A cheerful, loud-voiced, likeable man. Well known locally for his kindness and good humour.

A woman-dominated man, me. Out-numbered and out-manœuvred. Mind you, I'm not complaining! Too late for complaints. And my girls, all four of 'em, bless 'em, are as good as gold. Two married (I've got seven grandchildren!) and one on the brink. The youngest, Rebecca, I don't think wants to get married. Still, you can never tell.

One of my sons-in-law is in business with me. We bake bread and smoke fish. As my father did before me. And where we work is perfect for it. Just above Tiberias. We supply all the northern districts, and with the fish an even wider area. Anybody can bake, I reckon, but smoking fish is something else. 'Out of the sea and into the smokehouse' is our motto, and it is fact. We are right on the shore, and the Sea of Galilee is full of fish, full. Also, just inland from us, a lot of the thornbush and hardwood grows that is best for the smoking. God is good.

You know, in this part of Israel the fishing is done by families. Over the years we've traded with most of them. For a long time with the Zebedees, whose elder sons decided to follow their cousin, Jesus of Nazareth. For even longer with Jonas of Capernaum – whose sons Simon and Andrew did the same. Although I'm told Simon is called Peter now. Good fishermen, all of them. Nice families, nice people.

Andrew, you know, was first a follower of the Baptizer, John. A remarkable speaker, John was, remarkable. Strange-looking man. Lean as a twig, with hair which had never been cut and skin like sun-baked leather. A wild man. Yet no one ever laughed at him. Or, if they did, they stopped when he turned those eyes on them. Never seen eyes like it. I can't recall what colour they were, only the glow – especially in the brown face.

Jesus was a cousin of John, I'm told. Most of what I'm told I'm told by Rebecca, my youngest. Prophets and such are not my kind of thing at all. I know about baking and smoking. About loaves and fishes. But Rebecca knows more. She was there when John baptized Jesus – and when the four fishermen, whom she's known for years, decided to follow Jesus, she wasn't in the least surprised. She sort of did the same. She's no fool, my Rebecca. Hard-headed perhaps, obstinate – like her mother – but no fool. When she's in the bakehouse or working with the fish, she works as hard as a man. So, when she wanted a few days off to go on a trip with the Fellowship, as she called the followers of Jesus, I didn't object. A wandering preacher and his followers need looking after. It's best done by women.

Romantic figure, you know, Jesus. Pleasant, sympathetic sort of personality, a simple speaker – and a good voice. Warm and strong. And, of course, he came from these parts. One of us, sort of. And yet not one of us, somehow. This feeling he gave of being alone, by himself, apart, was perhaps the most fascinating thing about him. I miss him. Although I only met him once. The Zebedee boys brought him in once when they bought some loaves and fish. I heard him speak a number of times. Worth listening to. Most people aren't.

I always felt him to be a strong man. Not so much physically, although he was well made. He was a joiner-carpenter, and that makes muscles. No, I mean in character. He gave you the feeling that nothing would get him down, make him low in spirit.

But one day, and I was as close to him as I am to you, I saw that man very low in spirit indeed. And in circumstances which you'd think would have made any man happy. It was towards the end of one of these tours he used to do. He would speak and lead great prayer meetings and sick people would be brought to him and he would do these remarkable cures. Rebecca saw many.

Well, he was just outside here, on the jetty. All along the shore and spreading up into the streets, thousands of people.

Nearest to Jesus, his closest followers, the Twelve, as they were called. Jesus looked tired, but at peace. Then Rebecca came in, very upset, with two young men who both looked as though they'd been on the road for days.

'They've killed the Baptist,' she said. 'They've killed John. They cut off his head.' I made her sit down, and the young men, who'd come all the way from the western shore of the Dead Sea, from the fort of Machaerus, told me the dreadful story of how that terrible wife of Antipas got her revenge on John for his criticizing her wicked ways. The young men, who were exhausted, told me that they had come to tell Jesus.

I sent one of my bakehouse boys, young Jonathan, to fetch Andrew. He came in and the young men told him the story. Andrew was shocked, and was silent for a while. Then he went out on to the jetty. I watched him go up to Jesus, and he did a gentle thing. He turned Jesus, so that they both faced out across the water, and then he told him.

The Carpenter was absolutely still for a moment, and then said something. Andrew came back with Peter and the Zebedee brothers.

'Jesus wants to get away by himself for a time,' they told me. 'We're going to sail him across the lake to Bethsaida. One of our boats is right outside. We are going now.' I told them to wait a moment, and I packed up five loaves and two freshly smoked fish for them. Even sad people get hungry.

And off they went. A lonely sight. Jesus by himself in the bow, and the others in the stern. No other boats anywhere.

The great crowd was puzzled, but the Fellowship went among them and explained. I expected the crowd to disperse and go home, but not at all! There was a sort of meeting and they decided to follow the Carpenter by walking along the shore round the top of the lake. At least ten miles. Rebecca, who'd recovered herself and had been out among them, came in with her eyes shining. 'See!' she said. 'See, people just want to *be* with him, to share his grief, to make it less. To help, as he helps us!'

And off she went.

I didn't see her for two days. I wasn't worried. I pondered once or twice about how the great crowd had fared for food in Bethsaida, which doesn't much like strangers – and only has about three cafés.

Well, Rebecca told me that they didn't get as far as Bethsaida. When the crowd saw the boat, it was beached near a wide, grassy slope, at the top of which were some big rocks. The four disciples were by the boat and they said that Jesus was by himself in among the rocks, saying the prayers for the dead, for John. The great crowd gathered and waited. About five thousand, Rebecca said. It was late afternoon. Then Jesus appeared, and seemed deeply moved by the crowd's loyalty and sympathy. He moved among them, talking, smiling, laying on a hand here and there to heal someone, to cure someone.

I asked her what they did for food. After all, food is my business. I know the problems of large-scale catering.

'We all ate,' she told me, 'as much as we could eat. We were told to sit down in squares of about two hundred each. Which we did. I looked up the slope, I was sort of in the middle, and we looked like the beds in a kitchen garden. Down below, by the water, Jesus and the Twelve and a lot of the Fellowship men seemed busy breaking loaves and smoked fish into pieces and filling baskets they'd taken from the boats. Then the baskets were brought up to the squares and we ate. There was enough for everybody. In fact there were twelve baskets-full left over.'

Now don't start asking me questions. I don't know how it was done. A lot of the people must have had food with them, because people on a journey always do have. A number of people bought bread and fish here before they set off. And pooling and sharing is one of the things Jesus taught. Rebecca keeps telling me not to look for too many answers. Not to question too much. She says that the God who can make the blind see and the paralysed walk can certainly do a bit of simple catering. Well, maybe, but making a few loaves and a couple of fishes go *too* far can be very bad for business. I told Rebecca that, in a joke, and she told Jesus. He laughed.

Eliam

Old, thin, and weather-beaten. White hair and beard, uncut. Deep-set, grey eyes under strong eyebrows. A gentle expression. A slow, used-to-silence voice. A careful choice and use of words.

———————

I am not sure how it was that Simon and I first became friends, although I must try to remember to call him Peter, as everyone else does these days, I'm told. I am told also that my fisherman friend seems to be engaged in large and rather dangerous work. I would say rather to his own surprise, for I know him well – and the spreading of the teachings of a dead preacher is not Simon's sort of thing at all. Not the Simon – or Peter – that I knew.

It is, of course, possible that he has changed. It is said that the Carpenter, Jesus, changed many of his followers, as, indeed, a special sort of man can. I never spoke to Jesus, or heard him preach. I saw him. Once. In remarkable, almost unbelievable, circumstances. Peter was there. It was almost the last time I saw my kindly and considerate fisherman.

As you see, I am not young. At least thirty years older than Peter, who must now be nearly forty. He was about thirty-three or -four when Jesus died. They were much the same age. Yes, about forty Peter is now. I have known him most or his life, but not, as it were, to be 'friends'. He is like his father was, of the sea, of boats, of fish. I am of books, of words, of my first love, poetry.

So you see, my fisherman and I have little in common. Not even now, when he fishes for men, as he told me Jesus once put it. I do not fish for men, for 'readers of my writings'. I know few people. I live here on the side of the mountain, high up, alone, by choice. They tell me I am called the Hermit of Tabor. It's true enough.

Before I came here, to the mountain, I lived in Bethsaida, not very far from where Peter and his parents lived. I was very fond of his father, Jonas. A wise, quiet man. Peter's brother, Andrew, is very like Jonas, even to the voice and way of speaking. Peter was always the impetuous one, of great energy and strength. A vigorous, loyal man. The Carpenter chose his 'spreaders of the word' well.

I have always lived alone. I earned enough to keep myself by letter-writing for people, and by teaching children how to read and write, and to know their Scripture. I like children. I was a scribe and clerk to anyone who required such labours. Also, I had a certain skill in the drawing-up of a marriage settlement. On good paper, in pretty colours. I involved myself in no way with the arguments of the parties, only in their agreement – in pretty colours.

I think my friendship with Peter really began when he once brought a saying of Isaiah to me. He'd copied it down. He came in, big, handsome, not long married, in his middle twenties – and puzzled. He sensed a prophecy; about one who was to come as a 'Herald of the Messiah'.

Fishermen who think about such things are rare, and I was intrigued. We went into it. He got into the habit of dropping in, to talk, to tell me his news, to open his mind and his heart. He never came empty-handed. Fruit, vegetables, a chicken – and, most often, fish. I am fond of fish.

I remember his excitement when he first heard of the Preacher from the Desert, the Baptist, John. He was sure he was the Herald. He and Andrew made a trip south to see John, and to be baptized. It was on that occasion, or perhaps a similar occasion later, that he first met Jesus.

Not long after that, I moved away from Bethsaida, to live here on Tabor. This hut belonged to an old cousin of mine. He was dying; I looked after him till the end, and stayed on. Thus are 'hermits' made.

About two years later, at roughly the same time as I was

considering a trip to Capernaum, where Peter and his family had moved to, Peter came to the mountain. Not to see me. A coincidence – and a fantastic happening for the Hermit of Tabor to witness.

I recognized him right away, and two of the three others with him. These were James and John, sons of Zebedee. They were his partners in business. The fourth man, a little ahead of them, was Jesus, although I didn't know it at that moment. Not for certain, but I assumed it was, I felt it was.

As you see, this hut is much overgrown by the two trees that hold it up. It is almost a tree itself. It is very difficult to find, for which I am grateful. I can see and not be seen. I was going out to greet the four men, but something about their silent ascent gave me pause. Jesus led, and the brothers and Peter followed, as though bidden.

They crossed the slope below here and then began to climb again, until they were about fifty yards above my two trees. They stopped and Jesus lifted his hand as though to say 'stay', and he walked up another ten yards or so. No speech; in fact, no sound, nothing. No birdsong, no wind, no tree noise, nothing. Then he began to glow. There is no other word. It was as though he grew white-hot. All colour went; he was pure white, the purest white, from head to toe. It hurt the eyes and I turned away. The three men, nearer to the brightness, had dropped, face down.

In the shade of the hut, behind eyelids closed and smarting, I still saw the white figure. I turned again and opened my eyes. Now there were two more incandescent figures. One of great age and bearded, the other lean, in a coarse robe, leather-girdled. The three were speaking together, with Jesus listening more than speaking, as though receiving orders, or advice. With eyes nearly shut, I could just tolerate the brilliance of the light. Peter and the brothers lay still.

Peter raised his head first. In a second, he was on his feet, his voice thundering up the hillside. 'Moses!' he shouted, 'Elijah!' His voice was wild, hysterical, out of control. He shouted, out of wonder, in joy. I felt afraid.

Then the glow began to fade and the whole mountainside went into the shadow of a great cloud. I dropped to my knees and hid my head in my arms. Peter's voice died away and a voice a hundred times louder rang round the valley. 'This is my Son,' it said, 'my chosen. Listen to him!'

All was quiet then, and I got up and opened my eyes again. Jesus, by himself, natural, normal, was walking down to Peter. The brothers were on their feet. They listened as Jesus spoke quietly to them and then they all walked on down the mountain. They passed within twenty yards of my trees. I made no sound or sign. I felt weak and tired.

Living by one's self is conducive to visions, to fancies, to sounds in the head, to voices. I believe it happened. I believe I saw it. But when, about three months later, Peter made a journey to see me and I spoke of it, he denied it – after wanting to know every detail, as though for confirmation – and then said a strange thing. 'If such a thing happened,' he said, 'such a wondrous thing, it is not yet the time to tell of it. There will come a time,' he said, 'when it will all be written down, all of it.'

'Kwuz'

A nickname. Actual name not given. No age or origin. About sixty to sixty-five. Bald, with an untidy beard. Piercing, rather hard eyes in a permanently sun-darkened face. A thin, rather cruel mouth, the whole expression ungiving and watchful; sardonic. The voice rather loud, and hoarse. Barrel-chested, with heavily muscled arms. Poorly clad.

Somebody once said, so I'm told, that Jerusalem has more beggars than anywhere in the world. Whether it's true or not I don't know, I've never been out of Jerusalem. And I've been a beggar all my life. Certainly there are a great many of us. We supply a demand. People *need* to be reminded how lucky they are; to count their blessings. It makes them feel *good* to give a coin. You'd think people with a lot of blessings to be thankful for would give the most, wouldn't you? I mean, it follows, doesn't it? Rich people, big givers. Like hell. The givers are the poor people. Always have been.

As I say, as you can see, there's a lot of us. Local colour. Good tourist attraction. Though I must admit, looking around, a lot of us are not very pretty. We don't exactly beautify the landscape. High Priest Caiaphas doesn't like us cluttering up his beautiful Temple – and neither did King Herod, who made it beautiful. We've been cleared out a number of times, but we creep back, you know, we creep back. Herod's sons, Archelaus and Antipas, made similar noises. The Roman governors, Pontius Pilate, all of them, tried to get rid of us. We are still here. It's all a great game. Don't tell me that most of us are perfectly able to do other work. I know. I'm willing. What job would you suggest for someone with no legs who can't read or write? I can manage without legs – I've always had to – but once or twice I've wished I could read.

One time in particular. I think of that occasion a lot. When Jesus of Galilee sat as near to me as you are. Just the once, I remember it like yesterday – and it's nearly eleven years. It's about nine or ten since he died. Nasty business. He was a remarkable man, the Carpenter, in many ways. I always felt a sort of kinship with him. We had things in common. No money, no possessions – and we weren't fooled by people. I know he loved 'em all and I hate 'em all, but we *knew* about them, they didn't fool us. I've sat on this stone seat, in this corner near the gate of this part of the Temple for nearly fifty years. I've seen it all. If I tell you that most people are not worth twopence, it's not because I've got no legs and I'm all twisted, it's because I've been observing people all my life. All day every day. I can't write a letter, or read a book, so I sit and watch the whole stupid comedy. The way people rush about and hurt each other and think they're clever. The way people seem to think that no one knows what they're up to. The beggars know it all.

We beggars have the most accurate and the fastest news grapevine in Israel. We know everything. I knew about the Carpenter being baptized by his cousin John the day after it happened. The wedding at Cana with the water-into-wine business, the loaves and fishes, the healing of the sick, the disturbance he made here in the Temple with the money changers, how they threw him out of the synagogue in Nazareth, everything. I could have told you the exact day that the authorities decided to put a stop to him. From that day he was a marked man. They were at every meeting, in every crowd. Experts in the Law, high priests, the 'Establishment'. But he could handle them. As I said, one day he sat here next to me. In the open. Talking to a huge crowd. Teaching, making it simple. Suddenly a gang of Pharisees and lawyers pushed their way through, dragging a woman. I knew her. A man had left his wife for her. Not unknown, such behaviour. Plenty of it went on. The Pharisees, a holier-than-thou lot, were there to make the Carpenter look a fool. Or to say something that they could hang a charge on. They pushed the woman forward and made a half-ring round her.

'An adulteress!' they screamed. 'Proven! Great Moses said such women must be stoned to death. What do *you* say?'

The crowd were silent. Some of them edged forward, looking for stones. Very little difference between a crowd and a mob, you know. The woman and Jesus looked at each other. Then the Carpenter sat forward and reached down and wrote something in the dust by his feet with his finger. His head down. He didn't hurry. The Pharisees and lawyers screamed for him to answer. He got up and it went very quiet. Then he said, 'Yes, she sinned. Let the first stone be thrown by the one among you who has never sinned.' Then he looked at the crowd, and they went as still as he was. After a moment or two he sat down again, very calm, and again he bent down and wrote with his finger in the dust. As near to me as you are. Very quiet.

Then people began to shuffle and the eldest of the party

who'd brought the woman walked away. Then another. Then another. Soon she was by herself. Jesus lifted his head from the finger-writing and looked at the woman.

'All by yourself?' he said. 'Everybody gone? No stoning? No sentence? Did no one condemn you?'

'No one,' she said. She was crying. I wasn't surprised. Jesus got up and went to her.

'And I don't condemn you either,' he said. 'Go home and don't do it again.'

She went out by that gate, and the crowd moved forward to surround the Carpenter, to be near to him. Soon the writing in the dust was gone. And, because I can't read, I shall never know what it said.

Rivka

About twenty-eight. Dark, good-looking, with a rather serious expression. Fine eyes. Slender and graceful. A direct, open way of speaking, with level gaze.

———————

I suppose Martha and Mary told you where we live. They must trust you. That's good – although I hope they didn't give you the impression that Lazarus would speak to you. He won't, and I don't want him to anyway. Poor soul, it's best if he's not reminded too much of those times. The butcher told him last month that Governor Pilate has been recalled to Rome in disgrace and that was enough to stir it all up again for poor Lazarus. I'm not saying it's all nightmares and sadness for him, he can be as cheerful and loving as any other husband, but I do my best to leave certain doors closed. Believe me, I know best. He's out on the hills with our two kiddies and he's at peace. Talk to me. I know it all and I saw it all.

In one way Lazarus is right. The whole thing was full of echoes, of samenesses, of signs of things to come. When Lazarus gets in one of his states over it, it's mainly that aspect he's talking about.

It started with Martha's husband, Simon. He was a leper. He picked it up at the leper caves, where he used to take food and drink. He was a very good man. He was put away and in the first winter in the caves he caught some sort of lung fever and it killed him. About twelve years ago, just before Jesus first appeared.

Martha and Mary took me to one of the first faith healings Jesus did in this area. I don't know if you ever went to one. No? Well it's difficult to describe. It's not what you think. It was very quiet, for a start. Jesus was a calm sort of person. Unhurried. He never seemed to have any doubts about anything. He never doubted that he could heal – and he passed that feeling on, and the sick people believed too, and got better.

We saw remarkable things that day. When the meeting was over, Martha asked Jesus – who looked dead on his feet – and some of his followers, whom she knew, to come back for a meal, and they said yes. Now, mark this. Martha's house, 'Simon the Leper's House', is right at the end of the market street in Bethany. Beyond it, the path up to the top of the Mount of Olives, through the groves. As we came over the top and looked down at the house, Martha stopped and said to Jesus, 'If you had been here, Simon would not have died.'

Jesus looked at her without saying anything, then he kissed her and we went on down to supper. Martha as usual fussing and cooking and making everything just so, Mary just sitting and listening to Jesus.

Lazarus is the youngest of the three. He came about four years after Mary. He's never been very strong and I think his sisters spoiled him a bit. He and I are the same age. We grew up together. It didn't surprise anybody when we said we were going to get married. We set a date and started to get things together, and then Lazarus became ill. This was about two years after we'd met Jesus. He was a friend of the family.

People made jokes about Lazarus taking to his bed with 'marriage fear', but he got worse. He stopped eating and started terrible sweats and then after a few days went into a coma. The doctors were useless. Then Martha sent a message to Jesus, who was away to the east where the Jordan meets the Salt Sea. Fifteen, twenty miles. We thought he would come right away but he didn't. And Lazarus died. My father arranged the cave-grave with the rollstone in front and Martha and Mary prepared the body and put the bindings on. I helped. I insisted, and it is woman's work. Poor Lazarus. He was like wax. He'd given me a silk handkerchief about a month before and I bound it round his head. Then there were the prayers and the procession and he was put to rest in the cave and the stone rolled across. And still no Jesus. We couldn't understand it. Not a word – and my family is big, mostly living in Jerusalem, which is only about a half-hour's walk from Bethany. So every day there were dozens of people coming to sympathize or for prayers. But no Jesus.

I don't know how many days went by. Three or four. I just sat and cried. I was just nineteen. Then, on the Thursday I think it was, about midday, Martha came to me. 'Come,' she said, 'Jesus is coming.'

We met him at the top of the path where he had first kissed Martha. He kissed her again and she used nearly the same words as the first time. 'If only you'd been here,' she said, 'my brother would not have died.' Jesus didn't say much to us and then told Martha to fetch Mary. He and I stayed on the hill. Soon Martha came back with Mary and with them were a lot of friends and relatives who'd been in the house. Mary was in tears and so was everybody else. Then Mary sank down on her knees in front of Jesus and used the same words as Martha. 'If only you had been here, my brother would not have died.' Her voice was sure and her tears had stopped – and she's the emotional one.

By this time Jesus was in tears. It's very moving when a man cries. A lot of the people remarked on how much he must have loved Lazarus. Others spoke of his great cures, even the restoring of people seemingly dead or dying.

Then, as though by command, everyone turned and went down and across the hill to the grave. When we got there, everybody stood quiet. Jesus stood looking at the great stone with a strange expression. Frowning, thoughtful.

'Take away the stone,' he said.

'But he's been dead for days,' said Martha. 'By this time he will be decaying.'

'Take away the stone,' said Jesus, quite calm, like at one of his faith healings. 'If you believe, you will see the wonder of God.'

The men in the party rolled away the stone. The cave was a black hole. No one spoke.

Then Jesus looked up to Heaven and spoke in the same calm voice to God, calling him Father. Then he shouted in a tremendous voice like a great roar of trumpets:

'LAZARUS, COME FORTH!'

And Lazarus did. Not right away; after a moment or two. It was very natural and quite unfrightening. Rather endearing, in a way. A young man, very pale, rather sleepy, rubbing his eyes, blinking in the sun, with a silk handkerchief round his head.

Jesus looked at me. 'Take those clumsy grave-bindings off him,' he said, 'and take him home.'

Lazarus was perfectly well, and has never been ill since. Not in the body. We were married very soon after, on the date set. I've never known Lazarus so gay and happy. And then it seemed no time at all before the arrest, and the trial, and the terrible whipping, and the crucifixion, and we were standing in front of Jesus's grave, with the stone rolled back, and Lazarus started to talk about God giving and God taking away and echoes and samenesses and signs. I know all the stories about resurrection and so on, and of course Jesus, in the spirit, *does* live on, but Jesus, in the flesh, was *gone*. Lazarus is still here, and Jesus isn't, and Lazarus sort of blames himself. Poor Lazarus. He works very hard for the Fellowship, we both do, and he listens with sweet patience to everybody's wonderful stories of Jesus, but he'll never be happy again. It's worst late at night. He cries in my arms, like a child. 'Maybe Jesus was allowed just so many,' he says, 'and Lazarus was the last. Lazarus came back and Jesus didn't.' Poor Lazarus.

Chapter 5

THE BEGINNING OF THE END

Benjamin

Plump, rosy-cheeked, wide-eyed. Much younger in appearance than his twenty-five years. A gentle, high voice. A child-like innocence of manner. Left hand and foot slightly spastic.

For quite a long time, I thought my brother would get into trouble for letting the Carpenter and the Twelve eat their Passover supper upstairs. The way things turned out, I mean. With the Carpenter being arrested the same night and executed the next day. Sailing *very* close to the wind that was, I'd say. But my brother's like that, he's not afraid of anything. He's the strong one. He tells me what to do and I do it. He looks after me. He brought me up, pretty well, after my father died. He is nearly eight years older.

He's not really a follower of Jesus. He owed him a debt. Sharon, my brother's wife, was very ill. Dying in fact. No one could do anything, no one knew what it was. About two years ago, Jesus put his hand on her head and told her she would get well, and she did, in two days. My brother told Jesus that the big room upstairs was his whenever he wanted it – and for any purpose. For holding meetings, or for hiding in, when things got hot. My brother knows how things go in this city. In Jerusalem things can get hot – especially if you run foul of the Temple lot, or Governor Pilate. Jesus did both, I'm told. I only met Jesus once to talk to. On the night of that supper, upstairs. Nearly a year ago. It'll soon be Passover again. I like Passover, it's a happy feast, especially the Suppers of the First Nights, when the 'freedom from slavery' story is told.

The supper upstairs wasn't a very happy one. It was all rather strange. The whole day was odd. At breakfast my brother told me to clean the big room and put the long table up. I asked him who for, and were we going to have a Passover party. No, he said, the Carpenter and the Twelve were coming. I was surprised because Jesus had made no use of the room. 'When did you hear from him?' I said. 'Never mind,' said my brother. Sharon was pleased, and got busy cooking, getting all the big bowls out, making bread without salt, unleavened.

About midday, my brother told me to take a big water jug and go to the market well and fill it. Very odd. We have our own well in the garden. I was going to ask why but sometimes it's best not to. My brother usually has a good reason and the market is not far, and the melon-woman is by the well. I like melon.

I bought some melon and sat in the sun whilst I ate it. Then I picked up the jug and started back. And two men started to follow me! Both big, strong-looking men. It was obvious, they weren't secret about it. I tried to shake them off, I was a bit scared, but I couldn't. So I came home, so that my brother could handle it.

As I got to our door, they came right up and stood on either side of me, both looking down at me and smiling. The larger one put his hand on my shoulder. Then my brother opened the door and greeted them by name. Peter and John. It was two of the Twelve. Peter, the one with his hand on my shoulder, said he had a message from his Master, and we went inside. I took the water up to the room and, after a minute or two, they came up, with my brother, to see the room, and then they left.

I went on doing the room and helping Sharon with the cooking and in the late afternoon they all arrived together, just as the sun was going down, just as we'd finished the preparations. They stayed downstairs with us for a while and I served them with wine and nuts and dates. Sharon came in wearing her new Passover dress and they were nice to her and the Carpenter asked her how she was keeping. She looked very pretty.

They were a very assorted lot of men. About the only thing they had in common was a Galilee accent. Except one, a dark, rather tense-looking man called Judas who didn't smile at all. My brother told me that Judas came from the far south, from Kerioth; that his name, Iscariot, meant that. Man of Kerioth. I didn't like him.

Some of the Twelve were cousins of the Carpenter. There were two pairs of brothers, all fishermen. They were all rough sort of men, even the one Sharon said had been a tax-collector. She said one of them, who was quick and fiery, was a Nationalist, anti-Roman, a revolutionary. There were two called James, one a little, cheerful man. The biggest of the Twelve was Peter. His brother Andrew was like him, but not as tall or heavy. And he was quieter.

I suppose the quietest of them all that night was Jesus. He listened more than he spoke, and seemed rather sad. Not very Passoverish, as I call it, at all.

When I asked Sharon if she and my brother and I were also going to eat upstairs in the big room, she said we had not been invited. We were to have our own Passover supper downstairs with some family, as usual, but I would help a little upstairs with the serving and taking up of food and so on.

Then, when the sun had nearly gone, Jesus stood up. He seemed rather tired. Everyone stopped talking and he led the way upstairs. It seemed to be very solemn for Passover.

After a few minutes my brother told me to go up and make certain they had enough water and towels for the hand-washing before food. When I went in, it was feet that were being washed! Jesus, the chief one, the head of them all, was on his knees in front of Peter washing his feet and drying them on a towel. He'd already done about half the Twelve. There they sat, with clean feet. It was most odd – and all rather serious. The Twelve seemed rather embarrassed. Except Judas, who was scowling and looked angry. I went down and brought up more water and two fresh towels. When I offered to help, Jesus smiled and said no, and Judas gestured with his head for me to go out.

Our own supper, downstairs, was, as always on Passover, very happy, with lots of songs and wine. Every now and then I would go up to the big room with the large dishes of each course for them to serve themselves. They didn't seem to be enjoying themselves as much as we were downstairs. No songs at all. The second time I went up, they were just finishing the dish of savoury dip that Sharon always makes on Passover to start the meal. You dip bits of bread in, to give you a happy year.

As I walked in, about four of them were dipping and Jesus was saying, in a calm sort of way, 'One of you is going to betray me.' They all looked at him with their mouths open. I felt very out of place, and went out immediately. As I got to the bottom of the stairs, I heard the door to the room open and shut and then Judas came down. He was in a hurry, he nearly pushed me over – although I don't think he even saw me. He looked terrified – and sort of guilty. He rushed straight out into the street and up the road. I told my brother and he said it was none of our business and that I should take up a flask of our best wine with his compliments. I wasn't keen, and left it for a bit, then took it up when I took up the meat, the Passover Lamb.

I was almost afraid to open the door. When I did, the Carpenter was on his feet breaking pieces off a new loaf and passing them along to his friends. 'Eat,' he said. 'In memory of me; in memory of my body.' Then he saw me. 'And we will drink good wine,' he said, 'and it will also be in memory of me. Of my blood, which is soon to be shed for you.' I poured the wine in absolute silence. Jesus drank his and said, 'I will drink no more until I drink it with you all in my Father's Kingdom.' I thought he meant his father was a king and he was a prince soon going home. He didn't look like a prince. As I went out, they were beginning a hymn, a rather sad one. Not a Passover song at all.

The last time I went up was to ask if any more of anything was needed and to take up some of Sharon's cinnamon and almond cakes. I knocked but there seemed to be a lot of raised voices and I wasn't heard, so after a moment I went in.

Most of the Twelve were on their feet, all talking and protesting at once. The Carpenter was in the middle. Then he spoke, without raising his voice at all. 'It is written in the Scriptures,' he said. 'You will lose faith in me. All of you.'

The noise started again and the big man, Peter, spoke the loudest. 'Not me!' he said. 'Not me! Even if all the others do, not me!'

Then Jesus spoke again. 'I tell you, Peter,' he said, 'that before the cock crows tomorrow morning you will have denied you even know me – three times!'

The big man could hardly speak. I put down the little cakes and went downstairs. Not long after, they all came down. Jesus thanked my brother and Sharon and they all went out into the dark. They were all very quiet, not in the least like they'd been to a Passover party.

I went up to the big room and started to clear up. The little cakes were where I'd put them, untouched.

Malchus

About forty-five. Rather bald. A pale, bony face. Light hair and eyes. A sharp nose and a rather pursed mouth. A precise way of speech.

It would be as well, I would suggest, for you to understand fully that in the matter of the recent arrest and death of the Galilean I had no personal animosity toward him at all. None at all. And neither have my colleagues toward the ill-advised followers of Jesus, against whom they are at present drafting regulations. We carry out orders. We are servants of the Temple, with civil authority and influence. Civil servants, if you like.

We are bedrock; foundation. The leaders, the spokesmen, the ministers, change; governments change. We do not. It was ever so; it will be always so.

Nothing personal. When my master, Caiaphas, said some time ago that it would be better for Jesus to die than the whole nation should suffer and be destroyed, he was speaking good sense as he saw it. As a high priest he has a difficult job – even with our help. Jesus is dead; the thing is done. Soon he will be forgotten, but there was nothing personal. When Caiaphas made that statement, I don't think he'd ever met or seen Jesus. But miracle-workers and faith-healers and raisers-from-the-dead can be very disruptive and troublesome – and the Romans are touchy enough on the subject of what my master calls matters religious. Pilate hates all religion, all priests – high priests in particular. An impossible man, Pilate.

Certainly I have reason to be grateful to the late Jesus. He attended to a head injury of mine that could have been most disfiguring. I would like to have repaid him in some way, but it was far too late in the day. Very apt statement that, far too late in the day. And a fact. And what a day, too. I would have liked to have spared him at least the flogging, but that was by order of Pilate. A Roman touch; crucify, but the scourge-whips first.

I'm told that the Galilean prophesied his death. So did I, friend, so did I. I don't have prophetic powers, or second sight. I have records. I have on record the exact day that one of his closest friends, one of the so-called Twelve, came here to give him to us. I say give; to sell him to us. It's always a money transaction; it's allowed for. There's a fund. Cash; unreceipted, in silver.

We took Jesus in a garden, at night. A detail of the Temple Guard. Two officers, ten men, and the informer, to positively identify. We knew that he would be with others and we wanted no mistake. I went along really to see we got our money's worth. Jesus, the leader. We were not interested in the Twelve. Our experience in such matters is that, once the ringleader is picked up, the 'followers' stop following and fade away. We were right. They are all in hiding.

The big surprise was that one or two of them were armed. Most unexpected. Could have been fatal in my case. When the informer, Iscariot, had identified by touching, we went forward to make formal arrest. At that moment one of the Twelve, a huge, bearded man, stepped forward with a short-sword and very nearly took my ear off. I was covered in blood. The blow had clubbed as well as cut me. I was dazed. I heard the guard rush forward and a lot of shouting, and then the Galilean's voice, speaking quietly. Someone put a bandage round my head, almost holding the ear back in place. I remember thinking to myself, 'Well, Jesus, if you're such a healer, do *me*.'

It was almost as though he heard me. He put his two hands up, over my two ears, and said, 'It will heal, there will be no pain.'

He said other things, about prophecies coming true and why were we so busy with guards, when we could have picked him up in the Temple any time, and was he a bandit or something. I paid little attention to him. I had no pain but I hate the sight of blood and I was messy and sticky with it. I left him to the men, who took him to the senior high priest, Annas. Annas, my master's father-in-law. The Old Man, we call him. The real power behind the throne, that one. He's been high priest, *the* High Priest for years and years. He made all five of his sons high priests, too – and when his daughter married, his son-in-law, Caiaphas, as well.

Well, anyway, one of the soldiers took me back home to the palace of Caiaphas and I went to my room and changed my clothes and washed away the blood. I was going to change the bandage, too, but didn't. Our reports said that Jesus had positively cured people by the laying on of hands, and he'd touched me. And certainly the pain had gone. I felt fine. I looked down into the courtyard below my window. The palace guard had made their usual bonfire. It looked cheerful. I saw one of the arrest officers come through the gate on a horse and I went down.

He told me that the Old Man would question Jesus and would send him across to us, to Caiaphas. The officer told me that he'd left as the interrogation began – and that the prisoner and escort would arrive in about two hours. I thanked him and invited him in for a drink. We talked, and he was surprised that my wound was giving me no pain, that I seemed unworried by it. He suggested that the garrison medical officer might look at it, perhaps put some stitches in. I refused. He didn't insist.

After a little while, one of the maid-servants came in and told us that one of the Twelve was in the courtyard warming himself at the fire. I asked her how she knew. She said she'd been to hear Jesus many times and the Twelve were always with him. She knew them all by sight.

'Is it the informer?' I asked her, 'Iscariot?'

She said no. I gathered she had no opinion of our informer. 'Are you sure?' I asked her. 'Did you speak to him?'

She said, 'Yes, I am sure. And I did speak to him. He denies it. He says he doesn't know Jesus.' She seemed upset. I sent her away.

I was amused. It seemed a foolish action on the fellow's part, whoever it was. I looked out of the window. There were quite a few people round the fire, many with their backs to me. I was curious, and I asked the officer to go down. I watched, and saw him speak to a rather big man for a minute or two and then leave him. He came in and went back to his chair. 'I think the girl is right,' he said. 'In fact, I think it's the man who hit you with the sword. He denies everything, and there's no blood on him. It was dark in the garden, and there was a lot of confusion, and I'm not sure. What do you want me to do?'

I looked down again at the man. He showed no signs of wanting to run away. He sat hunched, bulky, his back to me. I left it for a while until the officer said that he should go down to meet the arrest detail. I went with him.

The man had not moved. I went across to him. He stood up. He topped me by a head and a half. He looked down at me, at my bandaged head. I wasn't sure. I asked him his name, address and trade. Simon, he said, of Bethsaida, a fisherman.

'A Galilean,' I said, 'like Jesus of Nazareth, a troublemaker we now have under arrest. I think you are one of his gang. An armed bodyguard.'

He was looking across the top of my head. Jesus and the escort were just coming in. I kept my eyes on the big man's face. The good timing was not accidental; I know my job.

'Well?' I said.

'I don't know what you're talking about,' he said. 'I don't know Jesus.'

I turned and looked at Jesus. He was looking straight at the big man. A sad look, but nothing to prove he knew him. I turned back to the fisherman and saw an astonishing thing. Tears were pouring down his face. He tried to speak, twice, then he turned and ran like a madman across the yard and out of the gate.

I let him go. If he is one of the Twelve, and the movement, or party, or whatever it is, starts to get out of hand, we shall have him. I shan't charge him with bodily harm or offensive weapon. No point. The ear is as new. Perfect. No scar, nothing.

Janus

Early fifties. Fit-looking, of a military bearing. Medium height, clean-shaven. Grey hair, cut close. A feeling of authority; also of tolerance, and humour.

Well, Pilate has gone. Cold-eyed Pontius, Procurator of Judea, rough-shod rider extraordinary, rode rough-shod just once too often and is on his way back to Rome. Good! Good riddance! Pilate, with pals in high places and appointed by Tiberius himself, is in disgrace and going back to a dying Tiberius, perhaps already dead – with new faces in the high places. Serves him right! Tiberius' favourite will be nobody's favourite, for that is the way of Rome.

I know Rome. I did my military service there and was born just outside, to the south. I came here, to Jerusalem, when Gratus was Governor, about fifteen years ago. He taught me my job. Personal assistant, aide-de-camp, right-hand man, dogs-body, beck-and-call merchant, doormat.

You must forgive me my rather undiplomatic use of words. Five days ago, when Pilate sailed away, I retired – and have not been quite sober since. The feeling of holiday is enormous. Marullus is the new man and he is bringing his own dogsbody. I shall see them in and that's it. I shall retire to my villa in Galilee, and my Galilean wife and my three sons, and I shall grow vegetables and fruit.

Where I was born we had a saying: 'You have to know a man really well to hate him.' Well, I knew Pilate very well indeed. He was by nature hateful. He had no friends, not really. Ten years here – and eight people saw him off. 'I like to leave a few reliable enemies wherever I go,' he used to say. He's left more than a few here.

He started off wrong. This country is really run by the religious groups – and he ran foul of them in no time at all. He used holy money, as they call the Temple treasury, to build waterworks, he ignored all the 'graven image' regulations here, he insulted people, he put the troops in at the drop of a handkerchief. The waterworks caused a riot and he killed rioters. He was a merciless man. Obstinate, and cold. Human life meant nothing to him. He once threatened me. I told him I was an army shortsword champion, and also that I kept a private journal to be forwarded to Rome upon my death. True, both statements. There's enough in that journal to hang him ten times over. He would execute without trial, condemn without evidence. He loved cruelty and pain for its own sake. He was corrupt and could be bought. He was crooked, but he was the law, Roman law, respected the world over. He was a bloody-handed disgrace. As you can hear, I knew him well enough to hate him. And I do. And believe me, I am not a good hater.

He was. He hated with a sneer, with contempt. He hated Antipas, and Caiaphas, the High Priest – and the High Priest's father-in-law, old Annas – who, I think, was a good match for him. An old fox, Annas. Completely unafraid of my splendid chief, he was. Pilate hated the Sanhedrin, the Pharisees, the Sadducces, all of them! 'I don't care what their labels are,' he'd say, 'they're *Jews*, the lot of 'em!' He had absolute contempt for Antipas – and *all* the royal family – and showed it! Not in a vulgar way. Never vulgar, my chief. A raised eyebrow, a curled lip, an expressionless look, like ice.

I suppose that one of the biggest disturbances in this last ten years was the business with the Carpenter, six or seven years ago. Not from Pilate's point of view, he didn't care one way or the other – and his killings were usually much bigger affairs, with him on his white horse and the troops in there with the swords.

No, when I say disturbance, I mean the whole city seemed to be in uproar. All the religious parties, the Temple lot, the councils, *everybody* seemed to be involved. Over a poor preacher from Galilee, who it seemed, could cure people. If Pilate had kept his temper and used a bit of sense, that preacher would have been put out of harm's way for a while and been forgotten. Instead of which, his followers have got a whole movement going which is right out of hand. We lock up ten and twenty more appear.

I often think that if the crowd with the preacher had waited till morning – and kept their voices down – we could have got some order into it. They came screaming into the forecourt at *dawn!* Hundreds of 'em! I swear that half of them were a paid mob. Shouters. We've used them ourselves. Confusion-makers.

Friend, I tell you that that was positively *not* the way to wake up my late chief – who used to indulge himself in various little ways till the early hours and normally opened the office at noon.

He came into my room white with temper. He looked mad. I dressed and went down, and the lunacy started. First, the accusers of the prisoner wouldn't come inside because we were a gentile building and they didn't want to have their Passover holiness contaminated. So Pilate went out to them and told them to clear off and judge the fellow themselves. The shouters started then, wanting a death-sentence, which only Pilate could give. So he had the prisoner brought inside and questioned him.

The preacher either wouldn't answer, or answered in a way almost guaranteed to annoy Pilate. I was doing the charge notes. As far as I could make out, the preacher was accused of misrepresentation, fraud and blasphemy. He said he was King of the Jews and the Son of God. After a few minutes Pilate stopped asking questions. I think he could hardly believe that his sleep had been disturbed by the sort of case that usually was settled in a district court, with the prisoner given a week of cold-water immersion, starvation, and a straitjacket.

Pilate looked at me. I knew the look. It usually meant that some mad private joke was being invented. Jokes in which pain for others always played a part. Pain, ridicule, often death. That was his humour, his stimulant, his aphrodisiac. I do not joke.

And it began. First, out to the mob, and the listening, with inclined head and cold eyes, to the different party spokesmen. A tall, correct, sharp-nosed Pilate, saying, 'I see nothing criminal in the prisoner.' Then, when told the preacher was from Galilee, sending him over to Antipas, official Tetrarch of Galilee. Armed guard, all the trimmings. 'It won't wake Antipas up,' Pilate said to me. 'He's got his cronies in. One of his ghastly wife's three-day parties – with the "special entertainers". Well, here's a new one for them. A Son of God.'

When the preacher came back from Antipas, he was dressed in a gorgeous cloak. Obviously some pretty rough fun had been made of him. The mob went crazy, howling for death. Pilate was enjoying it. He made a speech about his custom of always releasing a prisoner at festival time. Anyone. Even the Carpenter. The shouters started to scream for a rioter called Barabbas, very popular in the city, to be set free, and for the preacher to be crucified. 'Are you sure?' Pilate kept on saying to them, 'Are you sure?' He got them screeching like children at a pantomime play. A Roman procurator, a governor. Disgraceful.

Then he told the crowd that, as crucifixion seemed rather too severe a punishment, he would give the prisoner a sharp lesson. 'He will be flogged,' he told them. 'Fifty strokes. With the Roman scourge-whip. Right away.'

The garrison yard is alongside the forecourt and the whipping could be heard. The mob counted the strokes. Pilate was watching them. He was absolutely relaxed, expressionless. He was sweating a little.

Two sergeants brought the preacher back. Still in the robe, with a ring of thorn twigs pushed down on his head. He looked half-dead. He couldn't stand up, he was held up. Twenty strokes is standard – and will take most of the skin off a man's back.

Pilate turned his head and raised a hand. 'Behold,' he said to the crowd, 'the King of the Jews.'

They screamed like wild animals when they've smelt blood. There was plenty to smell. They wanted a death, not a whipping.

Pilate got up and told the sergeants to bring the preacher inside again. 'For further interrogation', he said over his shoulder to the spokesmen. I think he was curious, as I was, to find out why what seemed to be a rather mild man should stir up so much riot.

He discovered little. The preacher was conscious, but obviously badly hurt. He was calm, and showed neither fear nor anger. Pilate asked him certain questions but he gave no reply at all. Just the calm, almost thoughtful, gaze. Pilate went closer. He was angry, a kind of cold anger, his own kind. 'Don't you realize,' he said, 'that whether you live or die is entirely in my hands?'

Then the preacher spoke. 'You have no power over me at all,' he said, 'except that allowed you by God, my Father. Indeed, in this matter, you are guilty of little. You do only as he tells you.'

It was said quietly, from a bruised mouth in a dead-white face. Pilate was speechless. I could see why. It was almost funny, unique. Here was a prisoner judging *him,* a prisoner flogged nearly to death, covered in blood, in a gory fancy dress of kingly robe and crown, assessing *his* guilt. And worse, here was the pawn in the game, the middle of the joke, seemingly the least disturbed – and the only one showing any sort of dignity.

Pilate said no more. To match the dignity, to show his own, he sent for the silver basin. The abstaining bowl. Warm water. We went out and the crowd went quiet; something new for them to see. I held the bowl, and Pilate, facing the priests, said in his formal voice: 'The charge is not proven, I wash my hands of this matter.' And dipped his fingers, with a sideways look at me.

Then it went bad. The old fox, old Annas, stepped forward. The mob, which had begun to go mad again, stopped.

'In this country,' said the old man, 'we have no kings any more. We have tetrarchs, and princes. And procurators, put here by our rulers, Rome. Who *do* have a king, an emperor. The accused says he is *our* king, enthroned by his Father, Almighty God. Thus greater even than the Emperor, than Caesar. If you release this man,' said the old fox, 'it would seem you agree. It would seem you are no friend of Caesar.'

It went dead quiet. Pilate was now the middle of the joke. It had blown up in his face. He had lost command, and the mob knew it. Mobs always know. And Pilate knew, as I did, that the old man had power, and could send a report to Rome, using that reasoning, that could make a *lot* of trouble. The hand-washing could be made to seem both incompetent *and* disloyal, both serious matters.

It was very quiet. The old man was absolutely unaffected by the hatred pouring out of Pilate, who tried to match the cunning of the old fox.

'Am I to kill your *King?*' he said to the old man.

'We have no king but Caesar,' said the old man, without blinking.

And that was it. Pilate walked across to the raised dais in the forecourt called the Pavement. He sat down on the small throne where judgements and sentences are given. He formally found the prisoner guilty and sentenced him to be crucified. He used the correct words, put his seal on the order, stood up, and walked past me without a word.

I didn't go to the crucifixion. If you've seen one, you've seen them all. The Carpenter wasn't the first, or the last.

Lydia

Housewife. About thirty-eight years old. A rather buxom, good-looking woman. A ready smile, and a pleasant, low voice. The face, in repose, is serious and strong. Brown hair and eyes.

Pilate and his wife, my mistress, were in Israel about ten years and I can honestly say that I was as frightened of that man at the end as at the beginning. He was never cruel to me, or any of the house servants, but he did some terrible things. As Governor, or Procurator as he was called, he had absolute power. He killed many. He followed Gratus, whom we all liked better. Gratus used to talk about bringing more water to Jerusalem but did nothing. Pilate built an aqueduct – and took the money from the Temple treasury to pay for it – and put the city under martial law when it nearly caused a riot!

It was during that period I met my husband, Barabbas. He was well known in the city as an anti-Roman agitator. There was a whole bunch of them, and they caused a lot of trouble. They were called Zealots. All sorts of people called themselves Zealots, from the roughest gutter-boy to highly educated scribes. Even lawyers, and priests. My Barabbas, bless him, was nearer gutter-boy than priest. He's quieter now, but when he was younger, before Jesus was crucified, he was a terror. And very handsome and popular with the ladies – and he knew it! I disapproved of him entirely. I come of what is called a respectable family. We've been in service to the royals or the Roman governors for generations. I was a lady's maid, first to the wife of Gratus, and then, when Pilate came, to *his* wife. I miss her very much indeed. A lovely person, Lady Claudia.

Barabbas and I are both followers of Jesus. They shouldn't have killed him. He did no harm. But killing him made him live, if you know what I mean. Oddly enough, I first heard of Jesus from Barabbas. On my days off I used to go to a social club in the West End of the city. I liked it, it was lively. A lot of servants of the palace and Government House and so on used to go. It was well run. It was there I met Barabbas, as I said, just after the aqueduct disturbances. He and his friends had been trying to stir up the unrest into a full-size war against the Romans. Very naughty, very silly. When things quietened down he and some of the other younger Zealots used to come to the club. Very earnest lot, most of them. Lot of students among them, wanting to change the world. Fat chance, it was a Roman world.

Well, I was telling Barabbas about Pilate's wife, my mistress, and her bad dreams and nightmares. She used to suffer terribly. She would wake screaming and rigid – or for days she would be afraid to sleep, and would get pale and exhausted, poor soul. Pitiful to see. And she hated taking stuff. Any sort of drug upset her. So I told Barabbas and he told me about this preacher, Jesus of Nazareth, who it seemed could cure people of anything. Leprosy, blindness, fits, anything.

I told my mistress and she went to one of Jesus's meetings. I went with her. She didn't get near enough to speak to Jesus, there was a great crush of people, but on his way out of those meetings he used to walk slowly, and the crowd used to keep running forward to form lines either side of him, and we did the same, and as he passed us he looked straight into my mistress's eyes. She didn't say anything and neither did he, but that same night she began to sleep better. I can't explain it. She believed; and it was enough.

I was grateful to Barabbas and I let him take me out a few times. Away from his wild friends he was very nice - and he respected me, too. A bit too much, I thought, for he had a wicked reputation as a lover, and I wouldn't have minded. But not once did he try to take liberties or go too far. He would have been the first. After we were married, he told me he knew that - and he wanted it kept that way, until he married me! Very sure of himself he was! Less so after Jesus died.

If Jesus hadn't died, I wouldn't have my Barabbas. Although it's about ten years ago now (Pilate's been gone nearly four years), it's well remembered how the mob screamed for Barabbas to be freed from prison and for Jesus to be killed. It could have been the other way round. Pilate had this rule of releasing one prisoner on every major feast day. Barabbas and two of his friends had been caught red-handed in some sabotage nonsense, and they'd stolen some arms from the Roman garrison. It was all very brave and stupid and dangerous and they were put in prison and became sort of heroes. They were sentenced to death, but Pilate set no date. He was waiting for things to calm down. Then, not long after, Jesus was arrested.

I remember every detail of the morning Jesus was questioned by Pilate, who was in a foul temper. Any sort of delegation or council or committee brought out the worst in him, and that morning it seemed that every elder and high priest and lawyer in Jerusalem was screaming and shouting at him. Pilate shut them up and made their spokesmen make the charges. Then he began to question Jesus, who hardly answered him, which made him angrier still.

I heard about that part later, because I had my own troubles. My mistress, who'd been sleeping normally for months, woke that morning screaming and terrified - worse than before she went to Jesus. She was in a dreadful state. I had to slap her and throw cold water in her face to bring her round, to wake her up properly. She babbled and wept, and when she'd quietened down she asked what all the shouting was outside. When I told her it had to do with Jesus, she jumped up, with staring eyes like a madwoman. 'Go to Pilate,' she screamed at me. 'Tell him to have nothing to do with this matter. Nothing to do with Jesus, that good, good man. I have had such dreams, such terrible dreams – of death and massacre and disgrace and banishment and blood and exile! Tell him to have nothing to *do* with it! *Nothing!* Go and tell him!' she screamed, '*tell* him!'

Well, I did as she asked, I went to the forecourt and told Pilate. He listened without changing his expression, his eyes as cold as ice. Then he turned to the great mob and asked them whom they wanted released, Jesus or Barabbas. They roared for Barabbas – and that Jesus should be crucified.

Which was done. Barabbas and I were at the crucifixion. How could we not be? It changed Barabbas. Me, too. We married soon after. Some people blamed Barabbas, which was stupid, it had nothing to do with him.

Six years after Jesus was killed, my mistress's dream came true, sort of – although she never told me the details of the dream. Pilate heard about a great crowd of harmless treasure hunters in Samaria and he sent in an armed force and killed hundreds. Death and massacre and blood. The Samaritans complained to Rome and Pilate and his wife were recalled to Rome and then banished to southern France. Disgrace and banishment. I heard he committed suicide. I doubt it. My poor mistress. She changed, also, you know, after Jesus died. She was a follower, too, in her own way. She helped the Fellowship a lot, on the quiet. And she never had another nightmare.

Sylvanus

(A second visit. See page 271.)

_____

I think I may have told you, at our first meeting, that Great Herod liked continuity in his court. He trusted no one, but liked the faces of those he didn't trust to be familiar.

It was often said at court that it was better to be a servant of Herod than a relative of Herod. You would live longer. It is an over-simplification, but not without some truth.

I served Herod till he died; then, in the sharing-out between the sons, Archelaus – till Rome got rid of him – and then Antipas, until Rome got rid of *him*, about two years ago. Antipas the Tetrarch, part-ruler – for after Great Herod, Rome wanted no more kings. And after Archelaus, even the tetrarchs would have Romans to show them the way it was to be done. Roman governors, procurators.

When Antipas was officially made Tetrarch of Galilee, some months after his father died, it was one thing. After ten years, when Archelaus was sent away, it was another. The governors came. Coponius, Marcus Ambivius, Annius Rufus – during whose time Great Augustus died – then Gratus, of whom I was fond, and after him Pontius Pilate, of whom I was not. When Pilate came, Antipas had been a part-ruler, a tetrarch, some thirty years. Procurators had been in the country for twenty. I knew them all. They were in some ways alike; bred for the job. A sort of regulation-book courtesy, but with a certain hardness.

Pontius Pilate was the fifth – and the hardest. He took one look at Antipas and saw him for the weak, woman-dominated fool he was. I think they had met in Rome, where Antipas met Herodias – who did the dominating, but neither ever mentioned it to me, and, in a limited way, they both confided in me. I was an old employee, a sort of family retainer, privy councillor, and senior civil servant rolled into one. I did not mind. It appealed to my sense of humour to be a go-between. Antipas has gone now, in disgrace, but he was no fool. Foolish, yes, and weak, but he was able – and had inherited his father's love of creating fine buildings, even cities. Tiberias he built, and a lot of Sepphoris. I knew him so well. Pilate, less well. But the Roman was an enclosed, shut in, frightening man. He, too, is gone now. He went before Antipas, also in disgrace.

Such different men. In every way. Certainly in the matter of their private, off-duty, lives. Pilate was no angel, but compared to the occasional goings-on among the Antipas family and friends, he was ascetic. When Herodias, that dreadful woman, made Antipas kill John the Baptist, she did it at a *party,* a wild party. At which her stupid daughter, Salome, danced like a whore and her weakling of a husband had a good man killed so as not to lose face. Pilate was full of contempt. He had met John, as I had, and rather respected that fearless, wild man. As I did.

Not long after the Baptist was beheaded, we began to hear of another preacher. A man of Galilee, from Nazareth, Jesus, son of Joseph. Over a period of two or three years, he became quite famous. The orthodox and conservative groups didn't like him at all and finally arrested him. At night.

The morning following that night comes often into my thoughts – although it must be nearly ten years ago. There was a happening that morning that brought together Pilate and Antipas (whom he'd always detested) in a sort of closeness they had never shared. They became almost friends from that morning onwards. Very strange. I remember it well – and the happening – with a particular distaste.

It was Spring time, Passover time. Antipas and the court were in Jerusalem, as usual, for Passover. I had come with them from Galilee and seen them in, and had taken a few days off, to come here, to my own house.

It was a Friday, quite early. The sun was only just up. I was asleep. There was a loud knocking on my door. My servant came to me rather alarmed. It was a two-soldier escort, to take me to Pilate. As soon as possible. To do with the matter of the arrested preacher, Jesus. I did not know he'd been arrested.

When we arrived at the praetorium, the forecourt, the parade yard was full of people. Hundreds. Screaming, shouting, hurling accusations at the man I took to be Jesus, up on the steps, who was silent and still.

The soldiers went through the mob like a knife through butter, very roughly indeed. Pilate waited for me on the terrace at the top of the steps. He took me into an anteroom. He looked very angry. I assumed, quite rightly, that he had been awakened in much the same way as I had, but even earlier. Also, he was rather a stickler for correct procedure in the matter of judicial examination, and the mob outside were near to riot. I said so.

'And being whipped up, too,' said Pilate, 'I know the signs. Paid agitators, professional troublemakers. It's all out of hand. The preacher doesn't matter – there are too many of them anyway – but the charges against him are very minor by law. Obstruction, unlawful assembly and so on. I think he's some sort of religious maniac. The Temple lot are in a lather about him. Seems he says he's the King of the Jews and the Son of their God. Lot of rubbish. But I've just been told that he is from Galilee, which, strictly, is under the jurisdiction of Antipas. So I'm passing this little lot over to him. Let *him* handle it!'

Well, off we went, across town, to the palace. Antipas, as usual, had a crowd of guests. Parties at the palace were three-four-day affairs. Everyone was up – or hadn't yet been to bed.

A rubbishy lot. I knew them all. All looking a bit jaded. For Antipas, Jesus and the yelling crowd and the high priests and lawyers were just the thing the party needed. He'd never met Jesus, so he set him up on a throne.

'If he says he's King of the Jews,' he giggled to his guests, 'let's treat him like a king!' He had Jesus dressed in a gorgeous robe and he and his ridiculous friends danced and pranced and bowed and laughed themselves sick. Then Antipas, full of half-drunk self-importance, asked questions of Jesus, demanded 'proof', used long words. 'Do *me* a miracle,' he said. 'Raise somebody from the dead for *me!* I'll kill somebody! You provide the magic, I'll provide the corpse! What would you like, male or female? I can arrange it in a minute. Young or old? With a head or without?' He roared with laughter, and then stopped. John the Baptist had been a relative of Jesus.

To all this nonsense Jesus answered not one word. He sat quiet. Then the palace guard of Antipas had *their* fun – and the lawyers went on shouting. Every kind of charge.

I watched Antipas. He was very ill at ease. Herodias spoke to him and laughed – and he shouted in her face. Most unusual. I didn't hear what he said. She moved away, very drunk. He pushed his way through the crowd to me. 'Take the fool back to Pilate,' he said. 'I don't want anything to do with him. He bores me. Get him out of here. Get rid of him. Immediately!'

I asked him, because I could not resist doing so (and also I objected to his tone), whether he wanted the robe back. 'It is a royal garment,' I said, with a little mischief, 'and the preacher says he is a king. It might appear to Pilate that you in some way agree.'

He started to shout at the top of his voice. Half-mad, disconnected gibberish.

We took the preacher back to Pilate. He was crucified that afternoon. Pilate did not care one way or the other. He had no regard for human life at all. He had enormous power, and great cruelty. To scourge before execution was barbarous – and the preacher was not the first – or the last. I do not miss Pilate.

Although I do not think that Pilate would ever admit it, that morning he bowed to the mob. The Temple lot hinted at trouble if he didn't – and he did as he was told. It was to his interest, it suited his book.

As I said, from then on he and Antipas became quite friendly. He probably found that in the matter of weakness he and Antipas had a lot in common.

Alexander

About fifty. Tall, heavily built, with big shoulders and a hand-some head. Black hair and eyes. Dark skin. A musical, deep voice. Friendly, warm.

———————

When I look back, it seems to me that the whole thing had a sort of pattern, a shape. I'm not a superstitious man, or particularly deep-thinking, but I'm not young either, and age gives a sort of perspective. Paul of Tarsus said that to me a year or two ago and he is no fool. Indeed Paul's own life has had a pattern and a shape that no one could have foreseen. He and I had been talking of my father. He knows my father very well, and loves him. Most people do. He's old, my father, but he's a bit special. And in his own way he's rather famous, even now, after nearly twenty years. Simon, who carried the cross for Jesus. My father, when he is sad, or thinking back, makes a little joke: 'The heaviest work I ever did,' he says, 'and I didn't get a penny for it.'

My brother Rufus and I were born in Cyrenaica, in this city, Cyrene. My father's family has been here for generations. Fruit farmers, as we are; as my father was. A perfect place for fruit, Cyrene. About two thousand feet above sea level, with the sea, the Great Sea, only five miles to the north. And a fine city. My father always says that of the five cities, the Pentapolis, Cyrene is the finest. Only one other place in the whole world was, as far as he was concerned, more beautiful than Cyrene. Jerusalem. Which is how we came to be there on that day. The trip.

I grew up hearing about the trip. 'Alexander,' my father used to say to me, 'when we make the trip we will see wonderful things and places, we will see Alexandria, founded three hundred years ago by your namesake.'

Now, these days my father is rather frail, he has to be careful, his heart is not too good. But in those days he was all muscle. Big, powerful. A laughing, simple man, every inch a farmer, but when he spoke of the trip he became a dreamer. The trip was to spend Passover, just once, in Jerusalem. To pray in the Temple, to make an offering, to see the lovely buildings. Jerusalem was about a thousand miles away. As far as we, a farmer's family, were concerned, it might have been a million. The trip was something we grew up with, we grew up hearing about. It was my father's dream, a sort of family joke. But once, when Rufus and I were in our teens, and much given to scoffing, my mother said, 'No dream; no joke. Your father wants this thing; it will come to pass.' And a year or two later it did. We were astonished. We made the trip. We went overland, we joined the great trade caravans, we saw Alexandria. And Pelusium, and Gaza. It took a long time, but my father had planned well. We found a little house to rent in the pretty country near Bethlehem, about five miles south of Jerusalem. Rufus and I spent the week before the Passover exploring and seeing all we could. So much to see. The Golden City of Solomon and Herod. The gorgeous Temple; the palaces; the changing of the Procurator's Roman Guard; the Tower of Antonia; the Hippodrome and the theatres.

We listened as well as looked. We understood everything. In Jerusalem the Jews speak both Aramaic and Greek, as here. There seemed to be a lot of excitement in the city; a lot of talk of 'Jesus the Carpenter', the 'Miracle-worker', the 'Healer', the 'great Preacher'. We heard about him everywhere. Marvellous stories. From all sorts of people. We took it all home to father. He listened, and said, 'Yes, I've also heard of him. Don't believe all you hear. And go to bed early. I want to be in the city at daybreak. There will be thousands.'

He was right. First day of Passover and day before Sabbath. Big day. Mother stayed home, busy. But we were there; showing off our new knowledge to Dad. He was full of wonder. Everywhere huge crowds. Excitement. Then, suddenly we were in a different sort of excitement, absolutely unexpected. Round a corner came a screaming mob. In front, a square of Roman soldiers, one of them carrying a roughly painted sign saying 'King of the Jews'. We thought for a moment that it was a parade, a carnival. Then we saw inside the square a man bent under the weight of a huge wooden cross. He looked ghastly. He was deathly white and covered in blood. As we looked, he staggered and fell and the cross banged down on him. The soldier in charge shouted at him to get up but he couldn't. The soldier looked round into the crowd, drew his shortsword, and came over to my father. 'You look strong,' he said. 'Carry the cross.' My father started to explain that we were tourists, pilgrims. 'Doesn't matter,' said the soldier. 'Roman law. You're pressed into service. Pick it up. You don't get a choice.' And he whacked my father, not hard, as part of the law, with the flat of the sword. My father started to lose his temper but the man on the ground was looking up at him. It was a calm look. Very tired. My father went across and bent down and shouldered the cross. It was obviously heavy. With his free hand he helped the man to his feet and held him up. It was Jesus, although at that moment we didn't know it. The soldiers got into position again and the procession moved off again.

It was quite a long way. We walked along by the soldiers. Once or twice I made a sign to my father that I would take my turn with the cross (I was as big and strong as he was) but he shook his head and went on. I remember he looked rather proud. Jesus staggered along almost without a word. Once he stopped and spoke to some women who were weeping as they walked with him, but the soldiers got rough with both him and the crowd.

When we reached the place called Golgotha – the Hill of the Skull – the officer in charge talked to my father for a while and the soldiers took the cross away. Rufus and I wanted to stay but my father said no. He said no in a way that we never argued with. He is a mild man, my father, but like steel on some things.

'We will not stay,' he said. 'A man, that man, is to be stripped naked and nailed to that cross with iron spikes through his hands and feet. The cross is then to be stood up and dropped into a hole so that it stands upright. The man is nearly dead with one of the worst floggings I've ever seen, his skin hangs like rags. He is neither criminal nor traitor. He is a poor preacher. If this can happen in Jerusalem,' said my father, 'on the Passover, this is no place for us. We go home tomorrow. The trip is over.'

THE END

Rufus

Ex-soldier. Middle sixties. Medium build, upright, trim, muscular. A widower, living alone. A sad, indrawn expression. A lonely man, with memories. The slow speech of a man by habit silent for long periods. Well respected in his village.

This little village is a nice place to live. People in the main mind their own business. A man earns his living, does his job, and is left alone. I'm a sort of celebrity for something I'm ashamed of; for something I'd rather forget; and the village knows it and doesn't mention it. We are all Christians in the village. Me, too. But twenty years ago, when they crucified Jesus, no one was. Well, there was no such thing. I was told that you went to hear him and he gave you a sort of simple way of looking at things. Food for thought. It was after he was dead that the disciples really began to work at making what he'd said into a religion. Terrible death he had.

People say that he knew what was going to happen; that it was all in the Scriptures. That he was a prophecy come true. Well, maybe. But I'm sure there was nothing in the Scriptures about how we dressed him up and made fun of him and how we jeered at him and insulted him. All right, soldiers can get rough – especially with a convicted law-breaker, but we were *really* rough. I wish to God I could say I hadn't joined in. But I did. I don't know who first thought of dressing Jesus up to look like a king, but it seemed very funny at the time. None of our platoon was at the sort of trial they gave him. All we knew was that he was a troublemaker who'd gone around saying he was King of the Jews. We knew very little. We were a Roman garrison. Our orders came from Pilate. Pontius Pilate. The orders were clear. A scourging and crucify him with two other criminals.

Not many people have seen a Roman punishment scourge. It's one of the worst whips ever invented. It can kill a man. It's designed to break skin and wrap round and tear. I've been asked why scourge a man who's going to be killed the same morning. Well, it wasn't the first time – and Pilate was hard. Also, he was fed up with the whole business. I didn't do the whipping, a great big sergeant from Syria did that, but I put the robe on. One of the lads found it somewhere. A purple robe, to make Jesus *look* like a king. When we put it on him, he looked like a corpse. He was naked, and that sergeant knew his job. Jesus could hardly stand. His back was like raw meat. I often dream of it. One of the boys had made a crown of twisted-together thorn stalks and he forced it down on Jesus's head. More blood. Then we stood him on a vegetable basket and marched round him and bowed and saluted and shouted in his face – and when his head dropped we slapped it up again. We gave him a big onion for an orb and a twig for a sceptre and we spat at him and laughed till we were weak. Till we cried.

I've cried many times since. In my sleep mostly. I can't say that the shame began right away, it didn't. As a soldier you do many things that you wouldn't in civilian life. But out of the service, by yourself, with time to look back, you see things differently. About eight years ago, when I'd been demobbed about a year, I met Peter the Fisherman, who made me a Christian. I was in a bad way and told him all about that night and my shame. Peter listened and then said, 'I know about shame. On that night he was a stranger to you, a nothing, to be made sport of. On that night I'd known him three years and believed him to be the Son of God. I was his first follower and his friend.

Yet on that night, in fear, I denied that I knew him. Three times.'

I think Peter said it to comfort me. It did a bit. But not much. Nothing does very much. You know, I haven't talked about that night for years. I think of it often; I dream about it, but I don't often talk about it. It's strange how talking about it somehow loosens the memory. All sorts of other things come back. As I told you, my feeling of shame about joining in that night didn't begin till some time after. We were a rough lot. We were Roman occupation troops and we regarded the convicted prisoner as fair game. It broke the monotony.

So did a crucifixion. We didn't like the job but if we were detailed that was it. Our duties were clear. There were regulations; a rulebook. The crosses were ordered normally three at a time – because normally three criminals were done together. There used to be a joke, made first, I was told, by Pilate. Seems he said, 'Do 'em in threes, nice company for each other.' It's possible; he was a cruel, hard man, was Pilate, with jokes to match. The prisoner carried his own cross, or at least dragged it with the cross bar over his shoulder. Very heavy the crosses were. A long, up-and-down, winding route would be worked out, so that as many people as possible would see the prisoner and read his crime, written on a board and carried by the lead corporal. Jesus's board just said 'King of the Jews'. Another Pilate joke. When the Jewish elders asked him to change it, he refused and got very nasty.

Jesus was too weak to carry his cross. Not surprising, he'd been flogged half to death, so we pressed into service a man in the crowd. It was regulations; he couldn't refuse. There were regulations for everything. The distance apart of the crosses, the nailing of the hands and feet, the periods of watch, the crowd control, everything. There were also certain perks. Extra pay, extra drink ration – it could be a bloody business, the nailing part – and extra leave the following week. Also, we were entitled to the clothes and possessions of the prisoners. We would settle who got what by casting lots or gambling. Jesus had no possessions, and his clothes and sandals were poor stuff. We did better out of the two criminals we hung with him. They made a lot of noise those two, shouting and screaming, sometimes sensibly, sometimes like crazy or drunk men.

There were always women who offered drugged wine to those on the cross. Sisters of mercy. It was allowed in regulations. Jesus refused. He didn't say much. At one point I think he said a few words of comfort to the fellow on his left. There were some women a little way off who seemed to know him. None of his followers or disciples was there. They were all lying low, in hiding, out of sight. We put the three prisoners up at nine in the morning. Fine, sunny morning. But at noon the sun went in and it got darker and darker. And very still and close. Most unusual. Frightening. Never before, or since. At about three o'clock all three had been quiet for some time. They'd been up six hours. Suddenly Jesus raised his head and looked up at the sky. I was quite near. Then he shouted at the top of his voice. His face was alight, his voice and body full of power. It was impossible. The crowd, in the weird twilight, were scared and nervous. My mates moved in a bit. Then Jesus shouted again, with the same lift of the head, the same power. 'It is finished!' he shouted. He died magnificently. I've never seen anything like it. One of the things that got him hung was saying he was the Son of God. At that moment I believed he was. I've believed it ever since.

Ayala

About thirty. A well-made, handsome woman. Dark hair and eyes, which are rather sad. The smile is beautiful, but rarely seen. A throaty, rather rough voice. Poorly dressed, but with a certain style.

My mother-in-law, who lives with me, would probably tell you that her Josh didn't deserve what he got, that he was the most marvellous son in the world, as good as gold. He wasn't.

He used to hit her sometimes. His father did, and Josh grew up, I reckon, thinking that's how you treat women. It's how he treated me. Not all the time, but often enough.

I don't really know what 'getting what you deserve' means. Josh was a thief, and he was violent. Sometimes he would hurt people when he took things away from them. One day he killed somebody and he was caught and executed. 'Nailed' as he called it. On the cross. I don't know whether anybody 'deserves' that sort of death. I suppose if you were to kill somebody by nailing them up with great iron nails through their hands and feet and leaving them to hang in the sun, *then* you might deserve the same.

Josh was wicked, and very strong, and he drank too much – and had a terrible temper. But it was over in a minute. I bet the man he killed was dead in a minute. Still, as I say, I don't really know how to think about such things.

That's Josh. What about me? After all, I was his wife, I knew he was a thief. I wasn't proud of it, but I didn't stop him (no one could stop him doing *anything*!). So what about *me?* Surely I 'deserve' some punishment too? All right, I'm a widow, but it's the first peace of mind – and body – I've known for years. A 'bereaved mother' lives with me, but we get on well. She remembers Josh a bit rosier than I do, but, if she's honest, *her* life is better now, too. And my daughter is the prettiest ten-year-old in the street, with her father's looks, but only his looks. And now he's gone, his influence is gone. She'll be something, my Ruth. Something more than if Josh had lived. Call things by their right names, my father used to say, and that's what I'm doing.

It would be very funny if, after all the thieving and the hurting people and the murder, Josh is in fact not in Hell but in Paradise, like the Carpenter promised.

He and the Carpenter were executed on the same day. Four years ago next Friday. I'm a follower of the Carpenter, I belong to the Fellowship. Anybody can. It doesn't matter what Josh was.

My mother-in-law laughs at me, she says I'm trying to keep on the good side of the Carpenter so he'll keep his promise to Josh. Well, maybe. It wasn't *all* bad with my thieving husband. There were some good times. Not many, but they were very good. We were in the middle of one when he was arrested. I should have known, with him staying at home more than usual, that he'd done something bad.

There was a sort of trial, but only to sentence him. He was guilty; he did it. He was in prison about three weeks before that Friday. There's no appeal against the sentence – except to Governor Pilate, and that would have been a waste of time. He's a terrible, cruel man. Since the Carpenter, even worse.

We could take food, but not talk to Josh. On the day before the execution we were told the route, and where we could stand. Walking along by the prisoners was not allowed, in case of disturbance. We stood on a corner with four soldiers keeping an eye on us. We waited for hours. One of the soldiers said there would be two prisoners, Josh and another man, who'd also killed somebody. But when the prisoners came along the road, there was a third man. The crowds were shouting his name. Jesus, of Nazareth. The Carpenter. I knew him. Everyone knew him. Not that you would have recognized him. He was covered in blood, with a sort of hat made of spiky twigs pushed down on his head. He looked awful. As far as I could see, Josh and the other man had not been ill-treated at all.

Nearly all on our corner were women and most of us were in tears, some of us very noisy. I think I was more sorry for the Carpenter than for Josh. He looked half-dead – and what could he have done? He was a *preacher!*

As the soldiers and the three prisoners drew near to us, the wailing and crying got louder. Not just from our corner, but from both sides of the street. Hundreds of women. Jesus stopped a minute and spoke to us, of sad times to come, of what men do to each other (he was a good example). 'If this is what they do when the wood is green,' he said, 'what will they do when it is seasoned?'

It was as though he had spoken to me, because before Josh went to the bad he worked as a treefeller, for his uncle, who's got a timber yard. I knew about green wood and seasoned wood. Funny, isn't it?

One of the soldiers pushed him, and the party passed us. Josh and the other man – called Theo, I knew him, a foul-mouthed bully – were dragging their own crosses. The Carpenter's was being dragged by a man who looked as though he'd just been pulled from the crowd. A pilgrim, or tourist (it was holiday time). Poor Jesus didn't look as if he could carry a twig, let alone a great heavy wooden cross.

We were allowed to follow the crowds. The soldiers stayed with us. The place of execution is called the Hill of the Skull. The crosses were laid down. The stripping of the men, and the nailing, was done right away, quickly, with the crowd kept back. Fancy wanting to see it. But people do. The worst part was when the crosses, with the men on, were upended and dropped into their holes. The holes were deep. I shall never forget the sound.

Once the crosses were up, we were allowed nearer. I went behind, I couldn't look at the men. Josh hung like a broken doll. He'd fainted, I think, when the cross had dropped into the hole. There was no life in any of them. The Carpenter was in the worst state. He looked as though he'd been flogged half to death.

Then the mob started. Nearly everyone had heard the stories about the Carpenter being the Messiah, and the Son of God, and about his miraculous cures, and how he had saved lives. Not everyone believed the stories. The mob in general believes nothing. I know; I'm one of them. Or was.

The jokers in the mob were shouting for Jesus to save his own life if he was so clever, if he could do such miracles. And how come his Father, God, was letting him get nailed? And, if he was the Messiah, how come he was on the cross between two murderers?

Then the soldiers who'd been the escort, and had done the nailing and putting up, piled all the clothes together and started to gamble for them. It's traditional. It says in the Scriptures that the hung are the damned and their belongings are anybody's. I learnt that at Fellowship.

I went round to the side after a while. Nothing happens, you see. It's only waiting. The sun was high. Three black crosses with three naked men on them. Dying. You just wait.

All three of them seemed to wake up at the same time. The other man, Theo, started to scream like an animal, waving his head, using terrible language. The Carpenter heard the mob's remarks and seemed to be praying. Josh was still, turning his head carefully, licking his lips, looking for me. I was only about six yards away. I moved round to the front, closer to him. A woman made a remark about his body and I clouted her. Josh heard me and caught my eye. He nodded, and tried to smile. He approved of clouting, my thief did.

Suddenly Theo stopped shouting nonsense and started to direct his filthy words at the Carpenter. He didn't get far. Josh found his voice, told him to shut up, to do a bit of praying instead. 'What are you going on about?' he said. 'You're getting what you deserve, like me, but this man never did anything wrong in his life.'

Jesus turned his head. Above his head was a bit of board saying 'King of the Jews'. One of Governor Pilate's little jokes. Josh read it out loud and then said, sort of to cheer Jesus up perhaps, 'Jesus,' he said, 'when you come into your Kingdom, will you remember me?'

Then Jesus spoke. He said it. He made the promise. 'I tell you,' he said, 'truly, this very day you will be with me in Paradise.'

Well, there you are. As I said, it would be a funny thing if that's where my thief is. He must have felt very out of place, at first.

Ezri

Seventies. Of medium height, but stooped, and slight. Pale, and with thin, white hair. A sparse beard. A trusting, tentative expression. Slow of speech.

I have very few visitors and am somewhat out of practice in the matter of conversation. You must bear with me. I have a great-nephew, Jonathan, of whom I am very fond. He tries to shock me with the length of his hair, and his highly coloured and unorthodox clothes – and succeeds – but I like him very much. He loves to tell me of the full, eventful life he lives. How he has seen more in seventeen years than I have in seventy. He often asks me whether I feel I've missed a lot by spending my life in the Great Temple. Whether I feel I should have mixed more in what he calls 'the life outside the walls', the life of Jerusalem.

Well, perhaps, although I must admit that I was never attracted to the life outside. I am rather shy, and of a somewhat weak and timid nature. My father understood me very well and did not suggest that I follow any profession other than his own. A servant of the Temple. My two elder brothers, alas, both dead, were strong men, full of ambition and drive, and wanted nothing of the Temple. My father did not complain, one son to follow him was enough, as he followed his father, and his father, his.

It is difficult to find words to answer Jonathan, although he is well brought up and listens with respect, but, you know, to live and work in the Temple is not to be 'imprisoned'; it is to live among beauty and be close to God. Great Herod did many terrible things, but he also rebuilt the Temple – and he knew about beauty. His sons were not to be compared, or the Roman procurators, Gratus, Pilate, any of them. They did not care about the Temple.

And we are not so shut off, so cloistered. It is not a monastery, it is a wonder of the world, to which hundreds of thousands of people come each year. The world *outside* comes *in*. Once it came in in a way that changed my life. Not my *way* of life, my *mind*. I still serve, although I do less because I am old, but my *mind* is in some way changed. I don't often speak of it, but Pontius Pilate was recalled to Rome two weeks ago. And will not return. And my thoughts go back.

It does not seem like seven years ago. Passover time. I think it used to be my favourite time of the year. Until that year. So much trouble that year. We seemed to hear of nothing but the Galilean, the Carpenter, Jesus of Nazareth. High Priest Caiaphas seemed to be in a temper the whole time. On the Sabbath the procession of the Sanhedrin and elders seemed to be full of worried, tense faces. The Carpenter was a great disturbance. He seemed to have no fear. When he and his followers overturned all the money changers' stalls that time, there was nearly a riot. I never met him and never saw him. I would have liked to, I think. Many of his sayings and the way he put things in his teaching were collected by one of my colleagues, who is a scholar with a great regard for simplicity. In his opinion the Galilean had a great gift, both for simplicity and for picturesque parable. Certainly he seemed by his words to be a simple and honest man. Yes, I would have liked to have known him. But it was quite forbidden for us of the Inner Courts to attend any outside meetings.

Like my father before me, I am what is called a Servant of the Inner Courts. The Inner Courts surround the Holy Place, the Holy of Holies, where no man enters. We who serve the Inner Courts are all Levite, all of the direct line of Aaron, brother of Great Moses. As I said, I do very little these days. I am neither so strong nor, to be honest, so reliable. I forget things, or do them twice. Seven years ago, before the Passover, I did more. I had various duties, including the care of the gold and silver lamps and ornaments, but my work stopped at the great curtain that enclosed and covered the entrance to the Holy of Holies. I spent hours looking at that curtain. It was gorgeous. The work of a hundred women. My late wife was one. It was blue and purple and crimson, with a design of angels and cherubim in the most exquisite embroidery. Gorgeous. But strong also. Made to conceal; and to last. The finest linen, lined and thickened. Edged and strengthened. It hung, on golden rings, from a great rail. It was lit from above, with great clarity, by daylight. The blue sky and the sunshine of Israel.

Yet, seven years ago, on the first day of Passover, at noon, the blue sky turned dark and the sun went out. At a time of the year when the sun is always there, it suddenly wasn't there. An awful stillness began; a terrible feeling of silence, of foreboding. I realized that I had carried the feeling within me since I'd woken up that morning. As the darkness increased, I knew why. I knew that up on the Hill of the Skull, on Golgotha, Jesus was on the cross. Everyone knew. I carried on with my work. It got darker. Too dark to work. I sat and looked at my beloved curtain, which seemed to glow in the gloom.

The time passed. At about three o'clock the closeness and silence became almost unbearable, and then a terrifying rumbling began deep in the ground, which began to shake and move. Then there was thunder, and lightning. I could hear things falling and people screaming. I think I heard a great shout, by one voice. I was full of terror. As I staggered to my feet, there was a sudden pause, a hush. And then the curtain tore. From top to bottom. A violent, dreadful destruction, full of a sort of anger, of despair.

I was told later that there was no damage either to the walls at the side of the curtain or to the great rail it hung from. I was told also that at three o'clock, Jesus shouted, and died.

Chapter 7

THE BEGINNING

Zeke

Middle fifties. Powerfully built and weather-beaten. Deep-set, rather humorous eyes. Grizzled hair, big eyebrows. A deep, slightly hoarse, voice. A cheerful man.

It was an odd feeling, you know, to change jobs so late in life, after so many years. Very different jobs indeed – although still a council employee. A bath attendant, instead of a cemetery attendant. Swimming pool instead of graveyard. Surrounded every day by noisy people full of health, instead of dead people – who made no noise at all!

Except one. He didn't so much make a noise as *cause* a lot of noise and disturbance – and got me the sack! Although I'm not really complaining. To be honest, I like this job better. After that Sunday I prefer the living to the dead. I didn't always.

Councillor Joseph, of Arimathea, got me this job. Nice man. Said it was the least he could do after helping me lose the last one. I'm not sure what he means; it wasn't his fault. I don't know whose fault it was, really. But not his, the grave was his own property, he could do what he liked with it. No regulations broken.

Regulations. Doing things the right way. I believe in that. I've got no education – you don't need to be clever to work in a graveyard – but I know that things should be done right. It may be that I'm superstitious, but you don't bury a gallows body in a rich man's tomb. The hung are damned. It's written. In any case the damned and the stoned and the crucified have their own graveyard. Near the quarry. Pits, as is right. You don't put them in newly built tombs, with closing stones.

It was bad enough the graveyard being right next door to the crucifixion hill. People used to picnic on the graves, or leave their children with me whilst they went to watch the executions. I didn't mind, I like children, but the graveyard used to get very untidy, and I like order. Things should be tidy, and in their place.

If Councillor Joseph's friend had stayed 'in his place', I think I'd still be working up there! Lucky the wife's not with me, she doesn't like jokes of that sort. In any case, she says she knew the Councillor's friend – and even a marble tomb in the Temple wouldn't have been good enough for him! Women, bless 'em.

I spoke of the Sunday; the whole weekend was strange. What is it, about a year and a half? I remember it like yesterday. In some ways the Friday was more frightening than the Sunday, a thousand times more.

It started normally. Nice morning. Cool, fresh, usual for Spring. The usual one or two early-morning people, visiting graves. One of them told me there'd been a lot of noise in the city during the night. At the palace, at the High Priest's house – and at the praetorium, where Governor Pilate lives.

There was to be a crucifixion, he told me. Three, in fact. Very unexpected, that, on a Friday – and, if I remember rightly, it was the first day of Passover, too. Almost before he finished telling me, I saw the crowds coming up the hill. It was no more than eight o'clock. Three crosses being carried. I remember thinking 'somebody's in a hurry to cross them off!' (Don't tell the wife I said that.)

I got on with my work. I don't hold with crucifixion – or the people who go and watch. On crucifixion days I would plant flowers, and look after the dwarf trees and bushes – most of which I put in.

That day I was working on the Councillor's tomb. A nice piece of work. Cut into a natural rock outcrop up at the higher end of the cemetery – away from the crucifixion end, luckily. I was lining the little trench which guides the closing stone with pebbles, so that when it rolls across, on edge, it doesn't sink in. Those closing stones can be very heavy. I've seen as many as twenty mourners needed to move one. End of the service; male relatives and friends to the stone. The wealthier the man, the bigger the stone. Councillor Joseph is very wealthy.

I set pebbles and put in little plants. I occupied myself. From down the slope I could hear the crowd making mob noises. Nasty.

It began to get terribly close, and hot. And silent. I didn't notice it at first, but I like birds, and enjoy their song – and suddenly I was aware the birds had stopped. It was uncanny. Then I noticed the sky starting to change colour. It went red, like anger, then purple. Then dark grey – then black! At noon! I was on my knees. As I got to my feet I felt the ground move. I thought it was *me,* that I was fainting – that it was *my* things 'going black'.

It wasn't. The earth *was* moving, with awful rumbling, grinding, crushing noises. I could hear people screaming and crying. I lay down and hid my head in my arms. No hero, me.

It went on and on, seemingly for hours. Then it stopped, and it began to get light again. It was about three o'clock. I was stiff. I got up and walked around the graveyard to see what damage had been done. At first I could see nothing at all. None of the upright headstones, which you'd think would be flat, were different in any way.

Then I saw a very scary thing. One of the ordinary graves, with the headstone upright and tidy, looked as if it had burst open; as if the body had burst out – and gone! It gave me a funny feeling. There were about four like it. The earth pushed violently up and thrown to either side – as though from *inside!*

I decided that I would fill them in again in a day or two (they scared me) and went back to the Councillor's tomb, which was the same as before. Everything was; sunshine, breeze, birdsong, everything. When I got there, the Councillor was waiting. I was surprised. He looked very white and strained. He told me to get the tomb ready and cleaned for someone who had just died. 'I will go and get permission, from Governor Pilate,' he said. When I looked puzzled – for a Jewish cemetery is nothing to do with the Romans – he said, 'It's one of the three men just crucified,' and walked away, looking very choked up.

Well, I thought, none of my business, and I got busy. Most unusual. As I said, there are pits. That cemetery is rather a smart one. Titled people, upper-income groups. Old families, family tombs. Now, in a brand new, cut-from-the-solid-rock, rich man's vault – with a huge closing stone – we were to put to rest a felon, a convicted and executed law-breaker. I was quite put out by it.

The body was brought in the late afternoon, by some of the Councillor's servants, who were told to come back a bit later to help move the stone across. I looked around for the embalmers, but the Councillor told me that he and a friend called Nicodemus (I know him, his parents are buried there) would prepare the body themselves. They did it well, too. I've seen the best. No expense spared, the finest linen, the purest myrrh and aloes – about a hundred pounds of it! Fit for a king.

We laid the body in, said the prayers, and called the servants back. With the Councillor and Nicodemus, it took fourteen of us to put that stone in place.

The next day, the Sabbath, another surprise. A lot of coming and going of the High Priest's people, and the Temple authorities – and a lot of instructions. All in a 'my man' tone, as the wife calls it. 'You must be very watchful for any suspicious characters near the tomb, my man.' 'The stone is not to be touched in any way, my man.' 'We will be sealing the tomb, my man – and mounting a guard, my man.' A guard! for a dead felon! They meant it, too. Potter's clay sealing, and ten men with two officers. Well, I did my day's work, was 'watchful' and went home, leaving the soldiers to it. The only 'suspicious characters' seen had been some very sad-looking women, probably relations.

When I got to the cemetery the next morning (I don't hurry on Sundays), the place near the tomb had to be seen to be believed. All the soldiers either asleep or just sitting, as though in shock, the stone pushed right back – and the tomb empty! Well, I can't tell you the commotion that went on that day! And the stories that started to fly around!

My day ended with the sniffiest of the Burial Committee sending for me and telling me that the cemetery was to be closed till further notice, that my watchfulness left a lot to be desired, that great confusion and disturbance existed, for which as 'custodian' I had partly to accept responsibility – and, because of all these factors et cetera and so on, I was sacked.

I wasn't too upset. Neither was the wife. Especially as the Councillor fixed me this new job almost the same week. Anyway, the wife thinks a swimming pool's got more class than a cemetery. Certainly more cheerful – and I never had to fill in those graves. Good thing too, seemingly, for a lot of folk swear that the people who were in them have been seen around the city! Peculiar, the whole business. It was in my mind to ask the Councillor how he felt about the tomb being interfered with, and his friend's body disappearing – and all that expensive embalming stuff being wasted – but I didn't. He didn't seem too upset. In fact, he seemed happier than for a long time.

Maron

About twenty-two. Slim, handsome, fair. A well-brought-up, innocent, look. A 'good-school' voice. A sort of fledgling authority. Pleasant.

I'm perfectly willing to tell you all I know about the night the preacher's body went from the tomb, but all I know doesn't amount to very much. I know what I've been told – and it may be the truth – although those who told me weren't even there.

My wife says I worry about it too much. She says it often. She also says that, if it hadn't been for that night, we couldn't have afforded to get married and buy this little house. It's true. Second lieutenants earn almost nothing in the Temple Guards. It's all honour and glory. All father-to-son, if you're an officer. The men do better than we do.

It's very father-to-son in our family. We've been soldiers for generations – right back to Judas Maccabeus. 'More medals than money,' my mother says. She's also very pleased the money came my way, like my wife is. Women have a special sort of logic, I think. My father, who's Household Cavalry attached to Antipas's palace in Tiberias, has made it clear that he won't discuss the matter with me. He sees it as sleeping on duty, and that's the end of it. He's not easy to talk to at any time, my father. My brother, who's a major in the Infantry, is no better. He says it's the highest paid worst bit of soldiering in history. D'you wonder I worry about it? Another thing, my father and my brother are military; they deal with senior officers, the Cavalry and the Infantry. I get my orders from priests. The Temple Guard are really policemen. Our authority comes from the elders, the Sanhedrin Council, the religious parties.

That's where the order came from that Saturday morning. The officers of the High Priest Caiaphas, and the Pharisee Party. It's just over a year ago (we've been married about seven months). The order was simple and clear. A ten-man guard detail with two officers to proceed to the burial ground alongside Crucifixion Hill and mount a day and night guard on a tomb. Not a guard of honour; normal dress and arms. Not a lying-in-state guard; a watch guard. No details given at all as to occupant of the tomb, whose owner was Councillor Joseph of Arimathea, my father's second cousin. Uncle Joseph, who was very much alive.

We were up at the tomb by noon. When we arrived, two men from Temple maintenance were sealing the front stone with clay – and attaching the official tags. Seemed a needless procedure. They were sticking bits of clay round the edge of a slab of stone that looked as though it weighed fifty tons. It closed the entrance to the tomb, which was cut in solid rock. Official sealing, official tags – and a full Temple Guard. Somebody – or something – very valuable in there, my corporal said.

We sorted out our roster and settled in. Two hours on, four off. Always four men on guard, officers to share duty. A sunny, mild afternoon, a cool evening, a cold night. Normal for the time of year. As I say, what did actually happen I can't tell you – mainly because I was asleep. It was just before dawn. I'd done the third night watch and was off duty, asleep. What woke me was a mixture of things really. A blinding white light and men shouting in terror. My men, I'm not proud to tell you. There was a sound like a great wind, and a movement in the ground, like an earthquake – or landslide. I was dazed. As I tried to get to my feet, my corporal, in full flight, with his eyes staring out of his head, went straight into me.

We both hit the ground together. I caught his fear. I've never been so frightened – or known less why. I felt some great thing was happening, to do with the blinding light and the earth movement. The corporal and I clung together, then he went limp. I thought he had died of fright! I remember that just as I thought that such a thing is impossible – everything went dark and I fainted! It couldn't have been for long. It seemed, as I came to, that the whole troop was waking up. I got up to investigate, feeling very groggy. Zephah, the other officer, was as unsteady on his feet as I was. The great white light had gone. It was a pale dawn.

You know, sometimes you just don't believe what your eyes tell you. The stone had been rolled right back! Right back, as though it weighed a penny. Rolled on edge – *like* a penny! Not a lever, or a footmark, or a clue of any kind. The tomb was empty – except for some body wrappings. If there had been valuables – it was a rich man's tomb – they'd gone.

Zephah and I got much the same thought at the same moment. Court-martial. Twelve men guarding one small place against God knows what – and failing completely.

We questioned the men together. They all seemed dazed, in shock, stupid. Or drugged. There'd been a lot of talk lately in the city, of students inducing 'mind journeys' or 'trips' with hallucination drugs, and it occurred to me that our wine or water or food had been tampered with. The men's stories varied a lot but had certain things in common. All spoke of the brilliant light. Two said it was a man, or two men, who gave off the light. An angel, one said; the other, a 'white-hot' man. No one had seen anybody move the stone or leave the tomb. Some spoke of music from the sky, of great singing winds, or choirs. Others, of shooting stars, and explosions in their heads, and powerless limbs, and terror. Others still, of the stone 'leaping' to one side, and great groans from the bowels of the earth, great weeping noises from Heaven. All told of everything going black, of fainting, of terror, of collapse.

Zephah and I talked. We were in trouble. What could we report? If we wrote down what the men had told us, it would look like the burblings of lunatics – or men crazy-drunk. It would do nothing to hide the simple fact that the thing which we were there to prevent had happened. It was our fault. We were officers in charge. The blame was ours.

We decided to go ourselves to Council, and tell all we knew. We went first to tell our C.O., who went glassy-eyed, for our absolute failure of duty was certain to reflect upon him. He came with us to the Temple.

We told our story first to the elders, who sat like statues, then we went with them to the palace of High Priest Caiaphas, and repeated it all to him. He has an unblinking stare, Caiaphas, and eyes with no expression. Terrifying. When we'd finished, he nodded and told us to wait in a small anteroom. We were in that room about two hours, shaking, for dereliction of duty carries not only disgrace to the whole family, but punishment of a most severe kind.

Then we were called back in. Just the two of us, not our C.O. We were spoken to by one of the elders, I believe a cousin of Caiaphas, with a smooth, modulated voice – and the same eyes. He told us that we had been the victims of a diabolically clever plot, in which powerful drugs, magic and sorcery had been used to make powerless twelve highly trained men to whom no blame could be in any way attached. Indeed, he said, we were to be richly rewarded for our bravery – and discretion.

When I looked puzzled about the word discretion, he went on to tell us that he could now reveal that the body in the tomb had been that of the Galilean preacher, Jesus. The Carpenter. The fraud and impostor crucified for his crimes against the people and sedition against Rome. Tried and sentenced by Governor Pilate himself. The tomb had been sealed and guarded against a foreseen attempt by the dead preacher's followers to make the body disappear as though by a miracle and thus perpetuate the fraud and deception of the people. All was foreseen, he told us, and allowed for. No shame or dishonour; a reward. And that was the story. The only story. No other. Even if Governor Pilate himself were to ask us, that was the story. Drugs, magic and sorcery, and the stealing of the body by a large gang of trained agitators.

Then the elder gave us a bag of gold to share among the men, and a bag of gold each for ourselves, nearly as big. Before distributing the money to the men, the elder said, explain to them – and teach them – the exact, and only, story.

And that's it. You needn't tell me the other stories, of the Carpenter rising from the dead and meeting his friends and so on, I've heard them. Good luck to him. I'm grateful to him. Because of him I'm married, and we've got a nice little house and garden. As my wife says to tell you, if you don't like one story, choose another, there are lots.

We want to hear from you. Please send your comments about this book to us in care of the address below. Thank you.

GRAND RAPIDS, MICHIGAN 49530

WWW.ZONDERVAN.COM